FORTUNATE SON

THE BRITISH ISLES
Early 1700's

N

SCOTLAND

Aberfoyle

Edinburgh

IRELAND

Irish Sea

Manchester

Dublin

Sheffield

Kildare

Stafford

New Ross

ENGLAND

Waterford

Dunmain

St. George's Channel

London

Bristol

THE MIDDLE BRITISH COLONIES
Early 1700's

FORTUNATE SON

A novel by

David Marlett

THE
STORY PLANT

THE STORY PLANT
Studio Digital CT, LLC
PO Box 4331
Stamford, CT 06907

Copyright © 2013 by David Marlett
Jacket design by Barbara Aronica Buck

Hardcover ISBN-13: 978-1-61188-159-2
Paperback ISBN-13: 978-1-61188-077-9
E-book ISBN-13: 978-1-61188-078-6

Visit our website at www.TheStoryPlant.com

First Story Plant Printing: February 2014

Printed in the United States of America

For my father,
le do ghrá agus inspioráid

ACKNOWLEDGEMENTS

Go Raibh Maith Agat Go Léir

I am so very grateful to a number of people for their support, encourage-ment, editing, attaboys and assistance throughout the years of my researching and writing of this novel. I begin by thanking Thomas Haack, without whose singular vision, courage, and support my writing career might never have launched. Thank you Tom for rolling the proverbial dice. *Tá tú mo bhuíochas ó chroí.* In that same vein, I am warmly indebted to my steadfast friend and backer, Wesley Davis, for his unwavering encouragement and assistance. *A Prionsa I measc na bhFear.*

I am grateful to my parents, Dr. Robert and Carolyn Marlett (*tá mé mac ádh*),and my brilliant children, Meredith, Caroline, Kathleen and Jack. *An t-aer unseen faoi bhun mo sciathdin.* Their love and encouragement sustain me more than they will ever know. I am grateful to Michelle Wisk Marlett (*mo cara móide*) for her patience, support, and faith in my dedication to seeing this through. I am appreciative of Ruth Miller who tolerated early drafts and attended at least one research expedition with me through England, Scotland and Ireland. And I am also grateful to my literary agent, the incomparable Jane Dystel; my visionary publisher, Lou Aronica; and two thoughtful and highly skilled editors, Joanne Starer and Sue Rasmussen.

In addition, I thank Aidan Quinn, Josh Kesselman, John Davis, Mitchell Maxwell, Vincent Bugliosi, and David English for their unique contributions toward the completion of this work.

I am indebted to a host of people in Ireland, Scotland and England who were vital in my research. A specific thank you to Ann and James Conway and their children for graciously hosting me in the famous and historic Dunmain house in County Wexford, Ireland. Further I appreciate the support of the staff of Christ Church Cathedral (Dublin, Ireland); Library of Trinity College (Dublin, Ireland); National Library of Ireland (Dublin, Ireland); Irish Legal History Society (Dublin, Ireland); University College Dublin School of Law, Roebuck Castle—*An Coláiste Ollscoile, Baile Átha Cliath* (Dublin, Ireland); John F. Kennedy Arboretum (County Wexford, Ireland); The British Muse-um (London); National Museum of the Royal Navy (Portsmouth, England); Royal Historical Society (London); The Historical Association (London);

The Seldon Society—University of London, School of Law at Queen Mary (London); Historic Scotland (Edinburgh, Scotland); Highland Folk Museum (Newtonmore, Scotland); West Highland Museum (Fort William, Scotland); The Stair Society—The University of Edinburgh, Edinburgh Law School (Edinburgh, Scotland); The New Ross Chamber of Commerce (New Ross, Ireland). I am specifically indebted to the staff of The Kennedy Homestead (New Ross, Ireland) for the insight into the early pre-American Kennedy family and their association with the Annesleys of County Wexford.

In the United States, I owe a debt of gratitude to a number of institutions and organizations, including the Colonial Williamsburg Foundation (Williamsburg, VA); Colonial National Historical Park (Yorktown, VA); Virginia Historical Society (Richmond, VA); Mariner's Museum (Newport News, VA); Historical Society of Delaware (Wilmington, DE); Maryland Historical Society's Museum and Baldwin Library (Baltimore, MD); Pennsylvania Historical and Museum Commission; Cornwall Furnace (Cornwall, PA); Lukens National Historic District and Brandywine Iron Works (Coatesville, PA); Smithsonian Institution (Washington, DC); Library of Congress (Washington, DC); Harvard Law School Library (Cambridge, MA); The Museum of Printing History (Houston, TX); and The University of Texas School of Law (Austin, TX).

I specifically wish to express my appreciation for the Jamail Center for Legal Research at the Tarlton Law Library at my alma mater, The University of Texas School of Law in Austin, Texas. I am indebted to that institution and its premier faculty for my introduction to the study of law and legal history, for my introduction to this case, for having the ancient trial transcript in their extraordinary law library, and for not having better security such that I was able to get locked in the stacks overnight, reading the amazing transcript and meeting the incomparable James Annesley.

Tá súil agam gur féidir linn a bheith t-ádh a fhoghlaim a fírinneach atá againn a is iad.

PART ONE

Ireland

1727

Aide me, o justice! Be my guide, o truth!
While inspirited by the love of you, most amiable virtues,
I attempt to paint the distresses of helpless injured
innocence: to trace the mysterious windings of deep deceit;
the cruel paths of lawless avarice and wild ambition;
to show how fatal to their posterity variance between the
wedded pair may sometimes prove; and how attentive
villainy from thence may form the most successful projects.

The story I have to relate is full of wonders—all the
passions are concerned in it—I have to treat of strange
unnatural persecutions—accumulated sufferings—
numberless dangers—miraculous escapes.
O may my words have energy to give each incident a true
descriptive force to warn the gentle generous soul with
alternate pity and indignation, and make the guilty, tho'
ever so great in power, and wealth, and titles, start at the
reflection of himself.

> — *Memoirs of an Unfortunate Young Nobleman,*
> James Annesley, 1743

—m—

Alice Bates, examined — "I knew Lady Anglesea at Dunmain in 1714. She was then with child. I went to pay her a visit and when I came to the dining room door, Lord Anglesea met me and slapt me on the back and said, 'By God, Ally, Moll's with child!' I also knew her to be with child by seeing her pretty big. I wished her joy on being with child, and she thanked me in presence of his lordship."

— trial transcript, *Annesley v. Anglesea,* 1743

—m—

CHAPTER 1

Every man has three names:
One his father and mother give him,
One others call him,
And one he acquires himself.
— Anonymous, 17th Century

Sunday, November 16, 1727

Lord Arthur Annesley, the Sixth Earl of Anglesea, was slopped. He had been sitting alone at his oak table in the dark back corner of the Brazen Head Tavern since half-past ten that morning. Now, nearly five in the evening, he could hear fresh rain blowing across Dublin's Merchant's Quay, tapping the tavern's windows, dripping heavy in pools along Bridge Street. He was floating, his white wig askew, his fat fingers tracing the blood groove of his gold-hilted rapier lying on the table. "He's mine, he is," he muttered to no one. "B'god, James is mine! So he is. She'll never take him to England." He glanced up with his one eye, the other having been long ago shot out by his wife's cuckolding suitor. "My son's mine," he boomed. "Damn you all!" A violent cough overtook him until finally he lowered his chin, rivulets of perspiration trickling down his brow.

"'Tis well known, me lord, James is yer son," the tavern keeper offered. "Would ye like another?"

"Ney!" Arthur shook his head, muttering, "No more boys."

"Ach nay, me lord—would ye like another pint?"

"Ha! Ney, Keane. Best be on m'way." He stood shakily, steadying himself on the dark wall, sheathing his rapier.

"Well den, g'night sire," the keeper said, gesturing with his bar towel.

Arthur tapped the wrinkles from his blue Italian cocked hat. "Keane?"

"Aye, m'lord?"

"What be the cure...." He stumbled sideways, trying to buckle his sword sash. "What be the cure for a hangover? I'll wager you don't know."

"Sleep, most likely," Keane answered, moving across the small room, delivering a dram to a large man sitting alone. "What do ye think, sir?" he asked the man.

"I have no reckon," the man muttered, his Scottish brogue rumbling low. "Leave me be."

"I suppose a pinch o' snuff might do ye, Lord Anglesea," Keane guessed, wiping his hands on his apron.

"Ney, goddamn you, Keane!" His words a lather of grumbled mush, his arm a terrier in a fox hole, fumbling through the twisted coat sleeve. He spun, shoving his hand through. "I knew you didn't know, you damn thievin' Irishman. 'Tis t' drink again!" He staggered backward to the door. "That be the cure, b'god!"

"Aye, me lord," said Keane. "So I've heard." Now the Scotsman was standing too.

"T' drink again!" Arthur bellowed, throwing his arms up. "T' drink again, 'tis all you need!" Turning, he careened through the doorway, along the rickety boardwalks, lurching into the muck of Bridge Street. "'Tis all I need!"

A large hackney coach pulled by six horses was crossing the Father Matthew Bridge, gaining speed in the pelting rain. The horses snorted against the driver's whip as he yelled from the box, his cloak flailing in the wet wind. "Up with ye curs! Now! Up! Up!" Again and again he cracked the long leather across their backs. The loud roar and stirring commotion of the coach and six easily cleared traffic from the bridge, opening a wide swath up Bridge Street beyond, like a plow cleaving mud. When the horses reached the quay on the far side of the River Liffey they were pulling so hard and running at such a blaze that all four wheels left the ground before crashing back to earth to spin in the slurry sludge. Galloping past the Brazen Head Tavern, with nostrils flared and eyes mad wide, they would not and could not stop for anything in their path.

Against the whir of voices the ale had loosed in his head, Arthur heard charging hooves, people shouting, and through the stinging rain, he saw a maniacal blur rushing him. But he couldn't move. A black surging wall, yet he stood, stammering something about God. Finally one step toward the side, but it wasn't enough—the violent impact threw him back and down. Twenty-four hooves thundered over him, snapping his right leg like straw, driving it into the thick mud. Another hoof trampled his gut, his ribs shattering. Instant fire. Then the coach hit him, the splinter bar catching his chin, the front axle crushing his larynx, cracking spine, whipping his head into the path of the rear wheels which slammed over him, mashing his face into the filth and black ooze.

His one eye fluttered open, stinging, but he couldn't breathe. To one side he saw muddy boots and spurs—some standing, others moving away. His bloody mouth sagged, convulsing for air. He felt warmth trickle from his ears. Life abandoning him. Then, between the clamoring shouts and splashes, he heard the massive bells of Christ Church Cathedral begin their solemn peal, announcing the time. He stopped moving, and there in the shadows of his mind he saw James, no more than five, standing on a rocky hill, laughing, the sea air tousling his auburn hair. Suddenly James sprinted off, through an emerald field, clambered over a low stone fence, then raced on, away, toward a man who was waiting, watching—a man Lord Arthur Annesley, the Earl of Anglesea had never been.

—ᴍ—

Mrs. Henrietta Cole, examined — "My mother and I, being invited to Dunmain, went there about the spring of 1714. While I was there Lady Anglesea was with child, but she received a fright and miscarried. The fright was occasioned by my lord, Lord Anglesea, being in a great rage at some saucers being brought to the table contrary to his express orders, upon which he threw the saucers into the chimney just by my lady, who was seated at the upper end of the table. During the night my mother called up by Charity Heath, her ladyship's woman, who told her that Lady Anglesea miscarried that night. I saw the abortion in a basin next morning. Charity Heath must have seen it, because she was present. My mother said that, if Lady Anglesea was so easily frightened, she never would have a child. Lord Anglesea said it was her own fault."

— trial transcript, *Annesley v. Anglesea,* 1743

—ᴍ—

CHAPTER 2

But know, thou noble youth,
The serpent that did sting thy father's life
Now wears his crown.

— from *Hamlet*, William Shakespeare, 1601

Two days later the birds fell silent in the churchyard of Christ Church Cathedral, leaving only the heavy steps of shiny boots and shoes amidst the light clanking of silvery mourning swords and the rustling of somber fabric. Led by the priest and the cross, the clergy began a slow procession from the lich-gate at the churchyard's north end. Behind them, six men covered in dark grey frocks filed forward, lifted the mahogany coffin from its table and joined in step.

James Annesley, twelve years old and now the Baron of Altham and Earl of Anglesea himself, slowly followed, studying the path before him. A gust whipped his black hat and he snatched it back, covering everything but his tail of hair. He glanced across the crowd of no fewer than three hundred gentlemen and ladies shuffling along, awash in their black linen suits, heavy silk dresses and respectfully short ruffles. The women were suitably dour, a collection of black gloves and matching crepe handkerchiefs, hair pulled high under dark bonnets of silk. He could see the eyes of the men, a mass peering from under silver-ribboned cocked hats, white wigs and furrowed brows. They were fixed on him like the luminous piercing eyes of black cats, studying him, judging him.

A woman in a full veil was standing apart from the others, fidgeting. For a moment Jemmy thought she might be his mother—but of course she was not; this woman was too short, too heavy. Besides, his mother would not be there. Although his gaze dropped back to the path before him, he was too late to see the upthrust edge of a flagstone. His toe caught it and he stumbled, one foot across the other and down, smashing into the legs of the rear pallbearer. The man's knees buckled, he lost his grip, and the coffin shifted violently back. Thud! The sound echoed from within the coffin as the bearers struggled to keep it from hitting the ground. Jemmy sprang to his feet, his freckles lost in blush, imagining his father imperiously jostling about inside the box. As the bearers recovered their grips and solemn composures, the priest slowly proceeded forward, never hesitating in his recitation: "I know that my Redeemer liveth, and that he shall stand at the latter day upon the earth...."

Regaining composure, Jemmy focused on the back of the coffin. His father was finally dead, killed just two days ago, crushed by a runaway coach. He had heard it was murder— "A blood-damned, godless Catholic killed him!" But it could have been anyone. Who had not hated Arthur? Everyone had their reasons. Some had tried before. Even Jemmy—or at least he had thought on it. The man had been vile—a meanness that had enveloped Jemmy for so long that he was now calm, relieved the rage had been silenced under the booming hooves of six horses. The storm of the man had ended, the thunderclaps subsided, the torrential rain now dry. Relief. That coolness he felt in the hollow of his stomach was a certain contentment, the settled knowledge that the evil was gone, never to return.

But where one weight was gone, now another hovered, waiting to be assumed. Jemmy was the new Earl of Anglesea, the English owner of over fifty thousand Irish acres, four thousand more acres across in England, a member of both the Irish and English Houses of Lords—he had no idea what that meant for him. Where should he go? How to act? Could he remain friends with Seán, the son of Fynn Kennedy, a Catholic laborer? And what of Jemmy's mother? Could he now go live with her? Even on to England? She had not come to him in over two years—would she want him? He watched his shoes glide back and forth. Why didn't she come to this funeral? Even just for him. Yet, if she had, what would he say? He didn't want to talk to her or anyone else. Except Fynn Kennedy who now joined in step beside him.

Nothing felt more right. Though his father was lying in that coffin, the only man who had ever treated Jemmy as a son, who had ever loved him, was walking by him now, upright and proud, wigless hair tied back, jaw set, crescent eyes warm, one big hand on Jemmy's shoulder. Even though Fynn was Catholic, Jemmy knew the man would remain by him today, no matter the aristocratic grumbling it caused. The warm hand on his shoulder gave him strength, as if chain armor, as if it were the hand of Sir Lancelot on Sir Galahad's shoulder, the hand of valor, strength. Although Fynn's son, Seán, thought Sir Lancelot was the best knight, Jemmy knew the best was Sir Galahad—the young one, the only one who had found the Holy Grail, found it glowing in the belly of a ship. He wished he could find something like that. Another wind-burst snapped his state away, and he returned to the bleak churchyard, the cold people.

Behind the peerage, a small gathering of commoners had gathered along Fishamble Street. They too were in dark clothes, though mostly in browns and grays, with no wigs nor swords among them. These were the Catholics, no more welcome than Fynn, particularly at such a noble Englishman's funeral. Among them was Juggy, soon to be Fynn's wife. As Jemmy saw her, she caught him with her empathetic eyes. He gave a slight smile, pleased she was there. Beside her was Fynn's giant cousin, John Purcell, with his wife and their two young daughters, pulled in so close that they were almost lost in their father's enormous gut. To Jemmy they all seemed lost, uncomfortable. He wished they would just go back to their homes, back to whatever they were doing, back to their happiness. And just past the Purcells was Seán. He was hopping on one foot, tugging irritably at his brown coat. Jemmy watched him, longing to simply step out of the damn procession, cut across the yard and run down Fishamble Street with Seán. To run away. To disappear. Seán could give him that, that most precious of gifts, the gift of invisibility, the gift of vanishing into the Dublin streets.

The priest's droning faded in Jemmy's head. He looked up. There was no rain, no sun—only the low, spit-grey clouds of November clinging to the morning sky. Its hazy light draped the stones of Christ Church Cathedral, engulfing the high buttressed walls, throwing faint shadows across the Four Courts of Justice which adjoined the church's north side. The march slowed now, approaching the chapterhouse, which joined the Cathedral to the Four Courts. He expected the procession to turn there, to enter the church's nave through the side door, but instead the priest led the group to the left, toward Skinner Row, toward the far side of the Four Courts. "Where's he going?" Jemmy whispered.

Fynn leaned down. "I suppose t' enter 'round off the lane. No doubt these nobles can't squeeze their arses through that transept."

"'Tis the long way, 'round the courts."

"Aye, so 'tis, Seámus," Fynn said, addressing Jemmy by his Irish name. To Fynn Kennedy, Jemmy was not Jemmy, not James, not Jimmy, not barely an Annesley, not the Baron of Altham and certainly not the Earl of Anglesea. He was Seámus. And that was that. Seámus he had been since birth—Seámus he would remain. Their bond had formed over the years at Dunmain House in Southern Ireland, where Fynn had served as the Annesleys' stablemaster. But that service ended upon their move to Dublin a year prior. Fynn had been summarily turned out without even the bother of a fictive explanation.

According to Juggy, it was because Lord Anglesea had overheard Fynn teaching Irish Gaelic to Jemmy. They had all denied it of course, Jemmy the loudest. But the truth was he had learned much more Gaelic than just his own name. He was now fluent in the illegal language.

The priest paused to adjust his peruke wig, now flopped across his slumped back, then resumed recitations from the Book of Common Prayer for the Anglican Church of Ireland: "We brought nothing into this world, and it is certain we can carry nothing out. The Lord gave...."

As the group moved along Skinner Row, Jemmy looked up at the court building. He and Seán had often played here in the passages and the churchyard. They had sat on the stone steps leading up from Christ Church Lane watching the comings and goings of the high-wigged solicitors, chained criminals, justices of the peace, and other curious-looking people. But he had never paid much mind to the old court building itself. Nor had he ever thought it odd that it was built on the cathedral's grounds. Stretching up above him, the court's tall narrow windows were cracked and moldy, most threaded with lead latticework, the track marks of numerous repairs and fragile attempts to keep out the rain. Squinting his sea-green eyes, he noticed the parapet along the roofline was crumbling in places, the grey sky seeping through the eves.

Once inside the church, the procession continued into the drafty nave to where the coffin was laid on a stone table before the closed chancel screen, below the pulpit with its imposing canopy which appeared to rise out over the people. The clergy turned and waited silently for the laity to slide into their pews. Jemmy picked a pew in the center of the nave, scooting down the long wooden stretch until he came to the outer edge. Fynn eased in beside him, patting him firmly on the knee. The priest had climbed the rounding stairs and was now wobbling in the pulpit. "I will take heed to my ways, that I offend not in my tongue. I will keep...."

Immediately next to the end of Jemmy's pew was a black marble tomb shaped in the effigy of a medieval warrior. He studied it, cocking his head to read the inscription: Richard de Clare, Earl of Pembroke, STRONGBOW, 1176. And beside Strongbow's tomb was another one, though much smaller. Silently, he read the faint letters inscribed in its base:

> O graceless son, who left thy sire,
> Amid the battle's din;
> And the same moment, turned thy back
> On Country, Kith, and Kin.

'Tis his son there, the one he cut in half for running away from battle! He knew the story well but had never seen these tombs. The small one wasn't short because it held a child; it was short because it held only half a man, a young warrior killed and forced to lie forever beside his father, the very man who had sliced him in two. Suddenly a dreadful idea came to Jemmy as he stared at his own father's coffin, panic paling his face. Glancing over, he saw the reassuring glimmer in Fynn's narrow eyes. *Please God, let them bury me next to Mr. Kennedy. Or anywhere so long 'tis far from this cathedral, far from Da.*

The tombs of Strongbow and his half-son lay in the bay of a stone arcade that ran the length of the nave. Toward the top of the nearest column the stone arched up and over and down to the next column. Looking up, Jemmy saw the lower arches supporting higher levels of stone arches which in turn were hoisting the high vaulted ceiling—pushing it back to God, curving it out into the open air, denying gravity, tempting fate. The house of serendipity under the ceiling of castigated chance. The priest coughed slightly midphrase. Jemmy leaned close to Fynn. "Did he know Da?" he whispered.

"Who, lad?"

"The old priest."

Fynn shrugged. "I don't know. Perhaps so."

A cold breeze drafted across his feet. He watched the ancient man, studying the movement of the thin lips. "...shalt prepare a table before me against them that trouble me. Thou hast anointed my head with oil, and my cup shall...." After the prayer, a cool, echoing silence fell through the cathedral, interlaced with an occasional cough. No weeping. Not even a sniffle. But was he supposed to cry? He clenched his teeth, trying to feel sad. Was he lacking something, some care? Was he devilish, cold hearted? Was he just like his father? A devil? A gargoyle of a man. Did the priest know that man in the coffin had been a devil? Was his father still a devil, even after death? Maybe he should yell at the priest: *You're burying a devil, don't you know!* Maybe his father should be buried outside, not in the crypt of this cathedral, not below where Jemmy now sat. He had been to church a few times since they had moved to Dublin, but always to St. Patrick's Cathedral, and the dean at St. Pat's, Dean Jonathan Swift, was much different than this codger. Dean Swift told them how loving and caring Christ was. Jemmy looked again at the coffin. There lay mortality. There in that mahogany box lay his father, wrapped in death clothes, his fat head pushed against the coffin end. If Dean Swift was right, if Christ did die for everybody, was his father in heaven now, devil or not? Jemmy chewed his bottom lip, glancing away, up, anywhere. Dean Swift told stories about Lilliputians too, didn't he? Were Lilliputians in heaven? Or did they go to some other heaven, a much smaller one?

Retracing the arches down to the tops of the massive supporting pillars, Jemmy's wide eyes found others looking back. Circumscribing the summit of each column was a series of faces with deep-carved, stone eyes—forever beautiful, staring blankly at the nave people. A man in pensive gaze, an old man wrinkled and withdrawn, another much younger, frozen on the verge of speaking. Then he saw her. Almost directly above him was the face of a beautiful maiden, her head wrapped in a death shroud. Or was it a scarf to keep out the cold? Different from the others, her eyes were closed. The others were all peaceful men, noble faces, the old, the young, all with open eyes, all looking right back at him. And the lady's face was graceful, not threatening or warning, yet her closed eyes bothered him. Why couldn't she look at him? Did she not want to see the people there, not want to see him? She was welcoming yet still hidden. Was she dead or just sleeping? Suddenly, in his mind, the carving began to transform, swelling, trembling, struggling and flexing against its stone bindings. Then it became a living face—the face of his mother. Tears welled in his eyes as he silently pleaded, *Mother, where are ye? Where are ye?* As quickly as she had appeared, Mary Sheffield faded back to grey stone, the flesh hardening, the eyes closing. She was gone.

"Seámus." Fynn touched Jemmy's shoulder, whispering. "Seámus, m'boy, 'tis time for ye t'go. Up t' the altar."

Jemmy wiped his hot cheeks with the back of one hand as he stood, slipping into the aisle. He reluctantly walked to the front. Behind him he heard deep murmurs, but no distinguishable words. As he stopped at the coffin, a clerk took his arm, leading him to one side. People began to course by, men unknown to him, greeting him as the new Earl, calling him lord, saying things in memorial about his father, a man they had surely never known.

—〰—

Thirty minutes later, the eight bells of Christ Church Cathedral began their dirge, shaking the brisk Dublin air. Emerging up from the crypt, Jemmy walked up and out, into the light, beyond the stone columns, past the cold faces, through the door of the south transept, and out into the churchyard. The throng of the elite, the spectators, stood about, clustered in dark little pockets of self-appointed supremacy. To Jemmy they were more like clumps of black peat. The sun had broken through the grey sky at last, and Jemmy squinted trying to spot Fynn.

"James Annesley!" a voice thundered.

"Aye?" Jemmy looked up, shielding his eyes from the brightness.

"Just what do you think you're doing here, knave?" The man was advancing on horseback, two other horsemen close behind.

"What business do ye have with the lad?" Fynn was at Jemmy's side. Jemmy could now see the man, mounted high, haughty and proud, the angular face scowling down at them. He saw the man's gold cravat, cropped wig, blue three-corner hat. Nothing dark, no mourning clothes. The only black was in those eyes.

"My business is none of your concern, stable boy," the man growled at Fynn. "Remove your nasty heretic arse from this holy yard."

"B'God ye'd best declare yerself, if ye wish t' survive yer tongue!"

"A challenge!" The man spun his spirited mount on the churchyard turf, the hooves spattering wet clumps of mud on Fynn and the people crowded around.

The big Irishman, John Purcell, charged, brandishing a walking stick. "Get yer English arse down!" His guttural boom reverberating off the stone walls. Just as quickly, the other two Englishmen spurred their mounts toward him. Shouts and neighing erupted in Jemmy's ears. He stepped back from the commotion, seeing the glint of a steel scabbard, hearing the ring of a blade slipping free. Silence descended. Everything stopped. Except the bells which continued their tolling far overhead. Fynn was once again beside Jemmy, John Purcell was being held back by the tip of a rapier, and Seán was standing wide-eyed on the far churchyard wall.

"Now," began the man. "Now that you've closed your Catholic gobs, I'll speak t' the young runt." Infused with anger, a hint of brogue slid through the man's efforts to maintain his English composure.

Juggy stepped forward, clasping Jemmy by the elbow. "What do ya want with the young lord? He's just buried his father, so he has. Tis that not enough? Or didn't ya know?"

"Aye, so he's just buried his father." The man smirked, lowering his voice to a whisper. "But what do you know of it?" His lips curled to a grin. "I am the corpse's brother."

"Richard Annesley," Fynn said, reciting the name flatly.

"M'da has no brother," Jemmy said. "He—"

"Aye, but he did, Seámus. He did indeed." Fynn was slowly advancing.

"So Richard, where's yer black beard? Or aren't ye hiding behind no more?"

"Stand back!" Richard drew his pistol, cocking it. "Stand back, Irish cur!"

Fynn stopped, then raised his arms, smiling. "Wouldn't want t' be upsettin' ye. Ney. That wouldn't do—now would it? Considering how upset ye must be over the loss of yer dear brother." Richard shifted in his saddle, but kept his aim steady. "Let me think on this," Fynn continued, now feigning contemplation. "If I be right, ye've come t' claim the title and property of the Earlship for yerself. Aye?" He turned, patting the rump of the horse beside Richard. "And this here must be the arse of Captain Bailyn."

Bailyn jerked his horse around. "Get yer b'deviled hand off m'horse!" He spat at Fynn through two crooked yellow teeth. His thin face was pale, unshaven, smallpox scarred.

Fynn smirked. "Good God, Bailyn, ye're more ugly than last we saw ye."

Richard motioned Bailyn back. "Kennedy, the boy is a bastard. Ye know 'tis so."

"I am not!" Jemmy burst.

"Ye say he is, do ye?" said Fynn. "Of course ye do."

Juggy stepped in front of Jemmy. "So whose child ya say he is?"

"Ah, m'lady," Richard began. "I'd think you'd be the Betty t' answer that." Juggy's face tightened, her cheeks growing red.

"Damn ye!" Fynn erupted. "I'll not stand for yer insults against the lady or the lad."

"Lady, say you?" Richard spurred his horse sideways, placing his pistol against Fynn's temple, knocking off Fynn's hat. "I told you, maggot, step away." As Fynn took one deliberate step back, Richard grabbed Juggy by the collar, dragging her to his saddle, pressing her smooth face against the leather. He leaned down to her ear, his eyes and pistol still aimed at Fynn. "As you're aware, I speak true when I say the knave is the son of a whore. Aye, Mistress Mackercher?" He released her with a slight shove.

As Juggy stumbled back, Jemmy charged. "Ye're not my uncle! I have no uncle!" Just as he bolted by the third horseman, the man kicked out a spur, slicing Jemmy's right cheek, knocking him to the mud. He clutched his jaw, blood streaming through his fingers. Juggy was to him but he was already on his feet, backing up, refusing her, glaring at everyone.

"Now hear me, all of ye!" shouted Richard, straightening in his saddle. "This bastard boy goes by the name James Annesley, claiming to be the son of the widow Mary Annesley, once Lady Anglesea. But as you all well know, my brother was a drunken whoremonger and this boy is but a whore's son. He is a charlatan. An imposter and a liar. I am Lord Richard Annesley, the one and true Earl of Anglesea. And so help me, I'll hang the one of ye who says otherwise." He pointed his pistol at Jemmy. "Starting with you."

Jemmy stared back, eyes narrowing.

Catharine MacCormick, examined — "Lady Anglesea miscarried about six weeks after her coming to Dunmain. I heard it from Mrs. Charity Heath, her woman, who said that her ladyship would be as fruitful a woman as any, but for ill-usage by his lordship. About two months after I heard that Lady Anglesea was again with child. I was told so by Mrs. Heath, who mentioned to me, with a great deal of pleasure, that she had good news, that my lady was certainly with child again."

— trial transcript, *Annesley v. Anglesea*, 1743

CHAPTER 3

Alas, my Love! Ye do me wrong
To cast me off discourteously;
And I have loved ye so long,
Delighting in yer company.

Greensleeves was all my joy,
Greensleeves was my delight;
Greensleeves was my heart of gold,
And who but Lady Greensleeves.

— *"Greensleeves,"* Anonymous, 1581

Misty fog, aglow in the morning's half-light, settled over St. Stephen's Green, the vast open land on the western edge of Dublin. In a remote corner a meandering creek murmured along, slicing through a pale meadow, dividing trees—trees which sheltered the moist grass and the damp rocks which had tumbled from stone walls overgrown with ferns. It was early, yet the blackbirds were already beginning to fuss and caw. Time crept by, as had the five months since the funeral dirge that continued to play. Jemmy was sitting against one of those enormous oaks. He was focused, his mouth agape, the pink scar etched along his right cheek pointed to his hands where he was trying to count the legs of an orange centipede—he had not made it past seventeen. He would get the poisonous creature to cling to a small stick, its crittery back coiled into a tight ball. Then he would start counting. But whenever he would get to about seventeen, the vermin would uncurl, crawling quickly to the other end of the stick. With no desire to hold the thing, he would quickly invert the stick and begin counting yet again. "Ah, ye little turd," he whispered as it touched his hand, spawning a cold shiver. Hearing the sound of someone approaching, he peered around the trunk. It was Seán ambling toward him, carelessly swatting bushes with a sapling stick. "Seán!" Jemmy stood, his filthy wet clothes sticking to him. "Look at this!" Just then the centipede raced across his hand and up his arm. Jemmy shouted, flinching, whacking his chin with the stick, hurling the creature high into the tree.

"M'God! Get it off me!" Seán was immediately screaming. "Get it off me!"

Jemmy raced around the giant oak to see Seán writhing on the ground, kicking and swatting at the empty air, demon-possessed, wild-eyed and scared. "What's at ye?" Jemmy shouted. An orange flash tumbled from Seán's waistcoat, scurrying for cover under the leaves.

Seán didn't stop. "'Tis bitting me! 'Tis killing me!" He kept thrashing.

"Stop, will ye! Take in some air! 'Tis gone!" Jemmy suppressed a grin.

Seán was panting, his round face pink, blue eyes wide. "Jumped on m'face!"

Jemmy helped him up. "'Twas nothing Seán. Nothing."

"Nay, 'twas something big!" His hands wriggled over his head and chest. "Ye see it?"

"Perhaps just a little—" His mouth creased into a grin.

"'Twas nasty with big teeth! Fangs! Fangs, Jemmy! I saw 'em, I did!"

Jemmy was fighting back tears of laughter, struggling to keep control. It was nearly unbearable—Seán's terrified face and one orange centipede running scared.

"It had a million legs, it did!"

That was it. Jemmy roared with laughter, stuttering, "I'm sorry, Seán. Did m'best. But I counted only seventeen!" Then the dam broke and he dropped to his knees, lurching forward to the ground, giggling hysterically. Sean stopped and stared, totally confused, which only made Jemmy laugh harder. Finally Jemmy settled, feeling the cut under his chin. "So? Did ye bring me some food this mornin'?"

"Da wouldn't let me," Seán mumbled.

"Why not?" Jemmy soured rapidly at the thought of no breakfast. His jaw may have ached a bit, but his stomach burned.

"Said ye're being mule-headed to stay here. Said there's no reason to stay away from him. Ye aren't protecting nobody out here, least not yerself. Said ye should come back t' Mr. Purcell's."

"I don't care what he says," Jemmy blurted. Silence hovered and they sat in it, motionless, watching a man canter his horse across the far end of the green. The beast's snorts steamed in the early air. "If I'm there at Purcell's, that fathead Richard and his men will come. I know it. I'll stay hidden till this is gone."

Seán pulled himself to his feet. "'Tis not going t' just pass, I don't think." He walked a few paces to the creek bank. Swollen gusts whipped the leaves above, and a few wrens and yellow-winged hammer birds began to fill the morning with warble and echoing song. "I miss Dunmain."

"Aye," said Jemmy. They were thinking of the Annesleys' country estate in southern Ireland, the land where both he and Seán were born, where they had played the first ten years of their lives. Seán was born in the servants' quarters, the son of the stablemaster. Jemmy was born in his mother's bedchamber, one of the twenty-eight rooms of the lavish Dunmain House. Jemmy longed for the rolling green hills, the forests, the long stone fences, the random ruins and ancient abbeys lying in wait to be discovered. But he did not miss the house. The immense, cold house held a trove of bad memories—his father beating him, his mother leaving.

"Jemmy!" Seán blurted. "Look at this!"

As Jemmy stepped beside Seán, his eyes followed Seán's outstretched finger down toward the creek. Lying half-exposed in the slick clay was a human skull, peering back at them, peering up into the world, neither entering nor departing, the crown cracked slightly, polished white by water and sun. "M'soul!" Jemmy whispered, staring into its dark eye sockets. "Who do ye think it is?"

"Probably Friar O'Conner." Seán smirked. "After a night of ale. 'Tis begob." Jemmy's smile rolled into a chuckle, imagining the old, fat friar falling drunk into the creek. But the skull just stared back. Sean became serious and whispered, "Da says there's bones of Celtic giants buried in Dublin. All 'round us."

"Ye think this is one of Cuchulainn's knights?"

"Maybe."

"Perhaps, Seán," whispered Jemmy, "'tis Cuchulainn himself." Both boys plopped down on the bank, smiles dissolving, bright eyes warily returning the solemn stare of the great mythic giant.

"Nah," Seán said, recovering, shoving Jemmy. "Can't be. 'Tisn't big enough."

"Ye never know. Maybe 'tis." The skull made Jemmy feel strange, knotting his stomach. The stone image of the woman in Christ Church flashed in his mind—the bright effigy bursting upon him, white-hot light, then gone. Rolling to his back, he stretched his lanky legs across the grass and surveyed the living green rippling overhead. Flashes of distant cyan and white-blue glinted through the calico canopy, dropping down in wispy slants of gold that illuminated the boys below. Closing his eyes, he soaked the light in, the soothing coolness. Soon he began absently humming a tune that he loved, that haunted him. He could hear his mother's delicate voice caressing him with it:

Greensleeves was all my joy,
Greensleeves was my delight;
Greensleeves was my heart of gold,
And who but Lady Greensleeves.

"What are ye going t'do?" asked Seán. At that moment, like the aimless tune adrift, an indifferent emperor moth floated gracefully over their heads. Jemmy watched it, enchanted. It was a brilliant apparition, gliding, flicking its wings, disappearing as magically as it had arrived. Seán pressed on, breaking the spell, "Will ye go away with yer mum, now that—"

"What'll I do?" Jemmy grinned. "I'll put that skull on a stick and chase Juggy with it!"

"Ye know I wasn't talkin' about the skull. I meant—"

"Juggy'd forgive me. She'd beat yer measly arse, but she'd forgive me."

"Ye're a wee prick, ye are!"

Though Jemmy was only twelve, soon to be thirteen, he understood why the local men teased him about Juggy. Joan Landy, "Juggy," once the Annesleys' kitchen maid, had wet-nursed young Master James. Some of the cruder men had implored him to recount the experience, at which he would bolt away. Nevertheless, he loved Juggy like a mother and knew she treasured him in return. Indeed she showed him more concern than anyone else did, except maybe Fynn. She laughed with Jemmy, teased him, listened to him when he needed to talk. And though he adored Juggy, he knew his mother, Mary, flatly despised her, referring to her as "Madam Mack."

Juggy grew up with her brother, Daniel Mackercher, in an Edinburgh orphanage. When she was older she moved to London to serve the estate of Jemmy's maternal-grandfather, John Sheffield, the First Duke of Buckingham, working in the bowels of the Duke's new palace which he had only recently constructed. There she was taken in by the Landys, also serving the Duke. Hungry for a family to call her own, she took their surname, leaving Mackercher far behind. When Arthur and Mary were married, Joan Landy came to Ireland as part of the Annesley household. She had served them ever since. As far back as Jemmy could remember, a prattling of "lil' Scotty lass" tales and "Miss Juggy" stories had been bandied about. The one he heard most was when Juggy first arrived in Ireland, how she had been seen secreting about with his father. He was not sure what "secreting about" meant, but no doubt that was why his mother hated her so much. Perhaps it was the same "secreting about" rumored between his mother and a tanner named Palliser—his father sliced clean the man's ear, who in turn took out Arthur's eye. He would ask his mother, thought Jemmy. Someday. When he saw her again. If he ever did. No, he would ask Juggy. Juggy would tell him the truth.

"Ach." Seán's voice was tight. "Will ye be going away with yer mum, or won't ye?"

Jemmy sighed, rolling his eyes. There was no escaping Seán when he had an unanswered question, especially about Jemmy's mother. Seán's mother was Margaret Kennedy, the "matron saint" who had died giving birth to Seán. Juggy had been Margaret's closest friend, and Jemmy often saw Juggy cry at the mention of the dead woman. "Tell me, Jemmy!" Seán would not let it go.

"Tell ye what?"

"Ach! Ye bloody well know! What I keep askin' ye! Are ye going t' England? Are we t'be friends no more?"

"I don't know where she is, Seán." Jemmy felt his face flush as he conceded to the question. "I don't think she wants me with her. 'Tis been two years." He clambered to his feet, took a few paces, then picked up a small rock and began tossing it between his hands, shifting its weight from side to side, faster and faster. "Besides, she's probably already gone." He threw the rock at the skull, missing it. Then he snatched another stone and took careful aim before letting it fly. It hit just above the eye sockets and bounced away. Moving to the bank, he flumped down and found more pebbles to throw. One after another, slowly and deliberately, he tossed them, knowing all the while that Seán was still standing, watching him, confused. "Once, twice, thrice. Once, twice, thrice." Jemmy faintly counted his lofted shots. The small stones produced a hollow melody as they hit the ancient forehead then plopped into the shallow trickling stream and dark clay beyond. "Once, twice, thrice. Wants. Two eyes. Through ice. Eh?"

His friend was now sitting beside him. "Our codes."

Jemmy raised a finger. "Wants—"

"All be clear," Seán interjected, then paused. "Don't guess it'll mean yer Da's not around."

"Thank the gods." Jemmy added his middle finger to the other. "Two eyes," he said, pronouncing it like 'twice', "'tis me warning yer half-wit head to look about."

"Ach, sure." Seán elbowed Jemmy.

"And through ice," Jemmy exclaimed, raising three fingers. "We stand together. No matter the bastard."

Seán got to his feet. "Had we been at the Boyne, t'would've been our signal. Through the thick of it!" He thrust three fingers into the glowing air, as if commanding his men up the grisly hill of that most celebrated of Irish battles.

"True," said Jemmy with a smile. He returned to stoning the river. Much to his growing annoyance, and as much as he tried, he could not make the flight of the pebbles follow a consistent path. One would fall into the stream with a splash, then be washed clean and glide down the way. Another would veer to the left on its descent and land splat in the muck of the far shore, then slip from sight, swallowed in the ancient clay and silt. He became obsessed with the rock-casting, but it was futile. Only smaller and smaller pebbles remained, and they were increasingly unpredictable. As fate embraces chaos, order was not to be grasped, and the bitter issue about him leaving was still lingering, distastefully unresolved.

"So, what are ye goin' t'do?" Seán asked, as if on cue. He turned in a big circle, surveying the common green. "Ye can't rightly live out here. Anyway, Da said if ye want any more food ye'll have t' come back t' Purcell's." He started peeling bark from the oak that swelled over them like a colossus. "Besides, out here isn't much hidden."

"'Tis a fine place t' hide from that bastard Richard," Jemmy growled, standing and gathering his waistcoat. He warily watched two old men with a milk cow amble through the park, guiding the animal across a small rickety footbridge, then out through the north gate. Jemmy turned and walked the other way.

"Where ye going?" asked Seán, surprised.

"T' get breakfast. Ye not coming?"

Seán trotted to catch up.

—⁓—

Mrs. Dorothy Briscoe, examined — "I cannot charge my memory if Lady Anglesea was a second time with child. Lord and Lady Anglesea came to Dunmain after Queen Anne died. I do not remember her ladyship being with child. I had the smallpox when Queen Anne died, and my mother came to New Ross upon my sickness. (Did you ever hear that Lady Anglesea was with child?) Indeed, I can't tell, but I might, for Mrs. Heath tells me a hundred things about my own family which I am an entire stranger to, and an honest, worthy woman she is as ever lived by bread."

— trial transcript, *Annesley v. Anglesea*, 1743

—⁓—

CHAPTER 4

Richard Annesley, younger brother to the Earl, was a man
of whom it may be said, without any danger of being too
severe, that he had all the vices centered in his composi-
tion: He was proud and mean at the same time—vain-
glorious yet avaricious—ungrateful for good offices—
revengeful for even imagined injuries—treacherous when
trusted—mischievously inquisitive when not so—without
the least spark of honor, pity, or even common human-
ity—incapable by nature of doing any good, and qualified
by an extreme subtlety for all kinds of evil.

— *Memoirs of an Unfortunate Young Nobleman,*
James Annesley, 1743

That same morning, Richard Annesley, the self-proclaimed peer, stood in his
nightshirt, observing from his bedroom window, grinning imperiously as the
cold floor chilled his feet. Lowering his gaze, he saw little people and their
little horses moving along Anglesea Street below, parting the morning fog of
Dublin's Temple Bar. The street was named in 1659, in honor of his grandfather who had built Temple Bar—a development of homes, shops, taverns,
shipping docks, and even the Parliament Building itself, which towered over
it all, pigeons fluttering about its crowning roof. Below that he could see the
building's sweeping array of columns, its majestic courtyard. Now that he was
Earl he might build a new house, a mansion, a palatial residence. He smirked.
Perhaps he would build it alongside the Parliament Building, snug against the
law. That would erase all doubts. Then take a wife, some high-browed British bitch, some aristocratic daughter. No. Later. That can wait. Besides there
were plenty of fields open now for his plow. He would return to Dunmain
House, in County Wexford, the seat of Anglesea power, precisely where he
belonged—away from these factors with their spotted hands outstretched,
and the blue bloods of the pale, white-gloved, come to inspect both the manner and the ware.

A rustle behind him drew him to turn. Buried in the bed linens slept
an English beauty, breathing softly. He watched her. She was a servant, a

chambermaid, but not one from his stable of thirty-seven. No, Charity Heath was the ladyservant of Lady Mary Sheffield, his infamous sister-in-law, the banished, outcast wife, the recent widow. Richard had first seen Charity— this slender vixen nestled in his bed—two weeks earlier, from the foyer of Delaney's Clothier on St. James Street. For the past month, his men, Captain Bailyn and Patrick Higgins, had taken turns spying on Mary Sheffield's home from that clothier, watching for James to come slinking back to his mother. When Richard joined them briefly one day, he saw Charity step from Mary's house and climb aboard a small cart. He was captivated in the instant. Yet it was not just her graceful beauty that beguiled him. What intrigued him most was how she might assist his cause. Within the hour he had followed her, introduced himself, and was charming her, snaring her in his web. Bedding her was just a benefit of his ignoble efforts, the spoils of a successful hunt. Now she lay there, her brown hair swirled stormily across his pillows, the blanket rising and falling with the rhythm of her breath. He watched for a moment, smirking, wondering what Mary must think about her servant's overnight absence. Moving to the edge of the bed, he gently shook her arm. "Charity, my sweet, 'tis morning." Though the words were kind, they were laden with disapproval. She groaned softly and opened her eyes. "Ye must return soon," he added.

She whispered. "Do you wish for me to go?"

Her bare shoulders mellowed him. He slid on top of her and nodded. "I'll miss ye."

"So you'd have me believe."

"What have ye told Lady Sheffield, of yer going and coming?"

She pushed him off, rolling over, straddling him, the blanket falling from her bare shoulders. "Have I told her of us?"

"I know I can trust ye. I was—"

She squeezed him between her thighs, silencing him. "'Tis my choice to be here." She bit him playfully on the nose. "And if your intentions are...." She paused, then smiled mischievously. "If they are as I suspect, soon I'll have no need to return to her service." Her eyebrows arched to the silent question. To which he gently felt her breasts, then roughly flipped her onto her back, kissing her hard.

A soft knock resonated from across the room. "Lord Anglesea?" the butler inquired, his voice muffled through the thick wood door.

"What is it?" snapped Richard.

"M'lord, Captain Bailyn and Mr. Higgins are downstairs for ye."

"Put them in the parlor. I'll be there directly."

"Very well, m'lord." The butler's footsteps faded away.

Richard huffed. "I must go." He swung his feet off the bed.

—⚹—

Charity studied him as he dressed. She knew she was beautiful, tall and slim, similar to Mary in many ways. But could she be a gentlewoman, the wife of an Earl? She had served Mary since they were both fifteen, vicariously acquiring the habits and customs of polite society. In fact, Mary had kept her in such good dress that it was not unusual for Charity to be mistaken for gentility. But she wasn't. Her father had placed her in the Duke of Buckingham's service so she could help support her family. When Mary's mother died, Charity was there by Mary's side, supporting her. When the Duke then married Princess Catherine, who was the same age as Mary, the new Duchess took no time to expel Mary from Buckingham Palace. Charity left too, remaining the faithful lady-in-waiting to Mary. She had remained Mary's closest confidante ever since.

Nevertheless, Charity was lonely, having never married, having kept a hope kindled that a society gentleman would save her from a life of servitude. Years passed and no such gentleman came, only a few seedy requests for fanciful affairs which she usually accepted, hoping to massage them into more. Now it was Richard, the Earl of Anglesea. But this was different, she could sense it—he wanted to marry her. Didn't he? He needed a wife. And he was nothing like his hateful, dead brother, Arthur. Though she had disliked Arthur for being such a drunken monster, she had despised him more for never bedding her. God, and Mary too, knew Arthur had had many other women. So how was she that different from them, from Mary? What could Mary give a man that she could not? She was just as much a gentlewoman as Mary ever was, especially considering Mary's own vices. At least she had Richard now. He would elevate her to the same position Mary had held, till late. She smiled, watching him finish. Thank God for that coach on Bridge Street.

"You should get dressed," he said. The snapping tone was back.

"I will," she whispered as he left.

—⚹—

Richard hurried down the stairs and burst into the main parlor, finding Captain Bailyn and Patrick Higgins on opposite sides of the room, rising to their feet, hats in their hands.

"Did ye find him?" Richard demanded. "Tell me ye did."

"Nay, yer lordship," replied Bailyn. "Not a hair of the bastard."

"Then ye're clearly not looking!" snarled Richard. "God damn ye both!"

"M'lord," Higgins began, "we've kept a vigil at his mother's house and—"

"Blood and thunder! I told ye t' forget that. He won't be venturin' there. Not now." Richard turned and began filling his pipe, then tamped the loose tobacco.

"Aye, m'lord, but—" Higgins began.

"Good then." Using a tapered candle from the mantle, Richard lit his pipe, then exhaled a thick, aromatic cloud. "Where will ye look today?"

"St. Stephen's. College Green," Captain Bailyn answered. "Likely places."

"M'lord," Higgins interjected. "If James is there, we...." His voice trailed away.

Bailyn grinned wickedly. "Higgs is afraid we can't shoot the lad in a common as easily as we can in an alley. Ach, witnesses 'n all."

"'Tis easy enough," Richard said. "Take him to the back of St. Stephen's. There are places where even a foxhound wouldn't find the lad's corpse. Where ye dumped the other fellow."

"Aye, m'lord," sneered Bailyn. "Man's still bathing in the creek."

"Sire," Higgins interrupted, "Regardless of where Bailyn has done such foul deeds before, this lad's body will be searched for. And mind ya, it will be found. A murder charge would see us all hanged."

Richard shrugged, walking to the fireplace. Looking down at its cold ashes, he puffed his pipe. Blue smoke floated through the room.

Higgins continued, louder, "M'lord, it would be just as dangerous for yar neck."

Richard remained silent, turning to Captain Bailyn, studying him. "What do ye think?"

Bailyn's mouth curled. "Let's just kill him somewhere else, then burn him."

"Good Lord!" bellowed Higgins. "There are other means, with much less risk to all of us, m'lord. Have ya not considered to simply transport the lad?"

Bailyn chortled. "Boy-shagger Higgs is afraid he'll miss." He clapped a hand on Higgins's shoulder. "Don't fret, lassy, I'll hold the bastard while ye run him through!"

"Ya're a horse's arse." Higgins whipped around. "I won't be part of killin' the lad."

"Getting a wee bit bold for a highwayman, aren't ye?" Richard sneered, slowly pouring himself a brandy. "Ye don't wish t'be swinging from the Tyburn tree." Higgins moved to stare out of the window. Richard stepped behind him. "After ye and the honorable Captain Bailyn did such a fine job with my brother, 'twould be easy to have ye shittin' yerself in the gallows."

Turning slowly, Higgins looked directly into Richard's eyes. "I didn't know Bailyn was going to kill yar brother. I found him for ya, drunk at the Brazen Head. That was all."

"Ah, but ye drove the coach!" declared Richard.

"I bloody well did not!" Higgins protested.

"Ah, let's not quibble the details." Just then, at nearly half-past nine, the carillon bells of Richard's German clock began an unmercifully loud toll of the ten o'clock hour. Higgins took the shattering moment to gather his thoughts and to pull down his anger. He condemned himself to this walking prison the prior autumn, when he made the mistake of attempting to rob the wrong carriage—a handsome coach carrying Richard Annesley. Over-powered by Captain Bailyn and others, Higgins was taken to Kilmainham Jail, outside Dublin, where the gaol-magistrate was Richard's cousin. There he was given a bargain—to save his life he would have to sell his soul. Six months later he was now standing in Richard's parlor staring out into Ang-lesea Street, and he could see no end to the imprisonment. When the clock's bells finally stopped, he took a deep breath and asked again, "M'lord, let us transport him."

"To the Colonies?" Richard laughed. "Sell him like a slave? Like you?" No response.

"Just let me shoot him, sire," Captain Bailyn implored.

Richard laughed. "Which one?"

"Either one." Bailyn grinned. "Higgs first, then the lad. Or the other way round."

Higgins growled, "We'll put him on the next slave ship from Ringsend. Same as killing him. Ya'll never see him again."

"And what if I do?" Richard tone was bone-cold.

"Then yar honorable Captain can kill him," replied Higgins.

"Ney, I won't be needing Bailyn's services for that." Richard stepped close to Higgins. "Both of ye. Get the lad. Indenture him. Transport him. All that's necessary. But, Mr. Higgins, mind you, if James returns to Ireland, or England, 'twill be you that kills him. You!" He thumped Higgins's chest. "Ye'll squeeze his eyes out with yer thumbs and bring 'em to me."

Higgins turned to the door, grumbling, "'Tis an ill bird that defiles its own nest."

"Jacobite dribble. Go!" barked Richard. "Go before Bailyn makes sport of ye with his sword." Higgins donned his hat, gathered his coat, and left.

—⁓—

Upstairs, Charity Heath was out of bed, half-dressed, sitting on the front edge of a heavy oak chair. She was leaning forward, frozen, listening to the men below. Intently poised. A cat over a rat in the floor.

Major Richard Fitzgerald, examined — "I met Lord Anglesea at Ross, and he invited me to dine with him the next
day. I desired to be excused, as I was to dine with some
officers, but Lord Anglesea said that I must dine with him,
and come to drink some groaning drink, for that his wife
was in labour. I said that that was a reason I ought not to
go, but he would not take an excuse. He sent me word
the next day to Ross that his wife was brought to bed of
a son. I went to Dunmain, and dined there, and we had
some discourse about the child. Lord Anglesea swore that I
should see his son, and accordingly the nurse brought the
child, and I kissed it, and gave half-a-guinea to the nurse.
Some of the company toasted the heir-apparent to Lord
Anglesea at dinner."

— trial transcript, *Annesley v. Anglesea*, 1743

CHAPTER 5

If you be too wise, they will expect excess of you;
If you be too foolish, you will be deceived;
If you be too conceited, you will be thought vexatious;
If you be too humble, you will be without honor;
If you be too talkative, you will not be heeded;
If you be too silent, you will not be regarded;
If you be too harsh, you will be broken,
If you be too feeble, you will be crushed.

> — *Instructions of a King*, 267, Irish King Cormac
> MacArt, instructing his son Cairbre on the
> duties of a king.

Four days passed. Now the dark waters of the River Anna Liffey moved through another damp morning. It was Sunday and the array of brass church bells began clanging, rousing their flocks, summoning them. They were calling, like the harking screech of a falcon calls her young to follow, to stretch their fledgling wings, to engage their faith, to cling to hope, trusting the unseen air will hold them. Come to this church! they cried. Come all of you. Come trust that God is here. Come cling to the hope that only we can give you. Come now!

Jemmy was listening, but not moving. He was crouched behind a pillar supporting Ormonde Quay, waiting for Seán, watching the boats plying the river, his stomach growling angrily. He could see light traffic on Essex Bridge above him. Perhaps he should run, he reasoned. This morning. On his thirteenth birthday. The day he was born, so he'd been told, there came a solar eclipse—a day of promise. Or foreboding? He remembered the coldness of the full eclipse three years prior. It had harkened his mother leaving. Today felt the same somehow, an eerie coldness, a darkness, though the bright of day was upon them all. It was a good day to go, to leave Dublin. It would be his gift to himself. But go where? He pictured his mother. Why hadn't she sent for him? What about Fynn and Juggy and Seán? Could he simply leave them? He must. If only. Glancing back at the stream of people and horses crossing the bridge, he noticed a woman riding in a small cart—she was society, with a large, elegant hat atop her head. He recognized her. Something familiar. In that instant he knew her—his mother! He was certain! He scrambled up the steep steps, raced around the bridgehead, turning, tearing through the moving masses of horses, carts, carriages and people. The cart was already off Essex Bridge, moving south. Now he could see two women on the open bench behind the driver. One was his mother, the other one, the one wearing the bonnet, must be Charity. Heart pounding, he broke into a sprint. "Mother! Charity!" he yelled. Neither woman turned.

"Jemmy!" Suddenly there was Seán stepping into his path. Jemmy dodged past him and kept running. "Jemmy! Stop!" screamed Seán. "Da's lookin' for ye!" Jemmy ignored him, running as fast as he could on the crowded road. The cart turned left on Dame Street, directly abreast Dublin Castle. He sprinted blindly, knocking down two men with a sideboard, scattering chickens in the road. Finally, he rounded the corner where he had seen her turn. He slowed, panting. She was gone. Dejected, he walked into College Green and plopped on the pedestal of King William III's statue, the grand man riding high on a noble steed. Within seconds Seán came to him, deflating beside him. They were quiet for a while, just sitting, catching their breaths.

"I'm tired of running after ye," grumbled Seán.

"I saw her," said Jemmy.

"Don't think 'twas yer mum. She—"

"'Twas!" Jemmy blurted, "I know it!" He shoved Seán off the pedestal.

"All right!" Seán shrugged, standing. "As ye say. Ye win, today. She was yer mum. She was anyone. She was yer fairy godmother."

Jemmy sprang up, fist clenched. He slammed Seán backwards. "I'll bust your teeth Seán if you say more!. You don't know her."

Though evenly built with Seán, Jemmy had a bulldog's thickness to his bones. An unexpected strength matched with a simmering temper. But Seán was a better aim, and given the opportunity to fight back with a rock missile, Seán was the usual victor, or at least could keep Jemmy at bay till he stopped foaming. Today was different. Everything was different. So Seán just stood, in no mood to tangle with Jemmy. He stepped back, feigning a sudden interest in the looming statue. "I thought the O'Malleys were gonna pull this English bastard down."

Jemmy shrugged. He was from a long line of those "English bastards" and they both knew it. But Seán didn't care, and though Jemmy didn't acknowledge it, he could not find the courage to defame the English peerage out loud. It was always there, part of him, yet not. A lingering illness. A smell not to

be washed away. His father had been the Sixth Earl of Anglesea—and didn't
that make him the Seventh? Or since his shite-uncle Richard claimed it, if he
got it back, would that make him the Eighth? He was steeped in the smell
of peerage. Even on his mother's side, his grandfather was a Duke, living in
Buckingham Palace in London (he had seen a painting of it) and was counselor to kings and queens—even been counsel to this king, King William III,
under whose horse's massive marble cock he was now sitting.

Suddenly Seán announced, "Richard's shaggin' yer mum's lady."

Jemmy glanced up, his eyebrows peaked. "Charity?"

"That's not the worst of it. No." He sat again and waited for Jemmy to
nudge him on.

"Aye?" Jemmy huffed.

"Yer uncle...."

"What of him?"

"He has a mind t' sell ye. T' transport ye t' the Colonies."

"Who told ye that?"

"A Scot." Seán gestured to the south. "A coffin maker on Cook. Told me
t'warn ye."

Jemmy nodded, eyes wide. "I must be gone, Seán."

"Not yet ye don't. There's a barn, a loft in the Frapper Stables that ye—"

"Lads!" Fynn Kennedy called from Dame Street, driving a wagon toward
them.

"Shite!" groaned Jemmy, getting to his feet.

"I told ye. He's been lookin' for ye," said Seán.

Fynn stopped the team. "Come here. Both of ye!" Jemmy trailed Seán
to the street. He could see Fynn's eyes darting from one passerby to another.
"Climb in," Fynn ordered. "Keep yer head down, Seámus."

"Aye, sir," both boys said together, pulling themselves into the wagon and
hunkering below the rails. The horses started moving, bumping the wagon
along. Fynn kept them at an even clomp for awhile, along the mile back to
Purcell's shop.

"Seán," Fynn began, "have ye solved my riddle? As I inquired of ye
yesterday?"

"What riddle, Da?"

"Faith, lad! Can't ye remember? Lil' Jennie Whiteface has a red nose. The
longer she lives, the shorter she grows." Fynn glanced back at the boys. "So
lads, who is she? Eh?"

"A red-beaked warbler?" Seán guessed.

"Ach, Seán, ye're not trying. Birds grow shorter as they age, do they?" Several men walked close to the wagon and Fynn let them pass. "Seámus, what do ye think?" Jemmy didn't answer. "By japers lad! Are ye of the hearin'?"

"Aye, Mr. Kennedy, I hear ye," Jemmy drolly replied. "But I don't know."

"Humph! Well, maybe ye'll think on it," said Fynn, furrowing his brow.

As they stopped in front of the butcher's shop, Juggy rushed out. "Fynn, have ye seen—"

Fynn motioned with his head. "Seán. Seámus. Out with ye." They scrambled to ground.

"Jemmy? Seán?" She was half-smiling. "Where were ya Jemmy? And on yar birthday! Ya had us worried!"

Jemmy lowered his chin. "I'm sorry. I—"

"Seán," she interrupted, "lend a hand to Mr. Purcell. I must speak with Jemmy." Seán hesitated, staring at Jemmy as if looking at the condemned. "Go on! Shoo lad!" Juggy insisted with the brush of her hand. "He'll be along shortly." After Seán disappeared inside, Juggy took Jemmy's arm and led him to the bench on the shop's stoop. "Will ya sit with me?"

"Aye, ma'am," replied Jemmy, sitting. But she remained standing. He glanced up, seeing her holding a long object wrapped in brown cloth.

She gestured toward his cheek. "Never forget who gave ya that scar, lad. Understand me?"

"Aye, ma'am," he replied, confused by its mention.

She moved closer, tears welling in her eyes. "I want ya to have this, in honor of yar day."

"What is it?" he murmured, taking the object. It was heavy, narrow, about the length of a man's foot. His heart raced as he quickly unwound the dark-brown linen. Then his mouth fell open. Lying across his knees was the most magnificent dirk he had ever seen—gleaming brass hilt, richly oiled sheath. The dagger's pommel was an intricate acorn, the grip widening at the blade, forming a guard etched with ribbons. Grasping the hilt, he drew it from the sheath. The blade was single-edged with a thick spine of inlaid brass. Running two fingers down the leading edge, ever so lightly, he felt the deadly sharpness, then traced an engraving along the blood groove. "*Léargas sa Dorchadas.*" He read the Gaelic aloud, then translated it, "Sight in the Dark."

Juggy was now beside him. "'Twas my father's." She dabbed her eyes with a cloth and took a deep breath. "I want ya to have it. Please take it. But do be careful with it."

"Thank ye," he said, carefully resheathing it. "'Tis a marvelous thing."

"Aye. As ya are t'me." She placed a hand on his knee. Tears returning, she looked away. "I must go in," she said, standing. 'Happy birthday, son. Ya'll keep it safe?"

"Aye. I will," he said, standing with her. "Thank you." He watched her go.

Juggy hurried inside Purcell's, through a rack of hanging hare, past a customer thumping pork sides, and then silently by John Purcell and Seán slicing herring near the back. She sat on the stairs leading to the living quarters above and closed her eyes. She prayed Jemmy would be safe. When Fynn came, wrapping her in his big arms, she leaned into him and opened her eyes. Through the open storefront, she could see Jemmy on the bench near the street, studying the dirk. To her, Jemmy was everything. The son she never had.

"Do ya think his scar will go away?" she asked softly.

"No," Fynn replied.

"I wish something could be done," she murmured. "That boy has such a beautiful face." As a Scottish orphan, Juggy, Joan Mackercher, had survived by toiling in the fields and sweltering kitchens of strangers. At sixteen, with her youthful beauty in full blossom, she traveled to York in the service of her betters. There, John Sheffield, the First Duke of Buckingham, noticed her, abruptly declaring Buckingham Palace in need of another linen maid. And so Juggy, then Joan Landy, served the Duke until May of 1706, when the Duke's only child, Mary, was married off to Arthur Annesley, the Sixth Earl of Anglesea. At that time the Duke remarried, and his new wife quickly unburdened her new husband of the temptations of an attractive and young female staff. Thus Juggy (along with Mary's lady-in-waiting, Charity Heath) was carted to the southern coast of Ireland, joining the Annesley staff at Dunmain, near the towns of Waterford and New Ross. Among Arthur's most notable servants was Fynn Kennedy, his stablemaster. Fynn's wife, Margaret, became fast friends with Juggy, helping her settle into her new Irish home. They had giggled and wept together, worked side by side, shared intimate secrets.

Within a year, Lady Anglesea became pregnant. About that time, Margaret's and Juggy's bellies also began swelling. Juggy heard the women whispering about her unmarried condition. The men leered, calling her Juggy, claiming to have "shagged the Scottish wench." She ignored them. Having endured such banalities for most of her years, these were no different. And so that winter Mary was carrying Jemmy, Margaret was pregnant with Seán, and Juggy was to have an illegitimate baby boy, whom she would name Daniel, in honor of her brother.

Though Juggy rarely saw her brother, Daniel Mackercher, she loved him intensely. They had been separated when she was ten, seven years after their parents and six other siblings died in a wave of typhus that had rushed through the Scottish Highlands. She had only seen him twice since, once in Dublin, once in New Ross, and both visits had been wonderful. After serving in the Scottish military, Daniel trained as a barrister and had recently offered his sister employment in Edinburgh—an offer she might have accepted had he asked during her dark years at Dunmain. But now she was pledged to Fynn. She belonged in Ireland, with him. Wherever life would take them. All the same, nothing thrilled her more than a letter from Daniel. Each time, no matter what she was doing, she would find Fynn, sit in a quiet place with her eyes closed, listening to Daniel's soothing, transporting words.

When Juggy gave birth to the baby, Daniel, few around Dunmain House took notice, except when nursing kept Juggy from her household duties. The attention remained on the upcoming birth of the Anglesea heir. And thus it was with little mourning that Juggy's three-week-old baby became ill and died. Juggy was destroyed. Only the Kennedys comforted her, cared for her. Then on April 25, 1715, blanketed by a celebrated eclipse, Mary gave birth to young Master James Annesley. At the grand celebration, Arthur stood imperiously and announced Juggy would wet nurse the young heir as fate had so blessed her with "bursting breasts from the recent loss of her child." Within days a coach road was built from Dunmain House to Juggy's little cottage, allowing Her Ladyship to comfortably travel the half-mile to visit her infant boy. Meanwhile a glass window was installed, the thatched roof repaired, and a magnificent carved bed brought for the child-heir. As Juggy's smelly hay bed remained, along with her flimsy chair and table, she was directed to only nurse the child by the fire, near his bed.

One month later, Margaret died giving birth to Seán and Juggy's life fell black. Years later she still shuddered at the memory of holding her dead baby, of Margaret dying so soon thereafter. But she also remembered the pure joy of nursing Jemmy. Jemmy had been her light, her salvation when she might have otherwise lost her mind, her soul swallowed in despair. He made her smile. Always. Just as she was now smiling, leaning on Fynn, watching Jemmy outside, bathed in new sunlight. She closed her eyes, remembering him, a baby in her arms, thirteen years ago, suckling her breasts, his tiny pink toes. God protect her dear boy.

—ᴍ—

Outside, Jemmy had just finished wrapping the dirk and was now entranced, watching a tinker push a lopsided cart up the cobbled street. The cart's wheels thumped as they turned, clanging and jangling the tin pans and trinkets. Then, as if from a mirage, five men on horseback suddenly galloped up to Purcell's. The front man tipped his red hat to Jemmy, who sat petrified, instantly recognizing the man's choleric, thin face.

"Captain Bailyn!" shouted Fynn, stepping from the shop, advancing quickly between the horsemen and Jemmy. "To what do we owe this pleasure?" Jemmy noticed the man riding farthest back was the same man who had spurred his face at the funeral. As their eyes met, the man looked away. Jemmy slid the dirk behind the bench and stood.

"'Tis him," said Bailyn, pointing at Jemmy. "Shoot anyone who gets in my way." One of the men raised his musket.

"Come now," Fynn sneered, "what do ye think I'll do, unarmed as I am?"

"Keep yar place, sir," warned the man.

Juggy stepped outside, then Seán, with Kate Purcell and her two girls close behind. John Purcell burst past them, rolling up his sleeves as he did. "Get back inside," he snapped. Reaching into Fynn's wagon, he removed two large clubs, tossing one to Fynn.

"I've come t'get the bastard," Bailyn announced, pointing at Jemmy. He drew a pistol from his saddle holster. "Ye should all get inside." His saddle creaked as he leaned forward. "All except for lil' James here."

Fynn brandished his club, shouting, "I'll brain the one of ye who touches the lad!"

"Oh my!" Bailyn laughed mockingly. "What are we t'do?"

Purcell stepped forward. "It'll take more than a lead ball."

"Aye, ye're a big'un." Bailyn cocked his pistol. "But we'll find a coffin t'fit ye."

"There won't be any killing!" the horseman in the rear yelled. "Captain! We've no orders to do further."

Jemmy looked at Higgins, the man speaking, the same man who had sliced his face in the churchyard. Captain Bailyn suddenly began a rumbling chuckle, then lifted his pistol and fired at the butcher's shop sign, the ball splintering a hole through the wooden cow. He whipped his mount around, shouting with a flourish, "Good day t'all ye swine! I'll be back for the boy. I assure ye." He spurred his horse, cantering up Ship Street, three of the men riding close behind. Higgins tipped his hat, then slowly reined his horse around, walking it away. Jemmy sprinted furiously down the street, away from everyone.

Fynn shouted after him, "Seámus!" Jemmy kept running. "Seámus!" He watched Jemmy turn between two buildings and disappear. "Seámus!" Fynn followed him, stopping at the narrow passageway. Seán was close behind.

"Mind the rats," Seán offered, moving to take the lead.

"Lad." Fynn caught Seán's shoulder. "Stay here. Will ye?"

Seán huffed. "Alright, Da. But go to yer right when ye come out back there."

Fynn squeezed between the two walls. When he stepped out he was standing on the hillside behind the row of buildings that faced Ship Street. "M'God!" Two rats scurried over the rotting rubbish in front of him while a thick fog of flies buzzed about. Sewage odor burned his throat, setting his eyes to watering. He jerked his ascot over his mouth and nose. To his right he saw a worn trail along the top of the embankment. He followed it, crossing six waste ditches, then moved downhill through a clump of trees. There the trail disappeared, fading into the slick grass. He pulled his ascot down and stood in the shadows, his eyes searching the moat's bank. Rising on the far side was Dublin Castle, its enormous stone walls besieged by vine and moss. "Seámus? *Cá bhfuil tú*, Seámus?" he shouted, hearing his words echo off the English castle. "*Cá bhfuil tú?*" he called again. Slight movement on the ground caught his eye—the shadow of a boy, a young man. Looking up into the interlacing limbs above him, he saw Jemmy perched on a plank. Jemmy glanced down, then looked away. "*Tá athas orm tú a fheiceáil,*" said Fynn, telling Jemmy he was glad to see him. Jemmy nodded, a blank expression on his face. "Sorry I found ye, are ye?" Fynn asked, stepping forward to see Jemmy's face. He used a hand to shield the sunlight from his eyes.

"Nay," muttered Jemmy, scratching his chin.

"Hiding, are ye?"

"Wish I could."

"I reckon ye do," Fynn offered, smiling. "May I join ye?" Jemmy gave a faint nod. "Well, let's see." Fynn grunted, wrapping his arms around the trunk, attempting to pull himself up. But he lost his grip and slid back to the ground. Glancing back at Jemmy, Fynn sighed, frustrated. Jemmy almost smiled. Fynn tried again, struggling a little higher before sliding down once more. "Damnation," he grumbled with a huff.

"There's steps 'round the other side."

Fynn walked around the elm and climbed up the wooden planks he found nailed there. As he came to the rickety platform, Jemmy scooted to make what room he could. There was barely enough space for them to sit shoulder-to-shoulder, feet dangling in the air. Fynn wrapped an arm around Jemmy's back. They sat quietly. Then, like a breeze on a humid day, the moment passed. Fynn sighed deeply, studying Jemmy, seeing the midday sun flittering across the boy's light hair. It danced and shimmered there, shades of light then dark, shifting and swaying. Like a playful antic, the sun amusing itself with the innocent.

Jemmy was staring off, beyond the limbs above them, high over the castle, watching a peregrine falcon gliding effortlessly on its white-gray speckled wings. He studied it, observing its graceful, deadly actions. Suddenly, with speed-blurred ease, it dived for a small bird, flipped on impact, rolling midair, screeching as it missed its prey. "What am I t'do?" Jemmy asked.

"I don't know. Ye deserve t'be the rightful—" Fynn stopped himself, then continued, "Ye are the rightful Earl of Anglesea. B'God, ye are, indeed." He looked at the castle, lowered his gaze, then finally closed his eyes. "But we must prove it."

"Prove it?" exploded Jemmy. "Why must we prove it? I'm my father's only son! Shouldn't that arse, my supposed uncle, shouldn't he have to prove who he is instead? How can he say I'm a bastard? Juggy is not my mother!"

"Of course she's not," said Fynn, seeing Jemmy was close to tears. "But this matter won't be resolved easily, I'm afraid. We must—"

"I should just go away, and not be—"

"I won't have ye tuckin' yer tail and—"

"'Tis my choice." Jemmy's voice was surprisingly soft and far away.

Fynn took Jemmy's chin, forcing the boy to face him. "Aye, son. 'Tis yer choice." Jemmy pulled his face away. Not till Jemmy glanced back did Fynn continue. "Think on it. If we let Richard remain unchallenged, let him wrap himself in yer father's trimmings, let him take residence in Dunmain House, let him collect the Earl's rents...he'll be all the harder to remove. People will accept it if they see you accepting it, even if ye truly don't." He shook his head. "It doesn't make it right, Seámus. But ye shouldn't run."

"I can't stay either," Jemmy muttered. "To stay means to put the lot of ye at risk."

"Ye can't worry about that." Fynn closed his eyes, as if in defeat. Losing because he had no alternative, no hope, no promise to offer.

"What will Richard do t'me? Will his Captain kill me?"

"Nay! He'd have to kill me first. He would indeed."

"Or indenture me. To the Colonies?"

"He may try, but...."

Jemmy sat still, a slight breeze washing over them. "I can't stay in Dublin."

"Give us some time. To hire a solicitor. Stay hidden till we find a solicitor to take yer cause to the King's Bench. But we can't if ye're gone, Seámus. James Annesley himself must bring the charges, must make the accusation. In his very person." Fynn glanced quickly at Jemmy, hoping to see agreement, relief, something in those blue-green eyes. He hoped to see the boy believing the impossible—that a common Catholic like Fynn could afford an English solicitor.

But Jemmy was vacant, resigned. "Why do ye call me Seámus?"

Fynn hesitated before speaking. "Because deep inside ye're Irish. I see it in ye."

"But I'm English."

"Never in my eyes, lad."

Looking over the fetid valley and moat, Jemmy saw the rough ancient stones of the castle wall standing beyond. They had been there for over six centuries, protecting the Irish from countless attacks. But now they just held back the refuse of the people, protecting the English nobles inside from all others, from all else. What good were those stones? Who would want to wade through Irish sewage to capture an English castle that held nothing? Another fleeting wind whipped through the canopy of leaves, carrying the smell of rain with it.

"Best be going back, Seámus," Fynn prodded, his voice almost a whisper.

"Aye," muttered Jemmy, looking away, seeing the falcon had returned. Or perhaps it was different one. It climbed, dove, snatched its prey mid-air, then soared once again straight into the azure sky. He watched intently, pleased to be so momentarily distracted from his dread.

—※—

Dennis Redmonds, examined — "The child was christened James when it was about three weeks old, by Lord Anglesea's chaplain, Mr. Lloyd. The nurse who nursed the child was Joan Landy. Yes, I am familiar that she was on occasion known as Juggy. I was told that she was preferred because she had the best milk. There was a bonfire made and other rejoicing for the birth of the child. There was great drinking and carousing, and some of them were found drunk in the ditches next morning. The child was nursed about a quarter of a mile from Dunmain House, in Joan Landy's house, which was upon my lord's land. Lord Anglesea and his lady often went there to see the child and to bring him to Dunmain, and Lady Anglesea had a coach road made on purpose to go and see the child. The child, which was dressed like a nobleman's child, remained with the nurse about a year, and was then removed to Dunmain where Joan Landy continued to have charge of him, as dry nurse I believe, as if he were her own."

— trial transcript, *Annesley v. Anglesea*, 1743

—※—

CHAPTER 6

My grief and my affliction
Your gates are taken away,
Your avenue needs attention,
Goats in the garden stray.
The courtyard's filled with water
And the great Earls, where are they?
The Earls, the lady, the people
Beaten into the clay.

– from *Kilcash,* Irish Gaelic, Anonymous, 1700

By late afternoon, pelting rain had doused them, thrashing Dublin into the evening. But as the black of night settled in, the clouds passed and the moon and stars peered out, dropping their light on the quiet, wet city. Above the butcher's shop, the Purcells urged their girls to sleep, then excused themselves to another room, while Fynn and Juggy whispered near the stove. Jemmy and Seán were out front, sitting, plunking stones into a luminous puddle. Jemmy watched the reflecting ripples course out, an ever-widening eye in the dark. Pulling his cloak tight, he looked up, face to the night sky, studying the stars, white stones on a black veil. Glimmering jewels. Each out of reach. Then he saw something familiar in the northeastern sky. As he stared deeper, a shape gradually appeared. One he had recently seen. Subtle and returning. He would lose the image, then regain it. He could see the rounded crown, the hairline crack. "Seán, the skull!" he exclaimed. "B'God. The one in St. Stephen's." The starry skull flickered, staring back.

"Where?" asked Seán, looking up.

"The stars...there, near Jupiter," Jemmy said, pointing. But suddenly the star skull was lost in the wash of beady lights. He focused harder but it was useless. "I thought I saw it."

"I was thinking," Seán began, "when ye go tomorrow, if I'm trying t' find ye...." His voice faded to mask the emotion. "Perhaps if I'm trying t' tell ye something...."

"Aye?"

"A signal. If to say...."

"Aye Seán, we need a sign. The skull?" Jemmy offered. Seán nodded, roll-ing a pebble between his fingertips. Jemmy drew shapes in the mud, imagining how it should look. "Circles. Like this. Two eye holes, with an 'X' below them."

"That'll do." Seán turned to wipe a tear.

Jemmy put an arm around his friend, squeezing him. "Stop it." He took a deep breath. "Promise me ye won't say where I'm going. Not even t' yer da. I'll have no one hurt on my cause. I won't be having that on m'soul." He kicked a cluster of rocks from the edge of the street. "Promise?" Seán nod-ded. "Promise on the skull of St. Stephen's," Jemmy pressed, pointing at the muddy skull image before them.

Seán squatted, drawing another two circles and an "X." "Aye, I promise."

"Good. I'll go t' the barn on Frapper Lane," Jemmy said, nodding. "Then I'll leave Dublin when I can." His lip quivered. "Seán, ye're...." As his voice faded, he looked at the stars with newfound interest, as if they had just spun round, become new, trying to distract him. High over the two birch trees across the street, a meteor flashed through the blackness.

"Jemmy!" exclaimed Seán, startling Jemmy from his thoughts. "Look there."

He turned, seeing four horsemen guiding their mounts down the street, hooves clomping on the cobblestones, steadily advancing. The lead horse stepped through a puddle, then came into the full cast of the moon, revealing Captain Bailyn on its back. "Go inside, Seán," whispered Jemmy.

"I'll get Da!" Seán bolted into the shop.

"No," Jemmy tried, but Seán was gone. He slumped back into the shad-ows, focusing on the four men. He could hear Seán's feet pounding up the stairs, then loud voices.

Suddenly Fynn came bounding outside, turning back to yell, "Stay inside, Joan!" Purcell followed him out, brandishing a meat hook. Juggy was there at the door.

"Ya have no pistol, Fynn!" Juggy's voice was shrill, scared. "What are ya thinking? 'Tis madness!" Jemmy knew she was right—no Catholic was allowed to have a sword, dagger, or dirk. And certainly not a pistol or musket. When Seán maneuvered by her, Juggy came farther out, persisting. "Fynn, this is no way—"

"Hush!" he snapped, his eyes fixed on the approaching men. "Seán, go inside." Seán returned to the shop. The horsemen were now only two build-ings away, the hooves growing louder.

"Take this!" she pleaded, giving a shiny object to Fynn.

The dirk! Jemmy's mind raced, his sour fury rising.

"So what do have ye there?" Captain Bailyn's voice snarled in the darkness.

Purcell stepped forward. "Did ye not hear us this mornin'? Ye deaf lump of shite."

"My fat Irishman," Bailyn said, leering, "before ye start swinging that silly hook, trying t' keep yer oaths, let me introduce who'll be killing ye tonight." Jemmy studied the three other men, one being Higgins who was once again trailing the group—he appeared devoid of emotion, staring blankly at his companions. "Behind me, on my right," announced Bailyn, "this is Mr. Parks, the new chief constable of this stinking city. On my left is Mr. Byrne, another recent addition to the constables. We were in such need of more law, what with all the wretched Catholics and all." He tipped his hat at Juggy, adding, "And of course, all their whores."

"Coward!" Fynn thundered.

Bailyn grinned. "How are ye, m'lady? Still on yer game?"

Fynn charged Bailyn. "Come down! Deal with me directly!" He grabbed the reins of Bailyn's horse, forcing the beast's head around. "Get down! Or aren't ye man enough!"

"Fine," Bailyn muttered. He drew his pistol and then began dismounting. Just as one leg swung around, Fynn grabbed Bailyn's other knee, pulling him off balance, sending him crashing to the dark mud. The impact knocked his pistol away and sent his red cocked hat flying. Bailyn immediately curled, clambering to get to his feet, but Fynn stomped a boot hard on the man's chest, driving him deep in the muck. Before Bailyn could pull his own dagger, Fynn had the dirk against his throat. "If ye cut me, papist," Bailyn growled, "the boy will hang with ye tomorrow."

"No Fynn!" Juggy pleaded. After a long, prickly silence, Fynn slowly backed away.

Bailyn stood, shaking mud from his coat. "Now give me that blade." The constables had nervously drawn their pistols and were now cocking them.

Fynn looked around slowly, saw Jemmy, then scanned the rest of the crowd as if taking note of where everyone was standing. He eased forward, handing over the dirk. "Seámus," he said flatly, "'tis time t' run, lad. Be gone with ye."

Bailyn bellowed, "Shoot the boy if he runs!" Jemmy was paralyzed. Bailyn looked back at the dirk, studying it, the steel shimmering. "Fine Scottish blade ye have here."

Fynn stepped closer. "If ye mean t' take this boy, ye'll have t' kill me first."

"Very well." In one swift motion, Bailyn surged forward, lunging with the dirk. Fynn jumped back, stumbled, and everything exploded. Jemmy clambered against a stack of crates, ducking as pistol cracks lit the sky, and in the rush of mens' shouts, heard Juggy screaming "No!" Back to his feet, Fynn saw the long beef hook on the ground. He lunged for it, rushed and drove it straight through the chief constable's leg, deep into the flesh of the man's horse. The horse thrashed, whinnying loudly, throwing its rider into the air. Just as the constable hit the ground, Purcell jerked the hook free and thrust it into the man's neck. Blood splattered Purcell's face. Jemmy stood, scrambling to run. Another gunpowder blast exploded. Smack! A stinging slap ripped Jemmy's side, spinning him down. He crumpled behind the crates. *I'm shot! Oh God, I'm shot!* his mind squalled. He grabbed his side, cringing, his blood leaving him. He could hear the chaos of horses, men falling, yelling, the splashing, the ringing of swords. Then everything fell silent, except for the rapid clomp of a riderless horse running away. Jemmy crawled forward to cautiously peer around the crates. He saw the twitching feet of the dying constable. Purcell was holding a sword to the throat of the other constable, who was standing unsteadily. Captain Bailyn, still clutching the dirk, was on the ground, breathing hard, staring across his dead horse at Fynn, who was standing, panting. Behind Fynn was Higgins, still mounted, aiming a musket at Fynn's head.

"This has gone much too far!" shouted Higgins.

"Shoot the son of a bitch," ordered Bailyn.

Fynn looked at Higgins. "Are ye a demon too? Like him," he motioned to Bailyn. "Would ye shoot an unarmed man?" Higgins didn't move. Jemmy watched intently, feeling nauseated and weak as he held his side, the warm liquid oozing across his hand. Suddenly Fynn leaped over the dead horse and the blast of Higgins's musket shook the air.

"No!" Juggy shrieked. Jemmy saw Fynn falling, Bailyn hurtling forward with the dirk, Juggy throwing herself across Fynn, screaming. Then silence. A gurgled gasp came from Juggy. Fynn rolled to his feet, Higgins's shot having missed its mark. Captain Bailyn stumbled backward empty-handed. Juggy was on her knees by the dead horse, her back to Jemmy. He could see her long auburn hair fluttering, her body swaying.

"Oh God!" cried Fynn, eyes fixed on Juggy. She slowly slumped, pitched forward, then crumpled to the ground. Jemmy stared horror struck. The hilt of the dirk was protruding from her chest. Fynn wailed, kneeling beside her, lifting her head in his arms. Blood sputtered from her mouth as she coughed. "Damn ye!" Fynn yelled. "Look what ye've done! My Joan, my sweet Joan." A peal of cathedral bells announced the ten o'clock hour—a rhythmic knell from the darkness, wafting over them, metering out the agony, the disbelief.

"Let's go, Bailyn. Now!" demanded Higgins. He reined his horse around, spurring it into a quick trot. The staggering constable glanced down at his dead companion, then turned and ran after Higgins. Bailyn calmly walked to the remaining horse, caught the reins, mounted, and followed the men, disappearing in the dark.

Seán stepped into the street, then stopped—terror and tears on his face. No words, just petrified, fixed. Fynn was rocking Juggy, pleading, "Don't go, Joan. My sweet Joan." The moonlight cast a white glow over her dying face.

"Juggy!" Jemmy tried to stand, then collapsed. He crawled toward her, ignoring the searing pain, and grasped her limp hand. He pulled himself closer, pressing her muddy palm against his face, sobbing into the hollow of her hand.

"Jemmy. Seán." The names gurgled from her mouth.

"Right here," said Fynn, stretching a hand toward Jemmy, motioning for Seán.

"I can't...see him."

"I'm here," cried Jemmy.

"Juggy," sobbed Seán.

"Seán," she said with a wisp of a smile. Then her eyes focused on Jemmy. "M'lad, Jem.... Fynn, do care for him." Each breath a long wheezing heave. "He has no one else."

"I do. I will," said Fynn. "Of course—"

"Fynn...." She raised a hand, grasping his wrist. "Don't fret, m'love." She pulled herself against him, as if to rise. "Ya'll always be my husband."

"God! Don't take her! Don't—"

"I love...." Her last small gentle breath moved over Fynn's face and was gone, the flutter of a loosed feather, floating away.

"I love ye...my sweet," whispered Fynn, leaning forward, trembling. He kissed her, but he could not pull back, could not pull away, his mouth pressing her open lips, quivering, her blood smearing his face. He wept with his whole body, his whole soul shaking.

Her shimmering eyes were staring blankly into the black sky, and in them, Jemmy could see the faint reflection of the stars. "Don't die, Juggy," he mumbled. His brow tightened, another surge of tears slamming into him. "Please? Stay." The reflections in her eyes slowly faded, slipping into a haze. Finally all was gone and Jemmy could see the stars no more.

Mr. John Turner, examined — "Lady Anglesea told me
that she had a son. About a year and a half afterwards I saw
the boy at Dunmain: he was two years old then. I stayed
two nights or thereabouts at Dunmain, and I had the child
in my arms. I saw Lady Anglesea leading the child across
the parlour two or three times. I saw Lord Anglesea kiss
the child. I afterwards saw the child at Ross when he was
about three years old. (How was the child treated at Ross?)
He was dressed as the son of a nobleman, and the servants
called him master. He went by the name of Jemmy."

— trial transcript, *Annesley v. Anglesea*, 1743

CHAPTER 7

Are they shadows that we see?
And can shadows pleasure give?
Pleasures only shadows be
Cast by bodies we conceive,
And are made the things we deem,
In those figures which they seem.

—For the Lady Margaret, Samuel Daniel, 1610

The night Juggy was killed, Jemmy stumbled off into the black Dublin streets. A week later he was gone. Lost to everyone but himself. Except Seán. He knew where to find Jemmy. After a day of persistent effort, trying to get Seán to reveal Jemmy's hiding place, Fynn gave up. Though he would not say it, he respected Seán for keeping his word. But he did insist food, blankets, and clothes be bundled and taken to Jemmy, wherever the boy was. This afternoon, as he had done the previous day, Seán pulled the wagon off Frapper Lane, easing it cautiously down the stone-walled carriageway of the stables, toward the rear, where the hay barn stood. If anyone asked what he was doing, he was there to fetch hay. He leaped down and creaked open the big door.

"Don't worry. No one's about," Jemmy blurted.

"Ach!" Seán exclaimed. "Ye scared me!" He saw Jemmy's uneasy movement, his grimace. "What's hurting ye?"

"Nothing," muttered Jemmy. The musket ball had grazed his right side, and the wound had only begun to heal. He didn't want to say anything because Seán would be too worried and would tell Fynn who would undoubtedly demand Jemmy return. He had already disposed of the bloody shirt and was now wearing the shirt Seán had brought the day before. If only he had a different cloak. He tugged at it, yanked it around so the large hole and bloodstain could not be seen, then took the bundle from Seán. "Thank ye for the food." He gave an empty smile.

Seán glanced away. "Daniel Mackercher is coming from Scotland."

Jemmy furrowed his brow, to which Seán explained, "Her brother."

"Aye," said Jemmy. "He was coming for the wedding. Does he know about—?"

"Da sent a letter. He arrives tonight."

"He's coming for blood now."

"Aye. Da said if he had known Mr. Mackercher was arriving so soon, he would've waited with the funeral. 'Tis too bad he wasn't here for his sister's funeral. If I had a sister—"

Jemmy grimaced. "I should have been there too." He watched Seán fidgeting with a shoeing nail, scratching a line in the soft wood of the doorframe.

Seán dropped the nail. "I must tell ye something. Yer mum is here, in Dublin."

"I know." He looked puzzled at the statement. "But where—"

"She wants ye t' go t' England with her and—"

"Did ye see her?" Jemmy's eyes grew large. "I told ye I saw her that day on—"

"Nay. Charity came and told—"

"Charity is a lousy whore if there ever was one!"

"Aye, but...." Seán pulled a shiny key from his coat pocket, handing it to Jemmy. "She asked me t' give ye this," he continued. "Said it would prove 'twas yer mum."

Jemmy took it, studied the "B" engraved in the key's handle, then turned it over. As he expected, the word "Buckingham" was inscribed in the brass shaft. "What'd Charity say?"

"Said yer mum was sailing for England tomorrow on the *Courtmain*, a merchanter, ported down near Ringsend." Seán was less than enthused. "Wants ye t' join her."

"That's wonderful Seán!"

"She'll take ye overland t' it, t' the *Courtmain*."

"Where am I t'—"

"She'll be waitin' for ye in Christ Church tonight. In the chapterhouse." Seán's dejection was palatable, yet Jemmy scarcely noticed. His mother was going to rescue him. He could not believe his ears. She was taking him to England. He was going away with her. Hope surged through him. "When Seán? When this evening?"

"I don't know. Said tonight. When ye hear the bell of Christ Church. Just once. It'll ring just once. That'll be yer signal t' go to the chapterhouse. That's what Charity said t' tell ye. And ye're t' wait in Copper Alley. T' wait there for the bell."

Jemmy's eyes narrowed. "Why? Why should it matter where I wait?"

"So ye're nearby, I suppose. I don't know." They lingered in silence for a moment, each gripped by his own imaginings. Seán turned, looking out. "I've got t' get back. Da wants me t'go...t'do something for him. I think."

"Right," said Jemmy, watching Seán. He reached out and grabbed Seán's arm, then hugged him briefly. "Then I'll see ye in England. Soon. Someday soon, Seán. I promise."

"Aye. In England. Jemmy...." Seán's voice was fluttering again.

"Go now, will ye?" Jemmy urged. "Before we both start weepin' like lasses."

But Seán remained, his eyes fixed and glossy. "Will ye send for me? Ye comin' back?"

"I will. I promise. Seán, ye're my best friend."

"I'm yer only friend."

"So ye are." Jemmy's lip curled at the jab. "So don't ye think I'll find you soon? I will. London 'tisn't so far away."

"Far enough."

"Go on now," he said softly. Feeling the sadness mounting within, Jemmy gestured toward the carriageway beyond the half-open door. Seán dragged his feet out to the wagon, then climbed into the box. He stared at Jemmy, then gently reined the horse to go. Jemmy smiled, forcing back tears, holding three fingers high in the air—*through ice, together forever.*

Seán saw Jemmy's hand, then stood in the wagon, his arm up straight, waving three fingers back. "Good-bye, Jemmy!" he shouted.

"So long, Seán!" Jemmy hollered, watching Seán hold his balance as the wagon moved slowly up the carriageway. Both boys held their salutes high until Seán rounded the end of the long stone wall and was gone.

"Good-bye, my friend," whispered Jemmy. Taking a deep breath, he felt his throat tighten, tears rushing forward. He held the brass key, rubbing it methodically between his fingers, tracing and retracing the letter "B."

—❦—

Daniel Mackercher and his band of seven Highlanders stepped onto Merchant's Quay at a quarter-past five that evening. Fynn was there to greet them with horses for the men. He had been waiting for their currach's arrival since three.

"Mr. Mackercher," said Fynn, stepping forward. It had been eight years since he had seen Daniel and he was not entirely certain which one he was. All the Scotsmen were imposing, Farquarsons all, draped in pale brown and green tartans, basket-hilted broadswords strapped to their sides. Each had a pistol tucked into his kilt belt, along with one or two dirks. Fynn was impressed, having never seen such well-armed civilians.

"Aye, Mr. Kennedy," replied Mackercher. The two men embraced firmly. As they pulled back, a small chill ran through Fynn as he saw Juggy's eyes, the same lucent green.

"Daniel," said one of the Scots, pointing up Bridge Street, "we've wolves upon us." Five English cavalrymen were coming from the Brazen Head Tavern. Having spotted the Scots, they had mounted and were now approaching the quay.

"Good day to you sirs," said the lead officer, tipping his hat, eyes on Mackercher. From the insignia on the five red coats, Fynn knew they were guards from Dublin Castle.

"Good day, Lieutenant," replied Mackercher.

Another soldier moved his horse forward. "These men are Jacobites!"

Mackercher shook his head. "A man's tartan doesn't portend his politics. No more than yar uniform tells yars. My name is Daniel Mackercher. I am a loyal subject—"

"Daniel Mackercher?" exclaimed one of the soldiers. "Same man who captured the regimentals at Sheriffmuir?"

"Aye. Very same," said Mackercher. "I fought for the Duke of Argyle. I'm as loyal to King George as the one of ya."

"Mind you," growled the lieutenant, "do not weigh our sovereign loyalty."

Mackercher's good humor fell away. "Then mind ya not weigh mine, sir, and we'll get along marvelously."

"What business brings you and your men to Ireland?"

"'Tis a family matter," replied Mackercher.

Fynn listened, admiring Mackercher's boldness, his courage. He wished he had that nature of vigor, that spirited strength. Daniel Mackercher was tall, broad-shouldered, powerful. Even on foreign soil, the man was confident, certain of himself. How long had it been since he had felt that confident? Years. Now he had lost Joan. Now Seámus was leaving. He had never felt so fragile and drained. He hated the feeling. If Mackercher had been on Ship Street that dreadful night, things might have been different. Mackercher would not have been so foolish. Joan might still be alive. Seámus would be safe. Joan would be there with them. They would be marrying. He shook off the bitter thoughts. Mackercher was in Dublin now. For revenge. This would be dangerous, but it must be done.

The lieutenant eased his horse among the Scots. "Well armed for a family matter."

"'Tis a private affair." Mackercher was resolute. "Of no concern to the crown."

He stopped directly in front of Fynn. "What is your business here?" Before Fynn could answer, the officer turned back to Mackercher. "This papist with you?"

"He's here t' fetch horses," said Mackercher. Fynn gestured agreeably toward the horses.

The lieutenant continued to Mackercher, "Best be gone from Dublin shortly."

"I will not tarry in the *execution* of my affairs."

"Very well. Good day to you sir." After saluting Mackercher, and receiving Mackercher's salute in return, the lieutenant led his men away.

—⁓—

Within an hour it had grown dark, and Fynn was pacing Purcell's small kitchen, trying to reason with Mackercher, who was sitting in front of him, pensive and glowering. Purcell was listening, leaning in the doorway. "But ye can't," Fynn protested. "It wouldn't be just you who'd be hanged. 'Twould be the rest of us too. They saw me at the quay with ye. They'd arrest us all." He stopped walking, took a deep breath, then blew it out in a sigh. "Ye're far off yer native heath here, Mr. Mackercher."

"Ya must call me Daniel. I think I know ya," said Mackercher, rising to his feet. "But then, perhaps I do not. I know ya loved my sister." He turned to Fynn and nodded. "That much I do know."

"This isn't yer country, m'friend," Fynn began again. "No man wants t'rip the stinking entrails from Richard Annesley and that Bailyn more than I. Be assured of that. But at what price? At what price would ye kill these Englishmen? At the price of Mr. Purcell's family here? Pardon my sayin', but 'tis madness. Blind revenge."

From the window, Mackercher watched Purcell's girls playing in the street below. He mulled Fynn's words. He passionately hated Richard Annesley, a man he had never met. In a fit of greed, that demon had loosed his hounds on

Joan, butchering her in the street. Mackercher slowly shook his head. Richard Annesley, and every one of his men, deserved to die. Had this occurred in Scotland, their throats would've been cut days ago. The English in this country were protecting those murderous animals. Well, damn them all—he would draw them out and kill them. He would be done with it. It was proper. It was just. God ordained such killings. No one could find fault, and if they did, then damn them too. He would simply move Fynn and Seán to Scotland with him. He looked across Ship Street and saw Kate Purcell standing in front of a shop, talking to another woman. The Purcell's two girls were now next to her, the youngest tugging at her mother's dress. Kate bent down to talk to the girl, then glanced up and saw Mackercher in her kitchen window. Mackercher tried a pleasant smile, but Kate looked away, refusing to receive it. What would he do about them? Could he move the whole Purcell family to Scotland? Would they even want to go? Well, they would just have to go. But what about the English magistrates in Scotland? Could he truly ensure this family's safety there, even in his own glen? He turned back toward Fynn and John. "Then I shall challenge Richard. Kill him legally. Cut him down."

"Dueling is not entirely legal, as ye're aware," Fynn said. Mackercher didn't respond, so Fynn continued, "Even so, Richard is a coward. He'll assert his peerage and not appear. He'll aver a Scot to be beneath him, no doubt."

"That black dog," Mackercher whispered, pounding his fist on the wall. "The damn cur." He turned, glaring at Fynn, then shouted, "I don't give a damn about the Annesleys or which one of the bastards holds the claim to the Earldom of bloody Anglesea!" He slugged a hanging pan, clanging it to the floor. "What I do care about is that this *Richard* and his man Bailyn die." Mackercher's clinched jaw almost shook. "I'll kill them both. Mark my word."

Fynn nodded. "I have no doubt ye'll do just that."

"Good sir," Purcell addressed Mackercher from the doorway. "Ye're trained in the law?"

"Aye." Mackercher caught his breath. "Barrister."

"Ye say this matter could be brought before the King's Bench in London, or even here in Dublin?" Purcell's deep voice rumbled. "Fynn and I have spoke of—"

"'Twould be too costly," Fynn interrupted. "And wouldn't—"

"I might bring him to the bench on grounds of murder," mused Mackercher. "But another killing happened that night. A large Catholic man killed a constable." He raised his eyebrows, centering on Purcell. "With a meat hook."

Purcell hesitated, then said, "Aye. Something of that nature."

"I am certain he deserved it," Mackercher said. "But that will not be well received at the King's Bench. With the constable buried in the moat...." He glanced at Fynn, who nodded. "...that matter seems at rest, and there we should hope it stays. Nay, gentlemen, we'll never get Richard to the gallows by such means." He stared at the tin pots still hanging on the wall, tapping them softly. "Ya'd only be weaving yar own hemp—tying yar own noose."

They were all quiet for a while, sipping their ale. Mackercher liked both of the men, especially Fynn Kennedy. Fynn was a man whom Mackercher could admire, a simple man, plainspoken, yet proud. He could feel the strength emanating from Fynn—it filled the room. Fynn wanted to kill Richard as much as he did, but Fynn could see beyond his rage, could hold his reins in one hand and a sword in the other. For Mackercher it took both hands to rein himself in or both hands to attack. It had always seemed to be one way or the other, and he admired men who had mastered such self-control. They fascinated him, men like Fynn, yet irritated him—reminding him of what he lacked. Now he was against a wall again, wanting only to be free to attack, to charge forward...yes, as Fynn had said, blindly. He gave Fynn a brief smile. No wonder Joan had loved this man. A thumping sound came from the stairwell, and Seán came sulking into the room.

"How is Seámus?" asked Fynn. "Did ye tell him of his mother's plans?"

"Aye, Da. He was pleased." Seán then added under his breath, "But now he's gone."

Fynn held Seán, patting his back. "We'll see him soon, lad, in England. He'll be safe there." After another pat, he continued, "Seán, this man is Mr. Daniel Mackercher, Joan's brother. He's come from Scotland, with his men downstairs."

"Good t' meet ye, sir," said Seán, offering his hand, slightly bowing his chin.

"Ya're the good friend of young Master James?"

"Aye, sir."

Mackercher gave Seán an appreciative nod. "Everything will work itself out, lad." He tried to picture the other boy, James Annesley. From Joan's many letters (all written by Fynn), he knew James was bright and intelligent. She had often reported James's strengths, his curious mind—the "stargazer," she called him. Mackercher had hoped to meet James, but now the boy was gone to England. Rushed away by his wealthy mother, to safer ground.

Sell your books at
sellbackyourBook.com
Go to sellbackyourBook.com
and get an instant price
quote. We even pay the
shipping - see what your old
books are worth today!

Inspected By:guille

00015769198

0001576 **9198**

And who could fault him for that? Mackercher knew the feeling of being an orphan, and he knew what it was like to hide from men bent on killing him. But not both at once, not like what he imagined James was feeling. If only James could make his claim…. An idea burst upon him. "Where did ya say James is?"

"He's meeting his mum," Fynn replied. "She's secreting him away t' London."

"Where was she when all this—" Mackercher continued.

Fynn continued, "Arthur banished her two years ago, without a word t' their boy. Forbidden t' see the boy. And even now, Richard has placed a new warrant for her arrest, if she is found with the boy. She is a strong woman. This has been very difficult—"

Mackercher interrupted, "We should have the English boy, James, bring a claim against his English uncle. Aye, an English claim of property, to prove that he, James Annesley, is the rightful Earl. If we could prove it was true, then Richard would be ripped from his peerage protections."

Fynn nodded. "I spoke with Seámus, about such a thing, but how would the cost be—"

"That'd be my concern," barked Mackercher.

Purcell asked, "Can it be done without Jemmy?"

"No," explained Mackercher. "He'd have to be here, before the bench." No one spoke for a moment—this was Mackercher's decision, his money, his means. "Seán," Mackercher continued, "can ya find Master James?"

"I don't know, sir." Excitement filled his face. "But I know where's he's going! He might already—"

Fynn was moving. "Ye must go, Seán. Find him. Tell him t' not go with Mary, not yet. Tell him he must come here."

"I'll get him!" Seán bolted from the kitchen, clambering down the stairs and out.

Mary Laffan, examined — "His name was James Annesley, and he was kept like a nobleman's child. During the time that I and Joan Landy took care of the child, Lord and Lady Anglesea were very fond of him, and he was treated by the house and neighbours as my lord and lady's lawful child. In the morning my lady would order Miss Landy to bring the child, and would kiss him and call him a dear. About half a year after I ended my care of the child, my lord and lady separated, and my lady went to lodge at Dublin. She parted in a very angry manner about Tom Palliser, whose ear was cut off in my presence by my lord. She requested to have her child with her, but my lord would not let her have him. After the separation, the defendant, Richard Annesley, came to Dunmain and asked me, 'Where is Jemmy; where is my brother's child?'"

— trial transcript, *Annesley v. Anglesea*, 1743

CHAPTER 8

As we often see, against some storm,
A silence in the heavens, the rack stands still,
The bold winds speechless and the orb below
As hush as death, anon the dreadful thunder
Doth rend the region.

— from *Hamlet,* William Shakespeare, 1601

Dublin had descended into darkness. Its ancient dirty streets were all but deserted, the restless gusts whipping dust and whiffs of horse manure, announcing an approaching storm. Reaching Long Alley, near St. Winifred's Well, Jemmy heard the bells of Christ Church tolling the hour. He was close enough—only a half-mile from the cathedral, a distance he could easily cover. His heart thumped loudly. Captain Bailyn was in every shadow, Richard in every voice. About twenty steps down Long Alley, he hunkered against a soot-covered brick wall. In the blackness, under his dark green cloak, he could not be seen. But he could not see either. Couldn't see his hand outstretched before him. Couldn't see the source of the stench that wafted up around him. Above, through the narrow buildings, he could just distinguish the rooftops from the bottom of the menacing sky. Lightning ripped open the air and he looked low, getting a glimpse of the alley and the pile of rotting rats at his feet. He scurried quickly to the mouth of the alley. There he knelt behind an iron railing and peered across the nearly vacant Eustace Street, with St. Winifred's Well poking through the middle. A carriage lumbered by and Jemmy froze. After a moment, he peered around the corner, then stepped into the street, turning north toward the River Liffey. Should he go to Copper Alley? The questions flooded him yet again. Charity had specified it. But that didn't make sense. Why did it matter where he waited? Why did Charity say Copper Alley? What might be lurking there? Was it a trap? Who else knew he was going to Christ Church that night? He decided to get closer to the church but not go to Copper Alley. He kept walking, wondering what Mr. Kennedy would counsel.

The rain started slowly at first, thumping off wood, clinking the old slate roofs, splattering across Jemmy's forehead. He kept moving. Then it came harder, no longer falling in random plops, but now driving great sheets across his face. Though he hugged the building fronts, he was still getting soaked, the soot in his hair streaking down his forehead, face and neck. He could taste the raw coarseness streaming over his lips. He slipped into another alley. But once he was out of the wet blast, he realized he might not hear the bell in this storm. He cursed his foolishness. Why had he not gone directly to Christ Church? Why hadn't he just waited in Copper Alley as instructed? Why hadn't he simply done as he'd been told? He spun, sprinting into the street, running against the maelstrom, forgetting to be scared.

The rain and wind buffeted him, the water pelting his skin, washing him, biting at him, driving him on. As he rushed into an intersection, he was startled by a charging carriage and leapt from its path. His ankle twisted violently when he landed and the instant explosion of pain sent him tumbling forward, smashing into the slick mud, out of balance, rolling, and finally ramming his right shoulder into the base of an iron hitching post. He lay still for a moment, his clothes ripped, his body entirely wet and miserable. Then he heard it—the bell of Christ Church Cathedral. His heart raced, his breath shortening. He pulled himself to his feet and began a stumbling run, oblivious to the pain screaming from his ankle, and having long forgotten the ache in his side. As he reached Fishamble Street, directly across from the cathedral, the bell rang again. "Aye!" he exclaimed. But then it rang again, and Jemmy slowed to a stop. Then a fourth time. "Four rings?" he whispered to himself. "Damn. 'Tis on the half-hour." He backed away, panting hard, staring up at the gothic cathedral now looming over him. As he crossed Fishamble Street to Music Hall the rain began to relent.

Standing close to the wall, Jemmy shivered, lowering his chin, disconsolate, confused, feeling soreness throughout his body. Glad to be out of the rain, he knocked over an empty wood crate and plopped on one end. He tugged his cloak closer around his neck, huddling in the murky, wet darkness. Then he realized where he was—he was sitting in the mouth of Copper Alley. A coach rolled by. He moved back, off the street. He stood, peering nervously into the black reaches of the alley lit only by faint candlelight quivering from windows above. He considered the shifting shadows, then hobbled forward, eyes wide. After only a few steps, his attention was drawn to a wall recessed under an eve. There, scrawled in the dimness, was a chalky image—two circles and an "X". He froze, staring, his heart a thumping drum. "Faith be!"

he breathed. "Seán?" he called out as loud as he dared. Nothing. Only the smattering drips and splatters from the subsiding rain. "Seán?" His palms sweating, his mind a slurry of worries. He crept forward, then spun round, forcing his gaze into the corners of the alley, searching for movement, anything. "Seán, ye can't be gamin' me now," he whispered, unbearably alarmed. He prayed for a simple single ring from that damn bell. His next thought was a fist to his gut— *Did I miss it?* He peered up at the cathedral as if he could see whether the bell had already rung.

"Fine evenin' eh?" a voice suddenly broke from the dimness behind him.

"Auugh!" Jemmy jumped, then froze, still facing the street. His mouth agape, his eyes two harvest moons, jerky and nervous.

"Good evenin', Master James." The voice was still behind him, slithering through soot-black air. "I know what ye're thinking, looking up there." The man's steps were coming nearer. "Ye're wondering why yer mum hasn't saved her little boy yet." When the man stopped walking, he was just behind Jemmy, his putrid breath brushing Jemmy's neck, triggering a cold shiver down Jemmy's spine. "Ye're wondering what I'm going t'do. Aye, lad?"

Jemmy forced himself to turn around. When he did, he was looking squarely into the beady eyes of Captain Bailyn. He swallowed hard and managed to ask, "Where's Seán?"

Captain Bailyn smirked. "Oh, settle yerself. Lil' Seán has been most useful this evening. T' think yer friend would sell ye for a mere pittance."

Jemmy stepped back. "Ye lie!"

"Now lad, are ye goin' t' make this easy?" He moved closer. "Or hard?" Bailyn's breath was blistering. Jemmy didn't answer, his mind churning, devising an escape. "Doesn't matter much t'me," said Bailyn. Then he leaned close, whispering, "Frankly, I hope ye run. Then I get t' shoot ye."

Without thinking, Jemmy spun and ran as best he could on his hurt foot and was almost to Fishamble Street when the figure of a large man stepped in front of him, club in hand. Jemmy skidded, slowing, then cut into a painful, furious sprint. As he dashed around the man, Jemmy saw the image of Christ Church just ahead, and in that fleeting instant he believed he was free. Then he felt the club smash his head, followed by the impact of his face hitting the stone wall of Music Hall. His eyes fogged, a flurry of color, then everything was black.

—∞—

The next thing he knew, someone was tugging at him and Captain Bailyn was shouting, "Get up! Look lively, ye ragged arse."

He slowly opened one eye, then the other, the blackness yielding to faint light, his muddled brain telling him he was in a small boat, a currach, and above, on the docks, were shadowy images, silhouettes of men.

"Stand, damn ye!" Bailyn forced him to his feet. As he stepped out of the boat, fire shot up from his ankle, causing him to stumble, dropping to his knees. Then men were picking him up now, carrying him by the feet and shoulders, hauling him headfirst up a gangway. Looking up and back, he saw he was being hauled aboard a ship. Onboard, he was once again made to walk, a rough hand pushing him ahead, moving him toward the bow.

"Bind him well," bellowed a voice in the dark.

"Aye, Captain Hendry," replied another.

When Jemmy stepped around an open hatch, a man yelled, "Down there lass!"

Jemmy eased down the steep companionway, into the abyss, down to the between-deck, the putrid cargo hold. Though it was as black as any Dublin alley, it smelled much worse. He bumped his head, then reached a hand up, feeling for the low ceiling. A man came down with an oil lamp, and Jemmy could see the ceiling was about nose-high to the man. To Jemmy, it just barely skimmed his head. He leaned forward as the men escorted him deep within, pushing him along until he came to a thick post. There they shackled his wrists. He sat, leaning against the post, arms stretched back behind him, watching them leave, the light fading away.

When the deck hatch closed behind them, Jemmy thought he was in a tomb. Too exhausted and stunned to cry, he slumped over, moaning. The pain from his ankle squalled at him while his head throbbed unmercifully, and his shoulder and right side reminded him that they too had been damaged. He hoped for sleep.

"Eh! Bugger in de corner," said a scratchy voice, breaking the blackness.

Jemmy kept silent.

"Eh, new 'un! Ye breathin' or ain't ye?"

"Aye," whispered Jemmy, raising his head. He saw nothing, no one.

"Want t'be sure ye're alive. I'm tired o' talkin' t'de dead ones. So I am. So long as yer alive, I'll talk t'ye. Soon as ye die I won't talk t'ye no more."

"Where am I?" asked Jemmy.

"Ye don't know?"

He shook his head.

"De *Courtmain*," said the old voice. "Merchanter. But I think Captain Hendry intends t' take us indents back."

"The Courtmain?"

"Aye, so 'tis."

"Nay. Can't be," argued Jemmy. "This is not the *Courtmain*."

"Oh? Nay?" the voice asked with a crackly chuckle. "'Tis no other."

Jemmy's mind chased itself in confused circles. How could it be? Why would Richard put him on the same ship as his mother? What was happening? Had Seán betrayed him? No. Had his mother? Of course not! He hunched forward, everything quiet, only the sound of the ship creaking against the soft tide. Then he heard it. Resonating ever so faintly: a single, solemn toll, a bell ringing once, a clang from a cathedral far away.

—⚏—

Mary Laffan, examined — "Richard Annesley asked how my lady, James's mother, behaved toward him. I told him that she requested my lord to have the favour of letting her have the child with her, and my lord refused. He would not. 'Damn my blood,' says he, Richard Annesley. 'By my Saviour Jesus Christ, I would have let her have him, and she might carry him to the devil, for I would keep none of the breed of her.' I remember the oath as if I had heard him the other day. I am of good family, and I would not have waited on the child if I had believed him to be a bastard."

— trial transcript, *Annesley v. Anglesea*, 1743

—⚏—

CHAPTER 9

What shall we do for timber?
The last of the woods is down.
Kilcash and the house of its glory
And the bell of the house are gone,
The spot where the lady waited
Who shamed all women for grace
When Earls came sailing to greet her
And Mass was said in the place.

– from *Kilcash,* Irish Gaelic, Anonymous, 1700

Sometime during the night the rain became silky drips that finally stopped. Now the mottled-pea-green grass in the churchyard of Christ Church Cathedral was arching its wet back to the warm sun rising over the Irish Sea. Everything was quiet and still, save various fluttering birds scurrying through the air, their soft chirps claiming the churchyard as their own. Then a breeze slipped through, wrapping itself around the massive walls, brushing through the cool damp space between the cathedral and the Four Courts of Justice. And in that narrow passage was Mary Sheffield, standing between puddles, gazing absently toward the half-lit churchyard, an empty stare across an empty space below an empty sky. The night was over. Her boy had not come.

"Lord God," she prayed, whispering, "I beg of you to keep my Jamie safe." Then she added, "…and that he may forgive me." She stopped and bit her quivering lip, her chin lowering. "Can I ever be forgiven? My heart is broken. It is broken, Lord." She turned, walked back into the chapterhouse, then farther on, into the cold nave. Wiping back her tears, she made her way to the prayer candles on the back wall, and there lit two—one for each person she loved, smiling faintly at the one for Jamie.

Wasting no time, Mary returned to the chapterhouse and sat down at a large walnut table, where she found the items she had asked Father Pilchard to leave—a small sheet of parchment paper, a quill, and an inkwell. She softly dipped the quill pen, then alighted it across the rough paper, slowly and carefully drawing out her words, inscribing a letter to her boy. She wrote methodically, stopping now and again to redip the pen. She knew what she wanted to say, what she must say, what she had to tell him. He had to know the truth. Above the faint scratching of her pen, came her tender hum of *Greensleeves*, as if involuntary, as if it too sought her boy and his forgiveness. Time moved slowly as she wrote. When she was done she re-read her words, fixed one line, then blew across it gently. Convinced it was dry, she folded it, dripped candlewax to seal it, and placed it in her reticule draped around her waist.

Withdrawing outside, she watched the bleak sun rise unmercifully. She closed her eyes with a sigh, and rubbed her tired face, feeling old. But she also felt relieved in some peculiar way, having written words of confession, truths she had never before uttered. The cold breeze was growing stronger so she tugged the hood of her red cape, tightening it. Perhaps she was free of her secret, but she was still without her boy. She had failed him. She hated herself for being such a wretched mother, for letting Jamie ever feel abandoned. Now she must give up. It was time to go. If she lingered much longer, the *Courtmain* would sail without her.

—⁓—

A similar fast breeze was whistling over the deck of the *Courtmain*, the ship swaying softly against its mooring. The sudden sound of the stern hatch creaking open snapped Jemmy from his sleep. Light filtered into the between-deck. With his arms still bent behind him, shackled to the post, he sat up as straight as he could, groaning in pain.

"I'd have me a knot in me neck," said the old voice. Jemmy slowly looked in its direction. Sitting across the deck in squalid filth, bent under the low ceiling, was an aged, disheveled man. His lips were puffy brown and his leathery face was deeply wrinkled and splotchy. His hair was a mat of dingy grey tangled with sprigs of hay. One eye was blind white, but the other was light blue, startling in contrast to its moldering frame. It was gleaming with life, as if it belonged to someone else. This eye was staring at Jemmy. "A knot, I would indeed," the man continued.

"Would ye?" Jemmy asked irritably, feeling the pasty muck in his mouth. He desperately needed to urinate.

"Dis evenin', I'll show ye how t' sleep against dat pole. On yer side. Dere's art t'it."

Jemmy ignored the man. His mind hummed in a spiral of confusion like a child's top spinning wildly in a wooden box, ricocheting off the sides. What happened last night? Why was he on the *Courtmain*? Surely Richard was now giving him over to Mary. That must be right. Why else? But why would Captain Bailyn beat him and force him there if Richard was giving him over? Why not leave him at Christ Church? Because Bailyn loved to inflict pain. But where was Seán? Why was their skull drawn on that wall? Jemmy could not keep his thoughts straight. Surely Charity had said for him to be in Copper Alley so Bailyn could capture him. Yes. But why had Seán come too?

"So, dis eve, I'll learn ye, aye?"

Pain raged in Jemmy's head, throbbing, melding with the unbearable aching throughout his whole body. Touching his side, he found pus oozing. Then he looked down and saw his swollen ankle.

"Ye can't sit like dat, ye'll—"

"I'll be on deck by this evening," muttered Jemmy.

The skeletal man grinned, revealing his two crooked, mud-colored teeth. "Well now! What makes ye dink dat, lad?"

Jemmy let his head sag to his chest. He had no interest in continuing a conversation with this carcass. Surely his mother would be boarding soon. He would shout for her then. She would hear him, have him released, and by this evening he would be traveling with her safely to England. He soared at the idea of it. Speaking further to the old man was pointless.

But the man persisted. "Ach, do tell lad. Are ye goin' to break dose shackles and make fer de gangway? Eh? If so, den spirit us both from dis hole o'shite."

Jemmy kept his eyes focused on the floor. Suddenly he realized his cloak was gone. He remembered wearing it in the pelting rain. He pictured it—the bloodstains, the holes. Yes, he had been wearing it. But that was before Bailyn. Before he was taken.

"Ye'd have t'be a silky with a basket o' magic, t' do it. Ye would," the wretch continued, cocking his chin, the bright eye looking up at the low moldy ceiling.

Jemmy also studied the droopy beams, though he was not sure why. "A silky to do what?" he asked, surprising himself that he had spoken the thought aloud.

"T' spirit us out o' here, like I said. What's de matter? Ye deaf too?" Then the two ancient teeth started a cackling that Jemmy was certain would never end.

—⁘—

"M'lady, you startled me!" Charity exclaimed as Mary threw open the door.

"Why did Jamie not come?" Mary flashed, stepping into her own bed-chamber, a bit surprised to find Charity there.

"Did he not?" Charity's face flushed as she stood up from Mary's vanity. "M'lady, I know not! I spoke to the boy, Seán. He said he'd tell Master James." She glided across the room, taking Mary's hands. "You look so tired, m'lady." Mary pulled away.

The butler tapped on the open door, then entered carrying a small amber chest. He set it on the bed, then left. Charity stepped back, retreating across the room, watching Mary. Without saying a word, Mary pulled a brass key engraved with the letter "B" from her reticule and unlocked the chest. Easing the curved lid back, she lifted out some white damask that was lying across the contents and placed it on the bed. Then she removed a gold locket and popped it open. She stared at the little picture till her hands began to shake, then quickly kissed it, snapped it shut, returning it to the chest. Then she pulled the letter for Jamie out from her reticule and placed it gently in the chest, over the locket. After carefully returning the damask to its place, she closed and locked the lid with the key. Her fingers moved over the chest's smooth inlaid floral pattern. "You told Seán? As I instructed you?"

"I have so told you, m'lady." Charity froze for a moment, her brow wincing.

Mary looked at Charity, her servant, her friend. Forcing a smile, she crossed the room to give her a hug. It wasn't Charity's fault that Jamie hadn't arrived, right? How could it be? As they embraced, Mary suddenly focused on the dress Charity was wearing. She pulled back, running her fingers across the creamy-yellow brocade silk. "This is my Tresard dress?" she demanded.

Charity stammered, "Aye, m'lady. Faith be, I meant no offence. I was only trying it—"

Mary studied her face. Something was different. Something was wrong. Now she remembered she had startled Charity when she entered the bed-chamber. Charity was sitting at Mary's vanity table—wearing Mary's lip paint. Mary touched Charity's lips, feeling the pasty paint. "Charity," she began, her voice tense with rising anger, "What's about you this morning?"

Charity protested, "Nothing, m'lady. I was—"

"We said our goodbyes last evening...." Mary stepped back. "And this morning, when you must have thought I wouldn't return...you're wearing my dress and lip—"

"M'lady, I can explain," pleaded Charity. "As you had asked me to bring the remainder of your things to England. When I was to join you there in a fortnight—"

"And what of it?" Mary slung off her cape.

Charity began to undress. "'Tis nothing, m'lady—"

"Were you expecting a visitor? You were, weren't you?"

"My hand to you, nay, m'lady! Truly not." Charity's fingers were fumbling to loosen the long ribbon of ivory buttons. "I was wrong to do this."

Mary could see a tear glistening in the corner of Charity's eye. There was more to this. A faint suspicion began to emerge, but Mary could not quite see it. There was something deceitful here, something concealed, something foul. Charity must have believed Mary would not return, and yet Charity was to travel to London herself in only a few weeks, escorting Mary's furniture and other belongings. Was that it? She blurted, "You're not coming to England?"

Charity didn't answer, only averted her eyes, tears running down her cheeks.

"Do tell me what I am seeing here."

"I beg your forgiveness m'lady, I—"

"Am I right?"

Charity lowered her chin. "Aye, m'lady. I cannot go. I must retire from your service."

Mary turned away as the room filled with thick silence.

"Can you forgive me? The yellow silk rustled with a soft crispness as Charity stepped from it. "I was muddled. I didn't know how to tell you. You know my simple mind. I get confused."

Mary sat down, slumping forward in her chair. She rubbed her neck, then caught a glimpse of herself in the wall mirror. Trying to arrange her disheveled hair, she whispered, "I'm so tired." She studied Charity's image in the mirror. "You've a man. A new one. But you won't tell me his name." She raised a hand to stop Charity's objection. "You gave me a name, I know. But I harbor no faith in it." She pivoted around to look directly at her.

"Forgive me, m'lady," Charity murmured, "but I cannot betray his...his trust."

Mary watched as Charity began to dress in a dark blue gown. The morning sun was streaming past the long tapestried curtains, falling across the floor, lighting Charity in a glow at the center of the room. She considered Charity's beauty, her radiance. "We've known one another for over fifteen years."

"Aye, m'lady."

"For fifteen years we have shared our secrets. Both yours and mine."

Charity's jaw tightened. "This man 'tis truly not of your concern, ma'am."

"None of my concern! To the contrary, I do believe he is!" Mary stood, picking up the yellow dress. "Last night, I followed the plans *you* arranged!" She gestured wildly with the dress in hand. "I went to Christ Church. They rang the bell. I waited. Hours, Charity! But Jamie never came." Mary's blood-shot eyes glared. "I waited all night. Then I come home to this!" She slung the dress across the room. She felt her tears searing down her cheeks.

"M'lady!"

"And now you seem not surprised by the news that Jamie never came." Her face blazed anew. "Where is he, Charity? Where's my Jamie?"

"M'lady, please!"

"God help you if you had a hand in any harm to—"

"Upon my oath, I did not!" Charity clamored. Weariness overcame Mary and she stumbled backwards, collapsing in the drawing chair. Charity came to her. "M'lady, you are exhausted."

Mary could barely move, much less think. She forced herself to calm, taking deep intentional breaths, closing her eyes. Surely Charity would never betray her, she reasoned, and what did it matter that Charity had a new man, that she had tried on her dress? Mary's arms felt heavy. She leaned forward, resting her face in her cupped hands, mumbling through her fingers. "Perhaps I am wrong."

"I can assure you—you are."

Mary slowly lifted her head, attempting to regain composure. Another deep breath. "My Charity," she began, her voice much softer now, "are you not coming to England with me?"

Charity fidgeted, then answered faintly, "No, m'lady. I cannot."

Mary looked into her eyes—eyes she had trusted. After all the years they had been together, how could Charity leave her? Tears were returning, but she held them back. The time for that had passed. She stood, wavering not to flop back, regaining her well-practiced poise. She crossed the room, picking up her cape, wrapping it around her shoulders. She began to tie the hood with shaky fingers. Charity stepped forward to help. Mary watched her servant's pretty eyes as Charity fixed a knot, then tied it correctly under Mary's chin.

"He must be wonderful," Mary said with a conceding sigh.

"He is, m'lady."

Mary moved her arms around Charity's waist. "Kiss me. Then I must go." Charity hesitated, then kissed Mary's cheek. Charity smiled as they pulled back, each wiping the tears from the other's face. "I shall miss you," Mary said. The bells of St. Patrick's Cathedral rang the hour. "As you are remaining, I have a final request of you."

"As you wish, m'lady."

"See that this gets to Jamie." Mary placed her hand on the small chest. "I intended to give it to him." Her voice drifted away. "At my father's house."

"Be assured," Charity said, smiling, "I'll deliver it next I see him."

"To him directly. To Jamie. No one else."

"I will."

"My sweet Charity." Mary embraced her. "I'm sorry I ever mistrusted you."

Charity whispered over Mary's shoulder, "I am sorry as well."

James Walsh, examined — "I knew the late Lord and Lady Anglesea. Owing to some dispute between them Lady Anglesea came to Dublin, to the house of my stepfather. As she appeared to be in some trouble my mother took the liberty of asking what ailed her, upon which her ladyship said in my presence that she had a great deal of reason, for my lord used her ill. With that she sat down and shed a few tears, and she said that if it were not for two considerations, her heart would break. The first was, her ladyship said, that she thanked God she had a very tender, indulgent father, the Duke of Buckingham, who would not abandon her in her affliction, and the other was that she had a very promising young son, who, she trusted, if God would give him life, would be a support and prop to her in her old age."

— trial transcript, *Annesley v. Anglesea*, 1743

CHAPTER 10

Justice is a temporary thing
That must at last come to an end;
But the conscience is eternal
And will never die.

— Martin Luther, 1530

The morning sun's long reaching fingers slipped through the planks of the stable's eastern wall, gliding across the mare's back, across Fynn's face, then down to the dusty floor where they ignited in pools of light. Fynn had woken early that day, tied his hair tight with a brown velvet ribbon, put on his most presentable waist coat, and ridden directly to Mary's house where he anticipated finding her with Seámus. Instead, that morning he had been greeted in the foyer by a bitter tempered Charity standing imperiously in a yellow evening gown. She told him Seámus had disappeared and that Mary had left for England without the boy. Other than that she knew nothing, could be of no further assistance, and asked him to leave. He had then ridden to the stables on Chequer Lane where he was working that week. On the way, he mulled the confusion of facts, the flurry of unknowns. What Charity said fit Seán's account—he too had not found Seámus last night, having given up in the storm. He cursed himself for not going to Christ Church, for having sent Seán instead. He should have gone to Mary directly. Why had he not? She would have received him. This time, he was certain, she would have. Why had he hesitated till morning? When Fynn arrived at the stables, he found he was the first there and was glad for it. He stood awhile in silent slivers of sunlight, a daze of memories and loss. But not sadness—an emptiness beyond depression, a weight that defies all melancholy.

Finally, he started moving, hanging his waistcoat on an iron peg and re-tying his hair. Then he gathered his pick-hammer and cutters, a few shoes and a bag of nails, and prepared to shoe a highbred mare that had been brought in the day before. After looking the horse over, he touched her gently along her back and legs, sending a shiver across her withers. He chose the rear left hoof and straddled it, pulling it up. The horse sidestepped away from him. "Hold still hussy!" he bellowed, grabbing the leg. The horse stamped down, nearly stepping on him. "Nay! Stop it," he said, hitting its rump with the side of his fist. He walked to the front of the mare, staring her in the eyes. "Ye want t' dance? Do ye?" He grabbed the halter firmly. "I haven't the mind for yer antics. Not today. Settle down."

The crunch of footsteps on gravel grew louder behind him. He turned to see Seán and Mackercher entering through the giant stable doors. Seán was downcast, holding a cloak in his hands. Mackercher followed, giving Fynn a nod. As Seán came directly to Fynn, Fynn focused on the torn green cloak. He immediately recognized it and took it from Seán. A large russet spot was visible, with holes in the middle of the stain.

"'Tis Jemmy's, Da."

"Where did ye find it?" Fynn asked, still studying it.

Mackercher stepped forward. "'Twas left on the rail in front of the shop."

"What's it mean Da?" Seán's voice trembled as he stared into his father's eyes, looking for an answer, an understanding, anything.

"I don't know." Fynn shook his head.

"Is Jemmy dead?"

"Nay son!" He studied Seán's face. "Seámus is fine."

"That dog, Richard," Mackercher began, softly, "He's trying to scare ya, Seán. Wants ya to think some injury has come to Master James. That is all."

"I know," Seán said, trying to sound brave as his large boyish eyes filled with tears.

"When last ye saw Seámus in it?" asked Fynn, his voice thick as he rolled the fabric between his rough fingers, feeling the texture, examining the holes, reasoning with the dried blood, as if it might talk to him, might tell him something.

"He can't be dead, Da. He can't!"

"When last ye saw him?"

"Yesterday, when I told him about his mum's plan. He was wearing it then. He was."

Fynn held up the stained part. "And this? Was this there?"

Seán sniffed, his cheeks streaked with tears. "Nay, Da. 'Twasn't. I didn't see it."

"Last night, where'd ye say ye went t' find him?"

"Copper Alley. T'was where—"

"Ye did fine," Fynn began. He studied the blood, sniffing it. "This is older than that."

Seán's face flushed. "I tried, Da!" he sobbed. "But then it started raining and…."

Fynn squeezed his son tightly to his side and slowly nodded. How could Seámus be dead? What monster could kill such a boy? His temples tightened. His mind locked.

—※—

The sun was already warming the thick air of the between-deck, and Jemmy could feel the heat rising. Blessedly, his swollen ankle remained numb so long as he didn't move it. But his head was rippling with intense pain and holding it motionless didn't help. He had tried rubbing it, pressing it against the post, but the pounding would not leave. As the morning wore on with no food or fresh air, still shackled under the low ceiling with the one-eyed man still rambling and drooling, the pain had only worsened. He was sure his head was about to crack in two. At least the headache had made him forget the pain from the graze across his side, which was open and bleeding again. He felt the warm blood soaking his filthy shirt, wondering how much blood he could lose before he would die. Suddenly, a flash of Juggy's pale face rushed over him—she was falling to the wet dirt, lying dead in the street. He slammed his ankle against a crate and howled at the produced pain, letting it mix with his cleaving headache, welcoming the diversion, willing to take any pain. Anything to keep her dead eyes away.

"Name's John…John MacCullough," announced the old man, interrupting himself. He had been murmuring for hours about odd things mixed with vile fits against everything English. "What's yers?"

Jemmy glanced at him, unsure about answering, then said, "Master James Annesley."

"Aye? Master Jim?" The man's good eye rocked toward Jemmy. "Yer a young lord, are ye? M'lord!" he chortled. "*Tiarna Óige! Tiarna Óige* indeed!"

"Shut yer gob," Jemmy breathed. He had not been called *Tiarna Óige*, or "Young Lord," since Dunmain, where the local Catholic boys had teased him. He wished Seán was there to pummel this old man, as he had helped Jemmy do to some of those boys. No, Seán would think this was all funny.

"Ach, m'lord! Where be me breedin'? Can I get ye anything? Perhaps yer stinkin' arse wiped with me sleeve?" The laughter reverberated against the low beams.

Jemmy's chin fell. He wanted to relieve himself. To eat. To just sleep. "Leave me be, ye old stinkin' cur," he whispered.

The man became quiet for a moment, then started a bit calmer, "Ye're a little thievin' Irish lad, aren't ye? 'Tis nothin' t' be ashamed of, Master Jim."

"Good sir. Please leave me be," Jemmy pleaded, sighing deeply.

"Good sir? Me?" The decrepit cackling resumed. "Good sir!" he hooted.

—m—

"I don't know, Daniel." Fynn shook his head with resignation. "I just don't know." They were standing at the entrance of the stables. Fynn was brushing one of the Scot's horses while Mackercher held the reins. Jemmy's blood-soaked cloak was in Mackercher's other hand. Seán was sitting on a stool, staring out. "Richard wants us to think the lad's dead. That's all we know." The horse snorted softly, and Fynn scratched its large grey jaw.

Mackercher watched and said nothing for a while. He liked Fynn and though he had come to know him the past day, and through all of Joan's letters, he had never realized the depth of Fynn's affection for James Annesley, Seámus, the young nobleman now missing, possibly dead. He handed the cloak back to Fynn. "My friend," he walked behind the horse, gliding a hand over its rump, "we've both loved the same woman. Now," he grumbled, "we both hate the same man."

"'Tis true," muttered Fynn. He slumped against the animal, his face turned away.

Mackercher continued, "Ya're a good man, Fynn Kennedy. I'd count ya as a brother." He put a hand on Fynn's back. "But my sister's buried. And I'm held from bringing justice to Richard. And without Master James for a trial—"

"Ye may as well return to Scotland," Fynn finished the thought. He turned and faced Mackercher. As always, seeing Joan's warm eyes in her brother's face pained him, drawing him yet pushing him away. But this time he held his gaze. It was like seeing from a distance the flicker of a welcoming candle from his own house, only to come closer and realize the roof was on fire. Why not just let this man kill Richard? Because of the million reasons not to, he could not let his mind wallow through it again. He walked to the smithing table and pulled the dirk from behind a box of nails, then turned and handed it to the big Scotsman. "Take this. I don't want it."

Mackercher unsheathed the dirk. "*Léargas sa Dorchadas.*"

Seán turned at this and was now watching the men intently. Fynn nodded. "Joan gave it to Seámus. Said it was yer father's."

"Sight in the Dark," Mackercher read the inscription. "Been years since I held this."

As much as Fynn hated the damned thing, he knew it needed to be given to Mackercher, not buried, not destroyed. Joan had said the knife was a Mackercher heirloom—her great-grandfather was given it by a Scottish knight, Sir Alexander Dallas, whom the elder Mackercher had saved in an Aberfoyle battle. Dallas claimed the dirk had been Robert the Bruce's and used at the battle of Bannockburn. Yet now, its lineage meant nothing. Not to him. He loathed it for whom it last killed. He resumed brushing the horse, which leaned into Fynn slightly, no doubt enjoying the extra attention. Fynn hoped he would never see the dirk again, it only made him remember the horrifying image—the bloody hilt protruding from Joan's chest.

"When I see Master James," Mackercher said assuredly, "I'll return it to him." Fynn glanced at Mackercher, wondering at his optimism. "Aye. I will meet the lad someday."

"I'm glad ye think so."

"I do indeed."

"Seámus is a son to me, and..." Fynn stopped.

"I know," whispered Mackercher.

Fynn looked at the light streaming in from the open stable doors, then raised a hand, as if holding a glass, and closed his eyes. "May the road rise to meet ye, Seámus. May the wind be always at yer back. May the sun shine warm upon yer face..." He stopped momentarily, bowing his head. The tears were coming again and he swallowed hard. He sniffed, then raised his gaze once more. "And the rain fall soft upon yer fields. And until we meet again, may God hold ye in the hollow of His mighty hand." His chin was quivering, his fists clenched.

Mackercher embraced him. "'Tis a good blessing. Mark my words, friend, we will destroy Richard Annesley. We'll rip his goddamned heart out."

Fynn patted Mackercher's shoulder and slowly closed his eyes. "We will indeed."

Mackercher pulled back, but kept an iron grip on Fynn's arm. "Ya have my word. On my sister's grave, I swear it!"

Fynn knew Mackercher meant every word.

—m—

The empty day crept along, and the between-deck became crowded. Crew-men were loading crates, trunks, and large wooden boxes on board. One of them had heeded Jemmy's pleas, unshackling him to let him relieve himself through a porthole. Then he was quickly rechained to the same post. The threadbare man was still rambling and festering but had turned his attacks on the crewmen who slumped into the tight area. They seemed to detest the old creature as much as Jemmy did. Soon Jemmy heard people coming aboard, the clatter of their feet echoing through two layers of thick floors. He looked up, staring at the sounds, studying them, searching through them for her voice. Surely she was onboard by now. He envisioned how it would be—he would yell for her—she would have a crewman bring her down—she would have him unchained—he would be free—the nightmare would end—he would hold her, and she him, and they would never let go. Once more sailors clambered down, hauling more crates, shoving them into the hold, smashing them against Jemmy. He could not see the old man now. Couldn't hear him either as the ship was beginning to rock against the wind, swaying, creaking in protest. Just then, one of the trunks caught his eye. It looked familiar, dark blue with brass riveting—his mother had a trunk like that.

"Dead-eye!" Jemmy called out. "Ye still over there?"

"Name's John." The shaky voice emanated from the other side of the crates.

"Ye see that blue trunk near ye?"

"Aye, yer high holy lordship. What of it?"

"Anything on its front?" He heard the man's chains rattling. "Perhaps a letter?"

"Aye, Master Jim, I can see it. 'Tis the letter *B*. Hard t' see. But aye, 'tis a *B*."

Mother's up there! His heart began a hammering pound. "Mother!" he shouted. "Mother! Motherrr!"

"What in God's name!" screeched the old man.

Jemmy ignored him and kept screaming as loud as he could. "Lady Mary Sheffield! Motherrr!" He stopped to listen. Surely she would hear him.

"Screamin' fer yer mummy, are ye *Tiarna Óige?*" The crackling laughter resumed.

Jemmy strained against his shackles, listening. Nothing. Again he yelled, "Mother! Mother! Motherrr!" He screamed again and again, "Motherr! I'm down heerre!"

On deck, crewmen were bustling about. "All hands aloft!" was shouted and seconded across the deck as the mainsail and jib scurried up their ropes to guide the ship from the harbor. The few passengers were in the roundhouse, on the aft quarterdeck near the stern of the ship. Sitting, huddled among them, trying to find shelter from the wind's rush, was Mary Sheffield. As the wind shifted and the ship swayed to conform, Mary thought she heard a familiar voice, faint and far away. She stood, stepping around the other passengers, making her way down to the main deck. There she heard it again. Something distant. But she couldn't make it out. Moving back quickly, she dodged the elbows of a crewman spinning a massive wench. Then she leaned on the railing and looked up. Seagulls were riding the wind that streamed around the masts and booms. Again she heard the sound. Then again—and again. Something faint. It sounded like someone calling her name, saying "Mary" or was it "mother"? The wind whipped at her skirts, and the squeaking of the pulleys and wenches harmonized with the loud seagulls. Soon, she was hearing her name in everything—the ropes grinding against their blocks, the tackle clanging against the masts and yardarms, the sails popping like whips, the ship shoving against the cresting waves—everything resonating in a melodic moan, a unified sound of straining against the wind, against the unseen forces that bound them all—and it all sounded like her name. Feeling dizzy, she grabbed a rail to steady herself, slowly making her way back to the other passengers. There she sat down and leaned her head against a stack of rolled sails. Closing her eyes, she was convinced of her own delirium. She fell asleep long before the sound of her name left the wind.

Jemmy's throat was burning from screaming, but he kept calling over and over, "Motherr! Maaryy Maary! Down herre! Mother! Motherrr!"

"Shut your bloody mouth!" A new voice barked from the other side of the crates.

"Mother! Motherrr!" he continued, ignoring the order.

A crewman pushed the crates and trunks from his path and came straight for Jemmy, brandishing a crank handle. "Idiot lad! Simpleton! Your mother's not coming for you. You're on a ship, you stupid boy!" He raised the handle in his right hand. "Now, are you going to be quiet or aren't you?"

Jemmy could not be quiet. He would not. His mother hadn't heard him yet! She hadn't come for him. He was still shackled. It wasn't happening as it was supposed to. He couldn't stop yelling. How else could she find him? She hadn't come. She wasn't holding him. "Mother! Mot—" The handle smashed into his jaw, knocking him violently to the floor, unconscious.

—⁓—

Catherine O'Neile, examined — "His name was James Annesley. He was reputed and treated as my lord and lady's son. When the child came to Dublin he was over eight years old. Lady Anglesea was in Stable Lane while my lord was in Cross Lane, if my memory remains. When I saw him years later, it was after the death of my lord. He was in a very indifferent condition as to dress. He was being cared for by a once servant man of my lord, Mr. Fynn Kennedy, who was very fond of the child. Lady Anglesea called the child Jamie. She sent a letter by me to Mr. Kennedy about the child. I cannot read. My lady said that she was very desirous to see her child, but she knew if any of the servants brought him to her, Lord Richard Annesley would turn them out of their bread. After my lord died, my lady said she would be glad to see the child but he was not at liberty to go where he would."

— trial transcript, *Annesley v. Anglesea*, 1743

—⁓—

CHAPTER 11

Ní scaipfidh ar mo chumha
Atá i lár mo chroí á bhrú,
Dúnta suas go dlúth
Mar a bheadh glas a bheadh ar thrúnc
'S go raghadh an eochair amú.

My grief will not depart,
It presses on my heart,
Shut firmly in
Like a trunk that would be locked
And the key gone lost.

— from *The Lament for Art Ó Laoghaire,*
Eileen Dubh, 1773

The *Courtmain* was pitching and heaving in the rough northern sea, waking Mary. She opened her eyes, listening to the wind slapping the enormous square sails, luffing them through each tack. She was accustomed to voyages across St. George's Channel, even violent storms in that sea, but something was different about this. Rising from her pallet, she walked from the roundhouse onto the quarterdeck, scooting aside to avoid the crewmen buzzing around her. She found an open rail and held on, watching the organized chaos on the maindeck below. The crewmen were swarming the decks and shrouds, fighting the strong wind, and she found their intensity captivating. When the wind whipped her long loose hair, she pulled at the hood of her cape, tying it. Ahead was the nearing shore, her homeland, though it now seemed so terribly foreign. For the first time, she realized she would never return to Ireland. Never again. It would have been a pleasant thought, but she was leaving her boy behind. She felt wicked and ashamed. But hadn't she tried? What more could she have done? For a moment, the tormenting images absorbed her and she turned away from the movements of the crew, placing her face squarely against the stinging wind, toward England, and began to murmur a prayer. "Lord God forgive me...." She paused to cough, then closed her eyes, pulling the salt air through her nose. "I don't know what to do. I don't know what I've done. Please help me. Watch over my Jamie. Please send your angels to my boy."

"All hands! Calashee! All hands! Calashee watch!" the boatswain suddenly bellowed to the crew. Various octaves of deep immutable voices replied from just as many different locations across the ship's expanse, "Calashee watch, aye! All watches, calashee!"

"Ma'am, you'll need to get back. Ma'am?"

Startled, Mary turned to see a young deckhand pulling a thick rope through a block and up into the tackle of the mast. Before she could respond, another voice boomed from the poopdeck above, "Sailor, leave the good lady be!"

"Aye, Captain," the crewman replied smartly.

"Ma'am, ye'll have a better view from up here." The man smiled. "And there won't be any swabs swinging yardarms at ye while ye contemplate." Mary flushed with the realization that the captain had been watching her pray. "I'll help ye up," he went on, motioning to the steep steps.

"Captain." She acknowledged, curtsying politely before heading up the stairway. As she reached the top, the *Courtmain* began to come about, and she nearly lost her balance. The captain offered his hand, and she took it uncomfortably. "Thank you, Captain," she said. "You're very kind."

"Captain Thomas Hendry, at yer service, ma'am." He bowed, tipping his hat.

"Pleased to make your acquaintance," Mary replied with a forced smile. Her gaze returned to the nearing shore and the myriad of ships surrounding them. Feeling the captain looking at her, she tugged at the hood of her cape.

"Strangest thing, this wind," Captain Hendry said.

"How so?"

"'Tis usually a following wind, off St. George's. Not a head wind like this. Can be a right bit dangerous."

"Dangerous?" She feigned slight distress.

"Aye," he went on, motioning beyond the rail, "there are a few things we could hit out here, and she moves rather fast close-hauled like this."

Mary studied the flock of white sails overhead, each taut and straining against the frenetic air slipping by them in vigorous bursts. She didn't know what to say to the captain. He was obviously flirting with her, but she was in no mood. The sun's brightness forced her to look down again and she returned to watching the grey and white churning waves around her, seeing them as a mass of roiling, snow-capped mountains, as if she were a bird or a spirit, far above. Noticing Captain Hendry had stepped closer, she winced and stepped away. It was time to remove herself, she reasoned. Time to move back to her quarters. "Thank you, sir, for the explanation."

Just then the first-mate stepped onto the quarterdeck and yelled, "Captain, sir. It appears that Herrick's Quay is laden."

Captain Hendry pulled up his brass scope and extended it, then studied the far docks and quays of Bristol. "So it does!" he shouted back. Then he swung round, apparently exploring another area in the distance. Leaning on the fife rail, Mary noticed the first-mate below. He was wearing his own hair, tied at the back, and there was something familiar about him. Probably because he looked so terribly common, she reasoned. "Mr. Parker, take her into Bishop's Quay. That'll suffice."

"Aye, aye, Captain!" The first-mate was also looking through a scope, apparently studying Bishop's Quay. "Helmsman!" he yelled down into the dark wheelhouse. "New bearing—port three points!"

"Port, three points. Aye!" echoed a faint voice from somewhere below Mary's feet.

"Well done," Captain Hendry said to himself, putting away his scope. Mary started toward the steps. "Ma'am, are ye stepping down?" asked the captain, sounding disappointed.

"Aye, Captain. I must prepare my things. I do thank you for your hospitality. She is a lovely ship."

"Thank ye, ma'am." He tipped his hat, then followed her to the top of the railing. "If I may be so bold. I fear I did not learn yer name. May I have the honor of knowing it?"

Mary smiled meekly. "Lady Anglesea. I was." She paused, unhappy that she still reflexed so. "Mary Sheffield." From inside her cape, Mary pulled a black handkerchief, revealing her official state of mourning. Even though the custom, of which she was instinctively aware, dictated that she was to be fully attired in black for a husband so recently departed, she had decided to only carry the black handkerchief, which reflected the mourning of distant relative. It seemed more than enough to her.

"Oh...I'm sorry," stammered the captain, staring at the handkerchief. "My condolences." His face had died, falling white and empty, as if he had just seen the head of Medusa and was now reduced to a crumbling pillar of salt. "So, ye're the wife of Arthur...the late Earl—"

"Yes. You knew my husband?"

Hendry stared past her, not answering. The *Courtmain* was coming through another tack, but he seemed oblivious. Finally, he took a few paces back and muttered, "Aye, well . . . I suppose I do. I mean, I did." His eyes shifted away, then rapidly back again, then finally turned up at the mizzen sails as if they demanded his immediate attention. "Good day, ma'am," he blurted in a dull flat tone.

"Good day to you as well." Mary turned away, saddened. She carefully stepped the remaining way down to the quarterdeck and entered the round-house. She was accustomed to men hating Arthur, but Captain Hendry's reaction had been different somehow. Unusual. It infuriated her that she was still feeling apologetic for Arthur, even after his death. She hated him. It had been years since he had thrown her from Dunmain House, with his false allegations about Tom Palliser. He got what he deserved for what he did to that man. Arthur had been so wrong. And then he went too far altogether—forbidding her from ever again seeing her boy. Two long years. She hated him for that. But she had hated him long before then. She hated Arthur for what he had done to her, for what he had stolen from her—things that had never been his.

Mary's father had been Queen Anne's favorite secret lover, and as such had been granted the title of the First Duke of Buckingham. Having built Buckingham Palace, he was as elegantly rich as he was elegantly handsome, as powerful as he was loved by the royals. And yet he was a poor husband and a non-existent father. Mary's mother was of little consequence, having died not long after Mary's birth. Mary was raised in the splendor of English royalty, playing and schooling with Princess Anne and Princess Catherine, the haughty daughters of King James II, for whom Mary's father worked. Princess Catherine was Mary's age, and when they were both nineteen, Catherine married the Fifth Earl of Anglesea, a favorite friend and supporter of King James II. But that Anglesea Earl beat Catherine severely, leading her sister (by then Queen Anne) to authorize their quick divorce. Soon thereafter the Fifth Earl was murdered—whispers put it as the Queen's doing—and the Earlship transferred to the dead man's brother, Arthur, the Sixth Earl of Anglesea, and leaving the other, younger brother, Richard, fuming in the wake. After the divorce and death, Princess Catherine, then twenty-one, was once again available for marriage. Thus, Queen Anne arranged for her sister Catherine to marry the Duke of Buckingham, then fifty-four—the Queen's secret ex-lover, a widower, and the absentee father of Mary, also twenty-one.

With her father impenetrably focused on matters of the royal court, Mary fell to the devices of her ex-friend, her new stepmother, now re-titled Duchess Catherine. Within a month of the wedding Mary was quietly banished to a country house outside London—far away from the new family that Catherine planned with the Duke. Though Mary had gone, dutifully with her servants, including Charity, she was heartbroken that no one had objected, not even her father. Then after a few years, even Mary's occasional visits to Buckingham Palace became too much for Catherine, and a new plan was conceived. Catherine knew her ex-husband's brother, Arthur Annesley, was looking for a wife. The plan was born, and Mary's immediate dislike for everything about Arthur was of no relevance. They were married and she was shipped to Ireland with the drunkard, with his fists and virulent mouth. Duchess Catherine had calculated correctly—Mary was no better treated by the Sixth Earl of Anglesea than Catherine had been treated by the Fifth.

Now, journeying back to England, Mary had nothing to show for the years of misery and torment. She was returning with less property, less pride, and less worth than she had when she first left, over fourteen years earlier. And she had no home to go to in London. She doubted the country house would even be available. She would have to survive on the mercies of her stepmother Catherine and her aging father whom she barely knew. And most damning to her—she was returning without her son.

—⁓—

An hour later, in the between-deck of the *Courtmain*, Jemmy awoke to the fetid smell of bilge water commingling with his own vomit. His entire body ached with an abhorrent pain greater than any he had ever known. He had once heard that being burned was the worst pain a man could endure, and now he felt as though he had been burned from head to foot. As he tried to lift his head, the palpitations seared his skull. He was sweating and clammy. He lowered his head against the hard, wet, putrid floor. Managing one eye open and finally the other, he saw light and sounds enveloping him. Feet were moving on all sides of him, men's voices yelling over the scratching, bumping sounds of crates and trunks being dragged across the floor. After a while he tried to sit up again but the misery in his neck and head reminded him that he had been knocked unconscious twice in the last two days. He pulled against the stiffness, disregarding the pain, forcing himself upright, then leaned against the rough post around which his bruised wrists were still shackled. A short crewman came to him with a bilge mop, and Jemmy noticed the sailor was young, not much older than himself. He watched as the boy began dabbing at the vomit with the old broken mop, swishing it around, not absorbing much. The only thing he seemed to accomplish was to splash the muck against Jemmy's legs and stir the stench farther into the stale air. The young crewman, grunting in disgust, finally gave up and left. Looking around, Jemmy saw that most of the crates and trunks were gone, along with the wretched old man. Then he realized the ship was not under sail, only swaying lightly against its mooring. The soft lap of the waves caused a burbling echo throughout the hold. Where were they? Where had they been going? He tried to remember, tried to center his murky thoughts. Bristol, he realized. They must be in Bristol, in England. He brought a knee up to scratch his nose. Suddenly he understood—Bristol! His mind screamed, his matted eyes popped wide. Bristol! He turned to the right, examining the hold, searching desperately, frantically, scanning the few remaining trunks. He strained against the agonizing pain, peering at and past everything, hoping he had missed it somehow, hoping he was wrong, hoping his muddled head had forgotten something, something important, something that would explain the absence, some reason he was not seeing it. He stretched one way, then the other, then finally he slowed, slackening against the shackles, finally letting himself believe what seconds before he would have sworn could never be, could never have happened. But it was obvious. Quite simply the bleakness, the narrow hollow realm under that sagging ceiling, the dense nasty air, all of the nothingness, the worthless pain, the vast hopelessness of what surely was to come had all united into one singular agonizing truth. It had confirmed James Annesley's deepest fear—the large blue humpbacked trunk was already gone.

—∽—

James Dempsey, examined — "I am about thirty-seven or thirty-eight years of age. I went to Mass. My parents were popish. I was not acquainted with Lord Anglesea before I was employed as tutor to his son. Mr. Annesley wore his own hair—flaxen hair—when he was at school with me. I saw the boy in Dublin. I heard that he was in Dublin later, and that he was transported. To what place? I do not know; to where people are transported."

— trial transcript, *Annesley v. Anglesea,* 1743

—∽—

CHAPTER 12

I hate to be near the sea,
and hear it roaring and raging
like a wild beast in its den.
It puts me in mind of the everlasting efforts
of the human mind,
struggling to be free,
and ending just where it began.

— William Hazlitt, 1823

Later That Month
At sea — in route to the
British Colonies in America

Like a blossom closing for the night, the sea slackened, drawing in upon itself, relaxing, preparing to absorb the sun, which was hovering just over her furthest reach, over the very edge of the world. The thick waters rolled up against the *Courtmain's* red and gold sides, then receded again, easing her to slumber. The galley bell rang out calling the first-dog watch to eat. They quickly descended the ratlines, having flown the light kite-sails for the evening. Most of the crew and passengers had dined at noon, but the evening watch had successfully petitioned Captain Hendry for a later victual. For Jemmy, it was another opportunity to get a meal. Standing on the maindeck, he watched the sea slowly calm as he finished his small ration of salt pork.

He was beginning to like the grey-blue ocean, even when she was in a rage, pitching and buffeting them about as she had done for weeks since the *Courtmain* lost sight of England. The first days of the voyage had been a painful blur of raging headaches and wrenching nausea. On the sixth day, a passenger, chosen because he had registered as surgical apprentice, examined Jemmy and then informed Captain Hendry, in Jemmy's stunned presence, that Jemmy had "ship's fever" and would be dead before the morning watch. Jemmy was immediately unshackled and given a separate bunk in the halfdeck near the helmsman's berth. But then the storms hit and though the heavy sea had done no serious damage, it had managed to carry away a section of the port rails, wash two sea chests overboard, and jostle Jemmy unmercifully in his berth. But it was better than the between-deck. Anything was better than the between-deck.

He was not sure why he liked the ocean. Perhaps because he had stopped fearing her. Perhaps because she seemed to protect him, for a while, from indentured servitude, enslavement, or whatever it was that awaited him on the other shore. Perhaps it was her consoling touch, her rolling lifts and falls, holding him through his grieving. She lulled him as he wept in the dark, her waves whispering to him as he moaned alone, curled, imagining his mother, missing Mr. Kennedy and Seán, shuddering again and again through Juggy's death. Finally the images had subsided, lessening. He avoided thinking about them, letting the ever-present sea and the bounds of the tall-ship fill his mind, just as he was doing now, in the middle of the cold Atlantic, leaning over the railing of the *Courtmain*, studying the settling blackness below him, feeling both excited and soothed in the same bracing moment.

"What do ye think of her, James?"

Jemmy turned to see Captain Hendry approaching. "Who, Captain?"

"My ocean!" Hendry stepped up on a wooden box and swept his arm imperially across the vast expanse. "What do ye think of her?"

Jemmy smiled hesitantly, wondering if the captain might be drunk again. "Oh, aye," he said, nodding. "She's grand, sir."

"And my argosy? A leviathan, no?" He turned to Jemmy.

"Aye, sir," Jemmy agreed, wondering what either was.

Captain Hendry stepped to the railing and lit his pipe. They joined in a silent stare at the fire of the falling sun, each lost in his own secrets. The enormous deep-blue sky was streaked broadly with hundreds of golden-orange shafts erupting from one horizon to the other. The plunging sun ruptured, blasting all its colors free as if it knew they would be terminally lost in the blackness of the sea. It reminded Jemmy of Ireland, particularly Dunmain, of memories he had been trying to keep buried. He pictured the evenings he had spent with Seán climbing the Norman ruins atop the big hill south of McCreary's farm, and how they had tossed rocks, played mumblety-peg and dueled with wooden swords until the sun disappeared. They were sure that Dunmain had the best sunsets in all of Ireland. But then they moved to Dublin and neither seemed to notice a sunset again. Least not till this one, at sea. Would the Colonies have sunsets like this? Indentured slave—the phrase froze him. And with the sun nearly gone, a frigid emptiness bludgeoned him even more. He missed Dunmain terribly. Taking a deep breath of salty dark air, he closed his eyes and the image of Fynn Kennedy filled him, as if he had inhaled his face from that same temperate air. He longed to feel Mr. Kennedy's powerful grip, the weight of the man's arm on his shoulder. He missed his soothing voice telling him everything would be all right, all right in God's time. Even though it had not come true and perhaps never would.

Then his thoughts turned to Seán. He would love to be there, at sea. Seán had often talked of becoming a Royal Marine. If only he were there. *Aye, ye'd like this Seán, ye would indeed.* He breathed deep. He was tired of remembering them, but he knew neither of them would ever withdraw from him, never abandon his mind—they would never pass away. He was the one who was gone, gone for almost a month. Opening his eyes, Jemmy saw the sun had already vanished and was amazed at how quickly it had gone. Anger jabbed him—anger at himself, anger for having missed the sun's last few living moments.

"How are ye feeling today lad?" asked Captain Hendry.

"Fine, sir," replied Jemmy, looking up at the tall, square-shouldered captain. The man kept a proud air and spoke in a lilting Irish accent. Jemmy hoped that someday he would stand as tall and proud as Captain Hendry. They even shared a scar on their cheeks, though Jemmy's was on his right side and at five inches was twice as long as the captain's. In the last couple of days he had even begun to hope that he too would be a gallant ship captain, wearing the distinctive dark-blue fearnought jacket and tarpaulin cocked hat over a tight groomed wig, just like Captain Hendry—free to be true, free from the tangled evil of men like Richard. He could see himself skippering a crew of loyal men on a magnificent ship across an endless, peaceful ocean.

"How's yer foot?" Hendry continued.

"Aye, fine sir, that too. I've only a small limp to me now."

"Good. Ye're a strong one, ye are. I've seen many a lad succumb to her, but not ye."

"Nay, sir."

The captain slapped Jemmy's back. "Ye'll make a sailor yet, b'gob! Ye shall indeed!"

"Thank ye, sir," said Jemmy, smiling. He did feel better. Much better. He kept his beam for some time, proud to stand alongside the captain, even if the man was a bit drunk. As Jemmy stood there, braced against the chilly wind, he saw the sea change to a deep shade of crimson-blue, like aged burgundy.

The sun had long slipped below the horizon, and what was left of its blaze had become a smoldering gold fluorescence that shimmered across the dim expanse of settling waves, searing their small white crests with boiling orange and red, mirroring its lighter self overhead, still overspread in broad pastels, blushing against the darkening sky.

Again the captain cracked the silence. "I was told ye were a bit peevish today with the burials and all."

Jemmy turned away slightly. "'Twas nothing sir."

"Eh? Now lad, what was it?"

Jemmy hesitated, then softly said, "'Twas the old one, the man with the one eye."

"He was consigned to the deep. I hate to lose a passenger, but it happens. As ye've seen." The captain shrugged. "Always will."

"Aye," Jemmy muttered, then added, "I saw my first dolphin today," hoping to change the subject.

"Not a dolphin. Not in these waters. When we get to warmer water, I'll show ye. They'll be along under the bowsprit then. Ye'll see." He paused then announced, "I've got something to give ye lad." He motioned for Jemmy to follow him, and they both went up to the quarterdeck, then on up to the poopdeck where the captain staggered slightly, grabbing the chalk-marked rail. Then he bent over and picked up something next to the gunwale. "Now, look here, have ye ever seen one of these?" He handed a large brass object to Jemmy.

"Aye, Captain, I've seen one." Jemmy studied the object. It was about two feet long, a combination of brass strips forming two flat triangles.

"Well, have ye ever held one before?"

"Oh, nay sir. Never held one." Jemmy turned it over and back again.

"Do ye have a notion what it is, what it's for? Do ye?"

"'Tis a quadrant—a backstaff for navigation by the stars," answered Jemmy, still running his fingers over the worn brass. He had seen the first mate charting with one and had wondered how it worked.

"Very right ye are, a backstaff indeed. 'Tis yers."

"Mine?"

"Aye, Lord Anglesea, 'tis a gift from me."

Jemmy recoiled instantly. "Lord Anglesea, sir?" The title was hanging in the air, resonating, like the echoing aftermath of a single toll of a bell.

"What of it?"

"Well, sir . . . why'd ye refer to me as such . . . as Lord Anglesea?"

"'Twas nothin. You said that is your title. I was simply…." Even in the waning light, Jemmy could see that the captain's eyes flicking nervously between him and the heavy expanse of the sea. "Now, lad, let me tell ye about the quadrant. When I was…."

As the captain droned on, Jemmy's mind was elsewhere. Does he believe me now? Did he know before I was brought aboard? Nay, he's a ship's captain, not a kidnapper. Jemmy picked at a loose chip in the top of the chalked fife railing. Surely he'd spoken true when he said he had papers showing I'd registered myself for this. But why the particular treatment? The tiny chip wouldn't give and Jemmy tried harder to loosen it. He's been polite. But what if…might he have met Mother? Nay, he hadn't! He said he hadn't. Wouldn't he have known her? She was on this same ship from Ringsend to Bristol. He claims not to have seen her, nor to know Richard. Finally the small chip of wood flew free from the railing, leaving a dimple behind. Jemmy breathed hard and chewed on his bottom lip. So, why call me Lord Anglesea? The alternatives and potential lies of what he had decided were truths rolled through his mind like one wave crashing across another—a mass of confusion. Something was wrong, something spoiled, and now Jemmy wished he were older. If he were, he would know the truth and would not be so easily deceived by men such as Captain Hendry. Bitterness swept over him, for allowing himself to be hoodwinked, for not knowing if he had actually been deceived at all. It seemed as if something were being stripped from him—not just his trust in Captain Hendry—something more, something unknown. He felt as if he had been given his ration of hard tack only to find worms crawling through it. He reached up and felt the Buckingham key, that comforting piece of brass hanging from his neck on a strip of sailcloth. "I am," Jemmy finally whispered, interrupting the captain. "I am Lord Anglesea."

"Oh, aye, of course ye are," Hendry replied nervously,

"So ye believe me?" asked Jemmy, exhausting his last optimism.

"Well, nay. Can't rightly say I do."

Jemmy's face dropped.

"Ah, ye've gone chopfallen lad." The captain gently lifted Jemmy's chin. "Think upon it now—if I did believe ye, what then? I couldn't rightly take ye into Maryland as an indentee, now could I?"

"But what I told ye is true! Upon my oath, I am the Earl of Anglesea. Rightfully so!"

"Aye, and my mother was Athena."

"But I am, sir!"

"No more!" snapped Captain Hendry, raising a hand. "We've been through this lad. I won't hear it again. 'Tis ridiculous, indeed." He turned and started descending to quarterdeck. Over his shoulder he said, "Find the first-mate if ye want to learn that thing."

"Aye, sir," said Jemmy meekly. Once again, he felt lost—lost in the words of the captain, lost in his feelings of truth, lost in the past, lost in the unknown, lost on the cold black Atlantic. He looked up, staring blankly at the stars, which had come out to mock him, laughing in massive battalions of small white lights, flickering at his vanity, at his smothering ignorance. As he stood there, a group of stars near Capricorn caught his eye. At first he believed it to be the Druid constellation, as the sailors called it, but it looked more familiar than that. Something was different about it, something beckoning. He cocked his head one way, then the other. *I'll be—'tis the Skull of St. Stephen's, 'tis!* There it was, staring at him from on high. He looked away, focusing on the snapping mizzen sail, then back up again. The starry skull was still there. It had not disappeared as he hoped.

—〰—

The Right Honourable Hugh Montgomery, Earl of Mount Alexander, examined — "I was pretty often with Lord Anglesea drinking a bottle of wine. One night I was eating oysters with him and Captain Crow, and my lord said, 'By God, Crow, my wife has got a son, which will make that rake my brother's nose swell.' Yes, I saw the child. It was about three years afterward. The child was playing with a chicken and when the chicken ran away from the child, the child cried, and my lord said, 'Jemmy, Jemmy, don't cry.' "

— trial transcript, *Annesley v. Anglesea*, 1743

—〰—

CHAPTER 13

Whenever I cast my eyes on the tumultuous waves, which beat on every side of the vessel, and sometimes rose above it, the sight struck terror in my little heart. The dread of death seems implanted in the nature of human kind as a peculiar curse, since no other species of created beings are capable of it; but with us, the young, the old, the innocent, the guilty, the monarch on his throne, the wretch that groans in chains, all equally languish in one common apprehension of that tremendous change.

— *Memoirs of an Unfortunate Young Nobleman*, James Annesley, 1743

Footsteps tapped lightly across the deck. "So you want to learn the Davis Quadrant, do you?"

Jemmy pivoted to see Mr. Parker, the first-mate, approaching. Looking down at the quadrant in his hand, he mumbled, "Aye, Mr. Parker. If ye have the leave to show me."

"Well, I reckon I do, seeing how the ship is calm enough for a reading." He smiled warmly. "And seeing how the captain asked me to."

"Thank ye," Jemmy replied. He liked the first-mate, though he wasn't sure why, probably because the man was so affable and mellow.

"Now, of course," began Parker, lifting the quadrant to a ring hanging from a shank off the mizzen mast, "we can't use the stars." He dropped a plumb line and hooked a vane to one of the curves of the flat instrument.

Jemmy watched him intently. "Why not?"

"Need a shadow. See any shadows on deck?"

"Nay, sir."

"But, I reckon we can practice on the North Star—use it like a cross-staff. Where's the North Star, lad?"

"There!" Jemmy smiled when he spotted it, pointing confidently into the northern sky.

A night breeze whispered over them as they worked under the newly risen moon, and the mizzen topsail shivered overhead, empty and loose. By the time the watch bell rang eight times, signaling the end of the second-dog watch, Jemmy and First-Mate Parker had been working with the quadrant for over an hour. Just then, an urgent cry came down from the crow's nest: "Ahoy, Mr. Parker! Ship lying off the port two points, sir!"

Parker spun and quickly crossed the deck to the port side, with Jemmy close behind him. The first-mate pulled a brass scope from his pale green coat and peered through it, pointing it toward the far reaches. Jemmy stared hard at the horizon but saw only the moon, a full golden ball, igniting the black waters with its pale fire.

"I don't see it, watch!" Parker yelled aloft. "How far?"

"About a league, sir!"

Parker scanned along the horizon, then abruptly stopped. "Found it," he whispered. Then he turned and yelled, "Steady on!" across the maindeck. Moving quickly down to the quarterdeck, he shouted into the helm, "Ship on the port side, thirty-five degrees! We're on her bearing. Take her starboard one point easy, Mr. Lyons! Stay on our rhumb line!"

"Starboard one point easy, sir!" came a muffled reply from the depths.

Jemmy could feel the ship begin a slow yaw to the right, then watched below as Parker leaned out over the decks, ordering softly, "All hands on watch, keep your eye on that ship, but keep quiet about it." He climbed back to the poopdeck, pulled up his scope and studied the horizon, searching back and forth, then stopped. "There you are, you rascal," he muttered. "Now," he breathed, "just who are you?"

"What is she, Mr. Parker?" asked Jemmy, wishing for a turn at the scope.

"A full-rigger, a barque, best I can see." Parker handed the scope to Jemmy. "Here—you tell me."

Eagerly, Jemmy took the scope and peered into it until his eye gradually adjusted. Then he pulled the magnified image along the dark horizon until he saw it, another square-rigged tallship gliding along in the glimmering darkness—its sails glowing in the moonlight. "Looks like the *Courtmain*, Mr. Parker."

"Nah, that one's bigger'n us." He took the scope again and lifted it to his eye. "She's carrying cannon."

"Cannon!" Jemmy's heart thumped harder. "Will we pass her?"

"If we're lucky."

"Why...why might we not?"

"Lad, haven't you ever heard of privateers?"

"Privateers?"

"Aye. Pirates, lad!"

Jemmy's hands went cold. "Aye, I've heard of 'em." His eyes were as big as soup bowls. "What if…what if they see us?"

"Oh, I'm quite sure they already have," said Parker, matter-of-factly. He looked up at the crow's nest, calling out as softly as possible, "Watch! Can you make out a rogger jack?"

"Nay, sir," came the reply from the dark heavens.

"Ah, well," the first-mate whispered, "he'd probably not be able to see it, not in this dark. And they probably wouldn't be sportin' enough to fly one anyway."

"A rogger?" asked Jemmy, his gaze fixed on the inky shadow on the horizon.

"A pirate's jack, their black flag. Sometimes a corsair will put a skull and crossbones on it. Never seen one of them bleedin' things?"

"Oh, aye. Well, nay. I've heard of 'em."

"If they be pirates, we'll know soon enough. They'll turn into us."

"Then what?"

"Well, we'll have to ready the ship." Parker looked at Jemmy. "All hands will be piped on deck and defenses prepared. We'll load our cannons and muskets, distribute the cutlasses and pikes, strengthen the masts with chains, and make a breastwork of hammocks and beds against their small arms on the quarterdeck. Then we'll lock the women in the hold and make ready forty bottles o' rum to fill the men with courage! Will you help lad? Will you wield a cutlass for your good ship?"

"Aye, sir!"

"We'll see." He returned to his scope. Jemmy was frozen in a wide-eyed stare. "If they turn," Parker continued, "well then…soon enough they'll box-haul and come alongside us. Then I suppose they'll start firing their big guns. We'll have to stop on pain of losing our main mast."

"And if we do stop?"

Parker stood motionless, silently peering through his scope. Suddenly he looked down at Jemmy and said, "Then the rogue blood suckers will use a grappling hook and link us to 'em. They'll come on deck and, unless we fight well and give them the hell they sorely deserve, they'll kill the likes of us, saving only those they'll need to sail her." He paused for a moment, then returned to the scope and muttered absently, "Probably make you walk a plank." Jemmy swallowed hard. "Of course, on second thought, they might just take the cargo, kill us all, and scuttle the ship." He grinned.

"Should we wake Captain Hendry?"

"Nah, let's just wait and see what she does."

Parker said nothing else for a long while, just kept the scope to his eye, and stood there, still and calm, occasionally glancing at Jemmy. Jemmy could feel his own heart thrumming loud and his breath growing short. He could see it happening—they were stuck, abandoned, powerless, alone. Drifting on the near-end of a faint wind in the middle of the Atlantic, sailing to certain doom. Would they be sunk? Would they all drown? Would they fight the pirates? Was it Blackbeard himself just waiting to spring a trap? Was this it? Was this the end of it all? Here and now, on this godforsaken cold ocean?

The boatswain came up the steps. "Mr. Parker," he said, "she's bearing away."

"Aye, Mr. Samuels, so she is. So she is. Very good. Tell the helmsman to correct."

"Aye, sir." The boatswain stepped down and bellowed Parker's orders into the helm.

"So, it wasn't...." Jemmy began, his voice barely audible.

"No, lad. Just another argosy most likely, a merchant vessel like us. You weren't worried, now were you?" Parker gave a gentle grin, then lit his clay pipe.

"Me? Nay, not at all, sir," asserted Jemmy as he plopped down heavily on a side-turned keg. "Not at all." He drew in a cool breath that filled him entirely, like it was his first.

"Sure," said Parker. "Some things you can't change, lad. And those are the very things you have to accept. 'Tisn't fair. No, not fair a'toll. But we steer our course the best we can and let God protect us from the rest." He looked away, leaning on the railing.

Jemmy bit his lip, thinking about Mr. Parker's words. Looking back at the horizon, he saw the faint remnant image of the disappearing ship. He felt disappointed, somehow. What if they had been pirates, he wondered. What if they had attacked the *Courtmain* and he, James Annesley, had saved the ship? Or even, what if he had joined them? He pictured himself sailing the seas as a pirate, attacking innocent ships with a broadside of cannon-fire, collecting a wealth of treasure. He could see the battle, the swinging cutlasses, smell the smoke from the cannons—

"Time for you to turn in, lad."

Jemmy grimaced. He wasn't tired in the least. In fact, his heart had only begun to slow from its feverish pitch. "I'll bunk down shortly. I shall, sir."

"Aye, well then, good night to you." Parker stepped down.

"Good night, sir. And thank ye for teachin' me the quadrant."

"'Tis all right lad, we'll look at it again. Perhaps tomorrow you'll give me a hand with the chip-'n-log line."

"That'd be grand, sir."

"Very good." With that, the young man was gone.

For a few minutes more, Jemmy could still hear his voice down below, talking to someone on the maindeck. Mr. Parker's voice was familiar to Jemmy, comforting—the same dialect as his mother's. Jemmy stood and walked back to the poopdeck railing and leaned against a brace rope wound tightly around its bitts. He peered across the deep rolling emptiness but could not see the other ship. It was gone. He wondered where it was bound, then decided it was probably sailing to the Colonies, perhaps even to Maryland, like the *Courtmain.*

Earlier that week, Jemmy had begun thinking in earnest about their destination and what awaited him there. He knew the course was set for a place called Maryland, somewhere on Chesapeake Bay in the middle of the British Colonies. The land of Indians, untamed wilderness, freedom and warm air. He had known many people, especially some young men, who had waxed ardently about the Colonies. And though he had imagined going there, it had been fleeting. He belonged in Ireland, at Dunmain, in Dublin, where destiny awaited him. Seán had felt otherwise, saying he and Jemmy should be on the high seas exploring distant islands, fighting for the Royal Navy. If only Seán were there now—how grand that would be.

He also realized he would have to work for a few years. Nothing too long. Several passengers had talked about it. No more than five years, probably three, but they didn't know for sure. Apparently only Captain Hendry knew. But Jemmy didn't mind a little work. How many days had he spent in the stables with Fynn, tending horses? Uncountable. Yes, he could work. Until he would run away and return to Ireland. But then what? What would he do in Ireland? Would things be different? Regardless, he would still go back. He had to. When the *Courtmain* arrived in Maryland, he would jump off, and sail back. But maybe a week later. He had to see the Colonies first. Then go. But what if he liked Maryland? Most of the passengers were excited the *Courtmain* would soon reach the halfway mark. They couldn't wait to walk on the white beaches of the new land—the land of promise and riches. And in truth, after listening to them, Jemmy knew he had become swept up in their enthusiasm. But even so, he reminded himself, unconsciously standing taller, he was the Seventh Earl of Anglesea and he belonged in Ireland.

So his plan was set—he would see the Colonies, meet an Indian, do a little work, perhaps as a factor's assistant or tending horses, then sail home—all within the year. By next spring he would be back at the Anglesea Estate at Dunmain, the richest young man in Ireland. Richard would be in irons. His mother would return. Fynn would be happy. He envisioned himself regaling Seán with fantastic tales of pirates on the high seas, all of it. Seán would be completely awestruck, green with envy. A breeze wafted by and Jemmy's smile stretched to a yawn. He turned away from the rail and descended to the halfdeck. He would sleep well, dreaming of the white sands and the red Indians of Maryland.

Barnaby Dunn, examined — "In the year 1724 I kept a school in Bluecoat Alley, near the Main Guard, and Master James Annesley was recommended to me as Lord Anglesea's son by Mr. Cavanagh, a dancing master. I believe he was at school with me for eight or nine months. I cannot remember whether I taught him any Latin, but I am certain that I taught him to read and write. A young friend of his came to see him, but didn't receive my teaching. His name I believe was Seán Kennedy, the son of a popish fellow who had served my lord. I took a particular notice of something about Master Annesley's eyes when he came to my school, when he was ten or eleven years old, before the death of my lord. I thought I observed a little cast or turn in his eye."

— trial transcript, *Annesley v. Anglesea*, 1743

CHAPTER 14

When Britain first, at heaven's command,
Arose from out of the azure main,
This was the charter of the land,
And guardian angels sung this strain--
"Rule Britannia, rule the waves;
Britons never will be slaves."

—*Rule Britannia,* James Thompson, 1740

Five weeks later, the ocean floor was found. Then the lead-n-tallow, which had proven the proximity of the Virginia Capes, was cut off and fastened to the mizzen mast with "*85 fathoms*" inscribed beneath it in chalk. Within a day, the sweet aroma of pine wafted faintly across the deck, bringing smiles to everyone onboard. Then, two days after the bottom was discovered, a bony, smallpox-pitted crewman was bestowed with the customary bottle of whiskey for being the first to cry out, "Land! Land!" when the *Courtmain* finally made landfall beyond Cape Charles. Jemmy had stood on the quarterdeck, completely aston-ished. He had leaned against the marked rail, face to the west, marveling at the rising foreland. America was there, right before his eyes, just over that small expanse of grey-blue water. The day was warm and dry, and he was intensely happy to see the land, to breathe the new air of the new world. Crew and pas-sengers alike were yelling and dancing on the deck, rejoicing and thanking God for their preservation from the perils of the sea, from the evils of the deep. Even Captain Hendry had come to the maindeck for a reel. Jemmy knew he would be returning to Ireland soon, but on that day—there were the British Colonies, a wonderful apparition, stretching out across the horizon like an unexplored legend—like a wild-eyed, Connemara pony, daring to be broken. He became wistful, completely awestruck by the scene. They had arrived.

But that was two days ago, and now Jemmy was back in the hold of the fetid halfdeck, miserable, and chained to his bunk. The helmsman and his mates were busy in the steerage, immediately adjacent to Jemmy's berth, tak-ing and repeating helm orders up through the deck portal as the ship's crew worked the *Courtmain* into the long broad bay, slipping gingerly around the tricky shoals and sporadic islands. Jemmy sat listening to the crews, their loud voices tense with exhaustion and anticipation, and the incessant calls and echoes grated on him, like the cold wrist-shackles which were once again grinding against his flesh. At eight o'clock that morning, Jemmy heard the foc's'le bell peal eight times, closing the morning watch, clanging rhythmically, doling its rich tone across the decks, up the massive masts and down into the bowels of the ship. To him, it meant the helmsman would soon return to bunk in the halfdeck. Perhaps then he would get some answers to the array of questions which had stacked in his mind since he awoke, about two hours earlier, when one of the mangy ship cats had walked across his chest. He had seen the maps and sea cards, and as near as he could tell, the *Courtmain* was sailing north up the Chesapeake. But where was she heading, and when would they port? Why was he in chains again? When would he be allowed to speak to Captain Hendry? And where was the first-mate, Mr. Parker? He wanted to go on deck and see the land. He could hear people, ships, horses. But these damn chains. He jerked at them, then relaxed slightly, feeling his face hot with anger.

"Ye're awake squire!" said the helmsman, leaning forward so as not to rap his head as he entered the cramped quarters.

"Aye, I'm awake, and I shouldn't be in these." He rattled the chains again.

"Ye know," the man began unbuttoning his waistcoat to pull off his filthy shirt, "ye say that same damn'd thing every time I come down here." His sweaty, craggy face sneered at Jemmy.

"Is the captain—" Jemmy began.

"Is the captain 'bout? Ha! That's the other thing ye're always askin' me!"

"Aye, what of it?" Jemmy clenched his teeth. "Is Captain Hendry about or not?"

"What do ye think, squire? What'd I tell ye last?"

"Is he about?" Jemmy repeated firmly, tugging at his chains as if to tell the helmsman he would attack the lying bastard if only he could. When the helmsman sat on the edge of his own bunk, Jemmy could see the man's swollen legs and the sores on his shins.

"Nay, good Captain Hendry 'tisn't 'bout. Just as he weren't yesterdee."

"Did he leave the ship at Norfolk?"

"Nay." The helmsman was now unbuckling his shoes.

"Then where is he?"

"Like I said, lad, the captain's not 'bout." He began rubbing his bare feet gingerly.

"I must see him."

"Well, ye can't. He's not 'bout." The low roof of the halfdeck held the rancid odor of the helmsman's feet, and Jemmy could feel the pasty air crawling up his nose.

"Fine. Then let me see Mr. Parker," demanded Jemmy, recoiling from the smell. He stared at the man, then asked in a tense voice that belied his burning irritation, "Sir, would ye be so kind as to make arrangements for me to see Mr. Parker?"

"What fer?"

"None of yer bleedin' business!" Jemmy shouted in an explosion of anger. He hated to see those feet, with their red cankerous sores which were sometimes oozing, and the thin crusted blackness which gathered around the man's toes. And he dared not ask about the raw ball of flesh on the underside of the man's left foot, fearing the man might swing the hunk of dead meat closer to afford him a better inspection.

"None o' me business?" sneered the helmsman, stopping to pick at his brownish toenails. "Well then, I suppose that means the first-mate's not 'bout either."

"Ye're a stinking arse, ye are!"

At that moment, heavy footsteps thumped across the upperdeck, then descended into the halfdeck. It was First-Mate Parker, smiling at them as if all was well.

"Ach, Mr. Parker! What a delightful surprise," began the helmsman, "An' t' think we were just speakin' o' ye!"

"Oh? And just what might you've been saying?" The first-mate's smile lingered for only a moment, then the warmth abruptly melted from his ashen face. "What in God's name is that stench?" Jemmy nodded at the helmsman's open gangrenous feet. "Bless me!" Parker suffered a gasp and pulled his ascot over his nose.

"Come to unlock me, are ye?" asked Jemmy, ignoring the overwhelming odor.

"Well, lad, I wish I could," he answered, grimacing. "If only just to speak on deck." The helmsman gave an indolent shrug. Parker turned his head and breathed through the porthole. He glanced back, then turned and looked into Jemmy's eyes. With a slight sigh, Parker's black eyebrows lifted, then fell back in place.

Jemmy's face dropped. "Captain has the keys, has he?"

"Aye."

"Then surely he'll see the problem here."

"Lad, 'twas Captain Hendry who ordered you chained. He's the one who's going to sell you, and he won't be having any of you indentees jumping clear."

"That's right," interrupted the helmsman. "I told ye squire! Ye're nothin' but a dirty slave now." He cackled.

"On with you, McCauley!" Parker snapped with a glare, still shrinking from the smell.

"Sir, if I may . . . 'tis the end o' me watch, an' this be me bunk, an—"

"Out, McCauley!"

"Aye, aye, sir." The helmsman stood on his bare feet and started toward the hatch.

"And, McCauley, soak those appalling feet in your own givin's of rum."

"Aye, sir," he replied, then disappeared to the surface.

Jemmy and Parker were silent for a moment, then Parker waved at the stagnant air, trying to get it to move. "Why am I locked up," asked Jemmy. "I'm locked up like an animal."

"Do you know what's to happen in Chestertown tomorrow?"

"That's where we're going—Chestertown?"

"Aye. 'Tis the main northern port for trade, on the eastern side of the Chess, in Maryland. Captain wouldn't put in at Williamsburg, or even Cambridge, not this late in the year. Been too many others in those ports already this season for him to get a fair advantage. Not even Annapolis, but I'm not sure why on that account." Parker's brow furrowed. "'Tisn't usual for him to take us into Chestertown, except for Drummond maybe. He's—"

"A fair advantage?" Jemmy interrupted.

"Aye, a profit. You do understand profits, don't you?"

"Aye," answered Jemmy. "He wants to port where he can get the most for his cargo."

"He is, indeed." Mr. Parker looked plainly at Jemmy, as if studying him, then patted Jemmy's knee and stood. "I thought you didn't understand, but it sounds as if you do."

"I haven't seen much cargo aboard. Why didn't he sell it in Norfolk, where we ported earlier, and let the passengers decide where they want to be put off?"

"He should've sold what in Norfolk?"

"The cargo," said Jemmy, looking at the man curiously.

"James," began the first-mate, sitting again, "we've been at sea for over nine weeks now. Have you never spoken to anyone about being an indentured servant? You signed yourself over for it. The Tholsel officer told you what to expect. Aye?"

"I didn't sign for it—I was kidnapped! Ye know that!"

"I only know what you claimed." Parker rose to his feet. He walked to the hatch and stood there a moment, breathing the fresh air. "Such a proclamation will only discredit you here. You must put it from your mind...at least for the—"

"I can't! How can I?"

Parker returned to Jemmy's side of the berth. "You have to. If you stand on deck declaring yourself an Earl, no one will want you. They'll think you'll run, think you're a simpleton, a troublemaker. You'll stay on board for another two weeks till some soul-driver takes you, placing four pounds out for you, and lumps you in with a bunch of misfits and scoundrels. They won't buy a rough-hewn boy likely to run on them."

"Buy me?"

"I'll be damned," said Parker, faltering, shaking his head.

"I thought I was to work for a while," said Jemmy. "Am I not to pursue a labor of my choosin', to repay Captain Hendry for my transport?"

"It doesn't work like that," Parker said, clearly troubled. "Lad, the cargo I spoke of earlier, to be sold in Chestertown...." His voice was freighted down. "That cargo is you. And the seven other indentees on board. Did you truly not know that?"

Jemmy sat still, whispering toward his heavy chest. "Nay. Not entirely." He closed his eyes, feeling sick, smothered, as if the rush of the ocean were finally once and for all pouring over him, pulling him to the bottom.

Silcross Ash, examined — "I know the defendant in this case. Immediately after the burial of the late Lord Anglesea, I was in company with Mr. Hawkins, the King-at-Arms. The defendant had come to Mr. Hawkins, and in my presence got into a passion and called the plaintiff an imposter or a vagabond, or something of that sort, and said that he deserved to be transported. Mr. Hawkins refused to enroll his lordship on account of the rumour occasioned by the noise the boy had made at the funeral of the late Lord Anglesea. Upon that the defendant was very angry, and made use of some indecent expressions against Mr. Hawkins. As against the plaintiff, to the best of my belief the word 'bastard' was made use of. He repeated that the boy deserved to be transported. At a later date it was said Mr. Hawkins refused to enroll Mr. Annesley on account of expecting his honorary fees, whereupon the defendant said that if that was all, he would go and satisfy him."

— trial transcript, *Annesley v. Anglesea*, 1743

CHAPTER 15

All my past life is mine no more:
The flying hours are gone
Like transitory dreams given o'er,
Whose images are kept in store
By memories alone.

— *Love and Life,* John Wilmont,
Earl of Rochester, 1680

By the next day, the *Courtmain* was anchored and lying at rest in the Chester River, alongside a newly-built dock in Chestertown, Maryland. The mid-morning sun was striking the afterdeck, inciting the stuffy air of the halfdeck, where Jemmy could feel the heat rising. Crewmen had unshackled him and fed him. They had considered giving him a shave but laughed heartily at the apparent lack of necessity. Shortly thereafter, the helmsman brought him some clean clothes. In a lethargic daze, Jemmy put on the fresh white shirt and the light-grey linen breeches over his filthy undergarments, then a green-striped waistcoat that was much too big for him. Next, a man's blue wool coat was given to him, though he didn't want to wear it in the heat. As he began to slip on his old shoes, the helmsman handed him a set of stockings and garters, a pair of black shoes with shiny brass buckles, and a round, wide-brimmed, grey hat.

"Look, mates," the helmsman called, "Squire's dressin' purty fer market!"

"Shut yer mouth," growled Jemmy as he snapped his buckles and stood, now fully dressed. He set the hat on his head where it rode down over his ears.

The men started to ascend from the halfdeck. One asked, "What's that 'round yer neck?"

"Nothing!" Jemmy snapped, realizing he had not tucked the Bucking-ham key into his shirt. He hurriedly stuffed it under his collar.

"Wait here till yer called," the helmsman snorted, already out of sight. Jemmy felt something crawling through his hair and flung the round hat to the floor. He picked several lice from his matted light-brown hair, then scratched at the scrambling fleas. Finding a small piece of wood, he scraped his hair, trying to flatten it. Suddenly the helmsman's voice was back, yelling down from above, "And take care of that hat. Used to be mine." No surprise there, Jemmy thought. He kicked at it, knocking it further away. What choice did he have but to comply with these men? Perhaps he would chance it and run. He would look for an opportunity just as soon as he got on deck. After tying his hair in a short tail, he leaned back on his bunk, waiting, lapsing into a small trance, staring blankly at the nasty hat. Mr. Parker had told him about the sale, advising him to be attentive, to declare himself a stable boy skilled with horses, and to hope for the best. At least in a stable he would be out of the weather much of the time. Although Parker hoped the captain might sell Jemmy to a gentry house, he figured Jemmy's youth would make that difficult. He was to stand tall and answer the questions directly, and by no means was he to say anything about a claim to any House of Lords. The kindly first-mate had also explained that most of the indentured servants were committed to terms of three to five years, and the convicts to seven. But Jemmy didn't know his term. He had never seen his indenture papers. What then? Parker said he could expect three years—the typical time necessary to pay for one's transportation to the Colonies.

As thunder before a storm, a gathering of men's shoes and boots began to rumble overhead, jerking Jemmy from his haze. Then the helmsman was back. "Squire, get yer arse up here! What'd ye think—them good buyers would come callin' on ye down in this stinkin' piss-hole?" Jemmy picked up the quadrant and rose to leave, then saw the helmsman watching him. He gingerly picked up the hat, holding it away from his side, and climbed up through the hatch. On deck, he paused, instantly intoxicated by the bright morning sun, the pine-laden air. As he stood there, letting his eyes adjust, absorbing the sights, he noticed several well-dressed men onboard were look-ing at him, as if sizing him up. Near the foredeck, standing with their backs to the river, were the other indentured passengers, most leaning into raspy coughs, scratching their scalps, and tugging at their misshapen clothes—an assortment of dull patched coats and wrinkled hats which Jemmy noticed were not nearly as fine as what he had been issued. The women appeared to have fared better than the men, but not by much.

"Put on yer hat," ordered the boatswain, shoving Jemmy aside.

"Captain Hendry, this is yer prize bull?" A short man with fat red cheeks and a pate to match tapped Jemmy with his cane.

"I told ye to put on yer hat!" the boatswain barked.

He hesitated, then slowly lifted the infested thing. Just as the breeze caught it, he let go and saw it sail over the edge of the boat.

"Damn ye, Squire!" the helmsman yelled, watching his hat go into the water.

"Aye, Mr. Gunter. He is a fine one." Jemmy was surprised by the familiar voice and turned to see Captain Hendry behind him. "But ye're looking for a cooper," continued the captain. "This one'd be no good for that." The sun blazed behind the captain and Jemmy raised a hand to shield the light so as to see the captain's face. "Put yer arm down boy," Hendry ordered softly.

"He'll fetch a good price for you, I'm sure," said the fat man as he moved across the deck to the others. Hendry motioned to the boatswain, silently telling him to keep the other buyers away from Jemmy.

In that moment, a shadow fell over Jemmy and he looked up to see a boorish face staring down at him. "Lil' miss, how old are ye?" The voice was gravelly and slow.

"Sir?" Jemmy replied, startled. He recognized the southern Irish lilt, saw the Irish ruddiness, but nothing else was familiar. The man's nostrils were large and flared, his wig pulled back tightly over his broad expanse of a forehead, which dwarfed his narrow slit, yellowish eyes.

"Are ye hard of hearin'?" the man continued.

"Nay, Mr. Drummond," interjected Captain Hendry, smiling awkwardly. "He's strong. He hears well. Both of his eyes work. He eats and shites with the best of 'em. Nothing sickly about this one." Jemmy could hear the captain's nervousness.

"But Henry, the nit doesn't know his own age!"

"I do," Jemmy mumbled, looking down, seeing the man's shiny silver buckles.

The wealthy Irishman leaned closer, swelling his eyes. "Did ye fart? Or were ye talkin'?" Jemmy felt rage and humiliation at the same time. He had only one thought, *Run!*

"James!" barked the captain. "Speak yer age."

"Thirteen," he snarled, sarcastically drawing out the word.

"Thirteen? Bloody hell, Henry. What are ye bringin' me? I don't need children!"

"He's strong and agile. He can fetch wood for ye. Better yet, he has learning to him. Put him in the mercantile, Mr. Drummond. Let him count things for ye. He can even write."

"So ye say." Drummond was slowly circling Jemmy. He paused, inspecting the deep scar on Jemmy's cheek. "You had dirt in this cut. You English are as filthy as the French." He circled more, the asked, "This the one ye had me summoned for? This lil' lass?"

"Aye. He is," replied the captain.

Summoned? Jemmy's heart sank. *He planned to sell me to this oaf all along.*

Drummond snatched the quadrant from Jemmy's hands. "Where'd ye get this?"

"From the captain," replied Jemmy.

"Damn Henry, ye give these things away?"

"Nay, I just had—"

"How much, Henry?"

"For—"

"The runt, damnit! I don't want yer fackin' quadrant!" Drummond slammed the quadrant against Jemmy's chest, returning it to him. "I'll give ye ten pounds. Twelve tops."

"Oh nay, sir, ye're not seeing his breeding. I'd need much more."

Drummond frowned at Jemmy. "So ye have breeding do ye? If I buy ye, ye'll be dead in no time a'toll. Breeding or no. Breeding won't help ye at my iron works."

"He's strong sir," the captain protested, a bit weakly. "Make him a gutterman."

"What's yer time? Or are ye a bloody redemptioner?"

Jemmy looked directly into Drummond's ugly eyes. He was tired of this sort, the Captain Bailyn's of the world. This man was no different. He was tired of running from them, of being fearful of them. He had survived his father. He had survived Dublin. He had survived the voyage. This man could do what he wanted, but he would never get the satisfaction of seeing Jemmy scared. "I don't know my time," Jemmy replied bluntly, then turned his head and mumbled, "Blackguard's arse."

"Blackguard's arse? Ye lil' shite!" With one hand, Drummond nearly lifted Jemmy off his feet, then cuffed him on the head with the other. "Ye're in Maryland now, runt!" He threw him down. "There are severe laws against that kind of swearing and blasphemy. We're goddamned civilized! How'd ye like to get yer tongue bored?" Jemmy scrambled to his feet, keeping a stare locked on the man. Gradually Drummond smiled, nodding, then spoke in a forced Irish brogue. "Ye're tryin' t' get me not t' buy ye, eh? Tryin' t' be clever, aren't ye?" He pursed his lips, his yellow eyes squinting at Jemmy. "I'll ask ye again," he barked, dropping the heavy accent. "And, by God, ye'd better tell me direct this time. What's yer time?"

Captain Hendry stepped beside them. "He's a seven-year, Mr. Drummond."

"A convict? An unpreached convict at thirteen? I knew it. What'd ye do—steal some linens?" He jerked Jemmy's right hand over, looking at his palm. "No Bailey-burn?"

Jemmy scowled at the captain. "Seven years?"

"Hush, boy! Aye, Mr. Drummond, no mark on him. He's no felon." Backing up to the fife rail around the main mast, Hendry pulled a folded paper from his coat and held it high. "Sir, if I might have a word," he said. Drummond frowned, then stepped away. They whispered together for a moment, perusing the crinkled paper and glancing occasionally at Jemmy. Then Drummond's mouth creased into a wide smirk, his eyes gleaming at Jemmy. Jemmy was standing alone, his mind racing. *Run! Now is your chance!* His gaze darted to the gangway, but no, three men were there patrolling with muskets. *Leap the starboard rail and swim for the dock!* No, five redcoats were clumped there talking. Mr. Parker had said running could be a hanging offence. But would those infantrymen really shoot him? He had committed no crime. He looked back to the mast, wondering what the two were talking about. Perhaps Mr. Parker could help. He turned, hurriedly scanning the open decks, but the man was nowhere to be seen. By now half-a-dozen buyers had boarded and a general hum of conversation was swarming the maindeck. The other indentees were being tugged at and inspected. One buyer was looking at a woman's teeth while another waited impatiently for a man to strip off his shirt.

"Ye've got to be mad!" Drummond suddenly flared, drawing Jemmy's attention.

"Nay, sir. But I'll hear yer offer." The captain sounded urgent.

Drummond and Hendry spoke quietly for a few more minutes, then a bag of coin was handed to the captain and the two separated. Drummond walked back and resumed his stance directly in front of Jemmy. Now, in the shadow of the man's brown three-cornered hat, a wicked grin had emerged. Drummond was peering from under crooked black eyebrows as though hiding something, a tasty secret he could not wait to tell. "A bargain 'tis," Drummond said loudly, throwing the words over his shoulder. He curled his mouth, squinting at Jemmy as if trying to read his mind. Jemmy mockingly curled his own lips and squinted back. The man burst into a loud cackle. "Twenty-eight pounds 'tis a bargain indeed." He grabbed Jemmy's arm, his fingers digging in, pulling him close. Jemmy smelled the ripe gin as the gargoyle whispered, "A sweet price for one Englishman so nobly born. Aye, Master Annesley? Or should I call you Lord Anglesea?"

Jemmy jerked away wide-eyed while Drummond howled with laughter. But just as Jemmy whirled toward the gangway, Drummond's laughter ceased and he pulled a dagger from under his coat, sticking it to Jemmy's ribs. "Ye English cunt," he hissed. "Know this. If ye run, I'll kill ye. I will personally cut yer heart out and feed it to m'dogs." He smiled through clamped teeth. "Do ye understand me?"

Jemmy stared at him defiantly, then looked back toward Captain Hendry, but the captain was gone. With an unexpected surge of courage, he snapped, "Aye, ye'll kill me, I heard ye. But I still say ye're a blackguard's arse."

Drummond started to slap Jemmy but stopped short. He grinned. "Perhaps ye're right. Many an man better'n you has said so." Turning to a crewman coming up the companionway, he ordered, "Ye there, fetch me that hat." The sailor quickly complied, fishing it out of the water with a long pole. He handed it to Drummond, who in turn slapped it down on Jemmy's head, pulling it around his ears. The water coursed off of it, soaking Jemmy's waistcoat. "Of course, lad," Drummond went on, "whether or not I'm a blackguard doesn't change the fact that I now own yer noble arse. I bought ye—I can kill ye. Them's de rules."

"Poor waste of twenty-eight pounds wouldn't ye say?" Jemmy muttered. "'T' kill me before ye get any work from me."

"Nah, lad." Drummond slapped him on the back, ushering him to the gangway. "Whether I kill ye now or later, makes no difference to me. Either way, t'was the best sack o' coin I ever spent. B'God, 'twas!" He howled with laughter again.

As they made their way to shore, Jemmy asked, "Ye know who I am? Ye knew my da?"

"Oh, aye, m'lord! Although, I must say I was surprised by yer uncle Richard's thoughtfulness in writing me." He brandished the paper Captain Hendry had been holding. "Damned civil of him, even if he is a bloody Annesley. He almost asks me to kill ye. Imagine that!" The group of redcoats turned, watching them pass, hearing Drummond's threat. "Nice family ye've got. Still living at Dunmain House?" Jemmy didn't answer. "I reckon so," grumbled Drummond. "Land-stealin', murderin' English bastards."

They were about fifty yards from the gangway before Jemmy realized he was standing on firm ground—a moment he had been dreaming of for weeks on end. But he felt no pleasure or awe, just numb anger, his mind reeling, trying to devise a way to escape. Perhaps he would do it on the way to this idiot's iron works. He would jump from the coach and run, then stow away on another ship. He would get off this land, sail east, charge into Dunmain House, grab his father's old rapier and thrust it straight through Richard's black heart.

A carriage appeared to be waiting for them at the bottom of the hill. As they approached, the driver, in a dark-blue livery, stepped down from the box. "Sir," he said, opening the door. Drummond grunted and climbed inside. When Jemmy moved to follow him, the driver shoved him back. "What are ye thinking, lad? Ye're on that," he said, pointing to a large wagon several yards away. Jemmy saw several young men being ushered to it as its four draft horses stamped and shuffled, pawing the ground.

Drummond was suddenly back in his face, spewing, "Ye know, m'lord, I was thinkin'. Most of my runaways try it on the way to the furnace, thinking they'll find refuge with the thievin', godless Swedes. But I know I'll see ye tomorrow. Aye?" Jemmy refused to respond, even in expression. Drummond continued, unaffected. "If you try to run, my guards will kill you. Pick another day to die, will ye? If anyone gets to kill ye, let it be me. Fair enough? Besides, ye haven't even seen this virgin land yet. Most importantly, my silent Annesley, I want ye to see what a free Irishman can build when he's not under the stinking arse of an English Anglesea. Ye bloody invaders! Ye stole m' land in Ireland. Now ye can die working m' land in Pennsylvania." He shoved Jemmy away, slamming the door shut. The driver whipped the two horses and the carriage jolted forward. Two men remained with Jemmy, one holding a blunderbuss, the other a musket. They motioned him toward the wagon.

—✳—

Mark Byrne, examined — "I was a constable in Dublin.
I was told I had a good job to go upon and was to get a
guinea for doing it. My lord, the defendant, had charged
a boy with stealing a silver spoon. We took the boy away,
with the help of the defendant's man, Captain Bailyn. To
my knowledge Captain Bailyn is now dead. We were publicly known to be constables, though we had no warrant,
so far as I saw. I did not know what my lord was going to
do with the boy, but when I saw him going down the river
I began to be afraid, and I went no further. I apprehended
that it was not anything that was right that was going to
be done with him. I believed they were going to send him
over sea. Was I paid? I have never got any more of the
guinea than an English shilling."

— trial transcript, *Annesley v. Anglesea*, 1743

—✳—

CHAPTER 16

The New World now opened itself to view of me, in which
every thing I saw was strange: the habits and odd manners
of the Indians, the various birds, and four-footed animals,
so different from those of Europe, would have afforded an
agreeable amusement to my attentive mind for a considerable time, had I been permitted to indulge it; but that cruel
monster Drummond found me. O Heaven, can there be
such villainy in man!

— *Memoirs of an Unfortunate Young Nobleman,*
James Annesley, 1743

Jemmy held the quadrant close as the white freight wagon bumped and
plodded along the well-worn road. The trip from Chestertown, Maryland
to Coatesville, Pennsylvania would take the rest of the day, according to the
guard who was sitting next to him. The man's musket was standing muzzle
up between them, and the man's right hand was wrapped firmly around the
barrel. Jemmy let his mind drift, studying the musket's flashpan, noticing it
was somehow different—flatter and larger than any he had seen before. The
guard, a German immigrant, rarely spoke, and when he did his English was
garbled and thick. Jemmy learned his name, Karl Haack, and asked him why
Drummond's shiny black carriage was not with them. Colonel Drummond,
the guard explained, had gone to Annapolis to buy more indents. Karl then
slowly explained that he was indentured as a collier for the Drummond Furnace, and had six more months before earning his freedom, before he finished
paying for his journey from Germany. He had been asked to come along on
this trip to Chestertown to help the guards who did this kind of work for
Drummond. Jemmy made out most of this, but when he asked what a collier did, the reply was in such broken English that he could only nod as if he
understood.

Looking over the rumpled men riding with him, Jemmy noticed that
some were staring at him curiously. He casually scanned the worn faces,

glancing away when he saw eyes looking back. Including himself, he counted fourteen men and boys in the jostling wagon: four guards and ten indentured servants. All were in their own hair and a few had short tails. Their clothes were tattered, an ill-fitting array of patched browns and greens, all shaded by an assortment of earth-colored hats. Except Jemmy. He had removed his lice-infested hat as soon as he boarded the wagon, tucking the nasty thing down by his feet. Among the group, he saw three eye patches and seven chopped fingers, and almost every man was missing a few front teeth. And though most of them were young—not much older than Jemmy—he could see that he was clearly the youngest. He figured the burly one with the heavy smallpox scars was the oldest, perhaps even as old as thirty. Clambering to his knees, he peered over the wagon's tall sideboards and listened to the muffled low laughter from two men talking. From what he could hear, everyone in the wagon was either English or Welsh, with the exception of the young man who was clearly from Scotland, and the German beside him. Other than the occasional chatter passing between them, the passengers' attention was for the most part focused beyond the wagon. Most were turned out, each in his own fog, as was Jemmy, each absorbed in his own thoughts. Some even seemed to look beyond the virgin expanse now rolling past, as if they could see things unseen. Jemmy found himself so engaged in the spellbinding sights that the time eased by and he forgot he was famished. There were small farms dotting the landscape, wood split-rail fences snaking over the slight hills, and people who looked ruddier and healthier than any he had ever seen. Men and women were in the road, in the fields, chopping wood, herding cattle. Children were laughing, squealing in play. Most of the men were in plain dress, without wigs, wearing round-brimmed hats that reminded Jemmy of Ireland, making him wonder if they were all Catholic. As they ferried across the first river, Karl Haack leaned over the rail, looking into the deep water, summoning Jemmy to join him. "What's there?" asked Jemmy, peering over the edge.

"Ze fish," said Karl, pointing to a school of massive fish splashing and swirling just below the surface in a dazzling shimmer of silvers, greens and blues.

Jemmy was astonished. "What are they?"

"Ha! You don't know?" He asked, then saw Jemmy shrug. "Zemun, lad! Zemun!"

"Zeemun?" Jemmy struggled to understand.

"Zamun!"

"Ah, salmon," he said, suddenly comprehending. "That big? Salmon?"

He stared into the foaming water. "Truly?"

"Ze moder of zamun, lad. Ze moder!" Karl held up his hands, spreading his arms far apart as if to show the fresh-water salmon were almost five feet long.

"Aye, they're the *mother* of salmon. I understand, Mr. Haack." Jemmy still had his eyes on the fish as the ferry docked. "That they are, indeed."

"No, Karl."

"Eh?"

"Karl," the man said, touching his chest. "Mizter Haack, *nein*"

"Aye, sir. Karl," replied Jemmy with a nod. Once back on the narrow road, Karl pointed out the dark, broadleaved plants growing waist-high in the passing fields. The accent obliterated the word *tobacco*, but a Welshman pronounced it slowly when Jemmy winced in confusion. When the wagon lumbered through a community of Swedes, Jemmy saw a log cabin for the first time, and even the Welshman was hard-pressed to explain it properly. At the next creek though, when Jemmy stood pointing at a small, black-haired, ruddy-brown man in long leather breeches, the German's pronunciation of *Indian* was clear enough, and Jemmy's amazement nearly toppled him from the wagon. All around him, the passing land seemed to be flourishing with life, green and unspoiled, alive with a raw splendor that Jemmy had never seen before. And there was something else different. Perhaps it was the Indian or the Swedes. Perhaps it was all of the people. He could feel it, but he couldn't name it. He looked up into the colossal trees wondering if perhaps it was simply the sheer enormity of everything. The primeval forests awed him. He marveled at the epic size of the massive oaks, the stands of giant pine whose lowest branches began thirty feet in the air. Leaning back in the bumping wagon, he listened to the steady thrum of the horses' hooves and gazed straight up into the shifting coolness. Ascending hundreds of feet into the flickering blue sky, like pillars to God, the huge backlit trees formed a distant swaying canopy of a million leaves. And birds were everywhere, cawing, chirping, screeching out their shrill choruses as they swooped back and forth cutting the long strands of golden light that descended through the shadows. He rest his head on the side-railing, letting his thoughts drift. He tried to imagine how a man could climb such a gigantic tree. He wanted to try.

Faintly, he began humming a familiar tune—then suddenly realized he was humming aloud in a wagon of strangers and quit. But the tune had a mind of its own. It was unmistakable, *Greensleeves*, and it was holding him as a mother lion carries her young, in teeth both deadly sharp yet sharply forgiving. He couldn't get out of its clutches till it was ready to let him loose and any attempt to struggle might snag him on a tooth. Maybe he could block it out. He tried to think of a sea chantey he had learned from Mr. Parker, but it didn't work. The faint image of his mother crept into his mind, overpowering him. His mouth dried as he closed his eyes and stopped fighting her image, allowing it to consume him. There she was, bleeding, dead in the—"'Tis Juggy!" he blurted, his eyes popping open from sleep. Karl was looking at him curiously. Jemmy turned, closing his eyes again. Just as during its last few visits, *Greensleeves* had reminded him of Juggy, not his mother. But it was his mother's song, the song *she* had sung to him. He tried to picture her face, her smile, but she wouldn't come to him. His stomach tightened, a ball of sadness rolling over him. He clenched his teeth to keep from crying. Soon sleep returned.

Suddenly the wagon hit a rut, mercifully jostling Jemmy's head against the rail, the pain snapping him alert. Gathering his strength, he quickly wiped his eyes and looked around. For the next mile or so, he counted every meandering crook and bend in every split-rail fence they passed, careful not to let his mind slip into *Greensleeves* again and determined to think of something, anything, anyone other than Fynn or Seán. By the time he counted seventy-two bends, a measure of peace had returned. The wagon crossed three more creeks and was ferried across one more rushing river before the giant trees began to give way to a lush, flat land bordered by swamps. There he saw more birds, hundreds of them—ducks and geese in dense flocks overhead, their cries and wings a deafening roar. Jemmy sucked in the fresh warm air, savoring its taste. "What an amazing place this is," he whispered. "What an incredible land."

—m—

Another hour passed, during which he had roughly drifted in and out of half-sleep, lulled by the motion of the wagon. Then he heard strange voices coming from the road. Glancing up, he was startled to see two African men rolling a huge wooden barrel down the road, coming toward the wagon. Even on its side the barrel was taller than the Africans. He was impressed by how well they handled it. The driver eased the wagon off the road, pulling the team to a stop, waiting quietly till the enormous barrel passed. Jemmy wanted to ask Karl about the men and their load, but the German was taking his turn in the box alongside the driver. So Jemmy sat silently, staring, assessing the sight.

Though the barrel was baffling, he was more entranced by the two Africans. He listened to their deep, resonant voices as they spoke to each other in their peculiar language. As they passed, both Africans glanced toward the wagon and gave the driver a duteous nod. Jemmy had seen an African only once before, in Dublin, and from a considerable distance. These two were close and he could see them clearly. *How odd!*

"Slaves." The older boy sitting across the wagon spoke up, as if he had been reading Jemmy's mind. "They're slaves."

"Aye. Of course," replied Jemmy as the wagon resumed moving, then hit a large hole, lifting and crashing them all back onto the plank-floored bed.

"Negroes, they call 'em here," the boy continued, unaffected by the bump.

"I knew that," Jemmy lied.

"They're rolling a hogshead," the boy said with a mild cockney accent. "This here's a rolling road."

"A hogshead?"

"Got tobacco in it. About twelve hundred pounds." They watched the two Africans straining to extract the hogshead from a gully that cut the road behind them.

"Twelve hundred pounds?" Jemmy asked, impressed even though he was unsure how heavy that really was. "Where are they taking it?"

"To Chestertown, I suppose. Probably loading it onto your ship for the journey back."

He turned toward the young fellow. "What about yer ship?"

"Ours sank."

"Sank?" Jemmy's impish green eyes grew wide.

"Aye, sank." The boy nodded, then extended his hand. "Name's George. George Brooke." As Jemmy reached for George's hand, he noticed a round scar about the size of an Irish shilling on George's right palm. "'Tis a Bailey-burn," George said as they shook hands.

"I know."

"No, you didn't."

"I did so," protested Jemmy, tired of being corrected. "Yer a convict. A felon. Ye were in the Old Bailey in London. They branded ye before transportin' ye here."

"So you know something," muttered George, rubbing the mark. "It was either this or danglin' from the Tyburn tree." He looked away.

Jemmy watched him. He didn't look like a murderer. Probably just a thief.

Having looked into the eyes of Captain Bailyn he knew a murderer when he saw one. It was the Captain Bailyns, Richard Annesleys and Drummonds of the world who should be swinging from the Tyburn tree. "Pleased to meet ye. Name's James Annesley—" Just then the wagon hit another huge hole and crashed down, lurching violently with a fantastic creaking noise. As Jemmy started to right himself, the rear wheels hit the same rut. Then the band of the back right wheel popped with a loud twang, the wooden spokes splintering, shooting free, and that corner of the wagon wrecked to the ground with a medley of thunderous whomps and thuds.

"Whoa, damnit! Whoa!" the driver yelled at the horses. The wagon crunched, grinding to a halt as the men and boys clambered over each other, grabbing for the side rails to keep from sliding out. Karl had reached back and caught Jemmy by the wrist. Everyone was shouting, some laughing, and it took a moment for the agitated chaos to settle. Jemmy turned toward the sound of metal scraping against wood just in time to see his brass quadrant falling from the wagon, clanging against stones.

"Get you down!" a bearded guard bellowed, stooping to pick up the quadrant.

"Get out," yelled another. "Move lads!" All the servants including Jemmy quickly scrambled down the tilted wagon bed to the coarse road.

"Over there." The guard motioned with the quadrant, ordering the ten new servants to move to the low side of the road. Once they had all shuffled over, he continued, "You!" He was pointing the quadrant at George. "Get your arse under and fetch the other wheel." George hesitated, but for only a moment, then crawled beneath the still-creaking wagon. "You four big'uns get around this end and lift." The large men came forward and lifted the wagon, grunting under the weight, holding it up while George shoved the new wheel out from under the bed and then emerged himself. Jemmy started to move up and help pull the new wheel out but the guard barked at him to stay back. The four rested the wagon down again, then lifted it once more while others went to work hastily replacing the wheel. Jemmy saw Karl standing in front of the wagon, musket in hand. He wondered why a young man like Karl would endure the long voyage to the Colonies only to find himself working for Drummond. But that was followed quickly with the realization that he himself was no different—he was about to become a woodcutter for that Irish ogre. The bearded guard who had been directing the work now took notice of the quadrant in his own hands. "Whose is this? Who brought this?" he asked.

"Me, sir," replied Jemmy. "'Tis mine."

"Well, I don't know who you stole it from but I'll keep it till it's claimed." Jemmy stepped up. "I didn't steal it, I—"

"Stand back!" the man barked. Jemmy froze, his eyes burning with anger. It was that wave of rage that came easily to him now, perhaps too easily—one moment on, the next gone, ready to return. He wished these men would just leave him be. If they—

"Stop! You shite-bastard!" another guard bellowed from behind the wagon. Jemmy jumped and then realized the man was yelling at someone else. Everyone fell silent. Jemmy followed the direction of the guard's blunderbuss to the wide eyes of the young Scottish servant who was frozen atop a wooded rise by the road. "Boy!" another shouted. "Where do you think you're goin' Scot?"

"No Kelly. Not now!" pleaded George, shaking his head.

"I'm not going back, George. I'm not." The young man's voice was quivering. Watching Kelly, it occurred to Jemmy that the boy was not much older than himself, perhaps fifteen or so. Probably about the same age as George. Kelly slowly retreated, taking three scared steps backward until he bumped into a fallen tree.

"Get down here, lad!" a guard demanded.

"These bastards do the paddy's bidding," George implored. "You know what he did to Robert. It isn't worth it."

"Aye," Kelly replied, his voice taut and high, "and if we stay on that wagon we'll end up working for Drummond too, we will." With a shaky hand, Kelly slowly pulled a flintlock pistol from his torn waistcoat and held it by his side.

"Mother of God! Don't do this lad!" The guard's round flabby face was glistening with sweat. Jemmy heard the pop and click of the blunderbuss's hammer rocking into place.

"Damnit, Kelly!" George shouted again. "This isn't—"

"You damned runaway. Put down your squirrel gun," said another voice.

The bearded guard stepped behind the man aiming the blunderbuss and whispered, "Shoot up, over his head. That'll stop him."

"Kelly," pleaded George, "I'm begging you. They aren't going to just let you go."

"What are you holding there lassy?" a guard taunted. "Looks like an old Jacobite relic. Better check the pan!" Nervous laughter rippled among the others. Another joined in with a forced Scottish brogue, "Haven't ya any powder t' ya? What ya goin' t' burn—one of yar Highland turds?"

The young Scot narrowed his eyes and screamed, "Ya're all fackin' English scum!"

"Kelly!" shouted George.

With one fierce surge, Kelly jerked the pistol up and fired it while whirling around, leaping high over the fallen tree. The blunderbuss instantly erupted with a deafening boom and the back of the young Scot's head exploded red and he fell. Jemmy froze, staring at the crimson mist falling softly in the air.

—※—

John Broders, examined — "I dwelt in Pennsylvania, in America, fourteen or fifteen years ago, and I saw Mr. Annesley there. My brother and I were traveling on the road one cold morning, and we went into a colliers house to warm ourselves. As we were there a boy came in with a gun in his hand and a dead squirrel. He said he was a servant at the place and he told us that he came from the county of Wexford. We told him that we both came from that county, and were glad to see him, and asked him his name. He said that he was James Annesley, of Dunmain, but refused our further questions. Though we pressed, he would say nothing more."

— trial transcript, *Annesley v. Anglesea*, 1743

—※—

CHAPTER 17

The doubt of future foes
exiles my present joy,
And wit me warns to shun such snares
as threaten mine annoy;
For falsehood now doth flow,
and subjects' faith doth ebb,
Which should not be if reason ruled
or wisdom weaved the web.

— *The Doubt of Future Foes*, Queen Elizabeth I,
1568

Jemmy's foot slipped on a wobbly stone in the middle of Brandywine Creek, a half-day's ride from Coatesville, Pennsylvania. His split-sole shoe filled with cold water, sparking a flurry of curses. When he regained his balance it was too late. One end of the heavy log he was carrying slid from his arms and splashed into the creek, pitching water up to his waist. "Damn! Fack!" he bellowed. "Damn it to hell!" He stood still for a moment, the frigid torrent rushing around his ankles. "Damnit! Damnit!" he wailed into the surrounding trees. Finally, resigned to his wet fate, he ambled forward sploshing his way across the creek dragging the length of bulky cordwood behind him. Climbing the far bank, he quickly grew weary and the harder he tugged at the log the more his feet slipped and the slower he progressed up the slick slope. He fell on his rear and sat still, thinking about letting go—letting the log roll back down to the creek where it seemed so desperate to be. A rustle behind him caught his attention and he stretched up, panting heavily, trying to peer over the rise. But he didn't see anything. It was probably a rabbit. Perhaps a fox. He almost hoped it was one of those mysterious Iroquois Indians the others claimed were lurking just out of sight—coming to kill him, crack his head open with a tomahawk and relieve him of this withering fatigue which was equaled only by his fury, both of which had not waned a bit over the past four months. He turned and lay against the muddy bank, watching the cold creek gurgle by.

"Give it here," George barked from over Jemmy's shoulders. "Wouldn't want his lordship bruising an elbow, now would we?"

"Damn ye," groaned Jemmy, pulling himself to his feet. Now he was going to get that bloody log up the ravine if it killed him.

"Come now. Give it here, Master James," George demanded sarcastically.

Jemmy stepped forward, clutching the log, teetering on losing his balance. "Get out of m' fackin' way!"

A mocking grin came over George. "The noble command of the Earl of Anglesea!"

"Go to hell directly," Jemmy replied, clambering past George and over the top of the embankment with the log. He then heaved it into the wagon bed. He was furious at himself not only for having trusted George to be his friend, but because the night before he had made the mistake of telling George about his claim to the English peerage. He had said it at the tenant house, just after their evening victuals of hardtack and tepid stew. Sitting on the long front porch of the one room cabin that bunked fifteen woodcutters, including George and himself, they had talked, just the two of them. After George told, for the seventh or eighth time, his 'harrowing' account of being nearly hanged for stealing bread from a Baton Bar baker in London, Jemmy decided it was time to tell his own story. But he didn't make it past the first sentence, "My father was the Earl of Anglesea and when he died—" before the derision began. Now, a day later, after nine hours of trudging hickory logs from the cutters' area, over a densely wooded hill, across the Brandy-wine, then back up the far bank to the waiting freight wagon, George was still at it, still mocking him. Jemmy was ready to hit him. He tried to focus on finishing loading the wagon.

Finally, much to his relief, the sound of horses' hooves and the jangle of harnesses came floating through the autumn-draped forest. Then the beasts came into sight. Riding one of them was a teamster bringing the four horses to pull Jemmy and George's full wagon to the nearest charcoal hearth where the logs, along with the loads of twenty-two other wagons from throughout Drummond's timberland, would be carefully charred in giant smoldering mounds, making charcoal for the plantation's iron furnace. Jemmy started to help the teamster hitch the horses, but George got to it first, so he held back. He didn't want to be anywhere near the fellow. The day was through now, they would ride back on the freight wagon and he could get warm. Perhaps tonight he could talk to the foreman, Mr. Clowes, about switching crew partners the next day. He glanced back at the horses and saw George and the teamster grinning at him, whispering. He had no doubt what George had just told the man.

"Is that true, Lord Angles?" jeered the teamster.

Jemmy glared at them, then turned. "It's Anglesea, ye arse," he muttered under his breath. Perhaps he would just walk the three miles back to the hearth camp.

George was snickering. "He said he was the son and rightful heir—"

"I didn't say that!" shouted Jemmy.

"You did!"

"Ye lie!"

"I think he's goin' to cry, George," the teamster chuckled, finishing cinching the harness. "Best leave him be,"

"Little Lord Angles is gonna cry," sneered George. "Perhaps your mother will come wipe your royal tears!" Still looking away, Jemmy grimaced, his heart pounding. George continued, "But then, Lady Angles sold you to Drummond." He added a mocking gasp, making the teamster laugh. Jemmy picked up a big hickory limb near his feet. "So," shouted George, refusing to relent, "perhaps you're a bastard boy and Lady Angles wanted to be rid of you? Perhaps she's not your mum a'toll!"

"Goddamn you!" Jemmy spun and charged, brandishing the stick. George stepped aside, laughing, ducking under a horse, making it snort and move.

"Lads!" barked the teamster.

"I'm goin' t' kill ye!" Jemmy cried, running around the horses, leaping on George's back, pummeling him with the stick.

"Get off!" he shouted, waving his hands, trying to hit Jemmy, to knock the limb away. Though George was bigger, Jemmy's rage, speed and weapon gave him the advantage.

"Ye're a goddamned maggot!" Jemmy shouted as George fell forward. "It's Anglesea! And never say anything about m' mother again!" He whacked George again, feeling nothing, thinking nothing, just a frenzy of blind rage. George cursed and thrashed about, trying to repel the blows. Finally he managed to throw an arm around and knock Jemmy off, then scramble to his feet. Then Jemmy kicked him and George lost his balance, plummeting forward, his head smacking a stone. "Damn ye!" Jemmy was back on him, not noticing that George was no longer moving. "I'm sick of ye waggin' about m' family!" He smashed the stick across the back of George's head.

"Get off him!" demanded the teamster, throwing Jemmy aside to the wet ground.

Jemmy was no less enraged. "Ye're a fackin—"

"You've damaged him."

"But he said—"

"Shut your ignorant trap!" the teamster snarled. He rolled George over.

Jemmy sat back hard in the brilliant red and gold leaves, winded, staring at the blood trickling across George's forehead. The sight stunned him. The idea of it. His breath shortened to the point of dizziness for now he saw the terror of what he had done. "Is he...?"

"Nah," the teamster whispered angrily, still studying the unconscious young man. "You're not a murderer. Not today you're not."

—⁂—

By the time the teamster brought George and Jemmy back to camp, George was conscious. Other men took him from the wagon and rushed him up to the plantation house. Jemmy jumped down and ran inside the cabin to his bunk. He lay still, ignoring the curious glances of the others. He listened through the wall as the teamster stood on the porch informing Mr. Clowes of the fight. Jemmy's stomach tightened into a knot of swarming bees. Ben Clowes, the foreman, was the kind of man Fynn Kennedy would have enjoyed knowing, which made Jemmy respect Mr. Clowes all the more. He even looked like Mr. Kennedy, in a way, though Clowes was taller and a bit stockier. Heavily religious, Clowes was a compassionate, gentle giant who never cursed, never raised his voice. And he had taken to Jemmy, the youngest in his crew, in a fatherly way, giving him counsel on more things than just the art of felling trees. Jemmy liked the man's soft voice and the way he would spend time talking, teaching him things, telling him about Indians, the Colonies, Drummond and God, showing him how iron and steel were made, taking him to the workers' chapel on Sundays. Now nervous tears welled in Jemmy's eyes as Mr. Clowes stomped inside. Without a word the foreman grabbed Jemmy by the arm and led him forcibly out to the collier's hearth. "What happened, James?" Clowes asked in a grumbling whisper. He released his grip and ushered Jemmy to sit beside him on a giant, ten foot diameter stump. They were away from the others where no one could hear. Jemmy relayed how George had called him names and slighted his mother. "That was it?" Clowes asked. He leaned into Jemmy's face. "That was it? That was sufficient for you to club him over the head?"

"Aye, sir," replied Jemmy, looking down sheepishly. The smoldering smoke from the collier's hearth rose over them, casting a black veil across the evening sky, bringing on an early night. "That boy nearly died. Do you know that?"

"Aye, sir. I'm sorry."

"Sorry? You're sorry?" Clowes's voice was going deeper, tensing. "Do you realize what would've happened had you killed him?" Jemmy nodded, then looked away. A light autumn leaf landed gently on his head, then slipped to the ground. "This may be Quaker land," Clowes continued, "but they'll still hang a murderer."

"I didn't kill the fackin'—" Jemmy whispered.

"Watch your tongue! These Quakers don't take kindly to such vile language either."

"Aye, sir. So I've heard ye say," said Jemmy, hoping to keep the subject off the fight, even if they were now discussing something else he had done wrong. He glanced around quickly. "But there's not a Quaker within a mile, I'd reckon."

"It doesn't matter," snapped Clowes. "Quite frankly, your swearing offends *me*. No more. Even when I'm not around. Even when there is not a woodcutter or a teamster for a mile, and you think you're all alone. Especially then." He paused, glanced about, then back at Jemmy. "Lad, when you think you're alone…you're not. You never are. God is always with you, listening to you."

"Aye, sir."

"Mr. Clowes?" a man shouted from behind them.

"Aye?" Clowes stood. Jemmy saw the approaching man was at the far end of the collier's hearth, leading a horse.

"You're wanted at the furnace," continued the man.

"Very well." Clowes turned to Jemmy. "Stay here, lad. Don't move. Don't talk to anyone. I'll be back shortly. Then we'll get you something to eat."

"Aye, sir." As Mr. Clowes rode away, Jemmy began pitching bits of bark into an abandoned badger hole near his feet. Then he found a short, crooked stick and took to crushing a cluster of mushrooms. Once the mushrooms were decidedly dead, he leaned his head back and stared curiously into the canopy of leaves overhead. They seemed to be burning, roasting with flittering red, amber and golden-orange—on fire, yet not devoured. Then he focused on a gap in the canopy, a hole where the dim light from the greying sky fell through the brilliant autumn foliage. Was God truly up there, listening to him? How could God hear a man's words from way up there—way up there in heaven looking down through that unconsumed blanket of blazing leaves? He watched as the breeze made the burning trees drop their embers, floating them effortlessly down, filling the voids of the forest floor. Was that where he would go when he died, up above the forests, up to heaven? Where Juggy was? He looked harder into the underside of the trees, through them, beyond them. Was Juggy up there, watching him? Could she see him from heaven? What did she think of him? Was she also furious with him for nearly killing George? He focused on the brightest of the red leaves—a burning hell. That was where his father was, probably, and certainly where Richard, Bailyn, Captain Hendry, Drummond, and fellows like George deserved to go. No, he stopped himself—not George, and perhaps not Drummond either. No, Drummond too.

—⁜—

Nearly an hour later it was dark and Jemmy's stomach was complaining loudly. He sat illuminated by the massive mound of crackling embers at the base of the charcoal hearth just fifty feet away. They threw a peculiar reddish light, a warm glow, and in that light he could see Mr. Clowes returning. "You stayed." Clowes sounded surprised.

"Ye told me to," replied Jemmy. *Where else would I have gone?* he thought. He saw his quadrant in Clowes' hand.

"This is yours. So I've been told." He handed over the brass object.

"Aye, sir," Jemmy muttered, holding it. "Thank ye, sir." He wanted to know how and where Clowes found it, how Clowes knew it was his, why was Clowes bringing it to him now, of all times. But he was too afraid to ask.

Clowes sat in the same place he had been earlier. "So, tell me now lad, you said George called you a liar. What was it he said you were lying about?"

Jemmy hesitated. Earlier he had overheard the teamster telling Clowes some of the details. He sagged his chin and mumbled, "Might ye already know, sir?"

"Perhaps. But I want you to tell me."

Jemmy looked at Clowes, wondering if the man would believe him. "I simply told him the truth."

"Which is...?"

A deep breath, then, "My father was the Earl of Anglesea."

"But he's not now?"

"Nay. He's dead."

"So you are now the Earl?"

"I should be. But my uncle claimed it. Then he sent me here."

"So you're the rightful Earl?" Clowes's warm eyes studied Jemmy. "Are you?"

"Aye. I am." Jemmy looked away, wondering about the point of these questions.

"All right."

Jemmy looked back. "Ye believe me?"

"Can you prove it?"

Jemmy touched his chest. "I have a key from my mother. It has—"

"Let's see it." Clowes held out his hand. Jemmy pulled the brass key from around his neck and handed it to him.

"The 'B' is for Buckingham. My grandfather is the Duke. And—"

"Your grandfather is the Duke of Buckingham?" said Clowes. "My goodness!" Jemmy studied the man's face, weighing the sincerity. "A key 'tis hardly proof," Clowes concluded, handing it back. "'Tis nothing more than a fairytale meant to stir men's ire if you have not the means nor intention to prove such a fanciful claim. 'Tis best left unsaid."

"But, I can't prove—"

The foreman raised his hand, stopping Jemmy. "Then perhaps you aren't an Earl a'toll?" Jemmy's face reddened. "You're not going to pummel me for saying so, are you?"

"No. Sir."

"I'll tell you my mind, lad," Clowes added with a wink. "If I was a betting man, I'd wager a heavy shilling, if not two, that someday I'll be hearing 'bout you again, hearing that you are the Earl of Anglesea after all. That you'd proved it."

Jemmy nodded slowly, staring blankly at a clump of moss a few feet in front of him. The man was right; someday he would have to do just that. He would have to go back to Ireland. He would have to face Richard. He would have to somehow make this right, prove who he was. He scratched his cheek, then muttered, "Ye will. Ye will, indeed, Mr. Clowes."

"But in the meantime, if you're fighting again, I'll throw you in the blocks. Are you hearing me?"

"My hand to ye. No more fightin'."

"That's right. There won't be. Is that how you came by your scar? Fighting?" He pointed at Jemmy's cheek.

"Nay. 'Twas a spur." Under his breath he added, "'Twas a sort of fight, I suppose."

The foreman flicked a few ants from his boot. "You must watch that temper of yours, James. 'Tis yours, nobody else's. You're the only one to control it. Your temper is your sword—it can inflict harm and it can protect you, but if you do not respect it adequately, if you hold it too loosely in your grip, it will slip from your fingers, be taken from you, and used to take your very life." They sat in silence for a moment before Clowes announced, "You'll learn fencing. That's what you'll do. Let those angry passions escape you."

Jemmy glanced up. "I don't know how."

"Of course you don't. That's why you'll learn. You'll come with me tomorrow to Sands Furnace. On our return we'll stop at Mr. Bird's slitting mill. He makes swords. He can instruct you in the art of the weapon. We'll arrange lessons for you."

Jemmy nodded agreeably, but was confused. "Why do ye tell me not to fight, then want me trained in dueling?"

"Not dueling. Fencing. It teaches the mind..." he tapped Jemmy on the head, "as well as the heart..." he tapped Jemmy's chest, "as much as it teaches the body. Perhaps more so."

"Aye. Sir." Jemmy grinned, excited by the prospect but not certain how much to show.

"'Tis too cold. You go eat," Clowes announced, standing. As they walked back toward the cabin, he asked, "So that I may be certain, James—what are your plans regarding your claim?"

"I'll keep it to myself." Jemmy gave a slight smirk. "Till I'm ready to prove it. Ye have my word."

"Good." Clowes pat Jemmy's back. "Before you turn in this eve, go inquire of George."

"Aye, Mr. Clowes. Good night, sir."

"Good night, James. Hurry up before you get too chilled."

Jemmy walked fast up the muddy lane toward the big house. He smiled, feeling more at peace than he could remember. He would keep his promise.

PART TWO

Virginia

Fourteen Years Later

1742

I had now attained to twenty-seven years, more than
fourteen of which I had languished in miserable bondage,
but I was so far from being more easy by being so long
injured, that my impatience to be eased of it grew stronger
every day.

O time—in whose tremendous womb the seeds of all
things lie concealed, and who, sooner or later, ripens them
to full perfection, now fly swiftly, as when happy lovers
meet, and bring me opportunity and means of gratifying
the righteous, so as the event may give honor to justice;
and to oppression, fraud, violence and cruelty, the shame
and punishment they merit.

— *Memoirs of an Unfortunate Young Nobleman,*
James Annesley, 1743

CHAPTER 18

There is a lady sweet and kind,
Was never a face so pleased my mind;
I did but see her passing by,
And yet I love her till I die.

Her gesture, motion, and her smiles.
Her wit, her voice, my heart beguiles;
Beguiles my heart, I know not why,
And yet I love her till I die.

— Thomas Forde, 1607

The music filling the small Richmond farm house poured from a harpsichord, swelling against the papered parlor walls, soaring around the corner,
through the kitchen and up the straight staircase to the two bedrooms above.
In the larger bedroom the sound engaged Hanna Johansson as she leaned over
a bed, straightening the freshly washed linens. Her gauzy dress, cheese white,
matched her skin, wrinkled in places yet beautiful, worn yet elegant, aged
yet full of life. This bed would soon be too small for Pehr and Gunnar, she
reasoned. Her mouth creased to a small smile as she pictured them—her riot-
ous ten and eight-year-old boys. She retucked a strand of her graying, long
blonde hair back into its bun. They were probably down at the pond gigging
frogs. She left the room. In the front bedroom she retrieved more clean linens
lying on the bed she shared with her husband, Bjorn. Turning back toward
the door, she saw the little bed he had dragged into their room last night. It
was Sonja's, their youngest at the age of five. Though Sonja was still afraid
of the dark she had mastered the intricate subtleties of father-manipulation.
Hanna started to move it back, then stopped. Why? A few passionless nights
and Bjorn would return the bed himself.

Back in the children's room, she changed the last bed—Laura's. Laura
was the gentle one, the one who comported her father's mild-boar tempera-
ment. She had his contrarian, melancholy nature melded with his inscrutable

energy, his passion for all things. She would be leaving soon. Not this month and perhaps not this year, but soon she would be gone. Married. Perhaps moved away. Though they never spoke of it, they could feel it. It was as if to talk about Laura leaving the nest would only hasten the moment's arrival. So they silently found themselves holding their eldest tighter, longer. Watching her more. Absorbing these last months as if they were the last fall sunsets before the grey skies of the Chesapeake brought down the soft snows of winter. The music hit an ill-chorded bump, jarring Hanna alert. "Laura!" she shouted down the stairs. "He's not in the kitchen anymore!" After hearing the same yearning, lovesick tune of *Greensleeves* eight times over and again, Hanna had grown decidedly weary of it. Downstairs, the music stopped.

"Where'd he go, Mama?" The melody of Laura's soft voice rose through the floor slats.

Hanna moved to the casement window and leaned out, linens still in hand. "My mind he's with yar papa and Sonja, out in da drying barn." She heard the stool scoot back from their old harpsichord. What would Bjorn say if those two decided to marry? Certainly he would give his blessing. He loved that young man. But it would no less break his heart.

—∞—

Laura stepped into the dark barn, her golden hair carrying the radiance of the day into the cool shadows. "Papa? Is he out here?" Her blue dress glided across the packed dirt floor.

"Aya," said Bjorn, a Swedish giant, "up there." His fingers were thick, his arms the trunks of small elms, his bald head held by a neck the size of most men's thighs. He nodded up toward the drying loft. "Tying more sticks far me an'—"

"Can ya help me put this on?" Sonja interrupted, struggling to pull a burlap bag around her shoulders like a cape.

"Aya." Laura knelt to the task. "What a beautiful cape ya have!"

"It isn't a cape. I'm a butterfly."

"Of course! A butterfly," said Laura. "And never a prettier one vas seen." Overlooking their blonde hair and light eyes, Sonja and Laura would not have been easily paired as sisters. Sonja's face was oval, sleekly Scandinavian, whereas Laura's was round like her father's, almost English in breadth. Her small, freckled nose sat daintily over the seductive arc of her mouth, each lip drawn into a perpetual bow, two red ample curves. Yet, as pretty as her lips were, it was the perfectly straight white teeth behind them that set others in awe. She could not remember a time in her childhood when neighbors didn't come to see her teeth. "Smile Laura," her mother had instructed when she was eight. Two biddies from the competing quilting group were there to discuss a "rule infraction." Her mother wasn't smiling, but Laura had to. "Show them yar teeth," her father had ordered on her eleventh birthday, buying seed at the Elkton mercantile, the one that burned that spring. All the men muttered in admiration and debated the cause of such an aberration of nature. How could a child that lived among them, who ate what they ate, who was no more healthy, no less dirty, no different from their own children, have such astonishing teeth? Her father bought her birthday candy after each showing. Everyone was amazed and Laura soaked in the attention. By the time Laura was fifteen, Hanna was firmly whispering, "Close yar mouth!" as Laura fondly offered unsolicited viewings to passing strangers. Her mother was afraid some might think her oldest a simpleton, brandishing her white teeth at everyone.

When she turned seventeen and left her schooling, the suitors began to appear. Though their arrival disconcerted her father, it was Laura who was disappointed as none seemed the least impressed with her teeth, always fawning over her more feminine attributes. Now, over a year later, she was accustomed to the parade of purveyors of masculine wares. And she never made a fuss of her teeth. The suitors came by the ox-load. Since spring there had been three seamen, two merchants, an old school teacher, a minister, a toothless blacksmith, six farmers, eight soldiers, a French convict, a Spanish pirate who was later killed by one of the soldiers, two captains, and even one of the sons of the Governor of Virginia—who left his linen card in the shaking hands of her mother while she whispered, "Laura, show him yar teeth!"—each suitor more enthusiastic than the prior one, each no less discouraged nor deterred by rumors that a transported convict, a servant, and Irishman of all things, had stolen young Miss Johansson's heart.

A shrill whistle erupted from the rafters, snapping Laura's attention. "I know ya're up there," she cooed, scooting into the black depths of the barn. She peered expectantly into the loft half-filled with racked and withered tobacco leaves, the remnants of last season's harvest. "Little birdie, vere are ya?" she called, an impish smirk escaping. The short whistle repeated louder this time. She grimaced. "That's the verst attempt at a varbler I've ever heard!" she cried. She glided quietly to the corner near the scythes. When Sonja giggled behind her, Laura glanced back to see her baby sister standing on the milling floor, eyes fixed on the loft above. Her father, also smiling, remained focused on winding a spool of hemp between his knees. The whistle came again, followed by a loud rustling immediately overhead. She spun and looked up only to see a figure leaping down to the ground directly behind her.

"Aurrrgghh!" growled the young man as he landed, arms stretched wide and menacing, dust swirling all around.

"Ah! My word!" she exclaimed, backing to the corner. The man, now kneeling on the floor, was doubled with laughter. "James Annesley!" she scolded. "Ya shouldn't scare me like that!" She stomped past him dismissively, her eyes cobalt fire.

James was still chuckling as he came to his feet and trotted after her. "Can ye ever forgive me my lady? Can ye?" His affected grin disclaimed all sincerity.

"Go away," she chirped, running out of the barn. A fleeting look back assured her that he was following at a hormonal pace.

"Are ya helping me no more?" Bjorn asked haplessly.

James whirled to a stop. "Aye, Mr. Johansson. Quite right," he said, looking first at Bjorn, then out the cavernous opening where Laura had disappeared, vanishing into the brilliance of the day. He slowly returned his gaze toward her father. "Shall I wind that for ye?"

Laura peered around the massive door, shading her eyes to see the men in the dimness. "Papa!" she scolded.

Bjorn frowned grudgingly. "Go on. Nothing here my old hands can't manage." James held his breath as tight as his angst, his eyes shifting between Laura and her father. A multitude of proprieties and improprieties flashed through his mind as he sorted them, trying to pick the best for the circumstance. Bjorn's frown dissolved into a round smile, now forming its truer self. His eyes fixed on his impetuous daughter. "On with ya, son. Aya, on with ya. I want no trouble with dat one."

Already moving, James blurted, "Thank ye, sir!" as he pivoted around the corner and was gone. Behind him he heard Bjorn's bass chortle filling the barn.

—⁂—

By the time they reached the ox-grass road that led to Palkin Spring, James had slowed his half-hearted run to keep from passing the prey of his pursuit. She was laughing uncontrollably, her hair having fallen from its combs now fluttered behind her, an enchanting golden pennant swirling in the air. He stayed close. Finally, she slowed, then collapsed against a birch, breathless.

"Ya're a rogue, James Annesley," she panted. "To chase a lady such."

He bowed handsomely. "No more a rogue than ye'd desire of me."

"Ha!" She pushed him away.

He approached again, glancing quickly to confirm they were unobserved, then took her hands and eased her toward him. Where she had practiced keeping polite space—room enough for Mama to see daylight—she now let him in close, his waistcoat brushing her breasts. He willed himself not to look down. *Be a gentleman,* he admonished himself. He forced his eyes not to leer as they otherwise wished, down into the warmth of her cleavage which rose and fell against him with each of her easing breaths. He knew of its presence, her smell, her warmth, so close. He wouldn't look down. He let go of her hands and embraced her, encircling her small waist with his arms, his hands careful to stay north of the forbidden line, his eyes focused where they belonged and inhaled, filling himself again with her sugary smell.

As she had done so many times, she reached up and silently traced the three-inch scar on his right cheek, touching it, deciphering it, as if to construe its story, reveal its true origin. As if by her caress she could extirpate it from his past.

"I love ye," he said, confidently and soft.

She withdrew her hand. "I know," she replied, affecting the coquette, the brooding look that turned away.

"Ye're wicked." He smirked softly, keeping a firm, almost carnal hold of her.

"Nay," she whispered, her ocean-blue eyes meeting his directly. "It's just—"

"Aye? Just what?"

"I just don't know if I can love a man who can't visal a varbler. It was pitiful James!"

"Ah, ye're a mighty fine one t' be sayin' such! What about me? Eh? I've fallen for a lass who says 'visal' for 'whistle' and 'varbler' for 'warbler,' so I have!"

"What's it my concern if da Irish or da English, whatever ya are, can't speak with da tune of a Swede."

He marveled, slowly shaking his head, befuddled, bemused, altogether in love. She was right—he loved to hear her talk. It was as if listening to a melodious, graceful song. She daunted him, mystified him. She was his world. He studied her eyes, those pools of glimmering blue, watching her gaze glide gradually down the length of his nose to where it stopped and lingered on the creases of his smile. He eased in and kissed her deeply.

They first saw each other at a Mayday celebration in Philadelphia eight years before. James was nineteen, a thin attempt at cutting a dashing image, and Laura was a radiant fourteen-year-old lass, as mischievous as she was charming, a devilish combination. Her family had come to town with a group of other Swedes from their community in Elkton, Maryland. Among their group were three stableboys, one of whom was known to George Brooke. After one stunned glimpse of Laura, James quickly made his request, George made the arrangements, and the stableboy made the introductions. Despite the brevity of their encounter—she was whisked away by her officious father—it was magical to James. He was spellbound. In that single moment his world transformed. Up became down, right was wrong, and nothing else mattered but her.

Within a week of meeting her—the one, the rapturous smell, the curves, that face, those teeth—James did the one thing he would most regret for the rest of his life: he ran away from the Drummond Iron Furnace. He had convinced himself that the loveliest girl he had ever seen was worth all risks, all chances, was beyond all disregarded sensibilities, all logic, all glaring impossibilities. Or so he told himself. In truth his decision to run had been founded on far less noble grounds. That May he had been at the Drummond Furnace six years and ten months. He was a collier at the charcoal hearths, running a crew of ten. In a mere two months the hell would end, his seven-year servitude would be over and he would regain his freedom. He would be an English citizen, a free man. Free to own land. Free to marry. Free to charge a wage. Free to have property. Free to have that property taxed by an English government an ocean away. Free to be a full subject of that Crown. Free to return to Ireland if he chose and if he were to afford such a passage. All he had to do was wait, to bide his time. For two months. But two things occurred first: he met the most beautiful girl he had ever seen, and five days later his Methuselah master, the insufferable Colonel William Drummond, finally died.

That May night after the hearsay of Drummond's painful death was cheerfully bandied about, every indentee and slave alike wished to lift a pint or two in remembrance. By midnight, the Wolf and Hen Tavern in Coatesville was stuffed with swilling servants staggering about bellowing chanteys, two urinating just beyond the back door, many more comatose and sprawled on the tavern's ale-slick floor. Though James and George were also on the floor, they had somehow managed not only to remain conscious, but were sitting up against the far brick wall, each into their twelfth tankard of ale. It is precisely in such moments that the gods amuse themselves with mankind.

Perhaps these lesser gods, these gods of fate and subterfuge, are weaker than might be expected. Success for them is only assured when a young man has just puked and is now swaggering in his ale-and-vomit-soaked-waistcoat, adrift in that sublime state of voluble courage and confused vision. It was no different for James, for it was precisely then that divine opportunity came into focus, like a golden chalice handed down through the thick clouds floating through his mind. This was his time, his moment. Now. With Drummond dead, James saw himself free to pursue both his Swedish passion and the shiny promised spoils of an ocean adventure (as spiritedly described by George who was no less drifting). It was the convergence of promise where his dreams collided hard, muddling him, unmercifully beguiling him. Though in later years he would be loathe to admit it, he was the one who decided that morning would be too late. No, he and George should go now. They rose and stumbled from the Wolf and Hen, supporting each other as they lurched into the cool Pennsylvania night. Swearing at the moon, they went away, all along screeching a grievous rendition of *Rule Britannia* at the top of their voices.

In principle, their ill-devised and poorly executed plan might have worked. With only a few months remaining in their terms and no master to announce their escape to the newspapers, few would notice or care. Only a man as virtueless as Colonel Drummond would more than scold an indentured servant who ran away under the pall of drink. Drunk servants often wandered away only to be quietly returned the next morning. It was staying away that got the man in trouble. If he planned to stay away, he had better get far away, fast. So, the incapacitated James reasoned that they had nothing to fear, no reason for speed as Drummond was dead and soon to be buried. They would make their way to Norfolk and sign on with the Royal Navy. And along the way they would pass through Elkton where he would call on Laura. George promptly agreed to the plan once James imagined Laura's friends aloud.

It was George's second run. His first attempt had failed when both he and Kelly, his Scot friend, were caught just as they arrived at the Chesapeake. A merchant had identified them from their descriptions in a runaway announcement and alerted the dockmaster, who also served as the sheriff. They were arrested, jailed, and sentenced to serve seven more years. Their original owner had not wanted them back, so he bargain-sold the unruly pair to Drummond, in Chestertown, on the same day James first came ashore, the same day Kelly was killed attempting to escape.

George Brooke had been transported to Maryland at the age of fifteen for lifting six pence of white bread from a London bakery. Or so he had told James. James was never certain of the truth in any of George's accounts, like the story about George's transport ship sinking off the coast of Cape Henry—an account which never fit, like an errant piece forced into the wrong puzzle. But the truth of George's tall tales mattered little. Their veracity was of no value. They were entertaining and that was enough. George's friendship helped mask James's blackness, the emptiness of the ever-passing, never-ending days. The friendship was the balm to his emotional cuts, slices extracted by those razor-edged images James carried with him—childhood pictures of his mother, of Seán and Fynn, of Juggy dying. The friendship served them well. It served to pass the months and years. The clubbing was long forgiven, though never forgotten. Fodder for unceasing jesting. And George never questioned James again about peerage or claims. James never brought it up. They became the kind of fleeting friends that only difficult circumstances can construct, hardships, suffering and war, years of struggle, imprisonment, the brotherhood of the oppressed, the chorus of the enslaved. Yet they knew the truth. They could sense it, feel it. Such friendships are accursed by the circumstances of their creation. Albeit unspoken, they knew it had its own span, its own term inextricably tethered to the adversity that fed it. Not like a life-long friendship that carries the hope of endurance beyond an immediate environment of privation. Someday they would go their separate ways, most likely never to see the other again. But it didn't matter. For that period they had their fleeting friendship, that class of brotherhood, and they clung to it with clenched determinism. Because it was all they had.

The morning after their "glorious" escape, they were discovered by one of the local constables. They had fallen asleep in a roadside ditch only two miles from Coatesville. As bad as it may have been, the horror of that morning was not the blinding sun, or the pulsating fire in their heads, or even the nauseating wagon ride back to the furnace—it was the sight of the man who met them at the gates of the Drummond Furnace that snapped them into a state of immediate sobriety. Colonel Drummond had in fact not died, but had fallen seriously ill. By the following morning, he was feeling entirely too well and was now at the gates glowering at those servants who had fled, those random souls being brought back, forced back by constables, by wagon, by horse, by capture, by guilt, by fear.

Both James and George were sentenced to nine additional years of servitude, seven for the escape and two more because it was George's second attempt. The fact that it was not James's second flight was of no concern to Drummond, and thus of no concern to the local judge who, for reasons unknown, felt behooved to impose whatever sentences Drummond demanded. Within the month George ran away again. But this time alone. This time sober. And this time he never returned. Now, years later, James still found himself scanning the crowds for his friend. He added George to his imagination, the realm where Seán lived, his imaginary friends. In this realm George met Seán, and the two of them were happy, alive, and waiting for James. Both were in the Royal Navy, capturing pirates, discovering new Caribbean islands, enjoying the impure exuberance of the island's native girls.

James could scarcely remember the three years following his foiled escape. Resigned to his fate of apparently endless servitude, he abandoned himself entirely. He deemed himself unworthy of Laura and tried to forget having ever met her—albeit an impossible task, he was aided by copious pints of ale and by bedding any half-pretty prostitute to be found or afforded. Occasionally, a distraction could be mustered by rallying himself into a pub fight (drawing his sword once too often he received another long scar, this one across his chest). Miserable and despondent, he lumbered aimlessly through those dismal years.

—∞—

Then, one December day in 1738, under a light falling snow, a miracle happened. Ben Clowes, the old woodcutting foreman James had not seen for nearly seven years, strolled into the collier's hearth, giving James such a start that he nearly fell into the pit. Once James regained his composure and properly greeted the man, Mr. Clowes explained his return. As he listened, James's knees buckled and he dropped into the charcoal-stained snow, his eyes welling with joy.

Mr. Clowes had left the Drummond Furnace one frozen grey January morning three and a half years after James's arrival, his back straight with pride as he passed through the iron gates, his indentured term finally over. James could still see it clearly. Mr. Clowes had left as a free man, vowing to claim his portion of the rich colonial land. James had heard from him through occasional letters. Clowes had gone to Virginia, built a small tobacco farm and started a family, then eventually founded his community's little church. But the years passed and the last letter James sent to Clowes was one he wrote the day George disappeared. James told everything, venting and shouting with his pen, raging at everyone. He didn't hear back from Mr. Clowes for a little over a year. The letter he received was in a shaky hand, smeared, telling of Ms. Clowes burning to death in their small farmhouse, and that two of his girls had died from prolonged fever. He had gone on to say that he was moving, that his surroundings held too many painful memories. That last letter pushed James even deeper into his personal black abyss.

Then, many months later, this miracle happened: On December 3, 1738, three and a half years after James's second term began, and in the thick of James's seemingly incurable despair, Mr. Clowes walked into the Drummond Furnace and summarily purchased James's remaining five and a half years. Though James was elated to be freed from the monstrous Drummond, what was truly miraculous was *where* they were heading when they whipped the carthorses into action that afternoon. Mr. Clowes had recently remarried and was managing his new wife's tobacco farm near the mouth of the Susquehanna River, at the northern end of the Chesapeake Bay, only three miles from the Swedish community of Elkton, Maryland.

—␣—

A small bird chirped angrily as it flittered through the tobacco barn seeking a path of escape. Finally, it swooped by James and Laura's heads and disappeared. "James?" Laura whispered.

"Aye?" James eased Laura away and frowned when he saw a tear on her face. "What's the matter, *Acushla?*" he asked, calling her by the Irish endearment. "Did I say something wrong?"

"Nothing. My sweet James."

He was baffled, a state not unfamiliar to him, especially when her feminine emotions were swirling about, capricious winds that held him off balance. They had kissed until their mouths ached. When Sonja found them they had convinced her to scurry home and resumed their embrace. But when Pehr and Gunnar, Laura's tenacious little brothers, discovered them, James and Laura retreated to the vacant tobacco barn, climbed to the loft, and sat in a draft window, dangling their entwined feet high over the open expanse of empty air. Now the sun was disappearing, sweeping a royal blush across the tops of the pines bordering the Johansson farm. James pulled Laura close.

"James?"

"Aye, Laura? Where's yer mind takin' ye?"

"Ya know I love ya, don't ya?" Her eyes were still wet with tears.

"Aye, my love. I do."

"Then…then—"

"Then what, Laura?"

"Nothing." She lowered her chin and offered a weak smile.

"Nothing?" Why must God make these creatures so difficult?

"I was just thinking, that's all. Just vishing we were—"

"Vishing? Were ye 'fishing' or 'wishing'?" He thought humor might help, choosing to ignore the voice within him desperately waving off that course. "Let me see, I don't think ye could be *fishing* from up here, so must be—"

Laura yanked herself back, her eyes blazing. "Mind ya not to make sport of my talking! 'Tis meanness, Mr. Annesley."

James stammered, "I'm sorry. Truly."

"Ya can't toy with my feelings, James. I von't let ya!" She stood quickly and moved to the other draft window, eight feet away on the same wall.

"I'm not…I would never," he weakly protested, leaning out of his window to see her in the other. "Now ye've moved and I must risk m' bleedin' life t' see the prettiest—"

"Then fall if ya must, but don't be looking at me!"

"Acushla!" He sat back and frowned. What did that mean? He leaned forward, peering down over the edge. In one instance she's kissing me and then she's wishing I'd break my neck!

—※—

When James first called on Laura Johansson in Elkton, he found her wrapped in a horse blanket, sitting in a similar loft window, watching a grey December sunset. That was over three years ago, the first morning after he moved his meager belongings into Mr. Clowes's tenant house. And it was on that cold Saturday, as they talked under the watchful eye of both Mr. and Mrs. Johansson, that he knew he was in love with her. An unwavering courtship followed, and their love for each other flourished with the passing months.

Two autumns later, Ben Clowes died. When his widow told James she needed to sell his remaining years to relieve merchant debts, James was forced to go to Laura's father for help. But Bjorn Johansson could not afford to buy him. Besides, he was planning to move his family to Richmond, Virginia, a new settlement at the falls of the James River. This news put James and Laura in a panic—the falls of the James River was a week's ride from Elkton. But soon a solution was found. Mr. Johansson recommended James to Duncan Morris, an itinerant printer who attended the Johansson's Lutheran church.

Mr. Morris had his mind set on starting a newspaper in the burgeoning town of Richmond and needed a literate assistant. James found him at the White Horse Inn and within an hour had negotiated his own sale on behalf of the Widow Clowes.

Most evenings of the next two years, after closing the press house for Morris, James would clean the ink from under his nails, brush his teeth, comb his hair, then borrow Morris's old nag and make his way across the James River, then south to the Johansson's farm. There he spent innumerable hours cutting wood, clearing fields, and helping Bjorn build the house and barns. Hanna fed him most meals and he spent most warm nights in their new barn. Bjorn was grateful for the help, which James never minded to give. So long as he could be near Laura.

—m—

The sun was almost gone. James got to his feet and walked the few paces to Laura's window, then sat beside her and watched the shimmering deep-red ball disappear through the trees. "Reminds me of sitting in m' Da's stables at Dunmain, as a young lad, it does." He hoped the innocuous subject would not incite another request that he throw himself from the window.

"Do ya miss yar father?"

"Nay," her replied, breathing easier upon hearing the softness of her voice.

"What do ya miss?" Her entrancing eyes were studying him.

"About Ireland?"

"Aya, Ireland." She paused, then furrowed her brow. "Ya speak so little of it. After these years, all I know is that yar father was a stableman."

"Aye," muttered James, tensing at the sound of his own lie.

"And about yar friend, Seán."

"Aye," he replied, looking away. "Seán Kennedy."

"Did yar father tell ya about yar mother? She was lost birthing ya, I know, but—"

"Nay. Not much." He hoped she wasn't detecting his anxiety.

"Do ya think they loved each other? Like we do?"

"Who? Mother? My father? Nay. Most assuredly not. Why?"

"They got married younger than we'll be, if I added correctly, and…." Her gaze descended to James's hand, which was covering hers on the rough floor of the loft.

"Is that what's on yer mind? Us marryin'?" James stared at her beautiful chin, her smooth skin. "What can I say that I haven't already said? I love ye. Ye know that. But ye also know an indentee can't marry."

Laura's lips began quivering and a tear ran down her cheek. "I know."

"A year and a half. That's all," he continued. "What is left for me to say? I couldn't imagine life without ye. Ye know if I were a free man we would already be husband and wife."

"I love ya," she whispered.

He pulled her closer, kissing her softly on her forehead. "Ye're my life Laura. What can I do to make ye believe me? To make these tears stop? Command me, m'fair lady. I'll do it." His eyes widened playfully. "Anything. Just say it. When I first saw yer beautiful face, ye saved my life. I would die for ye." He lightly brushed a tear from her warm cheeks. "I would, indeed. Tell me, what—"

She put two fingers over his mouth, silencing him. "Ya might ask me," she breathed. James's eyes relaxed as he started to smile. "Ya've never asked me," she continued. "I want to know ya'll never leave."

James's hands began to shake, but he grasped hers anyway. "I would never leave ye. Never in a thousand lifetimes." Her tears came freely now, her mouth and eyes smiling. He brought himself to his knees, gently pulling her to join him. His mouth went dry. "Laura Johansson...Laura...." he began stiffly. The tree frogs had begun their chirping croaks that sounded like a choir chanting, "Ask-her. Ask-her. Ask-her." He whispered, "Laura, I love ye." He moved a few strands of her hair behind her little ears. The tree frogs were getting louder. "Laura, will ye do me the honor of marrying me?"

The gleam in her eyes said everything.

CHAPTER 19

What is love? 'Tis not hereafter;
Present mirth hath present laughter;
What's to come is still unsure.
In delay there lies no plenty;
Then come kiss me, sweet and twenty;
Youth's a stuff will not endure.

— *Twelfth Night*, William Shakespeare, 1601

Gunnar and Pehr bolted into the press house, panting and red-faced, screaming about an imaginary nasty beast with long sharp teeth that had just chased them up the dirty Richmond street. "Settle yerselves, lads," James greeted Laura's younger brothers with a chuckle. "Ye wouldn't want to knock over—" An earsplitting clatter ripped through the small room as a cluster of gutter sticks and drying poles crashed to the rough floor.

"My apologies sir," said Pehr as he began picking the wood pieces off the floor.

"Ya're a dafty!" exclaimed Gunnar, laughing.

"Am not!"

"Dafty! Dafty!"

"Lads!" James drew in a deep breath, then blew it out noisily. "'Tis all right Pehr, truly. I've done it myself." He offered a reassuring smile.

Gunnar was already by the press, inking his fingers. "What's this?"

"'Tis an English press," answered James, stepping closer. Something scurried across it. "Ah, 'tis just a bug!" He grabbed a turn-stick, presenting it as a sword. "On guard!" he barked at the bluish-black bug. "Ye devil! Stand t' meet yer doom!" Both boys were transfixed and chuckling at the same time. James put forth a grand flourish of parries and thrusts, then stomped his foot as he lunged, startling the boys. "Auuhhww!" he bellowed, pretending to have become impaled on the spindle-arm. "The rogue's bettered me, lads! Tell yer sister I won't be . . . making it home . . . for dinner." He slumped over the press-carriage, keeping one eye open to keep from the ink tray.

"Mama's making lutfisk," Pehr retorted dryly. "Ya're better off staying dead."

"Ha!" James sprang back, laughing.

"Good fight, James!" Mr. Morris called out as he entered the room. He had the shambling grace of an aging man.

James gave them all an elegant bow, then flicked the ink-sodden critter from the coffin-tray. "Best there's no paper in there lads or we'd had beetle prints crossing Mr. Morris's type."

"Read these for me?" Morris's tone being more demand than request, having resumed its flat-rock proportions—cold and grey. He laid a stack of newspapers on the table near the window.

"Aye, sir. London?" James regularly read the English papers, looking for items Morris might wish to copy into his Richmond Gazette.

Morris blinked in confirmation, then shuffled back out the same door. The Johansson boys pulled James's attention. They had taken to fencing with sticks. He watched them as they played, momentarily transfixed. They flung their sticks high, crashing them against the other. James's eyes blurred into a haze of memory. The boys were now drawing, painting with coal-dust paint, the darkest of colors, black images, memories of him and Seán, a flickering shadow, a memory that would not hold, a vision that would never go away. Suddenly, Morris's blubbery face and ill-fit wig appeared in the closed window. He shouted hoarsely through the glass, "Mind you do them before tea!"

James nodded as he turned to the boys. "Lads! Lads!" They settled from their duel, their sticks rattling to a stop. "I have a riddle for ye." He watched their eyes. "Listen carefully. Lil' Jenny Whiteface has a red nose. The longer she lives, the shorter she grows. Eh? What is she?" He studied their vacant expressions, awaiting one of the little brains to snap alive, to capture the answer from the delicacy of youthful reason.

"Don't know," said Gunnar. "What is it?"

"Nah, me either," Pehr piped.

"Ah, fie! Do ye think I'll let it slip so easily? Think on it awhile. Let yer minds stew. Maybe it will come to ye. Like a sudden flame. Like a candle!" He smirked at himself. "Now lads, I've work t'do. Ye'd best run along."

Pehr bolted for the door, then stopped when he discovered Gunnar was not following. "Can ya teach me to be a sword fighter?" Gunnar asked.

A transitory pall. "Me?" James's eyebrows peaked. "I am not a sword master." The boy's eyes were pleading, a plea for adventure, a plea belying danger, a boy's plea that so often begets his doom. James broke. "I'll have a go at it for ye. Fencing is a good discipline." He took a breath. "Yet, another time." As the boys scampered out, he called to them, "I'll be askin' ye that riddle again this eve, before yar Pa lights the candles. Think hard upon it."

Moments later, James was rifling newspapers. He selected several and carried them to the small bench outside, along with a quill pen and an inkwell. The first one was the latest issue of *The Daily Post*, dated August 2, 1742, now two months old. The paper fluttered in the air, causing him to shift his back against the light breeze. His gaze scoured down the long thin page. He skimmed the accounts of King George II and his entourage, slowed in the paragraphs mentioning the auspicious activities of certain Dukes and Earls, skipped stock quotes, notices of oratories, lease announcements, and court renderings, then flipped it over to review the listing of recently published books. What he would give to be able to read those books. Finally he set the paper aside, weighting it with the ink well. He had found nothing Morris would care to repeat. He perused the next one. After a half-hour of reading and marking only a few items for Morris to consider, he picked up a three-month-old issue of *The Daily Post*.

"Good day, James."

James looked up to see a giant reining a two-horse team to a halt. "Good day t'ye, Mr. Johansson. Did ye see yer lads?"

"Aya, they'll be along shortly," said Bjorn, pipe in hand. "Fine day."

"Pleasant. Is Laura in town with ye?"

He nodded. "She and her mama. At the mercantile. Join us?"

"Nay, but I thank ye for asking."

"Ya don't appear to be working."

"I'm working indeed."

"Reading papers?" Bjorn's inability to read often seasoned his humor. "I beg ya not to exhaust yerself. My own labor awaits ya."

"No doubt it does." James smirked at the man, his future father-in-law. He had met no kinder man. Not since Fynn. But he could only remember the sentiment of Fynn. A wisp of warmth. Safety. Gentility. Anger at men and things that had scared James. Bjorn was something the same. A confused reflection of Fynn, the thick butcher Purcell, and a bit of Mr. Clowes, all alloyed into one massive Swede. But without the aura of violence *obbligato*. That concomitant corona that enveloped his secret memory of youth. Pain, tears, cold, running, darkness, fear.

Bjorn tapped the reins and the wheels creaked forward. "I'll send Laura."

"Thank ye sir." James watched the wagon away, then returned to *The*

Daily Post. Finding nothing for Morris on the front, he flipped to the back. Again he skimmed the royal doings of court and slowed on certain peerage. Something snagged him. He read it again. He froze.

> York, July 28. On Wednesday last died Mary Sheffield, widow, in the 46th Year of her Age. She was married to the Earl of Anglesea, Arthur Annesley, died 1728, and was Daughter of the Duke of Buckingham, John Sheffield, died 1731.

Mother was dead. A cold tremor ran across his chest, down his arms and hands. He read it again. Motionless. Minutes passed. Fourteen years passed. Over and again he read it. All clarity of reason flushed from his brain. He fell void. He sat hollow. He thought he might vomit. He stared at the words. Mary. Duke. Died. Arthur. Died. Age. Mary. 1728. Died. His fingers loosed. The breeze cut in and caught the paper, stealing it across the street. He watched it go. He could still read the words. But he could not remember her face.

"James?" Laura was there. "James?" She was standing there. He could see the hem of her skirt, her boots beneath. "James? What is it?" He saw her feet walk by, saw her retrieve the paper. Saw her sit beside him. "Yar scaring me James." He couldn't speak. For the first time, he wished Laura would go away. "What is it?" She moved in front of him and crouched down, trying to see his face. She tried to lift his chin. "James?"

"I can't. I'm sorry," he muttered. He had to go. He pulled himself to his feet and walked away. The air crossed his face. He realized he had tears on his cheeks.

"James!" Laura cried, following him. "What happened?"

He walked faster. Angry at himself. Angry at his tears. Angry at Laura for being there. Angry at his mother. Angry at the years of his lies. Angry at the damn tears. He glanced back. Laura was no longer following. She was standing in the street. A horseman passed, blocking his view. Then a carriage. Then he saw her, her blonde hair loosed, her eyes down. What was she doing? God, she was reading the paper. He hurried away.

After twenty minutes of walking, he was across the James River, beyond Richmond, moving south. The whitewashed bell tower of the Mt. Olive Church rose over a hill. He walked up the front steps and opened the creaky door. He knew the place. He had helped build it. He knew it well. He attended its services, smiled at its people, sat in its pews each Sunday. Beside the Johanssons. An occasional wink at Laura when she sang in the choir. It felt right to be there. It was empty. So silent that his footsteps echoed. He approached the pulpit, moved past it, and leaned his back against the wall. His knees buckled, and like an autumn leaf loosed from its stem he slowly fell, sliding down the wall to the cool floor. He stared ahead. He had lied to Laura. He had lied to himself for so many years. After an hour, he had decided nothing. He had come to no conclusions. He was still trying to remember his mother's face but it would not come to him. His tears were dry, gone. But the coldness in his stomach remained. The church door opened. A silhouetted feminine form moved in the light.

"James?"

He looked away.

"Aya. He's here, Papa."

James heard the horses, the wagon rolling away. She was moving toward him. She gathered her blue skirt, knelt, then turned to sit beside him. "Vill ya not talk to me?"

"In time," he whispered glancing away. He could hear the tenderness in her voice. Her smell slowed his breath. He moved his hand to her knee and left it there.

"Vere ya reading this?" She gently laid the newspaper in his lap. He glanced down saw the passage and nodded. He read it again. She watched his eyes carefully, then asked, "Who was she?" He inhaled fully and held the air within him. Laura continued. "She was married to…" She re-read the words. "To Arthur Annesley. Were they relations of yars?" He let the breath out through his nose, closing his eyes, rubbing his eyebrow.

Over the years, since his fight with George on the banks of the Brandywine, James had concealed the truth from everyone, even from himself at times. When pressed, he had kept the stories of his past contained to a few veiled accounts of a stableman father and a mother he had never known. Laura had asked countless times, each time prodding from a new direction, always in search of more detail. But he had managed to keep her at bay. And the truth away. He had honored his promise to Mr. Clowes. The word he gave beside that collier's hearth so many years before. He had never again said who he was. And wouldn't. Until he was ready to prove it. He had kept his oath. He had not broken the pledge. That was honorable, right? Even against Laura's inquiries? That had been the right thing. Right? Perhaps. But now he could not remember why. He couldn't see the reason. Why the deception?

Had Mr. Clowes been wrong to exact such a promise? He hated the falseness of his stories. He hated the feeling. And most of all he dreaded the price he knew he was about to pay. The loss of his treasured silence, the ease of lies, the veil pulled back from memories. All was about to be lost to repurchase the facts. To be true to Laura. To reclaim himself.

"James, I love ya. Ya know I do. So why—"

"She is…" he began, still whispering. "She was my mother."

"Yar mother?"

"Aye." He rubbed his face harder, and now with both hands.

Laura reached for the paper. "Ya said she died birthing ya."

"I'm sorry." He listened to her silence. "I made a promise years ago t' never tell—"

"Never tell what? The truth?"

There it was. Reflexively, he surveyed the area for anything she might hit him with. He eased a copper pitcher away with his boot. Then began. "The truth is—"

"Ya couldn't tell me the truth?"

"I just—"

"So, who are ya? Are ya even James Annesley?"

"Aye."

She got to her feet. "Is that much true?"

"Aye."

"Was Arthur yar father?"

"Aye."

"So, I'm pledged to marry a man who lies about who he is—"

"Laura—"

"What else have ya lied to me about? What—"

"Nothing, *Acushla*. Truly—"

"Don't I deserve the truth? I'm sorry about yar mother, but…" She was against the far wall now, glaring at him. "Why couldn't ya have just admitted it? Ya're the son of Arthur Annesley…." She restudied the passage. "The Earl…and…Mary Sheffield. Why couldn't ya have just told me?" She stopped. She read it again. "The daughter of the Duke of Buckingham." Her brow furrowed. But it was not in anger this time. It was something else. "Buckingham Palace?"

"I suppose so. But I didn't—"

"Why James?"

"I'm sorry. Truly, I am." He saw she was reading it once again. "If ye only knew how much I hate to see ye upset like this."

She gently shook her head. "I am sorry about yar mother."

"'Tis all right." He half rose, then moved around to sit beside her, against her wall. She let him wrap her in his arms. "I should have told ye long ago."

"Yar father was an Earl. Not a stableman?"

"Nay, not at stablemen at all. He didn't do well with horses."

"And the Duke of Buckingham was yar—"

"I never knew him."

"Do ya have any other family? Any brothers?"

"Nay." He shook his head, knowing what she was thinking.

"So, ya're…." She peered at him. "Are ya an Earl? The Earl of Anglias?"

"Anglesea. Aye. I am. I would be." He stood and offered her his hand. "Let me walk ye. I'll tell ye."

Outside, they found Bjorn's wagon and waiting horses. He had walked home. They returned to Richmond with Laura sitting close, listening devotedly. He told her everything.

At the press house, he received Morris's forgiveness for the abrupt departure, followed by permission to return Monday. Before returning to the wagon, James brisked to his quarters behind the shop. There he opened his creaky trunk at the foot of his cot, rifled past the quadrant, and retrieved the Buckingham "B" key from its burlap wrap. Perhaps it would convince Laura of that same hope, that same truth, of which it had once convinced him: his mother loved him.

They resumed the road and the story. Time languished along, measured only by the slow, slack clip-clop of hooves. James talked gently, lowly, guiding them across the Virginia countryside, down the James River, crossing at Pinckney Ferry, then eased them back toward the Johansson farm. Laura sat quietly composed through most of his journey, slowly caressing the key in her small hands. She asked few questions. She wept when Juggy died. She smiled through the stories of Seán. Though the day's light had descended through the trees, James was feeling brighter with each passing fence, each hill surmounted, each event chronicled, memories loosed, pain avowed. All anew, like old letters pulled from locked trunks and read aloud. In a resurrection of candor, each memory arose to take its first breath in years. And he loved her for listening. She understood. She forgave. She blessed open those chambers of youth denied, damage unrequited, destiny unfulfilled. She held wide his heart's heavy gates.

When they arrived at the farm, they put the wagon away and sat silently on a stack of oak. Each still traveling that journey in their head. Each held by those stories said. He pulled her close, an arm around her slender back. He looked up. For the first time in years he was awed by that spread of diamonds overhead.

"When are ya going back?" she asked.

"I'll stay in the barn tonight. I don't—"

"To Ireland, James. When will ya return to Dublin?"

He sniffed and closed his eyes. "I don't know."

"Ya must return, James." Her voice was a velvet whisper. "Ya must claim what's yars." She held up the key.

"Not now. Keep it. I don't want to go now." He tied the sailcloth around her neck, letting the key slip into her cleavage. "Someday. Not now. I won't lose ye, Laura."

"Aye, you won't," she said, her blue gaze flickering up from her chest, squaring it on him. "I won't have ya staying on my account."

"Fourteen years I've dreamed myself on Irish soil, facing that evil man. But then...."

"Then what?" she asked. "Then me?"

"Aye. My dear Laura. Then God granted my greatest wish. I found ye. To marry ye. 'Tis all I now desire."

"Ya'll never lose me. Do ya not know that?" She waited for him to reply. He nodded. "Ya'll break my heart, James," she began, her voice losing its tenderness, "if ya don't return on account of me."

"I know, but—"

"I won't have it!" She scooted away. "I won't! How do ya think it makes me feel to be the one keeping ya from being the man ya truly are, from claiming yar very home?"

"When did I say being the Earl, having all that....when did I say that was who I really am? When did I say Dunmain or Dublin was my home? To marry ye and settle here, to make ye happy—"

"I'll go with ya."

He watched her eyes. Then smiled. Then began to quietly laugh.

"Don't laugh. We'll wait out yar term, marry, and sail together."

He could hear her heels sinking into the hardening earth. "Yer family—"

"Ya're my family, James Annesley."

"It would be a fight there, in Ireland. I might not win. I could never put ye in danger. Not for a title, or money or land. Not for anything. These men, if they're still alive—"

Laura pulled his face toward her. "Hear me now good sir. I agreed to marry ya long before I knew any of this. If ya never have a shilling more than ya have now, I wouldn't give a tinker's damn. Ya know that?"

"I do."

"'Tis who ya are that matters to me. I'll have no part in keeping ya from claiming what's rightfully yars, from righting this terrible wrong done ya. Ya have to go, and I'm coming with ya." He started to speak and she covered his mouth with her small hand. "I'll hear no more about it," she breathed.

A moronic grin came over him and would not go away.

CHAPTER 20

Then will thou go and leave me here?
Ah do not so my dearest dear.
The sun's departure clouds the sky;
But thy departure makes me die.

— *Valediction*, Sir Robert Ayton, 1604

Dead leaves whirled beyond the open kitchen door at the back of the small farmhouse. She was just inside, watching the orange and red ghosts play. Behind her, the sound of huffing and the hostile thumping of a knife proclaimed her mother's displeasure. Laura felt warm. Was she getting ill? A draft rounded through the house, wafting past her, flicking the pink linen of her dress. Her father was right. It was an odd autumn. Odd to be so warm this late in the year.

"So he'll go?" Hanna was saying, not pausing for a reply. "And ya'll go as well, I suppose." Her mother's disappointment had turned sharp. She was hacking so fast that bits of potato were flying onto the planked floor.

Laura wheeled around. "Vhat would ya've done, Mama? If it'd been Papa? Vhat if he had to go?"

"Laura!" Hanna glowered at her daughter.

"When ya and Papa came to America, Gran couldn't have been—"

"Laura, stop. When yar papa and I came here, we settled and built our family. Our new lives were to be *here*, with all our children. Never could we imagine one of ya going back. Across that godless, unmerciful ocean. Starting yar own life." Her voice trailed to a yielding, empty whisper. "So far away. I don't know."

"Mama." She could see the tears welling in her mother's eyes. "I want to be here. James wants to be here. He's a good man. Ya know that. We won't be gone forever. Only till he's reclaimed what's rightfully his. Then we'll be back."

"Humph!" Hanna sniffed and resumed chopping.

"Ya'll have grandchildren," Laura tried.

"Why would he give up all that wealth? Fifty thousand acres, didn't ya say? That's a country in itself. Why would he give that up?"

"It's not what he wants." Laura looked away, touching her forehead, a half massage against a pending headache.

Hanna went on, "Don't be naive. I'm happy for ya. If he regains it all. But I am scared for ya all the same." She shook her head. "I am scared for me, for yar papa. I'm scared we'll never see ya again." Now the tears were coming so fully that she had to put down the knife. Laura slid across the kitchen to hold her mother. They both silently cried.

After a moment, Hanna pulled herself upright, sniffed and wiped her face with her apron. "Ya're a fine daughter." They heard voices approaching outside. She wiped a tear from Laura's cheek.

"That's a rich field you have there, Mr. Johansson," said a man outside. Laura recognized Captain Blackwell, a merchant vessel master who came around once a year, bringing his men to roll Bjorn's tobacco hogsheads to a barge on the James River. From there they would be floated down to York-town and placed aboard Blackwell's ship, the *Kathleen*. Where Blackwell took them, she didn't know.

"A cup of tea and we'll seal our arrangement." Bjorn's voice was surprisingly formal.

"Grand," replied Blackwell. The men were on the other side of the door, stomping mud from their boots.

"James?" asked Bjorn.

Laura heard James say from a distance, "I'll be there directly."

The men stepped inside. "Hanna, look who's joined us. Ya remember Captain Blackwell?"

Hanna crossed the room warmly. "Ah, Captain. So glad to see ya're in God's health, as ya are." Laura admired the way her mother could so quickly rally after a cry.

"I am indeed. And Miss Johansson." Blackwell gave both ladies a slight bow.

"Hello Captain Blackwell," Laura offered.

Hanna turned. "Laura, fetch some muffins and tea for the gentlemen."

"Aya, Mama."

"I hear cheers are in order for the new couple," announced the captain.

"Yes," Laura said, beaming, then turned and disappeared into the kitchen.

"Captain Blackwell and I have come to an arrangement." Her father was shouting to make himself heard from the other room. "I think ya'll find quite agreeable, Laura. And fortunate!"

Laura returned to the parlor, placed mugs before the men and began to pour the tea. "Truly? What might that be?"

"The good captain has agreed to carry James back to Ireland."

Laura stopped pouring. She stared at her father, who was beaming.

He continued, "Don't worry. There'll be no fare. And he'll return him here by the same means." Bjorn was clearly proud of this idea.

"That's most generous of ya, Captain Blackwell," said Laura tersely. "Did Papa tell ya we intend to marry first and sail to Ireland together?"

Bjorn interjected, "Laura, the *Kathleen* departs in a week's time, so he'll be going—"

"Now?" Laura threw open her hands. "He'd have to go *now?*" Just then, James stepped into the house, and Laura spun to glare at him, shocked and angry. "Now?"

"Aye, Laura," James replied calmly, coming to her. "I couldn't o'erleap this opportunity. Think upon it. I'll be over and back before our wedding day. It will—"

"Ya'd be a runaway, James! I won't have ya a slave, and wait another seven years to marry ya." Her throat was tight with anger.

"Nay, Laura." Her father reached for her. "Mr. Morris won't find him."

"So this was yar idea, Papa, that he should go alone?"

James frowned. "How is this any different than—"

"Ya didn't answer me," she raged at her father, at James. Tears streaked her flushed cheeks. "I can't—"

"Laura!" Hanna snapped, silencing Laura's storm.

"Laura. *Acushla.*" James tried to put an arm around her.

"*Acushla, Acushla,* James!" She shrugged him off. "Ya did this without talking t'me!"

Bjorn whispered, "*Acushla?*" Hanna shook her head. Neither of them knew Irish.

James persisted, "Morris would never let me go, if I told him. He'd think t' sell my term. He may search for me, but won't look far. And not for long. By Wednesday, I'll be in Yorktown. I'll board and be away before—"

"It will never work," fumed Laura, shaking her head. "They always look for runaways at the naval docks first. Ya know that!."

He wrapped her in his arms and whispered, "It will be alright."

Laura was quiet a moment, then pulled away from him and walked out of the house. He followed quickly. They talked by the garden. She cried. He tried to explain. She had been right before—he had to go. But he would never risk her to the sea, to Bailyn, to Richard. He had to go alone. Couldn't she see that? And if some harm came to him, she would be free to marry. This was best done now. Not later. Not two years from now. Not after a wedding. Not with children on the way. Now.

"I don't know what I'd do without ya," said Laura as he finished. She had finally stopped crying and was now leaning her back against a hickory tree that stretched its tired old branches high over the road.

"Nor could I bear life without ye." He kissed her. "Whether I win or lose this matter, I'll be back for ye, Laura. I will. And I'll write ye as often as I can."

"I as well," she whispered with a pensive nod.

James inhaled deeply, then blew it out. "I'll have to leave in the morning."

"I hate this," she said, her bottom lip quivering. "Why did I ever tell ya to go? If ya get hurt I'll never forgive myself. Never. I'll hate myself forever."

He held her close, gently pulling her face to his chest, then stroked her golden hair. "Ye know ye were right. I have been running all my life from this. From Richard. I can never be the man ye need, the man I must be for ye, if I don't do this now. Ye gave me the greatest gift beyond yer love. Ye gave me myself. My truth. My life. My youth. *You* did that. Now I can only make good yer gift. 'Tis my duty."

"Yar duty is to return to me, James Annesley."

"Aye. Return, I will. I will bring myself back to ye, here in Virginia. I swear to ye."

She touched his mouth. "Don't swear upon it."

"But I do. We'll marry and have children. We'll grow old together. I promise, my sweet Laura. Ye must be strong now. Ye must let me go."

CHAPTER 21

October 6, 1742. RAN AWAY, this Monday morning, from Duncan Morris of Richmond, Virginia, an Irish servant man, James Annesley, straight, well made, and of a fresh complexion; about 27 years of age, five feet 10 or 11 inches, has green eyes, scar on left cheek, a smiling way of speaking to strangers, wears his own hair, light brown colour'd, which he mostly wears tied behind in a club; had on with him a half worn beaver hat, a blue great coat, silk scarf, white county cloth jacket, leather breeches, and is a tolerable likely fellow. Whoever takes up and secures the said Servant, so that his Master may have him again, shall have Four Pounds Reward, and reasonable charges paid by Duncan Morris.

— *The Virginia Gazette*, October 8, 1742

He was alone with her in an alley off De Grasse Street, obliged to keep his eyes sealed for her to appear. Embracing him. Tangibly there. She cooed at him vibrantly. She was proud of him. She said he was brave. Said he was right to go. He could see her eyes. Paired oceans absorbing him, glowing a nameless color relegated to stars, angels, to delusory dreams. Her warmth was near, brushing against him. He could feel her, that night, that last night they were together. When they made love. When only they were alive. Before he left. Now he was gone. He inhaled. Opening his eyes, he looked around. He blew the empty air from within him. It left him as she did. And now she was gone.

After five days and nights, covering ninety miles, he was finally in Yorktown. He had footed the mud roads, fields, creek beds, hid in barns, crossed the James River at Jamestown, spoke to no one, ate what he carried, avoided any eyes, slipped south of Williamsburg, across the soggy peninsula and down the Great Run Creek, over the crowded Tobacco Road to the endless wharves of Yorktown. Now he was tired and hungry and rethinking everything. He had only twelve shillings and his clothes, his boots, his hat, and the key on its leather wrapped in a paper on which she had written, *Be safe my Acushla*. And he had his wit, he reminded himself. Fourteen years earlier he had come past this point of the Chesapeake in shackles, carrying not much less. Four-teen years of struggle. He had lived as many years in the Colonies as he lived in Ireland, perhaps more. What had he learned? Or did it matter at all? No, none of it really mattered, he told himself. Not now. Not in this alley. He was where it had all begun, in a damn alley. But even that didn't matter. All that mattered was what was here and now before him. And for that whole quan-dary he chided himself. His clothes and twelve shillings indeed. What a fool he had been. Twelve shillings would not be enough. He would starve to death before ever seeing Ireland. And there what would he do? Hire a solicitor? He imagined himself wandering Dublin again—only now a grown man skulking from one solicitor to another, scrounging charity. Captain Bailyn pursuing him like a wolfhound. It was a dullard's plan. But he could not return to Richmond. Its constables were trailing him. He could feel them. And he had seen the runaway announcement. Now bounty hunters were surely in pursuit as well. But only a four-pound reward? At least it said he was tolerable and well made. He was committed, invested. Nothing could alter that. He must focus on one thing—not getting caught. Nothing else mattered. Not food. Not sleep. Not worrying. Not anything. He had made it this far. He must find the *Kathleen*, run her gangway, disappear between her decks and be gone. Blackwell said she would be tied alongside at the main wharf, flying an orange and white jack below her standard. After an hour of searching up from the south, James had still not seen her. He estimated he had another hour before dark.

The wharf, dock bay and harbor beyond were choked with more ships than he could have imagined in one place. There were hundreds. Maybe a thousand if one counted the small ketches and skiffs, the sloops, the frig-ates, schooners and in the distance the ships-of-the-line, coming in, sailing out, anchored in the mouth of the river. Almost all flew Union Jacks of one size or another, most massive and draping. Many with Royal Navy pennants and man-of-war flags. A monstrous British armada. Probably part of the West Indies campaign, he guessed. Perhaps the entire campaign fleet under the command of Admiral Vernon. Though he believed Vernon was already in Jamaica from the reports he had read. Recent newspaper accounts had detailed a new war with the Spanish. He had seen solicitations for seamen, promises of prizes, uncountable riches and immense spoils. That meant hun-dreds of men ambling Yorktown were also runaways, like him. Only they were attempting to find work, passage of some sort, to conspicuously disap-pear—which was risky at best as the streets were undoubtedly crawling with bounties. It was a dance between two starving lots, the poor runaways and the poor bounties, each seeking a reward, to return home with a jingle in their pocket. Who won depended mostly on raw instincts for the hunt, the chase, avoidance and capture. For many runaways the only hope was to be quickly pressganged onto a man-of-war. Always good for the Royal Navy. They needed more men to fight, to die. James thanked God for his fortune. At least he had his passage arranged on a merchantman. Though he feared the pressgangs more than the constables, he tried to force himself to not dwell on either. To worry was to stay still. To stay still was to get caught. To be caught meant seven more years of slavery, or to die of malaria off some Spanish island. Damn. Everyone passing the alleyway had the face of a pressganger or bounty. He was worrying again.

His body receded further into the shadows while his mind tried to rally him back into the open, back to the long open wharf. He studied what he could see from there—the forest of topgallants over the roofs, beyond Water Street. He scanned the thicket of poles and arms and ropes and flags for the orange colors of the *Kathleen*. He knew it was ridiculous but he stayed anyway. Up the alley a door creaked open, startling him. He turned, hiding his face from whoever was coming. He heard a metallic scratch. He glanced around to see a cragged old woman scraping a pan into the sewer trough. The image instantly transported him to the stinking alleys of Dublin, the Long Alley rats, Copper Alley with its chalked skull. He shuddered. It was time to leave the alley. To never return. The shriek of a man in severe pain split the air. James jumped, spun, crouched, turned, looking around wide-eyed. The sound had come from within the building behind him. The old woman was watching James. The man cried out again, then another voice shouted, "Hold him! Hold him!" Then more thrashing and moaning.

"Ye nocks?" the plump hag asked James. She was closer now. He could smell her foulness. She peered at him, awaiting an answer as if he had understood the question.

"Ye nocks?" she repeated with a gin drinker's crackle, a gnarled finger pointing away.

"Next? For what?" he muttered, turning to leave. The loud moaning continued.

"Doc's plierin' teeth. Ye nocks?"

"Nay!"

She waddled in front of him and her eyes came alive. "Lookin' for a lil' swivin', eh?"

"Swivin'?" He smiled meekly. "Nay, ma'am. I'm best on m'way now."

She curled her lips back in what might have been a smile and revealed her absent teeth. "Magic with m'mouth, I am. And only a ha'shillin' for ye," she wheedled, before erupting in a wrenching cough.

Giving her a half-smile, a bless you, and a tip of his hat, James was past her and out onto De Grasse Street where he turned on Water Street now filled with seamen, merchants, women and children, wagons and horses, streets smelling of horse manure and boiled beef. He brushed shoulders, kept his eyes averted, kept moving, crossed the street where he could, pacing quickly toward the wharves. Keep moving. Don't look at them, he told himself. He had to find the *Kathleen*. A symphony of ship bells rang out the first-dog watch, the sound echoing softly against the shanties, taverns, the Custom House, the churches and homes. He stopped, unsure if he was going the right way. Then resumed. It was getting darker quicker than expected. A waft of fresh bread tightened his stomach. Only a bit longer. He regained a swift step. Only a bit. Soon he would be aboard the *Kathleen*, eating with the second-dog watch. He walked past the colossal war ships. He would keep working north now.

A group of seamen stepped boisterously from a tavern and into James's path. He shuffled to avoid them, darting his gaze to the dirt. "Ho there!" one exclaimed in a loud Irish brogue. James kept walking, passing them into the street, into the maze of people. "Ye there! Stop!" it came again. This time James dared a glance back. The group was laughing about something. All but one—the one staring at James. Through the flicker of faces and wigs, horses trotting by, the sounds and dirt, a slight fog forming, James only saw the man's eyes. They were on him. An alley cat locked on a mouse. James kept going, but he felt the eyes remain. Compelled, he looked back again. He could scarcely see the man, the eyes now. Gone. Then back again. In an opening here and there, between the people. There they were. Not menacing, just fixed, almost curious in their demeanor. Why was he still staring? Damn, he recognized me from the announcement! He's a constable from Richmond! Damn! Another glance. There was something piercing, something familiar in the man's eyes, the way he focused on James. A jaunting car momentarily blocked their view, then cleared. The man was still there. Panic hit James. He picked up his pace, made three turns, backtracked down an alley, and didn't walk nor breathe easier till he was back on Water Street, well out of view of those eyes. He was shaking on the inside. Find the *Kathleen*. Find the *Kathleen*. He forced his mind back.

Fog was dropping, ushering the following darkness. He passed ship after ship docked bow to stern, their hulls moving up and down, tied alongside the wharf. He studied the jacks. He scolded himself for waiting so long on De Grasse Street. He should not have stopped. Now this was becoming useless. How could he see an orange-and-white jack in this thick grayness? He moved closer to the ships, reading their sterns. The *Montclair*. The *Fortitude*. He would find her. The *Monarch* and *Warwick*. He would not ask anyone. The *St. David* and the *Hillsome*. Certainly not one of these seamen or marines. Not anyone. The *Falmouth* and the *Breda*. They all had bounty eyes, the look of constables on the prowl. No talking. The *Good Hope*. Keep moving. She is here. *The Guernsey*. Somewhere.

And she was. Over an hour later, he found her. He couldn't help grinning, thanking himself for keeping going, for not giving up. She had been nowhere near the main dock. She was a half-mile north, sandwiched longwise between the hulls of what appeared to be two British warships whose seamen were crowding the pier. He approached slowly. By the light of the dock lamps he could see her, a merchantman, an orange and white jack, the name *Kathleen* on her stern. It was her. He watched the seamen closely, then slipped into the black space between round hogsheads, tobacco barrels standing eight-foot upright on the wharf. He would wait till the pier was mostly empty, then walk slowly along her bow, careful to not draw attention, then hurry across her gangway and find Captain…. Was he on board? What if he wasn't? Could he be sure? What if Captain Blackwell was spending the night ashore? The first mate might hand him over for the four pounds. He could not go till morning, till he was certain Blackwell was aboard. He felt in the dark, further in, finding a hidden gap where three hogsheads were pushed together. He gathered a soft pile of coiled ropes and plopped down. His stomach ached hollow. He leaned over, drifting in heavy nods. Soon he was dreaming of a ship named *Acushla*. A toothless woman shoving him overboard. A man with the piercing eyes pulling him ashore.

—m—

Awakened by an urgent need to relieve himself, James eased onto the pier. Cold first light set the mist aglow as it rose over the York River with the Chesapeake beyond. His feet were cramped, his right arm dead, and his stomach growled a cacophony of base expletives. A pair of red eyes were watching him. He stretched his back, then kicked at the rat, shooing it away. He could see the *Kathleen* a bit more clearly. Her name painted in orange on her green stern. She was quiet, rocking her inhabitants slowly, not a soul on her decks or gangway. He urinated off the pier then returned to his nest of ropes. He pulled the wrapped key from his pocket, considered it a moment, then slipped it around his neck.

An hour later he was again awakened, this time by a warship's morning bells. Now the fog was completely gone and the hogsheads were stretching long shadows down the wooden pier. He stepped into the open, then immediately staggered back, astounded by the sight before him. Docked immediately behind the *Kathleen* was a massive British war ship. He had known it was there, but hadn't realized the entirety of its size. He stared at the hull a city block long dotted with three decks of gunports, room for over eighty cannon, below towering masts, the massive Union Jack nearly touching the poop deck, the broad pendant flicking clouds. "M'God!" he muttered, humbled by the formidable strength. He had read about these. It was a Royal Navy man-of-war, first class. An armada in itself with over eight hundred men. He could see many of them high in her rigging, others along the rails. On her stern he read: *H. M. S. PRINCESS CAROLINE.* He leaned against a dock house wall, settling in to watch for the captain of the *Kathleen.* But his gaze was on the *Caroline.*

By ten o'clock, the three hogsheads had been loaded aboard the *Kathleen*, the wharves were crowded with seamen, and he still hadn't seen Captain Blackwell. The sun, stretching to get over the *Princess Caroline,* was throwing a gigantic shadow across the *Kathleen,* graying the smaller ship's rising sail, darkening her hull and the greenish water around her. He studied the decks, looking for Blackwell. He had to be there. He noticed crewmen in the *Kathleen's* ratlines working the rigging, setting her forecourse for departure. Below skiffs were in the water, tow ropes secured for... *Departure!* The *Kathleen* was about to get underway! He quickened. He had to get aboard. What was he doing? Why had he been standing there? Crewmen were near the gang board, preparing to pull it in. James sprinted along the pier, cutting through a group of seamen and ship-chandlers, and knocked over a stack of galley crates as he ran for the gangway. *Leave the gangway!* he shouted silently. Men stared as he passed and some shouted, but he ignored them, focusing only on boarding. He was almost there, almost to safety. He hit the wooden gangplanks at full speed, but then stopped short, avoiding a collision with two crewmen dragging a last sea chest up. "Pardon me!" he blurted, panting, his mind shouting at them to get out of his way. They ignored him. He was in the open. "Please sirs, I must get aboard," he barked.

The crewmen just scowled at him. "Hold yerself, lackey."

Then James heard the worst thing he could have imagined at that moment, or any other moment since he left Richmond. A voice shouted, "Jemmmmy! Jemmmmy!"

"M'God!" James shuffled back, head snapped around.

"Ho there! Jemmmy! Up here!"

James searched frantically, looking up into the ratlines of the *Kathleen*, back across the wharf, the piers, everywhere. But he couldn't see the fool who was shouting. Must be another Jemmy. Stop panicking, he scolded himself. Stop it!

"Jemmmmy!"

Yes, another James, another Jemmy. Keep moving.

"James Annesley!"

"O' Christ!" He said aloud, freezing, mind racing. *It must be Blackwell— the damn fool!* Suddenly he leaped on the sea chest and over it, shoving the crewmen aside, ignoring the hail of curses pelting him as he reached the ship. He sprinted for the stern of the *Kathleen*, jumping over chains and blocks, pushing men, pivoting around the capstan, then climbed to the quarterdeck and raced to the far side, sliding to a slippery stop beyond the shrouds. Panting, he leaned over the starboard railing, his heart pounding. Alright. At least he was safe on board.

"Jemmmmy! Up here!"

"For the love of Christ!" A dark fluttering motion caught James's eye. It was down the length of the *Kathleen*, beyond her bow, up, almost in line with the sun. He saw the silhouette of a man high on the poop deck of the *Princess Caroline* waving his arms wildly, swinging a black cloth in a wide arc over his head. *Who the bloody-hell is that?* James held up a hand, shielding his eyes from the sun. The seaman was gesturing something else, waving his hand. A signal of some kind. Then it came into focus. The man was holding up three fingers, sweeping them back and forth, high in the air.

"Jemmmy!"

"Seán?" The name tumbled from his mouth.

"Jemmmy!"

"M'God!" he breathed. No, the man was too old. "Seán?" he yelled back. "Aye! Seán!" came the reply. "Jemmy!"

Seán? He had to get off the *Kathleen* before she was away! James turned and ran down the weather deck, thinking of nothing but to get clear before they pulled the gangway. It was too late, the gangway was in, the bow was coming around.

"What the devil!" Captain Blackwell appeared from nowhere, putting out a hand to stop James. "What are you doing, Mr. Annesley?"

James didn't stop. Besides, how could he answer? He didn't know what he was doing. Only that he had to get off the *Kathleen*. "Sorry, sir!" he yelled over his shoulder. "Changed m' mind!" He shoved past a cook, then two crewmen manning the pier ropes. There was nothing left to do. He leaped from the side and fell, crashing into the cold harbor water. Flopping to the surface, unable to swim, he flailed, thrashing for the pier ladder. The water pulled at him, doubling his weight. Men on the wharf were pointing, but no one moved to help. Grasping the ladder below the waterline, he pulled at the rungs, lifting himself and his overflowing boots up to the top of the dock wall.

"Ye're a fool," said a man as James gathered himself to his feet, the cold water coursing down and off of his head and coat. His hat was gone. He soggy-stumbled toward the *Caroline*.

Two British marines in red coats were attending that gangway. "Halt!"

James quickly complied. "Aye. I'm stopped," he panted, dripping. "Need t' get—"

"Mr. Annesley?" The question came from a midshipman at the top of the gangway.

"Aye. I am," James said, his heart beating wildly.

"Seaman Kennedy cannot remove himself from his post. Wishes you to meet him on the hour at the Swan."

Seaman Kennedy Seán? "Very well," James mumbled. The midshipman was gone. "The Swan," James repeated. He looked at the two marines. "The Swan?"

"A tavern," one replied. "On Main. Near Ballard Street."

"Thank ye," James offered quietly, still shock stunned, astounded and shivering wet. He scanned the *Princess Caroline* again, but didn't see Seán. This was absurd. Astonishing. Clearly impossible. But real. Was it? How could it be? His mind bickered, an angry crowd of thoughts trying to shout the others down. Backing away, he gaped up into the warship's thicket of shrouds as if he might see Seán again. Finally, he turned, melding into the crowd and walked down the pier to the next row of docks. Near the end, he turned back. The square sails of the *Kathleen* were swelling in the morning wind, pushing her into the Chesapeake, to the Atlantic beyond, bound for Ireland. He watched her. Just below her billowing standard was her orange and white jack, fluttering, snapping, waving farewell. She was leaving without him. She was gone.

Richard Tighe, examined — "I heard no more of the boy after his leaving Dublin, a matter of fourteen or fifteen years ago, till I received a letter about him from a friend in Jamaica, while Admiral Vernon was in the West Indies, in which he related the most amazing story of James Annesley encountering a childhood friend by chance in Virginia. He then related the troubles and misfortunes that the boy had gone through. The friend assisted in the removal of Mr. Annesley from America. It was later related on to me the friend's name being Seán Kennedy."

— trial transcript, *Annesley v. Anglesea*, 1743

CHAPTER 22

Should auld acquaintance be forgot,
And never brought to min'?
Should auld acquaintance be forgot,
And days o' auld lang syne?

For auld lang syne, my dear,
For auld lang syne,
We'll tak a cup o' kindness yet
For auld lang syne!

— *Auld Lang Syne,* Robert Burns, 1788

The Swan Tavern was stuffed with seamen and sprinkled with whores. For a dire moment, James thought one was the old alley hag till she revealed a slightly younger face and full head of hair. He chose an empty table near the back, a step from the cavernous stone fireplace where logs blazed, crackling, sending sparks up the great chimney to battle the afternoon chill. Its warmth began to dry him. He sipped a jar of beer and waited, trying to slow his anxious breathing, to idle himself, keeping an eye across the raucous room, watching the door for Seán. As he adjusted to the golden smoky dimness, he began studying the faces around him. Was the bearded one a constable? The one in the fur hat, was that the look of recognition? Would one of them come haul him away at musket-point? But none seemed to pay him much mind, which pleased him immensely. They all appeared seamen of some sort or another, navy or otherwise, sun dried, wind battered, and salt-water hardened. Some quiet, playing whist or working the iron tavern puzzles. Most a rowdy lot. Except the ruddy-cheeked round man at the table beside him. The man was alone. Silent. A tankard of beer in one hand, the other clutching a soggy piece of bread turned soupspoon. From his attire he was plainly not seaworthy. Something landed, though not of money either. A tradesman perhaps. The man kept a sharp eye on the others, listening intently, then scribbling notes in a parchment book. A writer perhaps. He reminded James of Mr. Morris, how Morris looked when scouting stories.

Yet, of what consequence was it who these men were? Perhaps there was a constable among them. Or seamen seeking conscripts. What if this fat man wrote his runaway announcement for the Virginia Gazette? He had chosen this path, to stay in Yorktown, to see Seán, to let the *Kathleen* fly. The minutes passed. They ticked by slowly. No Seán. James weighed his options, the scenarios. Perhaps he should have stayed on the *Kathleen*. How could he? Knowing Seán was so near, of course not. He reasoned one of three things would happen now: he would be returned under arms to Richmond for an additional term—he would return by his own accord and plead Morris's lenience—or he would sail to Dublin with the Royal Navy. He shook his head with a silent chuckle—he was to be pressganged after all by his own choosing. He exhaled a sigh at the sheer absurdity of it all, then sipped his thick warm beer, wiped the foam from his lip and listened to the room.

"Ya're right, begob! T' hell with Port Royal!" a scabby exclaimed to his mates. They ardently echoed the sentiment. "Vernon will rot us all on that island, that cesspool!" A young crewman stood with hands clasped behind his back, then he puffed his cheeks and stomped about the wooden floor. The men around him hooted. "Aye, aye, Admiral!" shouted one. "Ahoy Ol' Grogam!," yelled another. The parading young man stuffed his right hand into his open coat, dramatically flaring the front flaps wide and marched about sternly. Laughter gushed the tavern.

James chuckled, feeling oddly at ease with this place, these men.

A swishy wench approached. "Nother pint fer ye?"

"That'd be grand," he replied, almost in a whisper. His gaze made its rounds—the clamorous seamen, the wigwagging whores, the long bar, the entrance, the plump beside him—snap back to the door. A man was there. Something familiar. Grizzled. Hair flattened wet, a hopeless attempt at civility. His beady, smiling Irish eyes were surveying the room, then locked on James. By the time James sprang to his feet and stepped from the table, Seán was already running toward him, oblivious of the men he dodged. He grabbed James, knocking him backward, laughing deliriously, hugging him. "Jemmy! I can't believe!"

"Seán, m'God!" yelled James, stammering, beaming.

"Damn ye, Jemmy!" Seán shouted, grinning. "I thought ye were dead, I did. Then I read the runaways and figured ye'd be headin' here. I've been lookin' fer yer ugly mug since! When I saw ye yesterday, I wasn't sure, but—"

"Kennedy?" asked one of the seamen.

Seán beamed. "Aye, Chester, this is the friend of m'youth, Jemmy." He shook James by the coat. "Jemmy Annesley! I thought he was gone from 'dis bloody world."

James could not take his eyes off Seán. It was too inconceivable—Seán Kennedy, standing right in front of him, the same mischievous eyes, the same smile, that same unruly mop of hair. Yet somehow, Seán had changed. "Ye've gotten old, ye old Irish sot!" James teased.

"And ye haven't?" snorted Seán. "M'God, how long's it been? Fifteen years? Twenty?"

"Fourteen."

"Bloody hell!" Seán shook his head. They stood face to face, grasping each other by the arms. "Ye look fit, Jemmy. Have ye been here all this time?"

"I have. Look upon ye, ye navy man!"

The tavern door flew open, and two men in white campaign wigs stepped inside with three aides and a marine in tow. Seán's smile disappeared as he released James and snapped to attention. The two men made their way toward the fireplace. Screeching chairs and rumbling shoes filled the room as every seaman jumped to his feet, eyes on the officers. The older one was a head above the other, menacingly large. The tavern keeper appeared. "Good day Admiral. Captain Knowles. May I offer ye gentlemen—"

"No thank you, Mr. Smithers," replied the admiral, removing his three-cornered blue hat, tucking it abruptly beneath his arm.

The captain also removed his hat. "Aye, Smithers, just a bit of rum would—"

"Nothing at present," the admiral interrupted.

Knowles winked at the keeper, then turned to Seán. "Master Seaman, this your man?"

"Aye, Captain." Seán nudged James forward. "May I present Mr. James Annesley."

"Is that so?" The tall admiral stepped closer with an inspector's gaze. The aides, two lieutenants and a warrant officer, stayed close, silently watching James, listening to everything. The marine remained near the door.

"Jemmy, this is Admiral Vernon," Seán said firmly.

"Sir. I'm honored," James offered with a faint tip of his head while looking directly into the man's green eyes. As amazed as he was to stand before the famous Admiral Vernon, he was still reeling with the inexplicable presence of

Seán. He extended a hand and was pleased the admiral shook it.

"And I as well, Mr. Annesley." Admiral Vernon's face was strong and imposing, with a broad forehead and long chin. He pointed at the scar along James's cheek. "The mark of a dragoon."

"Stirrup, sir. When I was a boy."

Vernon chuckled, nodding his approval. "Bless my soul, you are him indeed."

Knowles arched an eyebrow at Seán.

"And this is our flag captain," Seán interjected carefully. "Captain Knowles."

James turned politely. "Captain. Pleased to meet ye, sir."

"Shall we sit?" asked Vernon, stepping back, his question an order. The four moved to James's table near the hearth and took seats. The others remained standing, all close. Behind them the room also sat with another loud scuttering of chairs. The hum of conversation resumed, only now dampened, peppered with curious remarks about the admiral's presence and wonder about James. All but the lone man. He remained distractedly dabbing his soup.

"Mr. Annesley," began Knowles, "Mr. Kennedy is fond of stories. He has spun us many yarns of his youth. Including much of you, sir."

"Indeed? I confirm only my heroics are true," James said, hoping for humor.

"What heroics?" Seán huffed, playing along.

Knowles continued, unamused. "Upon discovering your presence in Yorktown, he relayed such to me, and I to the admiral. Thus we are here."

Vernon had two fingers under his wig, scratching his scalp. "I shall be direct. I am familiar with your family." He paused, watching James's reaction.

"If I may ask, which sir?" James asked. "The Annesleys or the Sheffields?"

"Both, assuredly," he replied, then smirked. "When I'm not smashing Spanish privateers, my favored occupation—" Several gave an approving cheer and he waited for them to settle. "Then I'm found in the House of Lords contending with that other breed of blood-sucking vermin. I can attest many are so aptly described." His eyes fixed on James again. "And they too tell stories, Mr. Annesley. Some true. Some lies. Some honestly retold. Some slanderous, contrived for political gain. Some told to set matters straight. A most curious one was that of a young lad, the son of an Earl, cut with a spur, sold into servitude, his title robbed of him."

"Aye, sir," James said solemnly, his breathing nearly gone.

"I am familiar with your story, Mr. Annesley." Vernon rubbed his crooked nose. Everything else, his eyes, his face, everything about him was fronting James, focused on him. "And I know Richard Annesley. I know his perjury. Of which I was never inclined to believe."

James was momentarily stunned just at the utterance of the name. "My uncle lives?"

"Aye. On occasion he takes that appearance. But not in quality. He's a chuff. An odious man. My fellow lords and I must transact with him in Parliament. An unpleasant endeavor as he is a liar of the worst class." The admiral raised his hand, materializing the tavern keeper. "Mr. Smithers, we'll have a brandy round."

James's mind ran the fence of facts and events, unable to hold on anything in particular. There were just too many horses in the corral. Everything was coming too quickly. He wanted to stop everyone and talk only with Seán. How had he become a seaman? When did he see him yesterday? What had he told these men?

"You are a runaway?" asked Captain Knowles, breaking the brief silence.

"Some might say so," James cautiously replied. "I am…was…returning to Ireland."

Seán cut in. "On that wee tub ye were boardin'?"

Just the sound of Seán's voice had James beaming again. To think he was right there, right beside him. "The captain's an acquaintance," James replied. He put a hand on Seán's shoulder. Both men smiled at each other and for a moment James felt as if he might choke up. But tears at this moment would never do, not in front of a White Admiral of the Royal Navy.

Vernon leaned in. "So, are you prepared to tangle with your imposter?"

"There is no better time, sir."

"That's courage, Mr. Annesley." Vernon gave an affirming nod. "Mind you remember it in England. Hold it tight."

"I will sir." James looked at the man curiously. In England?

The keeper returned with the brandy. "Here lads," said Vernon, standing, thus pulling everyone else to their feet. He distributed the small bumpers then lifted his high. The others followed. "To the health and courage of Mr. Annesley. The true Lord Anglesea!"

"To Lord Anglesea!" they all replied, including Seán, then tipped their drinks.

"Mr. Annesley, you are surprised?" Vernon asked.

"To be called Lord Anglesea," James said softly. "Aye, surprised."

"You are the Earl of Anglesea, are you not?" The admiral lifted his chin at James.

James glanced at Seán. "Aye, sir. I am."

"So you are." Vernon clapped James on the back, and with that the air decompressed, the sails luffed, formality slackening as if left where it stood. Before the toast James was suspect. Now he was avowed, accepted, and in this presence, an English Earl.

After everyone resumed their seats, Knowles began. "I was in Dublin not long after you disappeared. I remember the notices posted for you."

"They placed notices, did they?" James asked. "Who—"

"M' father, Jemmy," said Seán. "He had advertisements printed for yer discovery. Kept them posted for months."

"Fynn?" James brightened. "How is yer father?"

"He is in good health. In New Ross. He'll be so pleased t' hear ye're well."

"Perhaps you will see him soon," declared Vernon, reclaiming the conversation. "You'll sail with us on my flagship, His Majesty's *Princess Caroline*. Once to Port Royal, in Jamaica, you can transfer to the *Falmouth* and sail for England. Of course, you'll sail as an officer of your station. Will First Lieutenant suffice?"

James knew his mouth was again holding a ridiculous grin. He nodded. "Yes, Admiral. That will be most kind of ye. Far more than I could ever have imagined."

"And you, seaman." Vernon peered at Seán. "What is your name?"

Seán popped to standing attention. "Master Seaman Seán Kennedy, sir."

Vernon turned to Knowles. "This man is to serve as officer's mate for Lieutenant Annesley, responsible for his well being. See to it that he transfers to the *Falmouth* as well." He stood, and again the room clamored. He shook Seán's hand. "You've done the navy a great service, Master Seaman Kennedy, bringing this man to me."

"Thank ye, sir!" Seán was nodding, smiling.

"I am charging you with his health. Do you understand me?"

"Aye, sir."

"Until relieved you are to remain his aide."

"Aye, sir."

"Very well then." Admiral Vernon gathered his hat and Knowles gulped his brandy. "Lord Anglesea," Vernon continued. "May I beseech a favor?"

"But of course."

"When you've recovered your title from your imposter uncle, you'll take your place among your peers in the House of Lords." He hesitated, looking at James.

"I am certain, sir."

"When you do, then we'll talk as brethren, and I'll remind you of this day when I saved your arse." He winked knowingly. "Then perhaps you'll assist me in rebuilding His Majesty's fleets. How's that?"

"Aye, Admiral. And so I will."

"Very well. I'll see you on board, Lieutenant. After Cape Henry, I hope you'll dine with me and tell us the length of your story."

"Indeed, sir," replied James stiffly, still reeling from the whole affair.

Admiral Vernon walked away with Knowles and the other officers close behind. Just as they reached the door, Vernon turned back and announced loudly, "Men, your attention please." He dramatically shoved his hand in his grogam coat causing a flurry of chuckles across the room. "I am honored that you would name your new rum ration after me. Mr. Smithers, if you will, a round of *grog* for everyone!" He grinned, donned his hat and left as nervous laughter erupted behind him, with many asking "How did he know?"

As the commotion abated, James and Seán sat again by the fire and began to talk, to stitch together those fourteen years, to relive their youth, regaling stories of their lives apart, finding common threads, moments when they were near, weaving lost time and space together month by month, year by year, tragedy by tragedy, joy by joy, sewing the semblance of one past, the way it should have been, every significant event told through and through up and till that moment, that shared present, that whole cloth that dared not be questioned due the miraculous nature of its very occurrence. The tavern keeper brought them drinks and dinner for no charge. After two hours, James had had enough of the fat man's apparent eavesdropping and stood to confront him. But before a word could be exchanged, the man gathered his things, paid the keeper and left.

CHAPTER 23

October 10, 1742. A seaman lately entered on board the *Princess Caroline*, to sail to England on the *Falmouth*, is said to be the right Earl of Anglesea. He declares that he was sent from Ireland by a certain Nobleman, in his 13th year, and sold as a slave for seven years into Pennsylvania, before the expiration of which having attempted his escape, he was retaken and by a law of the country oblig'd for his elopement to serve nine years more. A gentleman who was his schoolfellow, and at whose father's house he boarded, believes him to be the same person. Another gentleman who remembers the advertisements published when the boy was missing, corroborates this account. Admiral Vernon has shown him so much regard as to make him a lieutenant. We can expect the *Falmouth* to arrive in Bristol early next year.

— *The London Daily Post*, Extracts from our
correspondent in Virginia. February 12, 1743

A cool breeze swept down the slope of an Irish hillside, swirling, gathering wintered leaf cannonballs to explode against the garden walls of Dunmain House. Scaling those defenses, the bluster whipped into the house, through the drawing room, puffing flames and riffling a newspaper held by lanky hands in lace cuffs. Richard Annesley's eyes, cold black marbles, twitched back and forth as he took in each phrase, each word, each threat, each breath, each tick from the parlor clock. He held his patrician's face taut, unexpressive. Then, with a priggish lift of his nose, he examined Patrick Higgins before him.

Higgins shifted his weight from one boot to the other, otherwise dissembling any regard for the summons. Seeing Richard's glare, he parried it with a turn of his head, glancing over his shoulder. Behind him, in a grey leather, wrinkled chair was a grey, wrinkled, leathery man with a face pinched at a crow's nose, beady eyes through sharp squints below a white wig that to Higgins seemed comical in its inaptness, gauche for the base man it adorned. Though the three men in that room were within five years of age, the previous fourteen years had imbued each entirely differently: no doubt who was richest, who most alive, who most inconceivably decayed.

"M'lord" asked Captain Bailyn, "what do ye wish?"

Richard sneered at Higgins. "This papist knows."

"Do I?" Higgins half-asked.

"You bloody well do," Richard growled. "You'll give the boy a dog's death."

Higgins shook his head. "James is no boy. And I am not yar lackey. Not yar hireling. Ol' Bailyn here may still polish yar apples, but not I."

"Don't be cocksure with me!" shouted Richard, jumping to his feet, the newspaper scrunched in his fist. "We have an accord." He moved around the table, advancing on Higgins.

Higgins stepped back. "T'was many years ago. I fail to remember—"

"Live up your end," Richard spewed, "or I'll cut your liver out and feed it to my dogs!"

Higgins stopped his retreat. "I made no bargain."

Richard's face suddenly eased. He picked at his teeth with a fingernail. Though the Earl's wealth might have assisted his fine features to appear young—the French crèmes, Italian soaps, the absence of weathering and hardship, the perpetual strolls through the park of paramours—the effect was outweighed by the alcohol, the thick tobacco, black deception, veiled losses, the cabalistic angers, all of which oozed to the surface in occasional spots and crevassed wrinkles, a pallor of strain and distrust assembling to make his forty-six years appear ten years greater. In repose his face fell into lines of haughty calculations. His eyes, his brow, his angular features all clinched, as if in a constant state of peering through sewer fog. He turned to Bailyn. "Captain, do remind the fool of his bargain."

Bailyn huffed. "If the boy surfaced, you, Scotty goat shagger, were t' kill him. If ye hadn't sworn such I'd have slit his throat years ago. Then yers for sure."

"Mongrels, caitiffs, both of ya." Higgins muttered, shaking his head. He walked to the window where the wind cooled his flushed neck and forehead. There was nothing to do but assent to these demons. Perhaps an opportunity would avail itself at a later time, another place. But not now. He should leave, go, think, get out of this foul, dispiriting house, away from these vile men. And did he remember that bargain? Certainly. Of course. How could any man forget the miserable moment he sells his soul? He was Richard's hireling years ago under a similar threat: serve or get a highwayman's hanging. Then came that other accord, that enduring pact that now returned with James Annesley himself, both seeking retribution. He promised to kill James if James set foot in England or Ireland again—an event apparently soon to occur. A *fait accompli*. He made his bargain to save the boy, and now he must kill the boy to honor his bargain. A devil's contract to be sure. After years of peace, away from Richard, now this: a London newspaper accounts James's pending return, Higgins is summoned from Glasgow, evil angels are stirred in the land. A bargain with the devil never dies. Like a sinister star, it never fades, never disappears; yet it can only be seen in the dark. It clinches your soul. An apostate's curse lifted on pain of death; the only vehicle to true transcendence. To keep the covenant, someone must be sacrificed. But who? James? Richard? Himself? He knew. There was but one answer. He gave a profound sigh, then turned to Richard. "I'll get James for ya. But when all's done, I'll owe ya no more. Our bindings will be undone. What's more I make a new accord with ya, much like the other. If I see *you* again, or this ugly lap dog of yars," he said, pointing at Bailyn, "I'll murder ya both."

"Good lord, man, stop!" Richard sneered. "You're frightening me." He flashed an arched smirk.

"As well I should. Even bunglers have sense enough to fear a man with nothing to lose."

"Take yer leave," Bailyn barked.

Richard spoke as Higgins moved for the door. "Find him in Bristol, Higgs. Take care of the matter there. And know this: I will have eyes on you."

Higgins knowingly nodded at Bailyn, then left.

Bailyn gave a small cough.

Through the open drawing room door, Richard watched his butler usher Higgins across the marbled foyer and heard the massive front door close. Then he moved to the window to see two groomsmen bringing Higgins' horse. "Follow him to Bristol," Richard muttered, glancing at Bailyn. "Once he kills the bastard boy—or by Christ, even if he doesn't...." He took a weighty breath and looked out of the window again. Higgins was spurring his mount to a gallop, kicking up the dead leaves, disappearing beyond the grey garden walls.

Bailyn coughed again, this time with grimace and phlegm.

"See to it," Richard continued. "Neither of them may leave Bristol alive."

"T'will be my pleasure," Bailyn said slowly, emphasizing each word.

Richard moved to the giant chimneypiece and leaned on it, stirring the fire with an iron. "You must not get me associated with it. Be discrete. There must be no suspect in this matter but Higgs. Do not be seen. Certainly do not be caught. If you are, I will not help you. Do you understand?"

"Aye, m'lord," replied Bailyn, rising to his feet.

Turning to warm his backside, Richard once again read the newspaper, then closed his eyes. When he began to speak it was in a guttural whisper, a growl that resonated distant fear. "Now he will be widely known," he said. "Kill him before he finds those cur dogs allying against me. Quickly. And before they find him." He wadded the paper and watched it burn.

—⁂—

The sea was calm at dusk and the brisk air smelled almost sweet to James. Ireland and England were somewhere beyond that darkening cobalt horizon. Not far. About six days away. They would be home. Some of them. At least to England. He filled his lungs with the crisp air, then breathed it out again. They would be sailing so close to southern Ireland he might see it, perhaps smell it. The smells of County Wexford. Waterford. New Ross. Even Dunmain. A matter of miles from the southern coast, yet leagues off shore. He wished to think he missed the smell of Dunmain, or even its sound, or the look of its stone fences, something, But he barely knew the place. Could only remember the green and yellow dampness, mud, the cold stables, and the dread he felt when he left it for Dublin at the age of eight. It didn't matter. Least not for now. The *Falmouth* was not to port at Waterford—they were bound on to Bristol. Seán would go from there to Ireland, Waterford and New Ross; and hopefully James would be there too within a month or so. But for now, it was Bristol. Last he had been in Bristol, he was locked in the hold of the *Courtmain*. Fourteen years ago. His young body aching from the blows. Awaking to find his mother's chest gone.

He was nervous about arriving. He wondered at what awaited him. Probably nothing. Probably this was all a waste—the horrible journey, the bloodshed, the ocean of death that he had traversed these four months. And now, for what end? What could he hope to accomplish in Ireland? Richard would not simply remove himself from the peerage, from the Dublin properties,

from the Dunmain estate. Why would he? James knew that sooner or later
he would have to reveal himself, to declare himself the rightful Earl, to pro-
nounce his arrival and stake his claim. But to what avail? For what result? To
be ridiculed as a madman? To be tossed on his ear? To be killed? He had rolled
this over and over in his head, circling the problem, mulling it, mouthing it in
whispers against the air. It was a milling wheel driven round and round in his
brain. Only nothing came. No clarity. No solutions. No visions of a golden
path. Nothing but deep groves worn into his grinding table, etched by the
endless circling of answerless questions.

At least he was alive. And so was Seán. They had survived. After the
worst four months of his life, first in the Spanish West Indies and now on
the open Atlantic, he no longer pondered the coincidence of Seán's presence
in Yorktown, or the wonder of their reunion at the Swan. Instead, the only
marvel was that they had both survived at all. That they were there, standing,
breathing, above the water. As usual, when the memory of the dead overcame
him, he let his mind drift into Laura's arms. If only she were there. Missing
her was a hollow, painful joy. A known place that was private in its agony,
its memories, its dark corners and warm despair. He took a deep breath and
held it. Slowly releasing it, he let his eyes lose focus, transporting himself to
a vertiginous state, far away, coming to rest near her, beside her, sitting in the
loft window, the sun setting before them. Laura smiled at him, taking his
hand. He could feel the warmth of her touch. He could see her tears, hear
her dulcet voice.

"I wonder what ye're dreamin' of, Lieutenant," said Seán, stepping onto
the foc's'le of the *H.M.S. Falmouth*. He walked along the rail, then leaned on
it beside James. "Laura, no doubt."

"Aye," replied James. He was nonplussed by interruptions. And he knew
Laura was the same. One thing certain in the monotony of the sea, there
would always be other times, other moments. A continuum of silence as far
as the ocean's width. Moments where he and Laura would meet. And talk.
Later, as he did every night after darkness fell, he would return to this same
place, the ship's quadrant in hand, and chart their position. Laura would be
there too. He could wait.

"Let me figure," Seán continued. "Tonight is it the barn or the day ye
met? Or is it the *Greensleeves*? Barn, I reckon 'tis."

James bleakly grinned. "Ye're a soothsayer now, are ye?"

"I just know ye. 'Tis what I'd be thinking of. Hell, 'tis what I *do* think
of. Lived these months with her in my mind. Sorry to offend ye, my friend,

but she's in love with me. We figured 'twas time we told ye." He saw James's faraway stare. "Oh alright, don't be so chapfallen, she's in love with you too. God knows why."

Now James chuckled lightly. "Spare me yer affair with m' wife."

"Now Jemmy, don't assume I have no chance. She's not yer wife yet."

James winced, his eyes and mind racing back to the horizon. "She is to me," he whispered. "She is to me." Silence overtook them as they studied the softly churning green waves, the ship lifting and lowering them through their thoughts.

"Mind if I see her again?" Seán asked kindly.

James pulled a strip of sailcloth from his waistcoat and at its end was a small brass locket. He popped it open and showed the image to Seán. With months of water damage and exposure to salt air a thousand times, the picture barely resembled Laura at all.

"Aging quickly, that one. Bit wrinkled," smirked Seán. "Mind ye, I'll still take her from ye if she gives ye trouble."

"'Tis enough," James replied, snapping it closed. This dialogue about Laura was old, a routine they had danced countless times. Now it was over, their smiles faded, silence overtaking them yet again. They could remain for hours in quietness, beside each other, observing nothing but the undulating ocean, the barren horizon, broken only by the occasional dolphin or jumping fish. "Shame she's not here," James offered under his breath.

"Ach, ye wouldn't have wanted her in the Indies. Not Cartagena."

"Certainly not," James snapped.

"M'God," muttered Seán, miles away, "How dire 'twas."

James nodded. "Horrible."

Not long after he and Seán had transferred to the *Falmouth* in Jamaica, the entire fleet of 124 ships, including the *Falmouth*, was ordered by Admiral Vernon to sail to the northern crest of South America. There they were to bombard the city of Cartagena, seize the port, and destroy the Spanish fleet. The campaign was a dismal failure as rampant malaria and other tropical diseases beset the entire fleet. Of the 24,000 seamen, only 7,000 survived. And of the 5,000 army infantry, only 1,000 would ever return home. James and Seán were extraordinarily lucky to have been on such a senior ship as the *Falmouth*, and thus not directly engaged in the feverish battle. Instead she became a hospital ship to be held at anchor off La Boquilla, three miles up the coast. Well within earshot of the relentless barrage of cannon fire. Within sight of the burning city and ships. During those two months more burials were serviced off the deck of the *Falmouth* than Seán had witnessed during his previous nine years in the Royal Navy. More death than James could have ever imagined seeing in a lifetime. The *Falmouth* was a fetid, cursed ship of death, loved only by the sharks for its leaking blood and daily service of fresh carrion.

James and Seán, along with Tobias Smollett, a fellow seaman who had risen the ranks with Seán, became surgeon's mates. Due to James's rank, he had been afforded the opportunity to remain on deck, but there was nothing to do there except stand, pace, feel awkward and useless, while listening to the mordant shrieks from below. His skill in sea-charting came back to him with some practice, but was of little use while anchored for weeks on end. So the three of them labored together, often side-by-side, through each agonizing, blood-soaked day. Their initial shock was eventually numbed by the sheer magnitude of the suffering and death around them, and they found themselves spending hours talking and laughing together, drinking gallons of grog and telling stories, running through endless fencing drills, anything to pass the days, the minutes. Anything to forget the limbs they had sawed, hacked off that day, the blood they had mopped, the tissue they had sewn, the eyes they had closed. Sleep was an elusive luxury dispensed in two or three hour stints. Meanwhile the dying kept coming, a relentless, lame march. The few that survived vomited and defecated with a stench that even the nose scarves and burning brimstone could not abate. Many of the surgeon's mates pleaded to go to fight. Their wish granted, most soon returned to die where they began. But James and Seán, and Tobias, remained. Not out of fear of being killed in battle, as the risk of catching disease was immeasurably greater aboard the *Falmouth*. They stayed out of a blunt allegiance to the dying. Guilelessly relishing the "rooks," those rare patients, one out of fifty, mostly amputees, who not only cheated death, they recovered sufficiently to give faith that they might live to see England again. While anchored off Cartagena, it was the rooks that kept the *Falmouth* afloat, supporting a withering optimism, maintaining any semblance of promise, of purpose, of merciful hope.

Finally, six weeks ago, the battle waning, the death toll climaxing, supplies depleted beyond repair, the *Falmouth* was ordered home. She was to set course for Bristol, her berth. She pulled anchor with 507 crammed aboard: 186 seamen, surgeons and surgeon's mates, and 321 rooks. But once to sea, disaster struck: a rage of bilious fevers and malaria, bloody dysentery and typhus, ran rampant, especially through the rooks. Now the *Falmouth* was approaching England with only a 223 aboard. Only 53 were rooks, and of those at least eleven would never see the shore.

"When I get to New Ross, I'll listen about. Hear the gossip of Dunmain. See if Bailyn's on the hunt," said Seán. "Still thinking he'll be there? Hunting ye in Ireland?"

"In England, most likely. If he's still alive. Richard will send him, or someone else. Once he learns of my arrival."

"Aye, most likely," Seán said. "I reckon ye'll have a month."

"Perhaps," said James.

Seán smiled broadly. "I can't wait to tell Da ol' Seámus is alive. He'd set fire to Dunmain House if he thought it'd help."

"So he would," agreed James, chuckling, imagining the rancorous, scrappy, gentle Irishman. "Pray he leaves it be. I may want to live there someday."

Seán's eyebrows peaked.

James saw it. "If he allows me that privilege, of course. After all, as ye've said, 'tis on Kennedy land."

"Aye, Lord Anglesea, so it is. Or was."

"So it shall be again," James said, clasping Seán's arm. He lowered his voice. "Do tell Fynn how anxious I am to see him."

"Ye can count on it."

"I've missed him. More than he may ever know. Faith be. 'Twill be grand to see him."

Seán feigned hurt. "I dare say ye missed my Da more than ye missed me."

"Miss ye?" James smiled. "I was glad t' be rid of ye!"

Seán punched James's shoulder lightly. "My arse! I was the one hiding ye in Dublin, doing all the damn work, taking all the bloody risks on account—"

"Ye didn't take all the risks, now did ye?"

Seán hesitated, then sniffed. "Nay, ye're right. I didn't. Indeed, I wish I'd—"

"Ah, Seán, I'm only ribbing ye. Let's not revisit it. 'Tis the past."

Seán stood motionless for a moment before he spoke. "Aye. 'Tis. For now. But once ye get to shore, ye'll be back in it. Back in the thick of it. Yer past will come searching for ye. Hunt ye down like hounds on a wee fox."

"Jaysus, Seán! Why don't ye just throw me over! Ye sure know how to cheer a fellow."

"Nah, I was just saying—"

"I know what ye were saying," James bristled. "And ye're probably right. But there's nothing to be done. Least not out here. As they say, whatever will be, will be."

—⁓—

That same evening the falling sun was scalding the Salisbury Crags, the red sandstone ridges on Edinburgh's eastern flank. And further west, across that valley, it was setting afire the parapets of the Scottish castle itself. Daniel Mackercher stood near the Nor Loch, at the foot of the castle and smiled, watching the amber glow move toward Arthur's Seat, a knoll past the Crags. Soon that knoll too was burning. His city, his beautiful Edinburgh, was being warmed by the embers of the fading day, red and orange sparkling off Nor Loch's glazy surface, igniting the streets and buildings, the trees, the cool air. Even the Union Jacks were flashing orange. (He still flew a St. Andrew's Cross at his Highland home.) He believed it the finest city on earth. Just as it should be. Just as it had always been.

He had lived in Edinburgh, in some form or fashion, for forty-one of his forty-eight years—walking these streets first in broken orphan shoes, then regimental boots, now polished buckle brogues. It had always been his. Thus it was to Edinburgh that he returned after Joan's murder in 1728. And there in Edinburgh his acidic detestment for Richard Annesley grew blacker, year by year, punctuated on each anniversary of her death when he would drink heavily, grandly reaffirming his Dublin vows to commit the ultimate revenge. And it did little for his opinion of all things nobly British—English lords smelled of Richard's ilk, that pungent culpa, those sons of whores.

In Edinburgh, he put away his broadswords and dirks, and set about building a small, successful law practice. Weapons aside, other than the occasional dress sword, he kept himself in his Highland tartan unless before the King's Bench. He wanted a peaceful life. So it was. Though punctuated with restlessness. Known to be genuinely cheerful, every few months an unseen shadow would nevertheless succumb him, delivering a two-week melancholic stew of resentment and depression. It was then that his unabating fury over Joan's death would burst upon him in a different way: a mopey, angry sadness. A polar volcano erupting from the ocean floor. A bleakness that kept him cold—the knowledge that Richard and his men would never pay for their deeds, their crimes. Not in this realm. Richard's mortal sins were to be relegated to the justice of the afterlife. But to Mackercher that was questionable justice at best. Indeed, it was a failure of true justice. Earthly deeds required earthly retribution. But he knew the irony of his captor. He had commissioned his professional life to the system of law that proclaims justice supreme. But it was only when unbound by that very rule of law that such honest retribution could be executed, and thus prove itself superior, more fair in its finality, more complete in the balance, than anything a heavenly adjudication would afford. The paradox fed his rumbling temper.

Not long after he returned from Dublin, he married a young Lowland widow. They had twin girls who both died before the age of three. They never tried again. Never spoke of it or much else. They built a fine home south of the burgeoning city, settled into a rhythm, an ease of kindness—from separate bedrooms on separate floors, along the length of their long dining table overseen by a duteous staff, across parlors at frequent social functions, beside one another on Sunday pews. It was a good marriage. Love had died with the girls; even earlier for Mackercher—during the war when he was young, then again with Joan fourteen years ago. He focused on his work, on friends at the shooting club, on Edinburgh, his city.

And his law practice grew. He took on another solicitor partner, then another, and soon the offices comprised four solicitors, counting Mackercher, and six barristers. But that was years ago. One partner died, another group split away, and finally it was just he and one other, which suited Mackercher fine. This other fellow balanced Mackercher in the way that north balances south, and fire balances the winter cold. The man was too obsessed for Mackercher's style, too involved with the rules and punctuality and specifications of the law. Whereas Mackercher enjoyed the areas of the legal profession where a bit of lawlessness ruled, where to win meant bending things, thinking fast, winning favor with the enemy and surrounding them before they even realized a battle was afoot. This was Mackercher's strong suit. While his partner practically lived at their offices, rehearsing opening arguments and rhapsodizing long with professors of law—Mackercher was out, preparing cases. He trolled taverns for loose-lipped clerks. He was ever-reprising his role as poker-fool at the gaming tables of opposing counsel. He sipped the silver quaich with Loyalists and Jacobites alike. He sponsored pheasant and fox hunts for judges at his Highland home near Aberfoyle. He negotiated impeccable settlements rivaled only in denseness by the smoky dens where they were inevitably signed. In this manner he and his partner were a formidable team, even if no one could remember the last time they were seen together. Never socially. Once or twice at an Episcopal mass, but never in open court.

"Mr. Mackercher!"

Mackercher turned to see his fellow solicitor's young son, sprinting down St. Giles Street, a newspaper flapping in his hand.

"Mr. Mackercher!"

Mackercher watched the boy come close. "Andrew. What have ya there?"

"Father told me…to find ya." The boy was panting as he came to a stop.

"Did he?" Mackercher forced a smile, mildly perturbed at the interruption.

"Aye, sir. Said business requires ya. That ya had to return. To yar office."

"What business? Did he say?"

"Nay, sir. He just told me—"

Mackercher raised a hand. "I'm on my walk, Master Andrew." He resumed his pace.

"Aye sir, said ya'd be 'round the Nor." The boy walked alongside him.

"And so I am."

"But father said ya have urgent business and that—"

"Aye. Ya said that already."

"Ya have a guest."

Mackercher slowed. "Do I? I made no appointment."

"Aye, sir. A man ya'd be wantin' to see. And he told me to give ya this." The boy handed the newspaper to Mackercher. "Suggested ya read the back."

"All right then," muttered Mackercher, stopping, flipping the sheet. As he read it, he froze, eyes wide, mouth dropping open. "Good God!" he exclaimed. "Tell me, Andrew, the man in my office, what's his name?"

"I don't know, sir."

"Is he Irish?" Mackercher had already turned.

"I don't know, he sounded like a Scot—"

"Come now, lad! B'jingo! Let's go!" He hurried up the street, the boy close behind, both disappearing against the lagging sun.

It was nearly dark when James saw Tobias Smollett, the surgeon's mate, strolling toward them on the foc-s-le. "Good eve to ye, Tobias," James offered.

"Lieutenant Random. Seán. Where's our minds tonight?"

Seán shrugged. "Pondering Jemmy's fate, what's awaiting him when—"

"Not much to talk about," James interjected. He had still not settled with the moniker Smollett had given him: Roderick Random. Upon first introduction by Seán, Smollett had confused James with another, named Roderick, and it stuck. The Random came when weeks later James and Seán were discussing a good alias for James to use in his travels across England. Smollett had remarked that any random name would be best, as a determinate name would seem just that, and thus lend itself to discovery.

"Ach, sure there is," pressed Seán. "I saved his arse, got him into this bloody navy and now he won't listen to my advice for going ashore. Doesn't seem fair, now does it Toby? Ye know these nobles and their highbrow ways."

Smollett gave Seán a dismissive shrug. "Right, Seán."

"Ye agree with the bugger?" exclaimed James.

"Have I ever?" Smollett smiled. "Ya know, Seán, seems to me the lieutenant did *you* the favor. If he hadn't been in Yorktown for ya to stumble upon, well then, ya might've stayed aboard the *Caroline*, and ya'd most likely be lying in our between-deck now. Worse, ya might've been sent to the *Boyne*. By now ya'd be shark shite."

"Well said, Tobias!" James patted him on the back. "Well said, indeed."

"Who the bloody hell invited ye up here, Toby?" snarled Seán. "We were just havin' a pleasant discussion on the weather, and up ye pop with yer bleedin' Scottish mouth."

Smiling, James pulled Smollett aside. "Still wantin' to be a writer, do ye?"

"Aye, Roderick. That I do."

"Well then, my friend, 'tis time ye heard the epic tale of Seán and the great centipede!"

"Ach, Jemmy, ye never tell it right," protested Seán. "Don't believe him, Toby. He's an Englishman telling an Irishman's story."

"The great centipede?" asked Smollett.

"Aye," said James. "It had seventeen legs and two enormous fangs."

"Seventeen?" Smollett was ginning. "And fangs ya say?"

"Nasty fangs, aye. Seems one day this odd orange creature 'twas minding its own affairs, just crawling along, ye understand, and the hoyden Seán here sees it and screams to—"

"Ach piss off! Ye threw the damn thing on me!" yelled Seán. "Tell the story right!"

CHAPTER 24

This is the heir:
come, let us kill him,
that the inheritance may be ours.

— Luke 20:14

The morning sun shimmered off a giant white sail fluttering loose overhead, snapping back and forth in the chilly breeze. A rhythmic pop, to and fro. Its duty done, its ship to shore, the mizzen sheet flicked anxiously, as if yearning to be filled again, to return to open sea. It flew in the air, regaling its grander moments from its voyage past; no doubt exaggerating its importance amongst its thirty-three fellows. Yet it too knew its fate. Within an hour they would come. It would be furled and tied, lowered and stowed in some dark, windless place. There to await its resurrection, its rejoinder with sun and wind. Suddenly a fresh gust hit and it snapped wildly in reply, its shadow a gray flurry across the boards, across James and Seán who were down the *Falmouth*'s aft gangway, walking to England.

The Bristol wharf sounds were rich and curiously intoxicating: the creaking of hawsers, the hoarse shouts of dockworkers heaving their loads, the crackle of sails being rolled, barking dogs, the clatter of wagons on cobbled paths, the aching creak of wooden cranes as they pulled and turned. In the distance, immigrants, indentured servants most, queued along another pier, for another ship, other indeterminate fates yet to be resolved. James and Seán neared the awaiting crowd, the ones come to greet those leaving the *Falmouth* —those men now shedding from the ship's hold. The last green leaves shaken from an autumn tree. Discards. Distinguished only for having survived this long. Unique for the life still found within them.

Shore eyes studied debarking eyes, all in hopeful recognition. Too much familiarity for James and he quickly lowered his nose, eyes dropping behind the sharp brim of his green three-corner hat. Though these were mostly women and children, they were staring nonetheless, disturbingly so. Peering at him with faces locked in anxious alert, open eyes, brows peaked as if to ask,

'Are you my father, my brother, my husband, so changed by the war and sea as to be unrecognizable? My God at least you are alive! Oh, no, you are not him.' And the brows would momentarily fall, till the next was likewise examined. Many were already in despair, already wailing at the news that their man would never return, their sounds melding with the ever present screeches of seagulls overhead. Mixed in, like a marbled concoction of the most discordant groups, were those who also cried, but deliriously, clinging with near faint to their loved one, resolved to not notice the missing limbs, the sallow gaze, the stench, the pallid vacancy that greeted them. They quickly shuffled their living away from that remaining mass, that ceremonial throng of mourners, where hope breathes its last.

James, with Seán close behind, moved with the departing, anxious to get off the docks. After endless months of standing on decks, the earth was a bizarre surface to his feet and legs. His knees were jelly, the dirt giving and swaying beneath him. He moved as best he could, his mind racing to remember how to walk on solid ground. When clear of the shoulders and elbows, he half-turned to Seán. They stood a moment, just looking. "I guess this will be it then," James said quietly, as if to himself.

"A couple of months." Seán nodded. "Then ye'll get the honor of seeing me again."

"Indeed," James murmured seriously. It was not that Seán didn't amuse him; it was simply an instinct. He was uncomfortable in the open. He saw no value in stopping to chat up each other regarding plans they had long discussed in detail. They knew where to go, where to meet, what they would do. He would secret away, hopefully to his mother's family in England. Seán would hop a sloop back to Waterford, on the southern coast of Ireland, then make to New Ross and survey the doings of Dunmain. They would meet at a later date, at a place to be designated by letter from James. It was that simple. Nothing more. James would travel under the name Roderick Random. There was no need to loiter, canvassing in front of who knows what unseen, lurking enemies. He felt his heart thumping, chill overcoming him, panic coursing his veins. He hadn't felt it since Yorktown. Not even in the heat of the sea carnage with all the pressing men aboard. That had been different. Those seamen had other matters at hand. No informer, no wisp of evil had been prowling behind them. Not as in a street crowd like this one, here on the Bristol docks, on Broad Quay.

If Seán shared, or even noticed, James's anxiety, it was disguised as he rested a foot on his sea chest and leaned over his knee. "My friend, when ye get to London, watch yer back. Do ye hear? Don't let a stranger get near ye. Keep yer sword within reach, Jemmy. I am still under the Admiral's orders to protect ye're bleedin' hide. Never forget. Don't have me brigged on account of yer foolishness."

"My foolishness?"

"Just keep it at yer ready."

"I will." James put a hand on the hilt of his rapier, a gift from Admiral Vernon. He wished he also had a pistol. "I'll have a week or so before there's word—"

"Ye stay hidden all the same."

"I can't well find a solicitor if I'm shriveled in a London boardin' house, now can I?"

"Hear me now, Jemmy. Ye'll have to watch out for that bastard Bailyn, and Higgins too. Ye never know where—"

"I'll be careful," said James, placing a firm hand on Seán's shoulder. This was not wise, rehashing this on the public quay.

Suddenly a hawker boy materialized. "Coach to London and all points between!"

James nodded, taking the boy's only flyer. Across the top, it read: Shelby Stables -- High Street. He refocused on Seán. "I'll write ye when I get in a place to do so," he said, gesturing with the flyer. "Give my finest to yer father."

"I will," Seán said, standing tall. He held up three fingers, pointing them at James. When James returned the gesture, he noticed Seán's hand was shaking. They embraced, gripping each other's shoulders tightly for a moment before pulling away.

James was surprised by the flush that now suddenly jolted through him. He felt his lip quiver and held it tight. "Seán," he began, his voice cracking despite his best efforts against it. "I don't know what I would've done—"

"Ach, what ye would've done? Ye'd already be in Ireland by now. And most certainly ye would've missed Cartagena."

"Ye know my meaning."

Seán nodded. "I do. But must ye be reminded? I'd be out there fighting the stinkin' Spaniards still, I would. If I hadn't seen yer ugly mug. Ye remember that."

"I will." James gave his friend a smile, then pulled in a breath. "See ye soon?"

"Ye will. Unless I see ye first, ye ol' rogue."

James chuckled, though he didn't mean it. "I'd best be gone. God speed,

Seán."

"God be with ye too, Jemmy."

James turned away, tugged his lips in, cinching his face, refusing to let the tears come. In a moment he was gone, melded into the thick crowd.

—m—

Up Broad Quay, past a merchant's counting house, a tavern, a small glass-house, then another tavern, stood a sugar refinery twenty yards offset from the bustling street. In the courtyard formed by that offset, hauliers worked their handtrucks from the quay to the refinery's iron gates and back again. Also there this day was a rickety faded green wagon, turned round to face Broad, its driver's box just visible; its driver, Patrick Higgins even less so. He was peering through a brass scope, observing the two seamen disembark, talk, take the flyer, embrace, then go their separate ways. He kept his focus on the taller, darker one in the green hat. That was James Annesley. Certainly no other. "I'll be damned," Higgins whispered, thinking he saw the scar he had long-ago rendered the man. The other young man, who was that? Seán Kennedy? Must be. Same reddish hair, boyish grin. Yet how could it be? It hadn't made sense when he had heard it predicted; yet who else was the 'schoolfellow at whose father's house he boarded?' Must be Seán, just as they had told him. Very good. He disliked surprises nearly as much as he disdained rash behavior. He turned again, searching the faces for James. There. Damn! He was startled to see James approaching so briskly. He collapsed the scope, dropped his chin, hiding his face behind his hat, and watched as James passed by. Then he eased his wagon forward, joining the stream of horses and people moving along the quay, the reins slippery in his sweaty palms. James was ahead, moving away. This was not going to be easy. If only Bailyn would keep his bloody distance.

But he knew it was too late for that. Bailyn was already near. He might have known by the feeling alone—the chill of a demon's presence. But it was the tail of that pathetic, brilliant white wig wagging in the breeze which alerted him: Bailyn was a hundred yards up Broad Quay, on horseback, watching them all.

Higgins pulled gently on the bit, slowing to keep a safe distance from James. At Corn, James spoke with a passerby, then turned toward High Street. "Very good, Mr. Annesley," he mumbled nervously under his breath. "To the Shelby Stables ya go." Higgins reined the old horse to the right, then whipped it to a corky run down a muddy alley leading across one street and on to the next where he turned left, still cracking the whip to keep on a stuttering pace. The wagon jostled, banging under him, pitching loose hay from the wagon bed. "Come on, ya colicky nag!" he ordered, whipping new life into the beast. When he reached another alley, he tugged hard left and charged. Directly ahead, down the alley, he could see stables across the coming street, the large doors standing wide. Higgins whipped the straining nag yet again, bolting across the traffic and into the stable's dim shadows where he pulled to a stop and leapt from the driver's box. As he faded into the dark reaches, a bald, white-bearded man gave him a nod and led the horse and wagon back to the street. There the old man cooed at the nag, patting its jaw, hitching it loosely to a post. He closed the giant doors, ambled to a bench and sat down.

—⁂—

Captain Bailyn was cursing himself for losing sight of Higgs. But as he rounded the last turn, he sighed. There ahead was the horse and green wagon Higgs had been driving; now hitched in front of a stable. No driver. No Higgs. Bailyn moved forward, cautiously trotting his mare past the stables, across the street and into an alley opposite. He turned to face the street. From there he could see anyone approaching, yet stay removed from conspicuous sight. He leaned forward, creaking the saddle's black leather, and peered around the corner. The sight down the street made him grin. James Annesley was coming.

Looking back Bailyn watched a disheveled old man sitting in front of the stable. He imagined Higgs lurking inside, waiting to spring out and slide a knife between James's ribs. No, Higgs wouldn't have that kind of courage. Higgs will shoot him in the back. With that thought, Bailyn raised his musket, removed the plunger and began loading the barrel. If James Annesley didn't go into those stables, or if he overpowered Higgs, or if that pathetic Scot botched this in any way, he would be ready. He took aim at the old man, judging the range. By damn, if James even sticks his head out, he could shoot the English bastard right through the eye and still stay mounted. He glanced behind him. This alley would allow for a quick flight. For all of Higgs' idiocy, at least the Scot had chosen an ideal location for a quiet killing.

—⁂—

James walked quickly, keeping a hand on the hilt of his sword. Finally, there it was, straight ahead, a swinging sign with the words SHELBY STABLES emblazoned in red letters across a poorly drawn white horse. But he didn't see any carriages or coaches in front, just an ancient hay wagon hitched to an obviously experienced nag. He slowed as he neared the building, noticing an elderly man who seemed to have about as much life left in him as did the horse. "Sir?" James said as he approached.

The man watched James carefully. "What do you want, seaman?"

"A coach east." He handed the flyer to the man. "I can obtain such a fare here?"

The man studied the flyer as if he had never seen it before. Suddenly he bellowed, "Of course! What'd you think this place was, a dancin' parlor? Eh?" The man grinned, baring his gums. "A dancin' parlor?"

James glanced at the sign overhead, then back at the wagon. "I just didn't—"

"The coach east, certainly. That's what you want. A hackney to Bath and on to London." The man stood on his shaky legs. "Begob seaman, you've come to the right place, you have indeed. To London you said?"

James stepped back. "I didn't say. But aye, to London."

"Well, come inside, seaman. Come inside." The man shuffled toward the entrance and opened one of the large doors. "I'll make your arrangements here, begob I will. Have you gone in two shakes of a dog's tail, I will. Two shakes. You'll see."

As James followed the old man, he brushed past the panting horse. "What sir," he began, "what is the fare for the—" He stopped as the horse fidgeted, sidestepping against him.

"Fifteen shillings. Never mind the old mite. She needs a bit o' hobblin', I'd say. Aye, a bit o' hobblin for the missus. Just fifteen, I said."

James noticed the horse's neck was lathered in sweat. He touched its withers, feeling the dissipating heat. Then he glanced at the old man who was already disappearing into the blackness. "Somebody drove this one hard," he said, studying the horse again.

"What'd you say?" the man called from within.

"This horse, sir. A bit ragged, wouldn't ye say?"

The man re-emerged. "I told you, seaman, don't mind that mite of a horse. She's not the one that'll take your coach." He showed his gums. "I can assure you of that. Nay. Not to pull the likes of you."

"Good," said James, not sure what was meant by 'the likes of you.'

"Humph! You coming in or aren't you? Eh? What's it to be?" The man again vanished into the cool stables. This time James followed. His eyes struggled to adjust to the darkness. The sound of horses' hooves pawing the ground reassured him, their snorts, the rattling of their harnesses. He walked farther, following the slow-trodding man who kept glancing back over his shoulder with a polite, uneasy nod. About fifteen paces in, the old man stopped abruptly and turned around. James stopped, immediately alarmed. But it was too late. He felt the cold muzzle of a pistol press hard on the back of his head.

—⁂—

Across the street, Bailyn was braced. "Come on, Higgs," he muttered, "just kill him. I'll get you on the road." As he said it, nodding to himself, the image hit him that someone might see Higgs's body, recognize him as James's killer, and that might bring it back to Richard. Thus he would need to disfigure Higgs's face. He would shoot him with the blunderbuss. No, he would use his broadsword. Or maybe a large branch.

—⁂—

James was frozen, the pistol jammed against his skull. "Come now, Mr. Annesley. 'Tis time for ya t'go," a voice behind him whispered in a brusque Scottish brogue. "Keep yar hands where I can see 'em."

"Ah, Patrick Higgins, ye've found me," replied James, trying to stay calm as he glanced over his shoulder, pushing his head against the barrel. "Well done. Shelby Stables and—"

"Shut yar mouth and move forward."

"By God, ye'd better pull that trigger, Higgins. I've waited a long time to kill ye and Captain Bailyn, and I won't lose my chance now," James said, daring, turning slowly, reaching for his sword.

"Face ahead!" Higgins pulled James's sword from its sheath and flung it into the darkness. He growled quietly, "Walk to the coach."

"What coach, Higgins? Where's yer buggerin' friend, Bailyn? He's in the coach, aye?"

A hand grabbed James's arm and spun him to face the stable's open door. "Look outside. Across that street. Who do ya see?"

James complied, bracing himself against a feed trough as he leaned forward, peering into the bright street. He saw a man sitting on a gray mare, holding a musket across his lap. "Ah, faith be! 'Tis Captain Bailyn, the devil incarnate."

"Mark my words, James. He wouldn't let ya live more than three steps outside. He can't see us here, but if ya try to run, or even—"

"Ah, straight to hell with ye!" James took another step toward the door. "I'll take my—" He halted at the sound of a cocking flintlock. "Higgins. Ye plannin' to shoot me in the back? Why not give me a pistol and we'll stand our paces?"

"I'm quite serious. Don't go another step into that light. I swear Bailyn *will* shoot ya."

James made a half turn. His eyes had somewhat adjusted. Now he saw a black carriage beside them, hitched to two horses, and beyond it was a large blue coach with a team of four. "Is that the coach?"

"Aye. Keep moving," whispered Higgins.

James walked forward, purposefully slow, hoping for an opportunity to run out the back of the stable. But where? Then he saw it: a flitter of light. In an instant, he pivoted, shoving Higgins against a post, slugging him in the stomach. Sprinting around the carriage, he found his sword and lurched ahead, further into the darkness. He lost sight of the rear exit. He stumbled over something, clambered to his feet, then heard boots scrambling around him. Raising his sword, he slashed at the sound. "Get back!" He sliced the blackness till steel found flesh.

"Auuggghhh! Damn!" a man screamed. Suddenly a pistol fired and the darkness erupted in chaos, a flash of gunpowder, horses snorting in fright. James ducked, dropping back to the dirt floor. Hands were grabbing him, snatching his sword, pulling him.

"Get him up!" a gruff voice commanded.

"Hold him," Higgins half-yelled. "Hold him fast!"

"Bailyn is taking his aim," another Scot called out.

"Now! Now!" came a muffled shout. Suddenly the massive doors slammed wide and a man in the driver's box of the black carriage whipped the horses to run. As it shot into High Street, another shadowy figure brushed by James and ran out through the open doors. The man untied the old nag and leapt into the green hay wagon, whipping the horse down High Street, following the carriage. James heard a musket fire and people in the street shouting.

"Bloody hell!" James stammered, stunned by the unexpected commotion.

No one said a word. The big doors began to creak closed. Just before they met, James looked out, across the street. Bailyn was gone.

"Bring him," whispered a Scotsman. The men fettered James and pushed him to the coach.

"Get in," barked another. "Sit in the back."

James hesitated. Behind him, he heard the shrill, distinctive ring of a military sword sliding from its steel scabbard. He quickly climbed aboard. It was utterly black inside, forcing him to feel for the backbench. Finding it, he sat down and waited.

—m—

When Bailyn heard the pistol fire, he cocked his musket, taking aim at the stable doors. When they flew open, a black carriage shot out. Was that James driving? Bailyn fired and missed. He was certain it was Higgs who was fast behind, clambering into the old wagon and cracking the whip. Bailyn spurred his mount, galloping after them. Ahead, the carriage turned onto Bath Road, the hay wagon following. He would pass Higgs at this rate. At least he would get James. He would overtake the carriage and kill them both just beyond the city walls. "Faster!" he shouted, digging in his spurs.

—m—

"Ya damaged?" a man asked outside the coach. Then came the sound of ripping cloth.

"Just a cut to my arm," said Higgins, climbing inside. "Let's go." He pushed next to James, slamming the door behind him, sealing them in the coal-black interior. Then James heard the heavy stable doors creaking open once again, followed by the crack of a whip. The coach lurched forward and the wheels hit the street's ruts with a jarring thud, the canter of the horses' hooves rippling through the seat.

"All right, Higgins, I'm game. Who were those Scots?" James asked the blackness.

Higgins didn't answer.

James's knee bumped another knee and a cold jolt ripped through him. Someone, besides Higgins, was in the coach, sitting directly across from him. It could only be one person, he realized. "So, Uncle, I see ye've hired the whole damned Black Watch to nab me."

"Lord James Annesley?" a warm voice replied from the other seat.

James noticed the man's accent carried a soothing Scottish lilt. Though it had been years since he had heard Richard, he knew it was not the voice of that pernicious man.

"Lookin' for someone else?" retorted James. "'Twould be a shame."

"True," snorted the man. "Patrick, ya going to live?"

Higgins mumbled, "Just my arm. Didn't know I'd be bellin' a cat."

"Perhaps Lord Anglesea delivered ya a scar to match the one ya gave him."

After a silent pause, James spoke up. "Ye also work for Richard? Like Higgins here?"

"No," answered the voice. "Neither does my clansman here. Not present-ly." Just then came a loud double-tap on the roof of the coach. "Good, we're out of Bristol. Pull the curtains for us, Patrick. Oh, aye, yar arm. Allow me."

James heard the rustle of fabric and the slight screech of curtain rings. Then a shaft of brilliant March light rushed in, filling the coach, momen-tarily blinding him. He squinted and shielded his eyes with a hand. Across from him sat a tall, broad-shouldered, older man with friendly green eyes, distinguished smile, wig hanging to his shoulders, wearing a bold tartan kilt. James glanced at Higgins beside him: he was dressed exactly like the man who raced out of the stables, after the black carriage. He was tying a torn rag cloth around his bloody arm. No one spoke for a moment as the coach lumbered along.

"Need some help, Higgins?" James finally offered. He had tended far worse wounds.

Higgins grunted a barely audible "No."

The stranger was still studying James, leading James to return his fixed stare. But then a metallic gleam caught James's attention. On the seat beside the man was a gleaming dirk, its brass hilt cast as entwined ropes beneath an acorn pommel. James frowned, studying it. The man picked it up, handing it through the flickering light. "I believe this is yars."

James unsheathed it. "M'God," he murmured, his fingers tracing a Gael-ic inscription along the blood groove. "*Léargas sa Dorchadas,*" he read aloud.

"Still know yar Gaelic?" asked the man.

James whispered, "Sight in the dark." Then a black image came to him: this dirk protruding from Juggy's bloody chest. He looked up at the stranger. "Who are ye?"

"Daniel Mackercher, at yar service, m'lord."

"Mr. Mackercher?" James's jaw sagged. "Brother of Joan?"

Mackercher peaked an eyebrow. "So I am."

"Faith be!" James shook Mackercher's hand. "Truly?"

Mackercher smirked. "I've prayed for years I'd might meet ya, face to face as this."

"Faith be," James repeated, shaking his head.

"I am the one shocked. You, in my coach. You were believed long dead."

"So I've heard."

"I must confess," Mackercher continued, "I believed it as well."

"Never mind that," said James. "Back in those stables, I thought so too!" He snorted a smile at Higgins. "Well, perhaps for a moment."

At that Mackercher chuckled, and Higgins, still tending his wound, finally grinned.

CHAPTER 25

Kind and true have been long tried
A harbor where we may confide
And safely there at anchor ride.
From change of winds there we are free,
And need not fear storm's tyranny,
Nor pirate, though a prince he be.

— from *Upon Kind and True Love*, Aurelian
Townshend, 1656

From the Shelby Stables in Bristol, the blue hackney coach and its comple-
ment of six guards, two in the driver's box and four on horseback, charged
north for Scotland, pressing their horses over sixty miles each day. By nightfall
of the first day, they had made it to Gloucester. On the second, they passed a
field of Cromwellian gibbet cages, then rolled through the lush forests to Stafford, where in the black of night they settled in at the Black Bull Inn, where
James found paper and a scrivener's pen.

My Dear Laura—16, March 1743

*Tonight I sit by a warm fire wishing I had words to say just
how much I miss you. You never leave my waking thoughts
or my sleeping dreams. You are my beautiful, precious love.
Since my letter last, of which I can only pray and hope you are
in receipt, we sailed for England in late February, arriving
Bristol only yesterday. I am in health, as is Seán.*

*I have the most wonderful news to relay. Upon my arrival, I
was obtained by the associates of Mr. Daniel Mackercher, a
solicitor of Scotland, whose kind sister, Joan Landy, is the one
I spoke of so often - by her name Juggy. Mr. Mackercher has
declared he shall finance a legal campaign against my uncle,*

and I have accepted his most honorable and generous offer. I dare say, you would not recognize me, as Mr. Mackercher has provided me a new suit of clothes and pintail wig. I fail to remember when I ever looked so presentable!

We are in route to a place I shall not name, where I shall be safe. I dare not be more specific lest this letter come into unclean hands of RA's associates. I received your letter of 15 December on the very day we sailed from Jamaica, and I must say I am most pleased at your father's persuasive skills. Carrying the knowledge that I am released from my servitude is most heartwarming and gratifying indeed. Please give your father my undying appreciation and gratitude. Pray tell him from his er-to-be son in law.

I miss you, my love, my sweet. I wish you were here, although I know it would not be best. I remain safe as I am now in the protection of a Highland band. Do not fret yourself. I will return to you, or send for you, just as soon as such is possible. I entreat you, my dear, keep me in your dreams, as you stay in mine. We shall see one another yet again soon - then we shall marry. My Laura, O what a glorious day that will be. My heart yearns for you, and I long to hold you once again, to sit with you in our loft window and listen to your tender voice.

Please give my greetings to your father and mother. Tell Pehr and Gunnar I am having a grand adventure of which I will surely relate upon my return. I wrote four letters to you during the voyage and I enclose those as well.

I am yours, always, and so shall I faithfully remain.

— James

He had fallen asleep in the front parlor of the Black Bull, slouched in the larger of two chairs, his mouth agape and drooling on the leather. The crackling fire had also faded, surrendering the room to a Scandinavian clock that filled the cool air with an echoing cacophony of ticks and tocks. The letter to Laura was lying on the floor, where it had landed after slipping through

James's fingers while he was reading it for the third time. One corner was lying under the floppy ear of a spotted spaniel breathing deeply, kicking and running in a dream, curled at the foot of James's wing-backed chair.

Mackercher entered the room carrying two chamber candles, the floorboards creaking gently under his fine Italian shoes. "James?" The spaniel rolled onto its back. "James," he said again, setting down the candles to shake James's shoulder.

"What?" James awoke with a start. The spaniel's eyes opened, but it didn't move.

"We must leave." Mackercher was picking up James's coat and hat.

"Now? What time is it?" James got to his feet, wiping his mouth with his linen sleeve.

"A bit after midnight." He plopped the hat on James.

"What's happened?"

"Some of yar Irishmen are in this town, asking questions." While he spoke, Mackercher held James's coat open, helping him put it on. "We'd best go."

"Mumph, my Irishmen?" James half-asked, buttoning his waistcoat's silk trim.

"Meet me 'round at the stables."

"I'll be there directly," James replied.

Mackercher took a candle and left. Alone again, James noticed the locket was open and hanging outside his shirt. He snapped it closed carefully, stuffed it down his collar along with the key on its leather, and tied his ascot. Shoving his feet into his shoes, he noticed the letter. "Hey, ye shouldn't be reading that," he whispered, leaning over. "Where's yer manners?" Patting the spaniel, he retrieved the letter from under its head. "Laura will wonder what English strumpet has such peculiar hair." He carefully folded the paper, tucking it in the pocket of his waistcoat. Then he picked up his sword, tied on the dirk, and went to the door. Yawning, he returned to the chair and blew out the candle. "So long, Chap. Thanks for the visit."

—⁓—

They traveled through the night, James half-sleeping in a miserable heap, bumped and jostled on the hard bench. Just before sunrise, they finally stopped and most of the men, including James, stretched out in an open field beside the road and slept. They reached Manchester that evening, and the next day they traveled on to Preston, where they replaced three horses. Four days later, the coach reined to a welcome stop near Aberfoyle, Scotland, where Mackercher's estate lay nestled in the sublime Highland foothills.

—⁓—

A gentle wind skimmed across tender shoots of spring grass, caressing them, touching them, like a mother's fingers through her baby's hair. James leaned his head back against a boulder, eyes closed, and let the warm scents of the Highlands wash over him. Mackercher, in his hunting kilt, strolled up the knoll to sit beside him, laying his musket in the grass. He picked up a dead grouse James had shot and inspected the feathers, spreading the wings wide, giving it an appreciative grunt. It was their second day of hunting, and already this morning they had three birds apiece.

"I'll be back in six weeks," said Mackercher, smoothing the tail feathers. "Think ya can stay clear of all contemptible behavior till then?" He set the bird down.

"Not likely," said James, grinning, moving his musket from his lap.

"I'll advise ya to stay clear of the Gregor Clan. Even with old Rob Roy dead these nine years, his band is still a bit o' trouble.

"A bad lot, eh?"

"Not evil mind ya, just outlaws. A crafty, unseemly sort. We can't have ya running foul of the magistrates." Mackercher smiled warmly. "Indeed, if ya're going to do anything reckless, I damn well want to be a partner in it!" His deep laughter bellowed. "B'jingo, I got ya here. Ya're stuck with me."

James chuckled, "I haven't much choice, as I see it."

"Nay, ya don't."

"When ye get to Ireland," James began. "Waterford?"

"Aye." Mackercher picked at a briar in his kilt.

"Ye'll be in New Ross within a fortnight."

Mackercher nodded. "Before then, but aye. That'll have Fynn and Seán here within three weeks or so."

James's eyes glinted. "I cannot wait to see Fynn."

"I'm certain he feels the same."

"So, after New Ross," James continued, "ye'll be on to Dublin directly?"

"I'll not tangle with Richard at Dunmain."

"'Tis only that if ye go to Dunmain, one of ye will most certainly die. Which will be the end of this, with no resolution of the estate."

"My, how very practical," Mackercher said sarcastically. He scratched at one of his bushy eyebrows.

"'Tis a deal then? No Dunmain?" James fixed his stare.

"Aye, aye Captain. Ya have my word."

James took a deep breath. "So then, how will our action be titled?"

Mackercher hesitated at first, unsure what James meant. Then it came to him. "James Annesley, Esquire, plaintiff, and the Earl of Anglesea, Richard Annesley, defendant. Filed in Dublin's Exchequer, in the Four Courts."

James remembered the building well. "The Four Courts is next to Christ Church. I'd be grateful if ye'd light a candle there, for my mother."

"Very well," Mackercher said with a nod. "Is not yar father buried there?" He waited till James nodded before continuing. "Perhaps I—"

"No, but thank ye all the same."

"All right then." Mackercher leaned his head back, gazing up at the clouds.

James sat quietly for a moment, tying his birds together, then did the same with Mackercher's kills. "Mr. Mackercher," he said suddenly, "Before ye go, I want ye to know, ye've been entirely too good to me. I am grateful beyond—"

Up popped Mackercher's hand. "Now, James—"

"Ye'll let me say my piece."

Mackercher huffed, then smiled. "What mettle they breed in America."

"I am enormously grateful t' ye. At sea, I must've told Seán a thousand times I could never afford such a thing—to challenge Richard for my title and estates. He'd say, 'Ah, ye'll find a way,' but I sincerely doubted it. Perhaps only with some joinder of the Sheffield's."

"Not likely," Mackercher interjected.

"Aye. Admiral Vernon gave me counsel about that family of my grandfather. Said they are no friends to the Annesleys. Never were. In fact it was out of that longstanding disdain that my mother was married off to an Annesley. Apparently her stepmother, Queen Anne's sister, disliked her. Or something of the sort. In any case, seems she fell victim to the families' disputes and plotting. Thus I am the product of that quarrel. Bully for me." He paused to see how Mackercher was taking all this in. But Mackercher was blank. A small nod. Simply listening. "And so," James continued, "according to the Admiral, it is precisely for that cause that I am to dislike them all in return, especially the current Duke of Buckingham. Distant relation or not. Seems childish to me. Entirely childish. But I presume the Admiral correct."

"Seems an accurate account," said Mackercher.

"Although I had planned to call on them, it was not with bated breath. I don't know them, the Sheffields, any more than they know me. Only that I am the son of Mary. Unless of course they believe Richard's claims. If so, then they will claim they are no relation at all. Besides, it truly seemed a lost cause, any attempt against Richard through legal means, through the courts." He gave Mackercher a slight smile, studying his chiseled face. "But now ye've made it possible. I fear I may never adequately return—"

"Nay, James, I—"

"Of course I will certainly repay ye. Once I regain my estate."

"James!" barked Mackercher. "Hear me now. I don't want yar money. Not ever."

"But sir, this will undoubtedly be expensive. Ye cannot carry the costs alone."

"Can't I?"

"When I go to the Duke, perhaps he'll indeed see it a worthy cause and—"

"I concur with the good Admiral. Keep yar distance from that brood. Richard has sentries in London. Certainly around Buckingham and the Sheffields of York. He'll be awaiting ya. Besides, Buckingham has his own matters pressing at the King's Bench. These are difficult times. Another Jacobite uprising is afoot here in Scotland and the Loyalist are loathe for distractions. Richard has pledged for King George; thus despised or no, he will have the public alliance of the Duke. If the Sheffields wish to contribute to yar cause, it will only be through hidden means. I'll send word, as yar attorney, making yar request known. But ya should stay clear of them."

"Thank ye," said James, flicking at some grass.

"I appreciate yar willingness to apply reason," Mackercher offered. "It will be asked of you as well—to declare yarself a Loyalist or risk a Jacobite's reward."

"I am not familiar with the whole of the matter," began James, shaking his head. He knew more than he let on, but enough to declare an allegiance? Either way, it was enthralling that his politics mattered to anyone at all. To the point, he had read the accounts of the Jacobites, pressing for the return of their Catholic "King over the Water," James VIII or III (depending on your politics). They wished for nothing less than to depose the Protestant, Hanoverian English king, George II, an imposter according to the Jacobites. But did he concur with their cause? James had both Catholic and Protestant rumblings within him; a play performed in two languages simultaneously. A confused jumble of legitimate scripts. A dissonant noise. He was Protestant, he supposed, and that might lead to a Loyalist position, but he knew the persecuted Irish Catholics were vying for the restoration of their freedoms, something they believed could only be attained through revolt. That seemed right to him as well. And for the Scottish Jacobites, it was more of a nationalistic cause, for the dissolution of the union with England, a matter which, for many, was beyond even the reach of religious concerns. "If I may ask, Mr. Mackercher, whom do ye—"

"An honest question. But no, Lord Anglesea, ya may not ask."

James nodded, then looked away, cuffed by the chiding, albeit a real or merely perceived admonition. Yet he would tolerate it from this man. How could he not? This was Daniel Mackercher, Juggy's brother, solicitor, military hero, the man who, with Higgins, had saved him. The man who pledged to finance and manage the pending battle against Richard. He drew a long breath through his nose, then let it go slowly from his mouth. Perhaps he should just remain quiet.

"I fought for the Loyalist at Sheriffmuir, in '15," Mackercher finally began. "The last time the Jacobite clans rallied against the English king. Many died. It is not something I wish to see again. I am an older, wiser man. I hope." He stood, stretching his back. "Now the clans are scattered. And though divided loyalties abound, they'll not let this matter rest." He paused, looking about, almost as if he might see a warrior clan crest a hilltop at any moment. But they were alone. "There is an admirable nature to their cause." His focus returned to James. "Yet to declare oneself a Jacobite can lead to the end of a rope. Not something to ask a man."

"Yet ye said I should declare myself—"

"Yes, declare *yarself*. On yar own. For yarself. Do not allow yarself to be asked. Do not let the unknown grow. Rumors fester and breed in silence. Say ya're loyal to King George. Silence lends itself to mystery, and mystery to distrust, and distrust to fear, and out of fear, yar fellow man will assume the worst on yar behalf. Do ya see my meaning?"

"I think I do." James also got to his feet. He gathered the birds and musket.

Mackercher continued. "It is best if we all know who we are, or at least whom we say we are. If ya don't declare yarself loyal, ya'll have a devil of a time convincing anyone otherwise. The thing is presumed by the absence of its denial. And have no doubt Richard will promote ya as a Jacobite. Especially as ya're in my company."

"In yer company? But ye fought, as ye said—"

"I did. But this Jacobite cause is ripping our country apart. And I have enemies as well. It is a cheap thing to accuse a man. Thus I am so accused. And some believe it so."

James nodded. "I've seen that men will believe as they wish to believe. They always will. We can only hope for truth to eventually reveal itself."

Mackercher looked at him, then smirked. "Well said. I do concur."

James started walking as Mackercher turned away. They had lunch awaiting them. He would talk with Fynn about this whole Jacobite mess. For now, he would leave it be. "With my mother dead, her parents as well, do ye think there's a Sheffield who'd assist my cause? Our cause?"

"I doubt it." They were both moving down the knoll. "None of them stand to gain by the outcome, either way it falls."

"I can see that," James muttered.

Mackercher turned back and nudged him. "Doesn't matter, all the same. God has blessed me with resources enough. I'd part with it all, if required. If necessary to see this through. To have that murderer brought to justice."

James pressed. "Despite that, ye can count on my repayment once—"

"Did ya not hear me?" Mackercher frowned. "I won't take Anglesea money."

"Then what can I do to—"

"All I'll ever ask of ya, is that ya remember Joan."

"I do sir," said James.

Mackercher stopped at the edge of a trickling creek. "This is not only yar fight. Not yar fight alone. 'Tis mine as well. That bastard not only stole yar estate, yar freedom; he stole Joan's life. He stole my sister. My family. How could any man rest till justice comes on such a thing? And at what price? If it was Laura, could ya ever stop?" James shook his head. "Right," Mackercher continued. "We'll win back yar estate and yar title. We'll right that wrong. But I want my revenge." He stepped through the water to the other side and kept moving. "I may be cursed for it. Damned for seeking it. But there it is. Plain enough."

James saw Mackercher turn to watch him scale the small hill. He could see the man's eyes. Though Mackercher was old enough to be his father, his eyes sparkled with a youthful mischief. Unless he was talking about Richard Annesley—then an icy glaze would seize him. Like at this precise moment. Perhaps it was best to talk of something else. "Do ye come into these mountains often?"

"Whenever possible," Mackercher answered quickly, pivoting away as James caught up.

"'Tis the most incredible land I've ever seen."

"Then ya'll not mind staying put till I return."

"Of course. Will Higgins stay as well?"

"He may go to Glasgow to see his family, but keep him in yar eye as best ya can."

After a moment, James asked, "Do ye not trust the man?"

"I do. In a manner of speaking. I believe his heart is loyal to ya. To us. To our cause. And undoubtedly black against Richard. Undoubtedly so. But once a man turns against his word, even if he has turned from a pact with the devil himself, it reveals his heart. It shows he is capable of bending. That he can be bought. For the cause of good or evil, he can be bought nevertheless. He follows his conscience."

"Is that not an admirable thing?"

"Yes, but ya can never trust another man's conscience. The conscience is not beyond change, and thus it is unreliable bedrock. It is a man's truth, his values that carry his soul. If he ever is able to compromise himself, to be the lackey of a man such as Richard, then the worm of deceit and treason is within him. And that, James, that worm of treason; when ya see it in a man, never grant him yar full trust."

"Ye don't think a man can change?"

"The worm of treason rarely leaves just because its host has chosen to live beyond blemish. The infestation remains. Unfortunately ya have to rout it out. Most likely." Then he added almost under his breath, "Often with a claymore's edge."

"But Higgins saved my life."

Mackercher stopped. "Aye, so he did. He also gave ya that scar." He swiped a finger over James's cheek. "Same man. He also helped Bailyn kill yar father. Pointed yar father out so Bailyn could run him down. Same man."

On that James paused. He had imagined such. But now no judgment came, which surprised him. "It is a choice, I believe," he said. "To choose to see the good in a man."

"So ya will," Mackercher shouted over his shoulder. "But always remember." He stopped on the cattle path and turned. "Ya can only be betrayed by the people ya trust."

"Aye, sir," said James, now passing Mackercher on the trail.

"And *m'lord,*" Mackercher snarled kindly with a sanguine wink. "No more of the 'aye, sir' muck. Ya're not a seaman, not a lieutenant now. Not here. Quite to the contrary, ya're a bloody English Earl. Ya should sound as one."

James laughed. "Aye, aye, Captain."

"Impertinent nobleman," chuckled Mackercher. He resumed his pace with James squarely ahead.

CHAPTER 26

Like to the blaze of fond delight;
Or like a morning clear and bright;
Or like a frost, or like a shower;
Or like the pride of Babel's tower;
Or like the hour that guides the time;
Or like to beauty in her prime:
Even such is man, whose glory lends
His life a blaze or two, and ends.

— from *Argalus and Parthenia*, Francis Quarles,
1628

Mackercher's heavyset cook rose early, preparing for the May Day festivities. She was making her specialty; the finest gooseberry cream tarts James ever tasted. Though the celebration that day in Aberfoyle, Scotland was said to be something to see, it was something else that had him up before dawn. Today he, Fynn, and Seán would go on their first *tinchal*, or stag hunt. Unable to sleep, the thoughts of the *tinchal* running through him, he came to the kitchen for coffee, his Colonial hot drink. He had tried it in Virginia but spit it out. Yet when Mackercher offered it with milk, he found it surprisingly agreeable. Now the cook ground and brewed it for him each morning, though Mackercher had been gone for weeks.

"Mr. Annesley, will ya fetch da eggs?" she asked. "'Fraid me burnt foot's got me wobblin' dis morn."

"For yer tarts, 'tis the least I can do," James agreed, then turned and stepped through the rear door. He heard pigeons cooing from the dovecote's upper dome, and just below them, a chorus of clucking hens. "Here I come, ladies," he whispered, "Show me yer good ones." Gravel crunched under his feet as the cold air rushed through his lungs. He was in high spirits, the day's events on his mind. He liked the newness morning brought, the promise offered by the rested world, a dark canvas poised for color. At the dovecote he stopped and surveyed the constellations now shifted west. There was the

Big Dipper still carrying water for Polaris. He looked for St. Stephen's Skull, yet it seemed to have already set. But just before he entered the coop, he saw it—the elusive star-skull was on the horizon, disappearing, almost gone. Two hollow eyes peering over the edge of the placid world, taking one long final look, unblinking, absorbing all, as if it believed it would never return.

"Mornin' Seámus," sprung a voice from the dark.

"Ach!" James jumped. Turning quickly, he saw Fynn sitting on a stack of cut wood by the duck pond. "Mr. Kennedy! What are ye doing out here?"

"Same as ye, so it appears."

"She sent ye for eggs as well, did she?" James grinned.

Fynn returned the smile. "Lookin' at the stars, I was."

"Didn't know ye watched 'em." James moved to the logs and sat. "I've always liked lookin' up at 'em."

Fynn nodded. "Ye've got it in ye. 'Tis an Irish curse, I reckon."

They both stared at the sky. "Do ye often rise so early?" asked James.

"Always have." Fynn's aged voice fell. "'Tis the best time o' day."

"Aye, 'tis. Reminds me of being at sea—the calm nights mind ye."

The kitchen door creaked open with the cook's head sticking out. "Mr. Annesley?" she called, peering into the darkness.

"Ah, aye!" James cried, popping to his feet. "I'll bring 'em right away."

He moved quickly through the lower coop, gathering eggs and causing a vociferous turmoil among the ruffles. Fynn helped, though much slower. Once the full basket was delivered to the kitchen, they returned to the wood stack. The sky was showing the first hint of its lighter self. They sat quietly, James watching the dimming stars, thinking about this man who had cared for him as far back as he could remember. When he had fallen as a little boy, it was this man who had picked him up, brushed him off. It was this man who had taught him so much, even risked death on his account. And only this man called him "Seámus," for the Irish he said was within him. He was reminded of his father's funeral: Fynn had stayed with him that horrible day. What bravery. An Irish Catholic in a Protestant, English church, head high, escorting the child of the dead English nobleman—murdered by a Catholic, according to the peerage mob. He now understood it had been an act of defiance, of conviction. An act of love. He wanted to thank him, but how? He sat motionless, silent, enjoying how right it felt to be there, beside him, watching the Scottish sun rise on a promise-filled day. He would do anything for him. It was his turn. He looked over at the aging man and silently thanked God Fynn was alive. After so many years apart. He added a vow to his prayer: he would to take care of Fynn for the remainder of Fynn's days.

"Do ye remember up in that tree?" asked Fynn. "Across the moat from Dublin castle?"

"I do. Ye came to find me."

"I can still see ye up there, smiling down as I tried to bear-climb the damn thing."

James slowly shook his head. "Rough days, those were."

"Aye," Fynn agreed, his voice lagging. "The day Joan died."

"Aye," whispered James.

"Seámus, when ye disappeared . . . . Well I thought I would go mad, I did."

James exhaled hard, hating to hear the sadness in Fynn's voice. He wanted to change the subject. "Today's *tinchal*, Seán and I—"

"I can scarcely speak the hell I went through, roamin' the streets like a mad man, searching for ye in the alleys, along the quays. That cloak of yers made us believe ye'd been shot, that ye were damaged, or even worse." He stopped. In the pallid light, James could see Fynn's lip quivering.

"But by God's grace, I didn't die," James tried. "To tell the truth, Mr. Kennedy, 'twas knowin' ye probably thought I *was* dead that kept me going. I had to get back here to show ye. To see ye." Now he too was succumbing to emotions. He sighed through clenched teeth, then continued. "I held on to the belief that we'd be together again. Someday. And sure enough, God has seen fit."

"So He has," Fynn sniffed, crossing his arms and leaning forward.

James put an arm around the man's shoulders. For the first time in the week since Fynn's arrival, he realized just how frail the man was. Fynn was probably not much older than Mackercher, but he seemed to have lived longer and harder than his years. He appeared worn, tough yet weak. Not the scrappy, vibrant man James remembered. *It's all right*, he told himself. *It's not too late. We're here together now. That's all that matters.* Though finding Seán had been a most amazing event, nothing compared to this moment. He knew he would never forget sitting on this woodpile, his arm around this gentle Irishman, both covered by a vast blanket of fading stars.

Suddenly, Fynn straightened his back, collecting himself. "This afternoon, Seámus, after the *tinchal*, I want us to ride into these hills. Just you and me."

"I'd like that."

"There's an important matter to be discussed. Something I need t' tell ye."

"What is it?" James asked, surprised by Fynn's tone.

Fynn pat James's knee, then pressed off of it to stand. "Time enough this evenin'."

"Then we will," James replied. He got to his feet slowly, reluctant to end the moment yet compelled to follow Fynn's lead.

—⁓—

By early afternoon Fynn, Seán and James were two miles from Aberfoyle. They were on foot, muskets in hand. They had not seen a deer, though in truth, they weren't trying very hard. Seán had shot the hare now slung across his back, but that was all they had fired on so far. Now they were laughing, their voices carrying over the sublime, ancient rolling hills, across the lea, that Highland meadow stretching before them in canty shades of emerald and lavender, dusted with saffron flowers, sweeping down to meet Loch Drunkie, its surface reflecting the Menteith Hills beyond. Drifting clouds hung low in massive puffy clumps, playing, shaping and forging the sunlight into Olympian columns, golden shafts exploding off water, hills, meadows and trees.

"Seán," Fynn called to his son a few paces ahead. "Weren't ye to wear a kilt this day?"

"We wouldn't want to see those wasp legs," shouted James. "Pray ye keep 'em covered."

Fynn chuckled. "We can thank the Lord that Higgins took his kilts to Glasgow."

Seán laughed but didn't look back. While walking, he reached down, picked up a pebble and tossed it high back over his head. James and Fynn laughed as they dodged it.

"Best mind yer manners, Seán," said James. "We've a good aim at ye back here."

"Lads, remember hidin' in my wagon in Dublin?" Fynn asked softly.

"Aye." Seán answered, turning to let Fynn and James catch up. "James and I were in College Green, thinkin' of pullin' down King Billy."

"Is that thing still standing?" asked James.

"Aye. Maybe the Earl of Anglesea will help me tear it down when—"

"Ye lads keep jabberin' and a fleein' arse is all we'll see today."

James hooted. "It'd be more arse than Seán's seen in...forever, I'd say."

Fynn suddenly raised a hand and froze, signaling James and Seán to hush. He leaned forward to a crouch and eased up an embankment. James and Seán stifled their laughter and joined him, peering over the rise. There in the clearing of the adjacent forest were a number of grazing deer. One of the larger ones lifted its head nervously, then eased it down again, returning to its feeding.

"All does and fawns," whispered Fynn. "The buck is sure t' be near."

"There," James whispered, nodding at a nearby grove. The buck was standing alert, about fifty yards away, carrying its mossy rack high, cautiously smelling the air. Fynn slowly brought his musket up and reached for the lock, snapping it back carefully. Though it made only a light clicking noise, it was too much. The vigilant buck snorted, stomped, then vanished. By the time James looked back at the does and fawns, they too had run off.

"Oh well, at least we saw one," said Fynn, sighing as he stood straight. "There'll be others around the lake."

"Did ye get a good look at his fleein' arse, Seán?" James chuckled.

"Shut yer trap."

"Lads," Fynn said, once they had rejoined the path, "Do ye remember my riddle? Lil' Jenny Whiteface? Used to tell it to ye both, when ye were but wee mites."

"Aye, Mr. Kennedy, I remember," said James. "And I know the answer."

"Ye do?" Seán gave James a playful shove, then looked away. "Tell me how it went again, so I'll remember."

"Right. Here 'tis," began Fynn. "Lil' Jenny Whiteface has a red nose. The longer she lives the shorter she grows."

James let Seán squirm for a minute, then answered, "'Tis a white candle, Mr. Kennedy."

"Aye, Seámus," said Fynn. "Well done. 'Tis a candle that burns bright, gettin' shorter and shorter as it does—"

"I knew it!" proclaimed Seán.

Fynn went on, "It gets shorter and shorter till one day 'tis gone. Vanished altogether."

"Admit it, Seán," James popped back. "Ye didn't know the answer. Indeed, the last time ye guessed at it, ye thought it was a bird."

Seán looked astonished. "How the devil do ye remember such things?"

"Bugger off," said James, pushing him. They all laughed.

Late that day, the clouds had thickened and were pooling in ever-graying masses, promising at best a good collaborative rain, at worst a maelstrom. The three men sat below them, on the shore of Loch Drunkie, the rich smell of Fynn's pipe wafting up and away. A cool breeze had just come up, harkening the coming storm.

"Is tobacco yer lure?" asked Seán. "They'll smell yer pipe and come runnin' for sure."

Fynn blew out a billow of aromatic smoke. "I reckon all the bucks within five miles have seen us by now. Rather, I'm sure they've heard the two of ye carryin' on." He smiled. "We may as well unload our muskets."

"Aye," James agreed, standing, picking up his firearm. He stopped. The sun was casting a perfect shaft straight down. He watched it, the solitary pillar of light drifting across the choppy grey surface, moving toward them.

Seán stood also, looking at the mounting clouds. "We're about to get wet." Seán lifted his musket, pulled back the flash pan cover and blew the gunpowder off. Then he pulled the ramrod from the barrel, attached a small flange-hook, and fished out his ball and wad. After he did the same with Fynn's musket, he tied the dead hare to the barrel ends and slung the muskets over his shoulder.

"Ye ready?" James asked Fynn, reaching down to help him up.

As he took James's hand, Fynn said, "Aye, 'tis time. I love our Ireland lads, but by God, I've never seen anything so pleasin' as this. I swear I could stay here forever."

"Aye," whispered Seán, "I do agree." He set off, tramping back down the cattle drovers' path with Fynn close behind. Low gurgling thunder rumbled over the hills to the west.

James, reluctant to leave, looked at the lake, absorbing the image. As the first raindrops hit, he turned. The Kennedys were getting further away. He started quickly after them. About a hundred paces down the path, where the trail bent gently away from the shoreline, James felt a pebble in his shoe, grinding the ball of his foot. Ahead, Fynn was crossing a low stone fence, Seán assisting from the other side. James decided he would sit on that wall to remove the rock. He shifted the musket from his shoulder. "Damn," he muttered, wincing, limping along, trying to hurry. He was almost there. The pain was intensifying, a knife in his sole. He wiped the rain from his face. Fynn was twenty paces ahead, just behind Seán. One step from the fence, James reached to lean the musket. Suddenly his right foot slipped into a hidden fox hole, forcing his full weight onto the offending rock. Fire surged up through his calf and he toppled forward, his face toward the wall. "Damn ye!" he cursed again, his hands flying out ahead to break his fall. His musket, slamming against the top of the stones, suddenly discharged. The lead ball fired straight, chest high, over the wall. A flash of gunpowder blasted into James's face, a black cloud of smoke engulfing him. He stumbled backward, ears ringing, momentarily blinded, falling behind the wall.

"Da! Da!" Seán's voice was shrill, almost adolescent. "Oh no, Da!"

James clambered to his feet, the pain forgotten. To his horror, he saw Fynn lying face down in the grass. Seán was kneeling beside him. James scrambled over the wall and bolted to them, screaming, "M'God! Mr. Kennedy!"

He came to a stop at Fynn's feet. Seán had turned his father on his back and was cradling his head. Fynn's eyes were open, staring through James, straight into the falling rain. "Ye shot him!" raged Seán, now sobbing. "Ye shot him!"

James was stunned, his body shaking, his mind filling with the terrible sight. He fell hard onto his hands and knees. "God, no! No!" Blood was streaming from a gaping hole in Fynn's chest. James clutched Fynn's twisted legs, crying for him to live.

Fynn's mouth moved slightly, a wheeze escaping his lips, a last, soft exhale through clenched teeth: "Seán. Seámus."

Seán wailed, "Don't die, Da! Don't ye die now!"

Fynn's face rocked sideways, thick red streaming from his mouth and nose. The pouring rain splattered the blood across Seán's arms, carrying rivulets into the earth. Seán suddenly glared, growling furiously, "Ye killed him! Damn ye! Ye killed him!" Then he collapsed forward, sobbing.

"M'God, Seán. It was an accident!" James shouted, tears streaming, mixing in the rain. He began to shake, lifting his muddy hands, staring at Fynn. "This cannot be!"

CHAPTER 27

O! that I were as great
As is my grief, or lesser than my name,
Or that I could forget what I have been
Or not remember what I must be now.

— from, *King Richard II*, William Shakespeare,
1595

Newgate Prison was a lively grave where the living smelled worse than the dead. James was squatting against the filthy wall in a dim room referred to by the others as "the l'ord"—the inmates' term for the lower ward of the prison. He had been there less than a day and already knew the l'ord was the nastiest ward in the prison, though not the worst. The worst was the pressroom, one floor below, from which he could hear the low groans and high screams of prisoners being pressed to death by cumbrous weights while guards stood about waiting for a confession, or the revelation of conspirators' names, or just to watch the ribs crack on account of unnamed transgressions. Of course, the l'ord killed its prisoners too, though the weight it used was disease.

James knew if he was going to stay alive for long he needed to be transferred to the middle ward. But to get there, according to the small, fretful, craggy shadow of a woman sitting about five feet away, he would have to pay the turnkeys a shilling and four pence. But he had no more money. The turnkeys who had dragged him through the entrance gate had each claimed six pence as their earned privilege, then turned him over to the convicts, who had hovered about him like crows on carrion, demanding a desultory garnish, which James quickly learned was six shillings and eight pence for them all. As he only had four shillings left after the turnkeys, the convicts took his remaining money, then stripped him of his coat, waistcoat, and shoes to pay the balance of what they deemed was owed. He found that two well placed slugs allowed him to keep the brass key and locket.

So he huddled in the dark iniquity of the l'ord with some thirty criminals—men, women, and children, most of them waiting for trial on hanging offenses. The room echoed their odious chatter, old sick voices and young brazen ones uttering profanities of heaven and earth, volleys of oaths discharged from a mixed collection of detestable throats that loosed both their abusive language and their diseases into the fat gray air. Most were drunk with prison-brewed ale and many were smoking, further blackening what was left to breathe. And from one dark corner came the desperate, relentless sound of at least one couple engaged in some form of a sex act.

He decided to ease his way to the room's one small window, a low, iron-barred hole in the wall. There he would press his face against the grate and suck in some fresh air as he had seen others doing. Standing slowly, he struggled a little against his ankle chains and shuffled across the floor. He could feel and hear the lice crackling under his bare feet, as if the path to the window were strewn with tiny seashells. He paused when a man stumbled from the darkness ahead of him and lurched to the window, then urinated onto the street three stories below. In the brownish light, James could see the urine splattering off the grate and back to the cell floor. The man farted loudly, took a few drunken paces, then veered back into the black hell. James turned around and began to ease his way back to his place along the wall.

"Mum. Mum," a cherubic voice cried. James peered to his right. There in the half-light sat a small boy in the middle of the floor.

James turned to the child just as the sad moan came again. He moved closer. "What'd ye say, lad?"

The boy mumbled something unintelligible, then screamed, "Mum!"

James knelt beside him. "Ah, 'tis all right, lad—"

"Get away! I won't be your bugger-boy!" A small fist shot out, slamming James's chin.

James recoiled, grabbing the boy's arm. "Nay! Ye were yelling for yer mother, lad."

"So what? I was asleep." The boy kicked at him. "Get your hands off me!"

James held tight. "Stop, lad. I won't hurt ye. Stop it now. Ease yerself."

"What do you want with me?" the boy asked, his thrashing beginning to slow, then stop.

Relaxing his grip, James sat. "I came to see about ye. How old are ye, lad?"

"I dunno."

"How old do ye reckon?"

"Probably eleven."

James found a smile to offer. "When I was about yer age, not much older, I too was alone, yelling for my mother. Only I was chained in a ship, not in a bleedin' prison like—"

"I don't care, you old Irishman. Leave me be."

James sighed, then stood. "All right. So be it."

But then the boy blurted, "What're you in for, anyway? Buggerin' boys the likes of me?"

"Nay. Of course not." He gave a fake chuckle, then took a breath of the reeking air and squatted down again. "I'll tell ye, but first you tell me. What'd they accuse ye of?"

"No accusin' to it. I'm guilty."

"What'd ye do?"

"Stole a silver tankard. My sister and I needed to eat. Couldn't stand her whorin'. So, you?" the boy pressed. "Your crime?"

"I've been charged with shooting a man," James explained, shaking lice from his hand.

"Murder? Truly?" The boy's eyes widened. "You're a murderer?"

"Only accused."

The boy gave a disappointed groan. "The man didn't die?"

This was a bit much. "Actually, he did." James lowered his head. "'Twas an accident."

"I can guess," the boy said with a pugnacious turn, "you shot him in the back."

James cringed, pulling himself to his feet. "I said 'twas an accident." He clinked his shackles back to his wall, muttering, "'Twas a horrible mistake." The room was thick with coughs and raspy throats. After a few minutes he felt a tap on his foot. It was the boy. James scowled. "Ye're an ill-mannered lad." The boy didn't move. "All right, sit."

The boy settled on the nasty stone floor next to James and leaned against the wall. "Gonna transport me to the stinkin' Colonies," he offered. "They gonna hang you?"

"If they don't believe me."

"Maybe they'll transport you too."

"Not likely," replied James, feeling his stubbly beard.

"Gonna swing from the Tyburn Tree?"

"'Twas an accident. I imagine I'll be freed."

"But if they don't believe you?"

"Then, like ye said, they'll probably hang me." James thought for a moment, then asked, "So, ye think ye'll be transported to the Colonies?"

"Aye!" The boy's eyes brightened. "Ever been there?"

James smiled softly. "Once. I have indeed. Ye afraid of going?"

"Nay," the boy professed grandly, then turned. "You afraid of dying?"

Sergeant John Giffard, examined — "I understood that it was my lord's resolution to destroy Mr. Annesley, if he could. (Was it not the intention of the defendant to disappoint James Annesley?) No, the intention was to put this man out of the way that Richard Annesley might enjoy the estate easy and quiet. (Did you not understand that he compassed the death of this man?) I cannot tell. My lord is very apt to be flashy in his discourse. He is a man subject to passion and heat, and he is hasty and rash in his expressions."

— trial transcript, *Annesley v. Anglesea*, 1743

CHAPTER 28

Sweet beguilings, cruel smilings
Tickling souls to death;
Tedious leisures, bitter pleasures,
Smooth yet cragged path;
Heavy lightness, whose sad sightness
Cheers, yet breaks the bearer;
Dainty treasons, whose quaint reasons
Teach, yet fool the hearer.

— from *The Cheat*, Joseph Beaumont, 1652

Though the whole of New Ross and the surrounding villages mourned the death of Fynn Kennedy, only a few courageous souls attended the funeral—being outlawed as it was. And no one, not even Seán, risked holding a wake. The Catholic rites were held secretly at Fynn's grave, on a paltry hill nestled among tens of thousands of Anglesea acres, four miles south of New Ross. Ancient Kennedy land, though for eighty years in the control of the Protestant Annesleys, under the presiding English Earl of Anglesea. A mere parcel in the vast amalgam known as Dunmain. And the fact that Richard was the current Earl made those few brave mourners in attendance all the more nervous. Under the existing penal code, which Richard was known to frenetically enforce, they could all be arrested, the priest hanged, and Fynn's body exhumed and burned. Thus the ceremony was a clipped affair, with guards posted to survey the mile expanse toward Dunmain House.

Now across the hill's crown, a small stand of ash spoke in Gaelic shivers, covering the last of the mourners as they quietly receded, having tossed their handful of black earth to Fynn and sober blessings to Seán. Then the guards returned, filled in the grave, and ushered Father O'Brady away. When done, all that remained was Seán and a mound of grey and earthy stones.

Though dauntless all morning, standing resolute with the others, he now let the emotions come. "Da," his voice quivered, "ye're with Juggy now and pleased. I'm sure." He closed his eyes, bitterness filling his stomach. "I'm not

sure of anything. T' tell the truth." He collapsed to his knees, tears overflowing in pain. Minutes passed. He rolled onto his back, wiped his eyes, and
stared past the ash leaves into the sky. "I'm sorry Da. So sorry. Everything's
gone awry. 'Tis terrible. Jemmy, Seámus, was arrested. He's in London now,
awaitin' his trial. They're callin' it murder. I could've stopped them." He grimaced. "I don't know why I didn't." He heard footsteps approaching, someone ascending the hill. He sat up quickly.

"You shouldn't torment yourself, Seán," said a man thirty feet away. He
was dressed neatly in an expensive suit, pintail wig, his accent a mix of English and Irish.

"Ye shouldn't slink up on others, sir!" Seán was on his feet. The man was
clearly English, landed, Protestant—a threat. Seán grabbed the pommel of his
sword, a naval cutlass.

The man gave a deferential nod. "I've come to pay my respects."

"Then pay them," barked Seán, "and kindly take yer leave."

The man stepped closer—a menacing move cloaked in gentility. "I know
why you left James to fend for himself. And truly, you know as well."

"Who are ye?"

"Ah, we've not been introduced." His gaze was firm. "I am Lord Richard
Annesley."

Seán froze, glaring.

"I can assure you, I am no fiend nor reprobate, as you've been told."
Richard smiled. "Walk with me?" He turned, gesturing in the direction he
had come.

"Remove yerself from my Da's grave," growled Seán.

Richard snapped, "Seems you've buried the fellow on *my* land. Pity. Now
walk with me. Perhaps I'll not snap O'Brady's neck. And I might leave your
Catholic 'Da' to rest."

"Damn yer mouth!" Seán clutched hard the cutlass hilt. "I'll not be
played upon, sir."

"But you've already been played upon, Mr. Kennedy. Mind you, not by
me." He took another careful step. "I regret the burden of bearin' such bad
news, especially on this day." He motioned toward the grave. "But you've
been betrayed by the very man you most trust."

"What are ye sayin'?"

"Come now, Seán. James Annesley has deceived you. We both know
what happened that day in Aberfoyle. My assistant, Captain Bailyn, was in
Edinburgh when they found James."

"Coming t' kill the lot of us, was he?"

"Ney." Richard looked across the open meadow. "Just James."

"Go to hell."

"Maybe I will," he said with a shrug. "Maybe not. But mind you, 'tis one thing to tell a man to go to hell. 'Tis a matter entirely different to make him go."

"I'd have no qualms in making ye go!"

Richard smiled, nonplussed. "I think you'd have to agree, had the good Captain arrived a day earlier, he might have saved your father's life."

"Ye're an arse," Seán snarled. "How'd ye know Jemmy was in Aberfoyle?"

He lowered his gaze, pretentiously dour. "'Twas Fynn, God rest his soul."

"Damn ye! And over his grave!" shouted Seán, drawing his weapon.

"Easy, friend." His voice now English gravy. "Shall I tell the charges against *you*?" He saw Seán frown. "Unless I prevent such, you're to be tried as the murderer's accomplice."

A flash of rage hit Seán. "Ye lie!" He jerked up his cutlass, lunging forward, driving the tip toward Richard's heart. Richard sidestepped, swiftly drawing his own sword. In a steel blur he had parried the lunge, brought his rapier to Seán's throat, and was pressing him against a tree.

"For a navy man, you're a bit rusty with a blade," Richard said with a reproaching smirk. "Do I now have your attention?"

Seán nodded with his eyes, feeling the tip of the rapier brush his neck.

"Two English constables are in route from Dublin to New Ross, as we stand here. They're coming to arrest you for your complicity in James's deed. Shall we have that walk now?" He sheathed his rapier, eyes locked on Seán, then walked away.

Seán followed, sheathing his cutlass. Descending, he shouted, "All right, damn ye."

"'Twas no accident," Richard offered back loudly, slowing his pace.

"That all ye know?" Seán grumbled, catching up.

At the foot of the hill was the Dunganstown-Dunmain Road, and as they broke from the trees, Seán saw a black coach standing in the ruts, its driver watching them intently. Richard stepped through an open a gate in the low stone fence defining the road, then walked toward the coach. He stopped and leaned against the stones. "You Irish like stories, don't you?"

Seán glared.

"As you know, your father wanted revenge for Juggy's death at the hands of the brutal Mr. Bailyn. Mind you, I had no hand in that unfortunate event. But Fynn needed, in a manner of speaking, a means for getting to Bailyn. Bailyn, on the other hand, was intent on killing the young boy, your friend James—though I most strictly forbid it. That leads us to Higgs, who hated Bailyn perhaps as much as your father did. So Higgs and your father agreed…. And please understand that I'm merely relaying what I was told— perhaps you'll make some sense of it." He waited for an expression to form on Seán's face, but nothing came. "Thus, fifteen or so years ago, Higgs agreed to kill Bailyn if your father located James. That way Higgs got the boy trans- ported. Mind you, I convinced Higgs transportation was best. Certainly bet- ter than leaving him on the streets to be killed by Bailyn, wouldn't you say? Captain Bailyn can be so unpredictable. One of his finer qualities. But I digress." Richard plucked fern tips that dangled from crevices between the tight stones. "So an agreement was made."

"My father would never—"

"Ah, now, he loved Juggy and he loved Seámus. Isn't that what he called him?"

"Ye know nothing," Seán fumed.

"Perhaps." Richard gave a dramatic shrug. "As I said, these are facts pre- sented to me. Apparently your father followed you to some alley. Regardless, James was transported. Higgs didn't kill Bailyn, though. Obviously. He can be quite the Scottish lass."

"You ordered Juggy killed. My father hated ye more than Bailyn. He would never—"

"James is a bastard child, born to my brother and Juggy, his wench. I had no hand in killing his mother. Think on it, son. Why would I want her dead? By now she would have admitted James was hers. There were only two options for young Master James: stay in Dublin, embarrassing the Annes- leys' respectable name, or disappear. I was generous. I did the kindest thing I could. Had he remained, he would have starved, been killed, come to some bad end. Your father and I both knew it. And we knew you were moving him around, protecting him. Or so you thought." He paused as a wagon approached. It was carrying high mounds of peat. Because Richard's coach refused to clear the road, the peat wagon squeezed along the stone wall, drag- ging loose stones and scraping ferns to a green smear.

"Ye're a lyin' blackguard," Seán murmured, after the wagon was gone.

Richard grinned. "I don't give a rat's papist arse whether you believe me or not. I'm not here to convince you. Trying to help you. Hoping you won't be hanged as an accomplice."

"I'm no—"

"Of course not, but you did bring your father to James, did you not?"

"I'll kill any man claiming my hand was in my father's murder."

"Murder. Yes, that is what it was. And of course you had no hand in such vile things. But I wonder if the Ross judge will understand. As best I figure it, Higgs told James in Bristol or Scotland. He clearly wanted James to know. He hurried off to Bristol though I advised otherwise. Must have told him your father helped get him transported. James then sent for your father."

"Why would Higgins tell James?"

"Perhaps it made Higgs feel better to confess the truth. He's an odd man. Again, I'm merely piecing together the cloth of the thing. Perhaps you'll come to some other conclusion. As soon as they arrived in Aberfoyle, Mackercher left for Ireland to stir up trouble here. Higgs went to Glasgow, leaving James there alone. That's when I'm guessing James devised his plan and sent for your father. You, unfortunately, brought the lamb to the lion. I'm sorry, but that makes you an accomplice."

"This is insanity." Seán felt woozy.

"Certainly you weren't aware of this, or that James was capable of killing for revenge. If so, you wouldn't have gone on that *tinchal*, of course. And you most certainly wouldn't have let James follow with his musket loaded. I know that. Rest assured."

Seán said nothing.

"If he gets out of Newgate, James will hunt Bailyn, perhaps even me. But most importantly, you." He looked away, a concerned scowl crossing his face. "That young man has lost all his senses. Such a shame. But he always did have his father's arrogant, vicious side."

Seán slowly shook his head, eyes closed. "This is bloody unbelievable."

"Aye. But thank the Lord I have sway with these English constables and Irish judges."

"Can ye call them off?"

"I can try. But you'll need to tell that London jury what you know is true. That you saw James shoot your father, in cold blood."

"James loved my father," Seán said, his voice trailing far away, "Perhaps more than I."

"Of course you loved him. You were his only son," Richard said, his voice warm and momentarily Irish. "And so did I. Fynn was a good man. For Christ's sakes, 'twas me who let you bury him on my land! And I have no mind at present to dig him up."

Seán slumped his face into his hands.

"So, you'll help right this wrong? You'll go to London?"

Seán stood straight and looked about. He stared into the distance. Over there, just past the next tree line, were creeks and fields where two boys used to play. Beyond that was a black forest where mysteries were discovered. And then there were the barns of Dunmain where they had sat, imagining the world. "I will," he whispered.

Richard sighed triumphantly, clapping his hands. "Very good. Swift justice." He picked up a stone that had been knocked loose and shoved it back into the wall. Then he wiped his hands together, cleaning off the dust. "James's trial is in a few weeks. Tell the jury the truth."

Seán kept silent, looking away.

"Find my solicitor at the White Horse Inn, near the Old Bailey. His name is John Giffard." Richard produced a sealed envelope from his pocket. "Give him this letter of introduction from me. He'll tell you how you can help." He gave a cold laugh. "He'd better—he's charging me ten thousand pounds for this prosecution."

As Seán took the envelope, he glanced up, astonished by the amount Richard has said.

"I want justice as much as you do," Richard popped.

"Ye're not in this for justice."

"For swear though, *you* are. Tell them James made certain you unloaded your musket, then your father's. That he saw his chance and fired. Deliberately."

"Said 'damn yer blood' before he fired," Seán muttered.

"No! Did he?" It took Richard a second to remove his smile.

Seán glared. "Don't look so pleased. Make no mistake, ye cur—this is a matter between me and Jemmy. Ye'll be dancin' in the streets when Jemmy's hanged. But not me. That'll be the blackest day of my miserable life. I'll do this thing, but not for you! I'll do it for my da."

"That's all I'm asking." Richard took off his hat and smoothed it, then popped it back on. "That's all." His voice was back to English propriety. "I'll return to Dublin, speak to those English constables, then travel on to London." He pulled a sack of coins from inside his coat. "Do take this. It should cover your passage and inn fees. You'll have expenses."

Seán knocked the sack away. "Keep yer blood money."

"'Tis yours." He placed the sack on the mossy wall. "Do with it as you please. Leave it here for the next passerby, if you insist." He looked at Seán

blankly, then shifted to a concerned, fatherly expression. "I know this is difficult for you. Do call on me if I can be of any assistance." Turning, he signaled
his driver, who quickly brought the coach forward. As he climbed in, he
looked back, tipping his hat. "Till London, Seán."

"See ye in hell."

Richard smiled, stepping inside, snapping the door behind him. Seán
watched the coach kick up gravel. Then he looked at the sack of coins resting
on the wall beside him. With slumped chin and eyes closed, he blew a long
huff. Finally, without looking, he picked up the leather sack and brought it
to his chest. He shifted it from one hand to the other, feeling its weight, considering its heaviness. A jingle sang from within. Gritting his teeth, he thrust
the sack into his pocket.

Sergeant John Giffard, examined — "(Did you suppose from that that he would dispose of that £10,000 in any shape to bring about he death of the plaintiff?) I did. (Did you not apprehend that to be a most wicked crime?) I did."

— trial transcript, *Annesley v. Anglesea*, 1743

CHAPTER 29

The violence of either grief or joy
Their own enactures with themselves destroy:
Where joy most revels, grief doth most lament;
Grief joys, joy grieves, on slender accident.

— from *Hamlet*, William Shakespeare, 1601

Three weeks later the Newgate turnkeys came to the l'ord and hauled the young boy away, along with nine others, all bound for the Old Bailey. Half the day passed before two of the convicts were returned, relaying the outcome of the trials. One of the nine was freed, they said. Four, including the boy, were scorched with the Bailey-burn, then hauled to the quays for colony transport as indentured servants. And the last three, sentenced to hanging, were already thrown in the condemned hold. The two tossed back into the hellish l'ord were given sentences of six years each. A rickety old man leaned close to James's dirty, bearded face and predicted disease would kill those two before winter.

A few hours later, when a set of keys jangled just beyond the door, the ward fell silent and a group of pus-filled eyes turned toward the sound, watching eagerly, anticipating a windfall perhaps, anxious to evaluate the new inmate's possessions. The door creaked open and a turnkey stepped in, followed by a tall well-dressed man, eyes widening then narrowing as he scanned the fetid room. He spotted James and moved toward him. "James! James Annesley! What am I to do with ya?"

James struggled to his feet, the pain from being crumpled on the hard floor searing his legs. "Mr. Mackercher," he called out. "M'God, how glad I am to see ye!"

Mackercher stepped over a few comatose bodies and clasped James by the arm, keeping him balanced. "I was sorry to hear about Fynn. How terrible ya must feel."

James's head sagged slightly. "Aye, 'twas horrible."

Mackercher sighed, peering around warily, wrinkling his nose. "This place is a hogsty."

"Worse. Far worse."

"Come now, let's get ya gone from here. I have someone who wants to see ya."

"Gone?" James eased.

"To the middle ward. At least ya'll be safe there, before yar trial." They moved to the door, which the turnkey cautiously opened.

"My trial? When is it?" asked James, shuffling past the guard. The man glared at him, as though James's move to another ward were a personal affront.

"Tomorrow," said Mackercher.

"Tomorrow?"

Mackercher stopped. "I arrived as quickly as I could." He put a hand on James's back as they resumed walking. "I petitioned yar civil cause against Richard, to the King's Bench in Dublin."

"That's grand, 'tis," said James, attempting the difficulties of optimism. "I trust ye know—t'will be all for naught if I'm hanged." He kept moving, albeit awkwardly in his leg irons.

Mackercher shook his head. "Precisely Richard's design."

James double took the man. "Not the reassurance I was hoping for, Counselor."

Mackercher pulled his mouth tight, saying nothing.

James's pitching walk nearly ran him into an oil lamp, one of the many lining the hall. Their fires lit the air, soot-blackening the upper walls and ceiling, turning the hall into a long, dim, smoky tunnel. His face fell somber. The irons clanged, reverberating against the stone floor, sending rough vibrations through his knees. "My trial, tomorrow—ye'll argue for me?"

"Aye, m'lord," replied Mackercher.

"Thank ye, sir. It will be simple? As it was an accident." When Mackercher didn't answer, James stopped. "Mr. Mackercher?"

Mackercher stepped in front of James, then turned to face him. "I'd hoped it would be a plain matter. Straight. Easily dispensed with. Yet...."

James turned his chin to the side, eyes fixed on Mackercher. "Yet what?"

"This way," a guard barked, urging them on. From a distance, the bell of St. Sepulchre's Church rang its hollow toll for the condemned.

"Something has happened," whispered Mackercher, resuming his pace.

"What?" James asked, alarmed. "What happened?"

"Let's get ya downstairs. We'll discuss it in private. These walls have ears." He turned to the guard behind them and asked, "Good sir, will ya please remove this man's irons." The guard stared back without speaking, unsure of what to do. "This man is my client," Mackercher explained as he advanced, his big frame looming in the flickering light. "Mr. Pilchard is commander of this watch?"

"He is," the guard confirmed, stepping back.

"Mr. Pilchard has assured me that ya'll comply with my requests."

"That's right Henry," a guard declared from somewhere ahead, down the hall. At that, the first guard quickly removed James's shackles.

"Much better," James sighed. The cool draft moving through the hall stung his raw ankles, but he thought it felt wonderful.

"Good," Mackercher said. Then he turned to the guard who was now holding James's irons and said, "Lead us on."

"Please," James whispered as they started walking again. "What has happened?"

Mackercher slowed, glancing back. James could see the worry in the man's gentle eyes. "I made a promise to yar guest that I would let them tell ya. Please be patient." He turned, moving on.

James followed. "Who? What guest?" As he asked, he realized the probable answer: the one person he most dreaded seeing. "Seán? Is it Seán?" His gut tensed.

"Here," the guard snapped, pointing as he stopped. "Down these stairs to your left. First room to your right." He left them standing alone in the corridor.

"No, James," Mackercher whispered shaking his head. They arrived at the bottom of the stairs. "It isn't Seán. Now step in here, if ya will. I've a fresh suit for ya." He motioned to an open door.

James gave a puzzled look, then stepped inside the small room lit by the flames of a little corner fireplace. A set of clothes lay on a wobbly wood table, and a bucket of water sat on the floor, a brush and soap beside it. "Who am I gettin' cleaned for?"

"Ya'll see. But ya need a wash and shave first." He tried a smile, adding, "Most desperately."

James looked directly into Mackercher's eyes, considering him. "This guest ye have for me; he must be carrying grave news."

"In a way, but an extraordinary individual none the less." Mackercher ushered James to the table. "I'll wait in the hall."

—m—

Richard paced the small dining room in the back of the White Horse, one of London's exclusive public inns. A square oak table was in the middle of the dim room, and on it were two goblets, one half empty, the other nearly full. The man sitting at the table took a sip from the nearly full goblet, returned it silently, then resumed smoking his pipe. His strong blue eyes focused on Richard, his chiseled jaw clenched, his solicitor's wig held in perfect place.

Richard broke the silence. "So Giffard, you think you're the best?"

"Do you think I am?" the man responded gently, eyebrows peaking.

"How in Christ would I know? Sure, you're the most expensive whore I've ever hired."

"But does that make me the best?"

"It damn well better! That bastard will either be shittin' himself at Tyburn before the week's out, or you won't be worth a ha'penny!"

"He will if the evidence exists," Giffard said, his voice calm and methodical. "And if we are allowed to present our entire case tomorrow morning."

"You're hedging."

"There are no absolutes with the law, Lord Anglesea." Giffard's steely gaze didn't flinch. The room was growing musty, filling with the smell of the rain pouring on Piccadilly just outside.

"You damn lawyers," Richard mumbled, walking back to the table for another drink.

"You want this man convicted of a murder that is dubious at best. Or worst, as it may be." Giffard took another drink, then continued. "And his relation to you is widely known."

"Assumed relation. Rumored relation. Goddamned lies."

"The judge will have read the newspapers. He'll know James's claim, even if James doesn't declare it from the stand. Though I presume he will. You will need to be clear of the Old Bailey during the proceedings. My client's identity should not be so blatantly obvious."

"Give me a straight answer, Giffard. Can you get a guilty verdict?"

"It will be difficult."

"Why, for Christ's sakes? There was only one other man there, and he's our damned witness! What more could we hope for?"

"More witnesses."

"Well, damnit, there aren't any! Just Seán! The best witness we could ever have—son of the very man James murdered."

"His testimony will be seen as biased."

"But his testimony is the damn truth!" bellowed Richard. "You'll just have to make that maggot judge believe it." He turned away, muttering under his breath, "T'will be a pleasure watching him hang. If only he had another neck for me to strangle with my bare hands."

"Dead is dead, m'lord." Giffard took another sip, then relit his pipe. After a few puffs, blue clouds billowing over, he returned his intense gaze to Richard. "How is it, Lord Anglesea, that the son decided to testify for us?"

Richard closed his eyes, then slowly reopened them. "You do your job. I'll do mine."

"It may come out, under cross-examination."

"Don't let it!"

"Lord Anglesea, let me explain procedure in the Old Bailey—"

"Damn you!" Richard slammed his fist on the table, upsetting the goblets. Fine brandy spewed over burnished wood and Richard was snarling. "Let me explain something to *you*. See that James is hanged, or God help you. You'll have me to deal with."

"I don't work under threats."

"No? You'll whore for a sack of silver. Ten thousand pounds, to be exact."

Giffard took another long pull on his pipe.

"I swear, Giffard, you'd better get it done," fumed Richard. "This is my chance to bury that bastard, and you will not fail me!"

—m—

James felt more alive than he had in a week. The bath, though tepid, had soothed his aching feet and numbed the split pustules and itching scabs that consumed him. When he finished dressing, he opened the door and smiled at Mackercher, who was leaning against the corridor wall.

"Better?" Mackercher asked.

"Aye. Thank ye." The clean clothes were tremendous; a fresh shirt and breeches had never felt so comfortable.

"Good. Come, if ya will." Mackercher extended an arm. "Yar guest awaits."

They walked down the stale-smelling hall for a short distance, then through another passage, finally stopping at a short iron staircase leading down to a sunlit courtyard.

James looked sideways at Mackercher, silently asking, *Out there?*

"I'll join ya soon."

James gave a wary, confused grin. "All right." He stepped slowly down the stairs and into the light, almost blinded by the brilliance. As his eyes adjusted, he saw several people sitting around, most under the covered areas, talking quietly. He scanned them, and immediately saw Captain Blackwell, who appeared to have just noticed him as well. Blackwell gave him a courteous smile, then turned away and whispered to a woman who spun quickly around, revealing her face. James's knees buckled slightly, his mind seized, giving him only a few words to mutter: "Ah, my God! Laura!"

Tears streamed Laura's smiling cheeks. "Oh, James!" she exclaimed, racing to him.

"Laura, m'God," James stammered.

She wrapped him in her warm arms, softy crying. "I've missed ya, *Acushla*," she whispered.

"I am...shocked. I am so pleased." He felt his body relax into her, stunned, amazed. He inhaled her. He embraced her. "Ye're here." He engulfed her, kissing her hands dizzily.

"I just couldn't..." she began, still excitedly whispering. "I just couldn't wait."

"M'God," he said again, his mind caught in a swirling vortex.

"I am no good without ya." She smiled, her teeth bright. "I cannot be without ya."

"No. No. Me as well. I cannot tell you. It means so much for ye t' be here."

She pulled back to see his eyes. "Are ya all right? Are ya vell?"

"Yes. I'm fine," he said, though not entirely sure. 'No' might have been the better answer, but how could he be anything but well and fine in this moment? With her so near he could actually smell her. No imagination required. "Let's sit."

"Of course." She kept an arm around his waist, leading him to a bench.

"My sweet *Acushla*," he whispered, sitting. "Ye needn't have come all this way."

"I had to," she insisted.

"Captain Blackwell, he brought ye?" James saw the man talking with an older woman.

"Oh, aya, he did. That's Madam Kristin, my aunt. She's my chaperone. The captain was most kind to give us passage."

"Indeed!" James nodded. "Deserving a rich reward." He studied them. "Yer aunt?"

"Aya. She arrived in Virginia not long after ya left. She was eager to travel and wanted to come." She paused. A smirk. Her head cocked. "Alright, so I pressed her tirelessly!"

"I'm so glad ye did. And Blackwell?"

"Once he returned, and with Madam Kristen my ally, my parents conceded."

"This is incredible," he said, struggling for the right words. "I love ye. I must say, I am overwhelmed ye're here. That ye're right here. Sitting here. Yer hands in mine." As he leaned to her, she brought her mouth to his, slipping one hand behind his hot neck, pulling him close. They kissed passionately, sloppily, almost painfully. As they had never done in public. But was this "public," the bowels of Newgate Prison? Besides, what rules of prison decorum could be thus-wise offended? Neither cared. And neither noticed Madam Kristen observing them, smiling meekly. It was the power of that moment, of those months, of their journeys, the heartaches and fears, the loss, the longing, all of it colliding, coming together to grant them release, loosing them, pardoning them, handing them over to the grip of insuppressible passion, pulling at them, each together—gravity grabbing sky, earth holding heaven near.

Their lips parted slightly as she took a breath, mouthing into him, "I love ya so, James."

He wiped the tear that slipped over her cheek. "I'll be out this horrible place by tomorrow morning," he said awkwardly. Then he beamed, thinking past the immediate moment. "We'll go to Ireland together! Seán will be there and—"

"Aya, my love." She glanced away, a soft frown forming.

"I scarcely believe my eyes," he said, ignoring her expression. "I'm afraid they're deceiving me. Do tell me this is not some dream. That ye'll not vanish when I awake."

"Shh!" She touched his lips. "Don't say such things. I'm here. I'll never leave ya. Never. Never let ye go from me, ever again. Not in a thousand years."

James kissed the rosy plum of her cheeks, tasting her tears. "I love ye, sweet girl."

"I promised ya last autumn. I'm yars." Her eyes were shimmering blue. "I was going mad without ya. I simply *had* to come. Ya aren't angry, are ya?"

"How could I be?" he exclaimed. "When did ye arrive?"

"We came through Bristol, at least a fortnight ago. I searched for ya everywhere. I was afraid I might not ever…. But, then I read about the shooting and learned ya were here. Captain Blackwell brought us immediately." She shook her head slowly. "My dear James, this matter, the thing that happened, with Fynn.... It is all dreadful and wrong."

"Aye, 'twas a terrible accident. I never—"

"I know," she interjected. "I cannot imagine how ya must feel." They heard thunder rolling, and across the walled courtyard a breeze whipped up, sweetening the air.

"With Mr. Mackercher's help, and you here, all will be fine. Ye met him, Mr. Mackercher?" James asked, then caught himself. "Of course ye have."

"Aya. This morning. He had just arrived from Dublin. He put my aunt and I up in the Bartle House Inn. Then he told me about...." Her voice faded. "He seems a kind man."

"He is, indeed. And London is a dangerous place. I'm glad he'll be looking out for ye, till I'm released." James glanced at the iron staircase, half-expecting Mackercher to be standing there. He wasn't. The courtyard grew gray as thick clouds settled above. "I wonder if he's found Seán. I forgot t' ask if—"

"Have ya spoken to Seán since then...since that day?" Laura stood, looking away.

James got to his feet. "Nay, but I must. He—"

"James. I...." Her voice faltered. "I have news of Seán. Mr. Mackercher told me."

He walked to her, then gently turned her to face him. "What is it, Laura?"

"Did ya need Seán to be here, in London, for yar trial?"

"Aye! He is the only witness. He can attest on my behalf." James's voice dropped, seeing her blank expression. "Will he not come?" Laura grasped his hands in hers. "Is he not well?" he continued. "What happened, Laura?"

"I know ya're very close to him. Mr. Mackercher said much. And from what ya said in Virginia, and yar letters and all...." Laura paused, sniffing.

He put his arms around her. "Let Mackercher bring this news. There's no need for—"

"Nay. I asked to tell ya." She was faintly shaking in his arms. She glanced up, then quickly away, whispering, "Seán is here in London, James."

"He is?" He released her slightly. "Where?"

"The White Horse Inn."

"That's good." He waited but nothing came. "Is it not good?"

"He's there as a guest of yar uncle."

"What?"

"He will testify against ya."

"Nay, ye heard it wrong. Not Seán. He wouldn't do that."

"He'll say ya killed Fynn on purpose." She crumpled to the bench and leaned forward, covering her face with her hands. "They'll hang ya, James. Oh God, they will."

James felt his blood chill, his shoulders slumping forward. Then he erupted, pacing about. "Jaysus! This can't be! He's under Richard's demonic spell, he is. I don't believe this!"

"I could hardly bear to tell ya."

He returned to the bench, growling, "Why'd Mackercher leave this to ye, for ye—"

"Nay," she said, crying, "I insisted. I—"

"I'm sorry, James," said Mackercher, suddenly near. "She can be most persuasive."

She dabbed at her vibrant eyes. "I was here. I wanted to help. I wanted to be the one to tell ya."

"I could hardly believe it as well," Mackercher whispered. "But let me deal with Seán."

"Mr. Mackercher!" James snapped, spinning to him squarely. Then stopped. He blinked, relaxing his glare. "Thank ye for tending to Laura. I wish ye'd told me this news, not her, but I understand. As for Seán...." He blew out a deep breath. "No harm should come to him."

The rain began in fat plops, forcing the three of them under a walkway—Laura to a bench, James and Mackercher standing. James leaned against a column, staring at the flagstone splatters. He could see himself and Seán, standing over Fynn's body as sheets of gray rain stung their faces, soaking the ground with Fynn's blood. "How could Seán ever fathom such an idea?" he mumbled. "How could he? That I would do such a thing, deliberately?"

"Madness," offered Mackercher.

"Richard," fumed James. "May God damn that man. He's the devil incarnate." Rage gurgled up, bringing another image: He was standing, holding a bloody sword, watching Richard's body spew hot blood into rain puddles. The image disappeared. It didn't matter. He would never get that opportunity, to exact such final revenge. Laura was right. With Seán's testimony, and no conflicting witness, he would be convicted of murder. He would hang at Tyburn before the week ended. He closed his eyes to the rain. "Damn ye, Seán," he muttered aloud. "We were as brothers."

CHAPTER 30

Hear you, sir:
What is the reason that you use me thus?
I loved you ever.
But 'tis no matter.
Let Hercules himself do what he may,
The cat will mew
And dog will have his day.

— from *Hamlet*, William Shakespeare, 1601

It is said fear makes a man sharp, but James's fear left him immobilized, thick, murky with dread. Behind him, the Old Bailey's gallery was crowded. Though Mackercher had counseled otherwise, James kept glancing back into that swarm of callous faces. From their scrutinizing eyes and pointing fingers, he knew whom they had come to see. Though the judge was late and the trial was yet to begin, James felt it well underway. These people neither knew him nor cared about him. They were here for the spectacle alone, regardless of the outcome. He could hear their drums rolling. Each no doubt hoped he would hang, hoping they could picnic on Tyburn Hill watching him swing; watching the man who claimed to be noble, ignobly piss himself and die. He wished they would go away, but he knew they would not—these kind of people never go away. He took a deep breath and sighed loudly, leaning back in his heavy oak chair, listening to it creak against his weight. How many had sat in this very chair and heard their execution proclaimed? The last chair in which they would ever sit. Cold fear jolted him, his stomach cramping, as if he had just swallowed a brick of ice. As if he were freezing to death from the inside out. Nothing could warm him. Even his heart seemed to shiver. He moved, stretching against his collar. Mackercher had purchased these clothes, insisting James dress as the Earl of his claims. Now his best clothes might well be his last clothes, here in his last chair—an expensive deep lavender suit with a silk cloak, silver buckles and a smooth white wig. When the wig maker fitted him, James smirked, asking who would catch it when the executioner threw it off. No one laughed. He looked again at the faces behind him, their snares still keeping beat. A memory filled his mind: He was in a little school near Dunmain, age nine, the Tiarna Óige dressed in pompous finery, assigned to a creaky oak chair by the wall, being stared at, mocked by the others. Then he saw himself at his father's funeral—cat eyes staring from a black sea, studying him, as if they knew then that this day would come. As if they knew his fate was sealed, from that moment on, there in the muddy yard of Christ Church.

"Come now," Mackercher whispered. "Leave them be."

James snorted in response, feeling Mackercher's eyes on him.

"They've come to gawk," said Mackercher. "They mean nothing." His long white solicitor's wig draped his black silk robe, and as he leaned near, the robe rustled, and the ends of the wig fell across James's shoulder, giving the appearance that James's wig was longer and curlier on that side. "Ya're in the newspapers," he continued. "'Tis all. These people have nothing better to do."

James gave a nod, then turned, looking into Laura's compassionate eyes. She was directly behind him, yet too far away for them to speak. She held him with a gentle smile. He tried to return it, but knew his was too meek to be believed. He was almost glad that she was not beside him, that they couldn't talk. She should not hear the fear in his voice. Yet at least she was there, comforting him, ten feet away. He closed his eyes and inhaled. How blessed he was. That she loved him so completely. Yet how difficult it must be for her. He turned and faced forward again, his eyes to the empty, open expanse of worn floor planks running from the accused's table to the judge's bench. Now that Seán had resolved against him, James decided it was a sign from God that Laura had arrived so fortuitously. But what kind of sign? A sign of hope—an angel heralding imminent victory? Or was she sent as a last comfort, a last earthly consolation, last beauty, last love, before his neck snapped, dispatching him to the feet of God? Perhaps God didn't have a hand in it either way. Perhaps it was nothing more than ponderous fate.

Deep voices drew his attention to the right side of the courtroom. There stood a man dressed similarly to Mackercher: long solicitor's wig, black silk robe. Except this man's robe had a scarlet trim. And something else was different—he was priggish, leaning on the barrister's bar as if he owned it, speaking to a pair of young lawyers who were wearing shorter wigs, no scarlet trims. Both were standing on the other side of the barrister's bar. Clearly not touching it. Almost respectfully so. No, fearfully. They appeared about James's age, perhaps a bit younger. They seemed transfixed, listening to the words of the elder solicitor as if each syllable mattered, as if they were hearing the secrets of the universe, the uttering of eternal truths, the voice of God. They were scared, James thought. Perhaps more than him. He wondered why. Yet he felt neither envy nor pity. He felt nothing more than slight contempt. The man they were worshiping had been hired to kill him, to see him unjustly hanged. Just as they clearly believed, they could be no better than that man. They too were aspiring murderers.

Mackercher leaned in. "That's John Giffard. The prosecuting solicitor."

"Why the red trim?"

"He's a member of the Lincoln Inn, an order of King's solicitors. A Prime Sergeant Solicitor of the King's Bench. That's all. Of no weight here, I can assure ya."

"What is that, that title?"

"Nothing important to us," muttered Mackercher.

James could hear the dismissive tone. "What does it mean?"

Mackercher smiled thinly. "He can represent matters on behalf of the King."

"Ye must be joking!" James strained to keep his voice muffled.

"It has no effect on us here, except...."

"Except what?"

"Richard undoubtedly paid a fortune for a Prime Sergeant to prosecute this matter."

"'Twas my fortune he paid," James growled. "Using my money t' see me hanged."

"Aye, James," Mackercher sighed. "All we can do is make certain the judge learns *who* hired that shylock. I'll try to get it out of Seán."

James considered the imposing solicitor a moment more. Just then the man turned to James and smiled, as if he had known all along that James was talking about him. James frowned, averting his gaze. "What was his name?" he asked quietly.

"John Giffard."

"Ye ever tried a matter against him?"

"Nay." Mackercher gave a slight shrug, as if to say it didn't matter.

"Nay?" James looked alarmed.

Mackercher grinned. "It doesn't mean he can't be given a good Scottish arse-whippin'."

James nodded slowly, unconvinced, then whispered, "Good."

Mackercher sat quietly for a moment, then turned around, scanning the crowd. "Captain Bailyn is here," he muttered, turning back.

"Are you surprised?"

"Not a'toll. He's here for Richard." Mackercher's eyebrows knotted. "I'm sure he's also come for Mr. Higgins."

"He'll challenge Higgins," James contended. "If he finds him on the street."

"Bailyn hasn't the decorum to stand for a challenge. Higgins must leave hastily. I offered him protection, transport to the Highlands. But he refused me. The man is troubled beyond what we know."

From the slurry of voices behind them, a man asked, "Are you Seán Kennedy?"

James whirled to see Seán facing away, talking in hushed tones to one of the young lawyers near Giffard. Then James noticed two beady eyes watching him from the back of the gallery. Captain Bailyn's viper eyes beamed, mocking James's hurt and anger. James glanced again at Seán's back. A cacophony of bilious rage and overwhelming sadness swelled up, forcing him to look away. How could Seán stand there so calm, so deceitful, treasonous to all they had ever held sacred? James felt his gut rock and gurgle.

"O'Yea! O'Yea! O'Yea!" the bailiff bellowed from beside the bench, his words drawing everyone to their feet. "His Majesty's Honorable Court of Common Pleas is now in session, the Honorable Lord Justice Westerfield presiding. God save the King!" The judge, obese and looming, ambled in with his thick red robe dragging against everything. Finally arriving at his big chair, he sighed dramatically, then plopped down. He tugged at his robe to straighten it, and everyone took their seats.

"Bring in the jury," Judge Westerfield grumbled softly. Twelve men streamed into the room from a side door, stepped into the jury box, and sat on the two long benches. To James, they all appeared tired, even drunk. This was their third trial for the day, he realized, but they seemed as though it was their forty-third. He watched for some sign of life, some glimmer of hope, something his direction. But there was nothing. Not even a glance. "James Annesley, laborer," the judge intoned, "is charged with the crime of murder of a certain Mr. Fynn Kennedy, and that James Annesley did unto him, against the peace of our Lord, and the King who now is, and to the damage of said Mr. Fynn Kennedy, commit that most heinous offense. How plead the defendant?" Now judge and jury were staring at James. The gallery was silent.

Mackercher nudged James, whispering, "As prepared."

James stood. "I am the rightful Earl of Anglesea and a peer of this realm. As such, I am not subject to this court." Loud murmurs flew through the crowd.

"Oh? Are you now?" The judge smirked. "You sound like a pilferin' Irishman. Lord Irish, how do you plead?"

Now the room rippled with laughter. James flexed his jaw. Mackercher, now standing, said, "Your lordship, my client, James Annesley, Earl of Anglesea, pleads innocent of the charges of which he is so maliciously accused. I too reiterate that his title precludes him—"

"Very well," the judge muttered. "And you are . . ."

"Sergeant Mackercher, your lordship."

"Humph!" the judge snorted reprovingly, then looked down at his bench as if he were reading something. Mackercher and James took their seats. The judge raised an eyebrow at Mackercher. "Counsel, are you a Scotsman?"

Mackercher got to his feet again. "Aye, your lordship."

"A Jacobite? The hell you say. In my court?"

"Nay, your lordship, a Whig. A loyal subject of our King."

"You're all the same," the judge sneered, then looked at his bailiff. "You let 'em all in here, don't you? Scots defending papists, even." The bailiff half nodded. Mackercher sat down, frowning. When the judge turned to the prosecution's table, his face softened to a fat, enveloping smile. "Well, if it isn't Prime Sergeant Giffard. I say, counsel, do come forward."

"Good day, your lordship," Giffard replied, moving swiftly to the bench.

As the solicitor approached, the judge asked, "Sergeant Giffard, how long has it been since you stepped foot in the Old Bailey?"

"Ah, Judge Westerfield, I—" began Giffard.

"Your lordship," Mackercher was back on his feet, protesting. "If you're going to speak with Sergeant Giffard at the bench, may I approach as well?" He was already around the table.

"Agh, damn! Ney, Scot. Make your own friends," the judge growled. "Step back." He turned to Giffard, who was standing resolute beside the heavy walnut bench. "Come see me, John, after this…this matter. We'll share a spot of gin and tea."

"Aye, your lordship. You are most gracious," replied Giffard with a retreating bow.

"Now, Sergeants, let's not drag this thing out," barked the judge, his expression reminding James of an angry bulldog. "I won't be tarried from my tea. Understood?"

"Aye, your lordship," answered Mackercher and Giffard, almost in unison.

"So, what do you have for me, Sergeant Giffard?"

"If it may please the court, this is but a simple matter." Giffard walked to the jury and began an abbreviated description of the case, facile with his language, relating in terse detail the misery to be told: On that fateful day, Mr. James Annesley had been hunting with the elderly Mr. Fynn Kennedy, and his son, Seán Kennedy, on the property of Mr. Daniel Mackercher (of note, the accused's counsel here today). For reasons known only to the accused (and perhaps Sergeant Mackercher as well?) as the afternoon ended Mr. Annesley effectively disarmed the two Kennedy men, then leveled his musket and fired it intentionally, willfully murdering the elder Mr. Kennedy without mercy or conscience. Barely five minutes passed before Giffard was once again in his seat.

Mackercher was next. In bare sentences, he told the jury the shooting had been an accident and that the evidence would show that to be true. Then he thanked the gentlemen of the jury and returned to his place beside James.

Mackercher had no sooner sat down when Seán was called to the front. James watched him carefully as he walked by, the gait, the uncertain stance, shoulders slumped, looking pitiful and alone. James felt anger rising again. After Seán swore to tell the truth and was warned of the penalties for perjury, he turned around, at last facing James. But he kept his eyes on the floor, as if also studying the long planks that ran to James. He stood solemn, motionless in the center of the witnesses box.

Giffard approached slowly, and after a few preliminary questions, he steered the subject to the hunt. "Mr. Kennedy, you were hunting with your father and James Annesley that day?"

"Aye."

"And at the end of the day, you came upon a small lake and rested there. Is that right?"

"Aye."

"What did you do with your muskets? They were still rammed and powdered, aye?"

Seán stared at his feet, then the far wall. "James unloaded our muskets and—"

"Yours and your father's?"

"Aye."

"What about *his*, Mr. Kennedy? What about Mr. Annesley's musket?"

"He didn't unload it, I suppose."

"Clearly he didn't. So he made sure you and your father had disarmed your weapons before he.... Well, you tell us what happened next."

"I was in the lead, walking away from the loch, when I heard—"

"You saw, or heard?"

"I...I heard Jemmy—I mean saw—"

"I know, Mr. Kennedy," Giffard interrupted. "The murdered man was your father. No doubt, this is difficult for you. But, please, bear up and tell us what you saw."

Mackercher was on his feet, his face like a fist. "My lord, I humbly request an instruction to Sergeant Giffard to refrain from the word, 'murder', as that is the very accusation in issue—"

"Sit down, Scot," muttered the judge, waving at Seán, silently telling him to continue.

"What you saw, Mr. Kennedy," said Giffard, spurring Seán.

"I turned and saw him level his musket at my da."

"Who, exactly, did you see?"

"Who I saw?"

"Mr. Kennedy," Giffard moved closer to the box. "We realize that it is with great effort that you come before this jury to relate the horrid facts of that day; that you wouldn't be here if you didn't feel obliged to bring the truth before us. But, please, do tell us: exactly who did you see level the musket?"

"Jemmy. James Annesley."

"Very well. So you turned and saw Mr. Annesley raising the barrel of his musket. Like this?" Giffard pantomimed the action, one arm outstretched, taking imaginary aim at the jury.

"Aye, over a rock fence, and then—"

"He was aiming like thus, at your father?"

"Aye." Seán's voice dropped to a murmur. "Then he said, 'damn yer blood' and fired."

"He shouted, 'Damn your blood!' did he?"

"Aye, sir."

Mackercher stood to object, but the judge waved him down.

"Damn...your...blood," Giffard repeated, emphasizing each word.

For the first time, Seán's eyes flicked at James, who had been waiting for that moment. James had his arm stretched out on the table before him, wrist bent, holding three fingers straight up in the air. "Through ice," he mouthed. "No matter the bastard." He saw Seán freeze.

"Good Lord, Mr. Kennedy," Giffard continued, unaware of James's signal behind him. "That must have been horrible, indeed. What happened next?"

"Hum?" Seán mumbled, breaking his stare from James's hand.

"I asked—"

"Sergeant Giffard," the judge interrupted. "I think this jury has heard quite enough. Mr. Kennedy saw the defendant shoot the man on purpose." He glared at Seán. "Were there any other witnesses?"

"Other witnesses?" Seán echoed.

"Aye, Irish. You know. Other witnesses."

"Nay, sir. Yer lordship," whispered Seán.

"Then step down."

Mackercher was standing. "Your lordship, may I not cross-examine this witness?"

"Ney, Scot. I see no reason. He was there and he was the only witness. The gentlemen of the jury have heard enough."

"But yar lordship!" Mackercher protested angrily.

"What do you want!?" the judge thundered.

"We have a witness who was also there and will testify otherwise."

"Ah, of course, Scot. I am certain Mr. Annesley will claim—"

"Nay, your lordship. Another man."

"Good God! You are trying to keep me from my tea, aren't you?"

"Nay, sir. I'm trying to defend my client," retorted Mackercher, abruptly stepping around the table. "Your lordship, if I may bring on my witness now, I do believe you'll find my questions to be brief, his answers exculpatory. But if—"

"Bring him, then."

"Aye, your lordship. But I cannot predict the time required for Sergeant Giffard's cross-examination. If he is allowed to question my witness, we may be here long past tea."

"Fine, no cross. All right, Sergeant Giffard?"

Giffard looked shocked. "Your lordship, since I don't know whom the defendant wishes to call, how can I waive my right to cross?"

"By saying 'Aye,' John," responded the judge, his voice laden with sarcasm.

"But your lordship…." stammered Giffard.

"If you insist on crossing, then I'll let this Scot cross that man who was just up here."

"Truly, your lordship," Giffard went on, sounding dismayed, "I would not mind if he did. In fact, I had rather expected he would."

"Did you?"

"Well, aye."

"So, you don't mind, then?"

"Well, nay," Giffard began. "Your lordship, Sergeant Mackercher has—"

"All right then, if you insist. Let it be mutually conceded and the waiver recorded. No crosses from either side. Very efficient of you both. Bring on your witness, Scot."

Mackercher turned quickly to the gallery, signaling a man near the back.

Giffard stood as if in a daze, stuttering, "Your, your lordship, no crosses? I thought you, just now, I thought you were going to allow Sergeant Mackercher to cross Mr. Kennedy."

"Then you bloody-well didn't hear me," the judge shouted. Giffard slumped back into his chair. "Prime Sergeant Giffard, you've been off arguing for your high wages in front of the King's Bench for too long. This is *my* court. There will be no crosses on this matter. Just as you agreed. You may not reverse your waiver." He shouted to Mackercher, "Scot, proceed!"

Mackercher jumped. "Aye, your lordship,"

"You'd better get your man up here now, or you'll miss even your direct exam."

"We call Mr. Patrick Higgins to the witness box."

The judge waved his hand irritably, as if to prod the man forward. James sat rapt, stunned by that flurry of verbiage between the judge and the solicitors. He was beyond thankful for Mackercher. Higgins walked through the courtroom, making his way to the front. Bailyn glared. When sworn in, Higgins turned to the jury, following Mackercher's lead, running through a hurried set of questions. With skilled alacrity, Mackercher was to the point: "Mr. Higgins, what did ya see that day?"

Higgins moved forward, facing the jury box. "I was hunting grouse beyond Aberfoyle. 'Twas on the first of May, in the early evenin', I do believe." He paused nervously. "Oh, I forget the time—you know how it is, only shoemakers and tailors count the hours." He smiled, glancing uncomfortably at the glowering judge, then continued. "As I said, I was grouse hunting. I came over a ridge, north of the loch, late in the day, and saw three men—"

"Mr. Higgins," the judge interrupted, "did it appear to you that Mr. Annesley shot Mr. Kennedy intentionally or by accident?"

Higgins paused, then recovered quickly. "By accident, your lordship."

"All right. You can step down."

"Your lordship—" Mackercher began.

"Ney, Scot. That's all you needed to ask. Damned if I don't have to do

your job for you. How a Scot becomes a Sergeant Solicitor, I'll never know."
He turned to the jury. "Gentlemen, you have heard enough. One witness
claims it was an accident, the other claims it wasn't. 'Tis up to you to decide.
You may find the accused guilty of murder, and for which Mr. Annesley will be
hanged. Or you may call the matter chance medley and set Mr. Annesley free."

Instantly, the jury box rumbled in soft discussion—the sound of a stream
after a storm, gurgling as it absorbs the deluge of chaotic torrents. Droll eyes
moved back and forth, to and from James, and he wondered what they could
possibly be discussing so feverishly: they had been given so little to discuss!
Nevertheless he prayed for them to say "medley." *Please God!* He turned and
saw Laura leaning forward, eyes closed, her lips quivering in prayer.

Higgins excused himself from the box, sluing for the door. First, a small
nod to Mackercher and James. They nodded back in gratitude. Mackercher
had said it was Higgins's idea to take the stand and lie. James hated, yet appreciated, the irony: Seán and Higgins. Friend turned traitor. Traitor turned friend.

"Your lordship?" a juror ventured after five full minutes had passed.

"Aye?" The judge sat straight, his enormous eyebrows raised expectantly.
"Mr. Foreman of the jury, have you reached your verdict?"

"Aye, your lordship. We find the event to have been chance medley."

"Very well, Mr. Annesley, you may go. We are adjourned." The judge
groaned as he levered his bulk from his chair, like an old fat dog getting up
from a nap. "Mr. Giffard, will you be joining me for gin and tea in chambers?"

"Nay, your lordship, I should think not." Giffard's voice was firm and
severe.

"As you wish." As His Lordship codgered out, his fat robe brushed a law
book. It teetered, then hit the floor with an explosive pop.

James slumped forward in his chair, relieved, entirely exhausted. He
smiled, resuming his breath, feeling Mackercher's hands, then Laura's, on his
shoulders. Then Laura's face was next to his, her warm wet cheek pressed
against his forehead. "Ya're free, James. Ya're free!"

James lifted his face and stood, embracing her, then turned to Mackercher and grabbed him by the arms. "Well done, *Scot.*" He grinned. "Well
done, indeed!"

"The damned judge is who you should be praising," said Mackercher,
shaking his head.

"And Higgins," James added.

Mackercher laughed. "Aye, b'jingo. Higgins. He stood by you."

James's smile vanished instantly. A flicker of light now gone. *Seán!* He
pivoted, looking, hoping he was still in the courtroom. But he was gone.

CHAPTER 31

All you that in the condemned holds do lie,
Prepare you, for tomorrow you shall die;
Watch all and pray, the hour's drawing near,
That you before the Almighty must appear.
Examine well yourselves, in time repent,
That you may not to eternal flames be sent;
And when St. Sepulchre's bell tomorrow tolls,
The Lord above have mercy on your souls.

— Speech to the condemned of Newgate Prison,
read from St. Sepulchre's Church, 1690-1762.

Seán shoved his way through the crowd and burst from the Old Bailey like
a drowning man breaking the surface of a boiling sea. He leaned against a
horse railing along Gilt-Spur Street, sucking air, rubbing the sweat from his
flushed face, feeling his stomach begin to seize. People were massed along
the walk, most trying to enter the arched gallery doors, straining against the
throng pushing to leave. He heard voices everywhere, calling out the verdict, that James Annesley had been acquitted, that the Earl was innocent,
that the young nobleman had bravely declared himself the Earl of Anglesea
and triumphed over his accusers. A few recognized Seán and were pointing and whispering. Then one spoke loudly, recounting, "He's the one said
Mr. Annesley done it." Those damning words. "I didn't say that," Seán tried,
turning away. It was a vulgar crowd. He felt terribly alone.

Stumbling, he stepped headlong into the street, wanting to clear the Old
Bailey before Jemmy emerged. He looked up at crows screaming across the
low-hanging clouds—the color of tombstones. Church bells rang out the two
o'clock hour. One church was to his left, across Hart-Row Street. St. Sepulchre's. Its bell tower hoisting four gothic spires high overhead, looming
them at him, the gargoyles grinning at him like he was family. Below, he saw
its white stone walls guarded by an infantry of elms along the churchyard
fence. He would go there, he decided. No one would find him there. No

one would question him. There he could think. There he would silence these voices pounding within him, condemning him. But to get to St. Sepulchre's forced him back, past the Old Bailey entrance. He turned, pushing against the crowd still shuffling through the gallery door. He lowered his chin and moved quickly, hoping for obscurity, praying Jemmy wouldn't come out. He shoved. He wormed. Reaching Hart-Row Street, he glanced up at another man hurrying away. The man was hugging the court wall, hood pulled tight, eyes following Seán. Seán studied the figure, then recognized him. Higgins. They passed each other, their eyes locked, emotive though void. Hart-Row Street was cluttered with traffic and Seán had to wait for a wagon of goats to cross in front of him, then a green coach, followed by two horsemen in livery. Behind him, a new commotion erupted but he didn't turn. He figured Jemmy had just come out. The traffic cleared and he walked, focused on the church. He could feel Higgins's eyes searing a hole in his coat. Reaching the far side, he followed the long iron fence, the elms interrogating him along the way. The arched entrance to St. Sepulchre's was just ahead. He picked up his pace. Hurrying through the ancient covered portal, he pushed open the church's massive ironwood door. It creaked a cautious welcome. Inside the narthex, the venerable cathedral was cool dampness. He heard his footsteps echo across the flagstone floor, his breath heavy and loud, yet slowing.

"May I help you?" a rector asked from the back of the nave.

"Nay, father." Seán kept moving toward the altar. "I know where I'm going."

"Very well, my son," the man said as Seán passed.

Two rows from the altar bench, he stopped. He surveyed the empty nave, as if expecting someone to be lurking there. Slowly, quietly, he stepped into a pew and sat. Leaning forward, he buried his face in his hands, shaking and feeling sick, the questions prickling his mind. He had told the truth, hadn't he? Clearly Higgins lied. But why? What did that man owe Jemmy? Had Higgins's guilt compelled him into such a tale? *Whatever his cause, thank ye Lord that Higgins said what he said.* Seán opened his eyes. He exhaled loudly, lightly banging his forehead on the back of the oak pew in front. This was horrible. But what choice had he had? Richard was only protecting what was rightfully his. Wasn't he? Jemmy had shot, killed, no it was murder, out of revenge, right? He had yelled 'damned yer blood,' hadn't he? Had he heard Jemmy wrong? Did Jemmy unload Fynn's musket? Or did he do it? Jemmy insisted Fynn go hunting that day, right? Or was that his own idea, to bring his father along? Though these questions had churned for weeks, only now could Seán let them fully rise.

Behind him, the main door creaked. Then came men's faint voices. One he recognized as the rector's. He didn't turn. Then the talking stopped and footsteps began moving his way, becoming louder and more resolved. They stopped at the end of his pew. Seán looked up, but kept his face forward, staring at the crucifix and the candles flittering on either side. He knew it was Jemmy. The man slid into the pew behind him, the wood protesting under the man's weight.

"What do ye want with me?" Seán mumbled.

"We have a sayin' in Scotland," the man began. "The breath—"

"Higgs!" Seán spun to see Higgins slouched forward in his pew, his tunic still covering his head like the shawl of an old woman. "Afraid for yer life, I see? Well ye should be. With yer lies and all."

"No less than you," Higgins calmly retorted.

Cold shivers ran Seán's back. "Not me," he said. "I spoke the truth. Ye perjured—"

"Truth?"

"Aye. Truth." He returned to the crucifix. "What do ye know of it?"

"Too little," whispered Higgins. "If ya be so pure, why skulk in here? Why not face the man ya used to call 'friend'? The friend yar words nearly hanged."

"Shut yer trap, Higgs. Ye're the one—"

Higgins interrupted. "I know what ya must feel."

"Ye know nothing of me, old man." Seán closed his eyes, listening for that rough Scottish voice to return. He sensed the man scoot closer.

"The breath of a false friend," Higgins iced, "be worse than the fuss of a weasel."

"Damn ye," Seán snarled.

"Ya ever heard the fuss of a weasel? Before it attacks?"

"Higgs!" Seán spun, grabbing the aged man by the collar. "I told ye—"

"You were wrong."

Seán eased his grip. "Nay sir, I was right."

"You were wrong and I think ya know it. In yar heart, ya do."

"Horse shite," Seán bellowed, shoving Higgins back. The rector cleared his throat. Seán was on his feet, retrieving his hat.

"Your father had not a thing to do with James's kidnapping." Higgins pulled himself upright.

Though Seán was already five paces away, he stopped.

"He didn't," Higgins continued louder. "James never had any evil intentions against the man. He admired him, held him in the greatest regard. Loved him, no doubt. You know that."

Seán returned, stood a moment, then sat across the aisle. He pulled in a deep breath and closed his eyes.

"What did Richard tell ya? Fynn gave up James that night? Eh?"

Silence.

"That's what he said?" Higgins pressed, his whispers feathering the silence.

Now Seán slowly nodded.

"He's a damnable liar, that one. 'Twas me. I spoke to Fynn on Richard's behalf. I know what was said between them."

Seán turned his face. He clutched the pew in front, feeling ill, his knuckles turning as white as his face.

"I remember you, as a lad," Higgins continued. "A more loyal friend, James never had. One time, a man came to ya and gave ya a warning—remember? A warning 'bout Charity Heath." He lowered his voice. "Told ya she was shaggin' Richard. Remember?"

Seán looked up at the soaring ceiling, the gothic windows pouring colorful light into the hazy cold air. "Aye," he whispered.

"'Twas me."

Seán again nodded, absently. A tear spilled onto his cheek and he quickly wiped it away.

"I was a fool." Higgins's voice trailed. "Thought Richard would see me hanged. Perhaps, but I sold my soul all the same. 'Twas fear that ruined me. I excused myself. Self-pardoned for having done no harm directly, ya understand. Aye, a fool I was."

The cathedral fell silent, and Seán looked again at the crucifix. The blood looked so real.

"How have ya justified yar own sins?" asked Higgins.

Seán pulled his lips between his teeth, his eyes again viced tight.

"Eh?" Higgins prodded.

"I thought I was right," mumbled Seán.

"I suppose ya did. Ya're more the man who chooses blindness, than the one who stumbles from ignorance. All the worse, I suppose." He pulled the tunic from his head, revealing his own tussled hair. "Seán, ya were a good lad. Took care of James. Richard said, 'Seán Kennedy is more loyal than all of ya. Someday that lad will work for me.'" He shifted in his seat. The bench creaked.

Seán clenched his fists. "Pray, Higgins, say no more."

Silence fell between them, like the hush of a dead wind at sea. Seán's mind tumbled through those Dublin days and nights. He and Jemmy had both been afraid, but they had stuck together. No matter the bastard. He looked down at his hand and saw only three fingers. "Tell me, Higgs, who told Richard where Jemmy would be that night?"

"As I said, 'twas me. Charity Heath told me. And I carried her messages to Richard. But there was one thing she said that I didn't tell Richard: James's mother was booked on that same ship. I told myself I was setting things right, keeping that to myself. I was certain mother and son would reunite on board. Thus by letting him be kidnapped, I was having him saved. But of course, I was wrong."

"Was she on that same ship?"

"Aye. James doesn't know how close he came to freedom. I haven't the heart to tell him now. But she was there, indeed. I saw her board in Ringsend. Yet somehow, it never came to be." He shook his head.

"It was that simple?" asked Seán. "What did Da know—"

"Aye, 'twas that simple. Charity deceived Mary, and that was that. Yar da had no hand in the affair. None a'toll."

Seán sniffed loudly, then sneezed.

"God bless ya."

"Humph," Seán mouthed, wiping his nose with his pocket cloth. He was feeling grave, and Higgins's words were only making him worse, like an axe falling on a rotten tree.

"Yar da did have his secrets though."

"Aye? Like what?"

"He knew Richard killed Arthur, yet never said a word."

"Richard killed his own brother?" exclaimed Seán, stuffing the pocket cloth away.

"Had Bailyn and me do it. I found Arthur in a tavern. Bailyn drove him down with a coach and six." He inhaled fully. "I watched him die in the mud."

Seán closed his eyes. "Da said nothing?"

"Avenging Arthur's cruelty, I suppose."

"How'd he know of it, that ye'd killed the man?"

Higgins shuffled in his seat again, then whispered, "I told him."

"Why? What could Da do about it? Richard was the Earl, and—"

"I know, Seán. I was a fool about many things." He drifted in thought.

Then he stood as if to leave.

"So, what will ye do now?" asked Seán, his voice warm for the first time.

"Me? Oh, Richard's men are out there, scouring London, ordered to bring my head to Dunmain House. Bailyn at their helm." Higgins smirked.

"Where will ye go?" Seán stood as well.

"Home. To the Highlands."

"Ye'll run?"

"Why does one sinner question another's penance?" snapped Higgins. "What do ya plan to do yarself if not run?"

"I don't know."

Higgins placed a hand on Seán's shoulder. "You were wrong, Seán. But to go away now would make in worse. Ya must make amends with James. Let yar friend forgive ya, if he will."

"I don't think he would," said Seán, his words softly echoing off the high walls.

"Ya're not Judas. Ya may prove to be Peter, but that's for you to decide. The bell's not cracked between you and James. There's still time."

"I hope so," Seán said meekly.

"Ya must go to James." Higgins pulled a scrap of newspaper from his pocket, then handed it to Seán, who took it and read:

> On Wednesday last, the 28th of April, before the King's
> Bench in Dublin, suit was brought against Richard Annesley,
> Seventh Earl of Anglesea, Defendant, by one James Annesley,
> Esq., Plaintiff, by and through Daniel Mackercher, Esq.,
> Sergeant Solicitor, on behalf of Plaintiff. Plaintiff sues to
> claim the title of Earl of Anglesea and the property forthwith,
> and is the same person who arrived in the kingdom last year
> after serving fourteen years slavery in our American colonies.
> We can expect the great trial to occur before the new year.

"Seán," Higgins continued. "James must win this. To do so, he'll need yar help. Will ya go to him?"

Seán sighed, returning the paper to Higgins. "Someday."

"Someday soon, I hope. Take some advice, Seán," Higgins continued. "Life is dreadfully short of days. Get married. Have a family while ya can. Make yar peace with James."

"I will," Seán said, though not sure he meant it. How could he face

James, after nearly sealing his death?

Higgins extended his hand and Seán shook it. "He's a good man," Higgins said, then added in a whisper, "and so are you."

Seán said nothing. He didn't know anything to say. Higgins turned and walked away. "God be with ye," Seán finally muttered to the old man's back. Higgins raised a hand in reply. How could he have been so stupid, Seán asked himself. What a fool he had been, not to see through Richard's deception. What must Jemmy think of him? He grouped three fingers together and stared at them.

Suddenly an explosion of loud voices ripped through the church. Higgins was yelling, then someone else, then the angry sound of sharp steel loosed. The rector was entreating, "No bloodshed in the house of God!" Seán sprinted the aisle, jerking his cutlass free. The silhouettes of men were just beyond the narthex, under the arched portal. Now closer, he saw Higgins and Captain Bailyn circling one another, round and round in the tight breezeway, swords drawn.

Seán stepped into the portal, brandishing his sword. "Stop! This is madness!"

A man burst from the shadows, threw his forearm across Seán's face, bending his neck back, exposing his throat. Dagger touched skin. "Stay back!" the man growled, "or I'll cut you open!" Though Seán was facing the arched ceiling, he forced his eyes down to see the back of the dagger. Beyond it, Bailyn and Higgins were holding each other off, each making his point known.

"There's no reason for this," Seán tried. "Let him be."

"Drop yer blade," the man behind him demanded. Seán's cutlass clanged to the floor. "And the dagger," he added. Seán pulled that blade from its sheath, letting it fall as well. The sweaty hold relaxed and Seán lowered his chin, turning to glare at the man. One of Richard's troopers, no doubt. "What do ye say we let these two lovebirds have their dance?" the man sneered. His dagger was inches from Seán's throat. Seán noticed other men just outside, beyond Bailyn and Higgins. More of Richard's men, guarding against unexpected worshipers.

In an instant, Higgins lunged forward. Bailyn parried, a blur, sidestepping, his rapier grazing Higgins's forearm. Blood trickled from the wound, but Higgins didn't seem to notice; he was intent, heaving like a wild beast cornered. He circled, pulling his dagger with his left hand. Bailyn laughed. "Ye'll need that, Higgs."

"Whatever is necessary," snarled Higgins. After another flurry of lunges and parries, attacks and counterattacks, both men were beginning to sweat. Then an opening appeared and Higgins thrust his weapon hard. Bailyn jumped back, but not in time, and Higgins's blade sliced his shoulder, blood immediately soaking the cloth.

"Jaysus Christ!" Bailyn shouted. He grit his teeth and lunged back again. Higgins parried but Bailyn's attack was a feint, and now Higgins's side was perilously exposed. Bailyn's rapier plunged through Higgins's stomach in one deadly instant, sending blood spurting from his back where it emerged. Higgins staggered backward, his eyes wide with shock. Bailyn jerked his rapier free, then drove it forward again with all the strength of his fury. The tip found the careening form, piercing ribs and chest. Higgins fell in a quivering heap, his hands still grasping his rapier and dagger. As blood streamed from his chest, back and mouth, he curled his body, moaning through a gurgle, as if the stone floor were cradling him, holding his blood.

"Goddamned traitor," Bailyn hissed, wheezing. He leaned over and spat on Higgins, then kicked him in the head, though the man was clearly dead. One of Bailyn's men came to him, helping him with his coat. Bailyn turned to Seán with a sneer. "Ye know, Kennedy, for a moment there, I thought ye might've forgotten who ye serve."

"Ye're a sick animal," Seán shot back.

"So what of it?" Bailyn said, laughing. "Eh?"

"Yer day will come. I swear upon it."

Bailyn stepped over Higgins's body, approaching Seán, breathing heat in his face. He stopped, then suddenly kissed Seán on the cheek. "Don't forget, Kennedy, ye're one of us now. Always will be. So don't be getting yer own mind." He gestured toward Higgins's body. "Ye can see what happens." He peered down his nose, looking Seán over like a butcher surveying a hog. "But then go ahead, why don't ye? Ye'd make a good corpse too."

Seán slowly shook his head, glaring.

"Go on, mourn for this piece of shite. If ye must," Captain Bailyn continued. "But ye best be at Dunmain House within a fortnight."

"Why so?"

"Pray Lord Anglesea forgives yer impudence. Ye'll need my petition on yer behalf."

"Ye can both go to straight to hell."

Bailyn smiled, then motioned the man to release Seán. Freed, Seán picked up his cutlass and dagger. Bailyn stepped into the daylight, his men following, and disappeared. The rector and another man were behind Seán now, trembling something about getting the constable.

Seán stared down. The cold portico was eerily quiet. Numinously so. He had seen men killed before, at sea. Even some who had died more violently. But this was different. This he would never forget. This gruesome scene demanded retribution. He owed it to Higgins. He owed it to James. With one act he would revenge this murder. And redeem himself.

—⁂—

Lord Chief Justice Bowes, summing remarks to the jury —
"Wickedness and weakness generally go hand in hand."

— trial transcript, *Annesley v. Anglesea,* 1743

—⁂—

CHAPTER 32

A little more than kin, and less than kind.

—from *Hamlet*, William Shakespeare, 1601

Three Months Later
Saturday, September 14, 1743
The Curragh Races — Kildare, Ireland

The horses were rounding the last turn, a rattling rumble onto the straight. Even from a distance, James could see the dirt and sod exploding from the cannonade of hooves, the jockeys' elbows pumping as they whipped their mounts, the horses' heads bobbing rhythmically, ferocious nostrils, eyes blazing through a rushing storm of chestnut and brown, flashes of bright orange, red and blue, an unyielding mass of flesh shaking the earth.

"Come on, Packet! Come on, boy!" yelled Mackercher, his eyes fixed down the track.

James leaned into the white rail, shouting, "Go Dover!"

Beside him, Laura was screaming, "Dover! Pick it up, Dover!"

"Packet's the one," Mackercher called over the roar. "He's in the lead!"

"Dover's there!" James was shouting louder now. "Look at him go!"

"Packet will hold!"

"Come on, put yar heart in it!" Laura was jumping up and down as the thunderous wave of horses closed in on the finish line.

"Dover's passing!"

"Come on Packet, don't let that English rogue take ya!"

"Dover!"

The horses shot by in an enchanting blur, the ground tremoring, the spectators pivoting to see them go, shouting, clenching their fists, throwing hats into the cool indigo sky.

"He won!" James grabbed Laura, picking her up, spinning her. "He won!"

"Aya, he von!" Laura said, her eyes sparkling, her beautiful mouth laughing. She kissed James on the forehead. "What a fine horse that Dover is."

"Ah, you two," grumbled Mackercher. "Packet had the field till he lost his courage."

"Better luck on the point stakes," said Laura. "Aya, Mr. Mackercher?" She gave him a teasing smile.

"Apparently, Miss Johansson," he said, tipping his hat, "I'm in need of yar counsel."

She gave a coquettish turn. "I'd be glad to assist, sir."

"Don't coddle the old man," James scolded with a chuckle.

Mackercher frowned, mockingly serious. "Miss Johansson knows how to treat elders."

"Ye'd think ye'd know pity from polish, at yer age," James said.

"Never mind him," Laura said, taking Mackercher by the arm. "He doesn't know swift from slow. Didn't put a shilling on Dover till I did."

"Aha!" Mackercher turned back, smiling. "Ya said *you* picked that horse."

"Well I did pick it. After she did. No less true."

Mackercher slapped him on the back. "Ya're a sly fox. First ya let yar bride gamble in the open day, then ya hide behind her skirt!"

James laughed. "Let her? Nay. She's a mind of her own, as ya know."

"That she has."

Laura reached between them, grabbing Mackercher's hand. "And my mind now is for you, Mr. Mackercher, to escort me to the vinning post. Don't ya be concerned—we'll keep appearances. We'll tell them all the vinnings are yars."

"Then I must take my leave, Lord Annesley," said Mackercher with a perfunctory bow. Letting the young beauty lead him away, he grinned back triumphantly.

James laughed, calling after them, "She knows who has the guineas."

"And how to choose a horse, b'God," Mackercher replied.

Laura smiled at James, then blew him a kiss. "And a husband. See ya in a bit, aya?"

"Go!" He grinned, brushing them away. "But mind ye bring my *vinnings* as well!" Three of Mackercher's Highland guards followed close behind the two of them, the remaining four staying with James. James watched Mackercher and Laura stroll away, through the crowd, arm in arm, her blue dress gliding over the trampled sod. He loved to see her happy. As clearly she was. Especially now, with a wedding date set. And he hadn't seen Mackercher in better spirits in over two months. Not since Higgins was buried.

—⁓—

The morning after the murder trial, James and Mackercher had been urgently summoned out to the street in front of their London inn. There they found Higgins's bloody body abandoned under a rotten horse blanket in the back of a hay wagon. A threat from Richard, most likely. Or a warning by some unknown ally. Yet perhaps, the deliverer simply hoped Higgins's body would be properly buried, not stolen away for surgical experiments. Regardless of the intended message, finding the corpse got them underway. Within the hour James and Laura were in route to Ireland, along with Laura's aunt, Madam Kristin, and accompanied by nine Highland guards. Mackercher promised to leave within a day; bound for Glasgow to bury Higgins. Then he would travel on to Edinburgh, where he planned to hire attorneys to assist in the impending trial against Richard. And there too he would recruit more Highland guards to accompany them all in Ireland.

—⁓—

Thus in the inky depths of a warm night, on the fifteenth of June, at Drogheda, north of Dublin—James Annesley returned to Ireland, Laura at his side. He never forgot the moment. He felt stolid, stepping onto the creaky pier, leaden yet unwilling to linger on the docks for long. From Drogheda, a hackney coach carried them to the Huntsman Inn in Kildare, about thirty miles from Dublin. They had stayed there ever since.

He was uncomfortable in Ireland, yet found few words to form his feelings. Laura strolled long walks with him, trailed closely by Mackercher's guards. But they talked mainly of insignificant things, never about his Ireland, his childhood. Tense at first, they eased into an understood rhythm of distance and careful silence. For the most part, he thought there was nothing of importance remaining to be told. He had never been to Drogheda as a lad. Never to Kildare. His father once promised to take him to the Curragh to see the horse races, but never did. Sure he knew the trees, the smells, the people, the sounds, the night sky, but what did that matter? Nothing about Ireland enthralled him, charmed him, made him think of quaint stories to tell her, fond memories once lost. To James, his boyhood was Seán, his Ireland was Fynn, and he refused to talk about either.

He wondered if he would feel different when he went to Dublin in a couple of months. He would be there for the trial. Would he hate Dublin? Would he hate Seán all the more? He ran the place across and through his mind. Copper Alley. The old butchery. Frapper Lane. The Annesley house. The taverns. The River Liffey. Anglesea Street. Temple Bar. Christ Church. St. Stephen's Green. The skull. The castle walls. None of it mattered. All of it mattered. Only the trial mattered. What if he didn't win? What if he didn't become the Earl? After all this, it was a maddening thought. But he held it. What would he do then? Yet, what if he did win? Did he want Dunmain too? It was the Kennedy's. He already had plans for that. But what of Dublin. The properties there. The memories there. Answers eluded him.

Seán was ever-present on his mind. He knew Seán had disappeared after the murder trial, but it was of no concern. Let him rot, he thought. Seán's image would come, sometimes as a boy at Dunmain House or in Dublin, or as a young man in the Royal Navy. Or he would see them hiding in Dublin. Or them in Yorktown. Bristol or Scotland. But then always came London: his friend in the witness box, betraying him. He tried to shake those memories away.

In July, he began writing his memoirs, of sorts, at the behest of London's *Gentleman's Magazine.* They had sent a fraternal, matey correspondent with ninety guineas and an adulating plea. James had agreed, albeit reluctantly. The writer added much fantasy to the Colonial portion, fearing the story needed charisma, what with all that James wouldn't allow—James told much, directly wrote many of the passages, but held back on most personal matters, keeping those for himself. Laura was private, not for the masses to read upon. And nothing was to be written of Seán or Fynn. It was too difficult, too overwhelming, too private. Besides, if he told anything of them, he would have to tell how they ended. And that was something he simply would not do. "Keep it about the Colonies," he thus told the writer. "Make it up, if you wish. Whatever might best sell," he instructed, which was disingenuous as he actually wished no one would read it. And so when it was finished, it became a story of James in love with Indian maidens mixed with passages of truth about Richard and his childhood. He disavowed it quickly.

—m—

Mackercher arrived in Ireland that July, a month after James and Laura. He brought three barristers, two solicitors, four servants, and seven more

Highland guards. He too moved into the Huntsman Inn, along with several other attorneys and guards. The rest of the entourage was settled at Kildare's Blue Crow Inn. Mackercher also brought fifteen pounds from the Sheffield family, for James, along with a cursory note from James's great-aunt instructing him that the Duke of Buckingham advised James never to admit the Sheffields gave any assistance in the matter, that they had in any way contributed to his cause. If such was to become found in the London papers, it would be vociferously denied. But, that said, in the happy instance of James's much anticipated victory, he was beseeched to "please come for a grand visit among peers."

When trial preparation began in earnest, James was grateful for the flurried activity. Though the focus was on proving his identity, proving his mother, he could nevertheless lose himself in it, the strategies, the legal machinations, the lawyers' discussions, the endless meals and bottomless drams. Witnesses came by the hundreds, though most liars. The newspaper accounts made James's story well-known and people streamed into Dublin from all over southern Ireland, seeking out Mr. Mackercher to claim they knew James as a lad. Each, regardless of their credibility or sobriety, venerated James, promising conclusive evidence that Mary Sheffield was indeed the mother. Most wanted money for those truths they felt so morally compelled to passionately impart. The greater the "truth," the higher the price. And so it went.

Those witnesses taken seriously were whisked off to Kildare. There they were hidden from corruption, flip-flopping, and any form of chicane resignation. The others, the clearly false witnesses, the boldest liars, were handled graciously, given a shilling, a firm handshake, and a perfidious promise to be called upon to testify—a tactic hoping they would not peddle a different story to the opposing forces, Richard's legal team, which had formed ranks on Dublin's Anglesea Street, in one of his hulking estates. Richard's claim, that James was the son of Joan Landy, was public knowledge, and a steady stream of liars plied their trade shuffling from one camp to the other and back again. Yet none concerned Mackercher as much as Charity Heath, well known to be Richard's lead and most damning witness. They had to be ready for her. To offset her lies, to discredit her, even the most spurious were considered.

—⁜—

They had been at the Curragh races for nearly two hours and James agreed with Mackercher: it was good for the soul to get out, to get some air, even if only for a day. He smiled, leaning on the railing, watching the young jockeys easing their horses through cooling laps. The Irish sun warmed his face. The smell of heather and horses balmed his senses. He was glad they had come. He glanced over to the race house, the grey stone building clothed in ivy where Mackercher and Laura disappeared. High on the upper end wall was the large posting board. In front of it was a redheaded boy on a long rickety ladder, chalking the prior race's results and the odds for the next one. James studied the odds between a mare named Yesterday's Bliss and a gelding called Borrowed Hope. Just then the boy abruptly stopped writing and turned to the west. He seemed to be peering into the distance, away from the racetrack, then pointed in that direction and yelled something to the people below.

"What's he saying?" James asked a guard nearby.

"Who, yar lordship?"

James pointed. "That lad there, on the ladder."

"Can't hear him."

"English…sod, something," said another guard.

The wind shifted and the boy's voice came clear. "Soldiers," announced James.

"Red coats?" asked another guard, straining to see. "What business would they have?"

"I don't know," James muttered. "Let's not stand here." He moved into the thick crowd, making his way to the building. Mackercher needed to be told. Laura needed to be away from here. Something was wrong. As he neared the building, the redheaded boy came down and a short man took his place.

"A squadron, 'tis!" the Irishman shouted. "The bleedin' Newbridge infantry!"

Spectators began retreating, shouting for others to follow, heading for their horses and wagons. James realized most of them were Catholics, always nervous about any show of English force. He kept moving, assuming his Highland guards were close behind. Suddenly a gun blast erupted inside. Then screams, followed by a rush of people through the massive main door, forcing him back. "Laura!" he yelled before someone knocked him down. He scrambled to his feet, looking for the guards. Only one—fifteen feet and fifty people away. To his left he spotted a smaller door into the race house, with only a few people emerging from it. He ran there, shoving a man aside, stepping over another, and pushed his way inside. He froze.

Laura had her back to the gaming window and in front of her was Mackercher, glaring at a man who was yelling feverously in Mackercher's face.

"Damn yer Scottish blood!" the man bellowed. "You're a damnable maggot if ever I smelt one." James thought he recognized the voice. He crouched, reaching under his coat for his dirk. Whatever was happening, whoever that raging man was, all that mattered was Laura, getting to her, getting her out of here. The man was still shouting. "For Christ's sakes, James Annesley is nothing more than a shoeboy, an imposter who should've been hanged in London. Indeed, mark me, Mackercher," he slurred slightly, "James won't leave Ireland, not alive. Piss on your lawsuit. I'll have you in chains."

Richard! James growled inside. The thought, the reality of that man being there, so close to Laura, pulled James up, standing resolute, adrenaline pumping. He gripped the dirk tightly, but quickly slumped down. He was too tall to stand straight without being seen.

Richard continued, "Your men have been arrested by my constables. English soldiers under my charge will be here shortly to see them away. Tell me where the bastard is and I'll leave you be."

James studied his options, the available paths, albeit few. He had to get into the middle, into the open, grab Laura and get her out. Though Richard's withering barrage continued, the stout Scotsman only stared, his eyes steely, unwavering. Laura was obviously frightened, looking around, to the main door, apparently hoping to see James there. From his position, James could see the back of Richard's head, the long wig flowing from under an expensive green hat. The man's right hand was holding a short horsewhip, twitching, making the straight thing flick and wiggle alive. His left palm was open, hovering over the gilded hilt of his sheathed rapier. Ten feet in front of Richard, near Laura's feet, lay one of the Highland guards, bleeding, grimacing, apparently shot in the leg, groaning, pulling himself behind the wagering pole. The other two guards were standing rapt, pistols at their sides, staring at several men behind Richard, each with an aimed musket.

"Why don't we go outside and take paces on the sod?" Mackercher challenged, his voice rigid and quiet. "Just you and me. Let these men stand down."

James quickly moved to his left, slinking behind the spectators, until he could see Richard's men. There were four. But where was Captain Bailyn?

"Pistols? I am without!" Richard bellowed. "Ye've one holstered yet ye seek satisfaction?" He spoke louder, turning as to be certain the crowd heard him. "Is this yer idea of Scottish honor?"

"McCauley!" Mackercher barked, "Give this man yar pistol." The guard flipped his pistol around, offering it to the Earl.

"Ney," balked Richard. "I could never trust a Jacobite's firearm."

"Of course ya wouldn't," whispered Mackercher. "Pious turds such as yarself have no honor about them. None a'toll. Ya're no nobleman. And these fine Irish can see that."

"Quiet yer tongue. Ye're the rogue!" He again addressed the crowd. "This is nothing more than a villain in second-hand finery. A vile lawyer hiding a criminal from justice. I've come to protect you from—"

Mackercher smirked. "Ya stole both land and title, and in the process—"

"Damn you!" Richard swung with the horsewhip but Mackercher caught it mid-air and held it fast. Laura stepped back, searching for an escape, and James watched her, surprised at how fragile her beauty appeared, her wild nature now flushed with alarm.

"Ya stole yar stinkin' peerage," Mackercher continued. "Ya're a lying raconteur. Ya kidnapped a boy and murdered my sister. I curse ya before all these men!" He jerked the whip from Richard's hand then slapped him across the face with it.

"Damn you!" howled Richard, recoiling in pain.

Mackercher threw the whip. It bounced off Richard's chest and fell to the floor. "You mark *me*, Richard Annesley," Mackercher breathed, a finger pointed in the other's face, "In Dublin, I'll show this country who ya really are."

"You're dead! I'll have satisfaction from you!" Richard screamed, his face red, jaw shaking.

"Any time. Any place."

"Do ye not realize on whose land ye're standing? Who do you think owns this bloody track? Who do ye think governs this area? I am the law here and you and your men are trespassers. I warned ye! Now you're all under arrest!" He spun to face his men. "Constables, throw these men in irons."

James burst upon them, charging Richard from behind. In an instant, he had hold and spun him around, using Richard's body as a shield against the muskets. He shoved the dirk firmly against Richard's side. "Think twice, gentlemen!" James barked, "Lower those guns."

Behind him, Laura cried, "No, James!"

"If it isn't my prodigal nephew," Richard snarled.

"I should run ye through, right here," replied James, his voice steady. "Get out Laura!" he ordered. "Soldiers are coming. Go, Mr. Mackercher!"

"You'll hang for this," Richard said bitterly, his black eyes boring a hole. "I'll tear you limb from scrawny limb."

"Shut yer mouth." James prodded him lightly with the dirk, cutting through cloth. As the constables took a hesitant step forward, Mackercher pulled his pistol and took aim at them. They stopped. Behind him, James heard the two Highland guards cocking their pistols as well.

"All right men," Mackercher said calmly. "There's no need for this. Lay down yar weapons and we'll all ease out of here."

"You're outnumbered," one rebuked, looking at James.

"Not while I'm prying these ribs apart," James snapped back.

"Don't listen to him," commanded Richard.

"Nay?" Mackercher said, enraged. He shoved the barrel against Richard's temple. "Do as he said. Tell yar men to back away. God help me, I'll blow yar brains all over that window. Leaving Lord Annesley with no need of slicing ya."

Richard hesitated, then growled at his men, "Stand down." The constables quickly complied. "When the infantry arrives, arrest these animals. And that bitch with them."

James eyes narrowed. He made a fist around the dirk's grip, cocked back and slammed it squarely into Richard's jaw, sending the Earl flying to the ground. "Say that again, I dare ye! Say it! I'll gut you like the pig ye are!" Now James was on him, dirk turned to slam its point right through the man's heart.

Mackercher's mass were there, lifting James, throwing him off. "He's not worth it."

"You won't get away with this, by Christ," Richard stuttered, struggling to his feet.

"Go fuck yer own self!" James shot back. He grabbed Laura and they rushed for the door, him leading the way, brandishing the dirk. The crowd split for them. His heart was pounding out of his throat. They hurried to the paddock, then raced into the stables. There they found two of the Highlanders' horses still saddled. Without saying a word, he led one into the open and helped Laura climb on, then re-entered the stall for the other.

"James!" she cried in a muffled scream. James spun to see Seán in the middle passage of the stable, holding the reins of Laura's horse.

James grabbed a pistol from a saddlebag and took aim. "What do ye want?" he roared.

"Ye gonna shoot me, Jemmy?" asked Seán, not sarcastically, but with resignation.

"I just might."

"Perhaps ye should."

"Why are you here?" James blurted, then realized the answer. "Ye're here with Richard." He moved closer, his voice menacing, cocking the pistol.

Seán stood still, watching warily. "No, Jemmy. I'm not."

Laura was pleading, "James, let's go."

"I didn't know Richard was here," Seán continued. "Until I saw Bailyn and heard—"

"Bailyn?" James's eyes widened. "Where is he?"

Seán shook his head. "If I find him, I mean to kill him."

"Horse shite! Ye're with them."

"Listen to me! I was summoned by Mackercher. To be here today. To talk with you. That you and I might reconcile."

James led his horse forward, keeping a careful aim on Seán's head. "Just back up, Seán."

"I didn't know about any of this," said Seán, retreating a few steps.

James had his horse to the middle of the stable and was preparing to mount. "Tell me one thing, friend, was it you who killed Higgs?"

"Jaysus, no. 'Twas Bailyn. I brought him to ye for burying. To warn ye."

"Sold yer soul to the devil, ye did. Ye bloody traitor."

"I'm telling ye true. I called on Mackercher in Edinburgh. He arranged us to meet here."

James glared. "I haven't the time for this or your lies." He waved the pistol at Seán. "I want ye to stand aside now. If ye've anything to say, find me in Kildare."

"How nice, finding you two lads here," announced Captain Bailyn, stepping into the stable, clapping his hands. Two men slipped in behind him, both armed with blunderbusses and blocking the exit. "Just like those olden days of yore."

James wheeled around, pointing his pistol. "Get yer arse back, Bailyn!"

"Oh, and look!" He smirked at Laura. "His whore. Ye carryin' this bastard's bastard?"

"I will kill you, Bailyn. I swear on it." James clenched his teeth, restraining himself from pulling the trigger.

Bailyn leaned to see past James, then smiled at Seán. "Ye still work for us, aye?"

Seán ignored him.

"Let's see, shall we?" Bailyn sneered. "Take his pistol." He motioned toward James.

James's eyes flashed to Seán, then back to Bailyn, then to the two men beyond.

"Let me have it, Seámus," said Seán.

James wheeled to see Seán's hand extended, palm up. "Damn ye!" James bellowed. "And don't ye dare call me such."

"I'm glad to be here, to see this," said Bailyn, grinning.

"Please. I'm asking ye." Seán moved closer. "Just let me have it."

The distinctive clomp of a military march resonated outside, followed by the distant order to halt. A voice commanded, "Affix bayonets!" James saw Bailyn's toothy smile.

"'Tis over," said Seán. "There's only one thing left to do."

James turned back toward Seán, his mind racing. Then, with a shaky hand, he lowered the pistol, defeated. Then he saw it, Seán's outstretched hand. His palm was up, his three middle fingers held tightly together, his thumb and little finger spread wide.

"One choice left, Seámus. And 'tis mine. Let me do what I must do."

James saw it all, everything the next minute would hold, all before it happened. He slowly shook his head, mouthing "no" as he withdrew the weapon.

"Let's have this done with," Bailyn ordered.

Seán nodded. "Soldiers will be here soon. Let me do this. I was wrong then. Let me be right now."

James glanced back at Bailyn, who was still beaming. Then he looked at Seán, jaw flexed tight. He gave a knowing blink and nod, took a deep breath and carefully handed the pistol over, butt first, barrel toward Bailyn. He hesitated a moment, giving Seán a small smile. Finally, he let go.

"Now!" yelled Seán. As James jumped clear, Seán lifted the pistol and fired.

Deafening explosions ripped through the stables, the echo mixing with men shouting, horses neighing in fear. Laura's horse charged madly for the light, James's close behind as he struggled to climb on. Once in the saddle, he spurred the animal into a thundering run. Laura was already a good distance ahead, her blue dress flapping wildly. When two more shots blasted out in quick succession, James looked back though the flying dirt and sod churning up behind him. Captain Bailyn was racing on foot from the stables, followed by one of his men. Soldiers were swarming the ivy-clad buildings, the track, the paddock, some rushing to the stables. James whipped his horse harder, finally catching up with Laura, then again looked back. Counting Bailyn, there were at least six men riding hard their direction.

CHAPTER 33

There must be something terrible in a situation such
as this—where a life depends on chance.

— *Memoirs of an Unfortunate Young Nobleman,*
James Annesley, 1743

They rode hard, galloping across the Curragh plain, through a shallow creek
and into the cover of trees. "James, stop. I must stop," Laura yelled breath-
lessly, slowing her horse in the safety of the slanting shadows.

James reined his horse around. "What is it?"

"I can't," she began, flushed and panting. "I can't go this fast. I almost
fell."

"Ride astride then. Can ye?" He turned toward the creek, watching for
their pursuers.

"I've never tried and at a gallop." She hesitated. "I might not—"

"'Tis all right," he said, flashing a reassuring smile and spurring his horse
up beside hers. "We'll let yers go off and split the tracks. Here, climb on." He
held his arm out and she took it, pulling herself up sideways in front of him.
"Whoa, stand," he ordered, jerking back on the bit, forcing the animal to quit
lurching forward.

"I'm set," she assured him.

James smacked her horse on the rump, shooing it off at a run, then
wrapped his arm around her and pulled her close to his chest. He spurred his
horse forward, out of the woods, across another field. Laura's blonde hair had
come loose from its combs and was now streaming back, across his shoulder,
her head leaning against the scar on his face, her small hands grasping his
arm. He couldn't push the horse to a full gallop, not with both of them on it,
not through the trees, not for long. "Do ye see a house?"

"What?" she shouted, not hearing him over the wind and hooves.

"A farmhouse or barn. Help me find one."

She nodded.

They rode for another mile without seeing a building of any kind, except an occasional sheep pen. James slowed their pace. He didn't know the land, and as it was mid-afternoon on an overcast day he was not entirely sure which direction they were traveling. Kildare was to the north, he knew, but were they riding north or northwest, or even west? At least no one was following them, as far as he could tell. They would stop. They needed to rest and figure where they were.

"There!" Laura pointed to the right.

"Aye, so 'tis," said James, relieved. Over half a mile away was a small cottage on a smooth green hillside framed by a stand of trees. He turned the horse toward it, spurring the beast hard. Laura leaned back and he held her tighter. Suddenly a flash of anger struck him. It had been foolish to take her to the races, too risky, and he had known it. He had even told Mackercher he didn't think they should go. But at Mackercher's insistence, he had given in. What a fool he had been to let her get anywhere near Richard and his damned gunmen. The thought of Laura being in harm's way was infuriating. A breach of an inviolable promise. But it was not Mackercher's fault, he reminded himself. It was his own doing. From that he pictured Mackercher standing there in the race house, declaring Richard's crimes for everyone to hear. I pray he got away. But what of Seán? Seámus? He called me Seámus. Damn. Don't let him be dead.

Nearing the cottage, he slowed the horse, trotting it around to the front and stopped. As he helped Laura dismount, an old, robust woman came wobbling out in a faded green dress and tattered apron, brandishing a large stick. "Get off dat beast or I bid ye ride on!" she ordered. She advanced toward the horse, walking directly past Laura.

"Ma'am, we mean ye no harm," James began. "We—"

"Well den," she said, smiling at the horse, "I'll spare ye harm in return."

"We thank ye," James stammered, smiling cautiously as he got off the horse. The woman had stopped near the horse's head and was now running her wrinkled hand along its jaw, murmuring something to it. As if they had mysteriously common bonds. As if this were not their first meeting.

Laura started, "Ma'am, I hope—"

"Ah, by Jaysus, the Lord Christ and Mother Mary!" The old woman jumped. "I thought ye on me other side."

"Sorry." Laura looked perplexed.

James studied the far tree line, looking for movement, anyone on horseback, but he saw nothing. "Ma'am, if it'd be no burden, I'd like to stable our horse here a bit? We must—"

"What's de name?" the woman asked, still stroking the horse's sweaty muzzle.

"My apologies, ma'am. James Annesley at yer service. And this is—"

"A horse named James?"

"Nay, ma'am," he said slowly, exasperated. "We need to use yer stables, yer pen—"

"So, what's its name?"

"I don't know. If we could use your—"

"Ye don't know de name?"

Laura moved quickly to the woman, gently placing an arm around her. "Its name is Dover, ma'am," she said, then turned to James and whispered, "She's blind."

James nodded with a slight smile at her, then tugged on the reins, prodding it to walk with him. The woman followed, keeping a hand on the horse's rump, while Laura walked beside James. They went around to the back of the thatched cottage and headed for a horse pen set off in a cluster of trees.

"'A cryin' shame, t' be sure, don't ye think, lassy," the woman said over the horse, "t' see an olden mare lose her precious sight?"

"Ma'am?"

"Yer horse, lassy. Dover. Ye said 'twas blind."

"Oh, nay, ma'am, I meant you. I hope I gave no offense."

"Why should ye have?" the woman snapped back.

"Indeed I shouldn't have," said Laura, glaring at James, expecting him to say something.

He silently tied the horse to a water trough, and the woman returned to its muzzle. Then James came to Laura and held her lightly, slipping back into those sullen regions of his mind where Seán never left, never died. There was nothing to be done for that. Except another prayer that it wasn't so. Nothing for now. They were here, out of sight of the roads and safe. They certainly could not return to the track. After an hour or two, when the sun was further down, they would head for Kildare. But did this blind woman know the way? Though he wished she would invite them inside, he didn't want to alarm her by asking directly. An idea came to him. "May we trouble ye for some food, ma'am? I'd gladly pay."

"Plenty o' hay 'round de back. Ye get it yerself, Mr. Seámus Annesley."

James shook his head. He wasn't of the mind for this nonsense.

Laura elbowed his ribs. "Thank ya, ma'am," she said. "Ya're most kind."

"Ma'am, I'm most concerned for a friend, that he might live, so please forgive me if—"

Suddenly the woman turned and walked directly to James, letting him see her cloudy eyes, white wax orbs. "Do ye think I'm blind, lad?"

"I don't know, ma'am," he said, releasing Laura. "Are ye?"

"Might be. Might be. Some days I am fer sure." The woman stopped and stared straight ahead, as though she were seeing right through his chest. "Are you blind, Lord Anglesea?"

"Nay, ma'am. Ye know me?"

"Ye sure ye're not blind?"

"Aye," James said, growing impatient. "How do you know me?"

"Humph," she snorted. "But can ye see all dis and everything?"

James glanced at Laura, then back at the woman's haunting eyes. "I can. I think."

"Don't be so sure wise, lad."

"Ye know of me?"

"Heard yer stories," she muttered. "And m' mother, she knew of yer family. She's served the Buckinghams. Now she be in Kildare. Lived in Dublin. Served your mother some time ago."

James and Laura exchanged looks, each asking the silent imponderable: If she's this old, how old must her mother be? James spoke up. "I'd like to meet her."

"As I said, she's in Kildare. Talked of ye all de time," the lady continued. "Said yer uncle is wrong of yer mother. As the facts are the other way."

"My mother? Aye, she was Mary Sheffield. Not Joan—"

"Ma said the truth was hidden from ye."

"What truth, ma'am?" James studied the woman. This was tiresome. Another useless witness and blind at that.

"Something she knew. Go to her. She's in a papal grave."

"Grave, ma'am?"

"Cemetery beyond Kildare, m'lord. Why do ye bother me with yer questions? Ask her yerself. She'd like yer visit but mind ye take lassy here along."

Laura spoke up with a soft smile. "I'd be honored to go to her."

James gave Laura a puzzled look. This was dizzying. How could Laura be so kind? Regal. The word came to him. Laura had a regal kindness to her. A well kept, well bred beauty. Tough, to be certain, yet gentle, unthreatened by such confusion. He pressed on, in the only direction he understood. "'Tis no secret of my mother. It will be seen—"

"Ye can see everything, m'lord? Can ye? We've heard of ye all round dese parts of Eire." She felt for his shoulder, and when she found it, she pulled down on it, raising herself to her toes, whispering in his ear, "De question is, m'lord, do ye know of us. Do ye know of me?"

"Should I?"

She stepped back. "Should ye, ye ask?" Her tone now crackly and sharp. "Why should anybody know about anybody, I ask ye? Tell me, sir, if ye can. I heard 'bout you, didn't I?"

James frowned. "I must apologize, but I'm adrift here."

"So be we all. Look under yer feet, m'lord."

He looked down, and noticed Laura was doing so as well.

"What do ye see?"

"The ground, ma'am."

"But whose ground?"

"Yers?"

"Nay, m'lord! For shame and swear." She pointed near his boots. "'Tis yers."

"Mine?"

"Yers, indeed. Ye're standing on yer own land."

"It will then be."

"Didn't ye be knowin' dat?"

"Well, nay. In truth, I didn't know the estate—"

"Learn t' see right from wrong, m'lord. I foresee soon I'll be bringin' me rents t' ye. They aren't much, but I know ye'll take 'em. An' when I do, I want t'know dat ye can see. Dat ye know of me. Dat ye can see dis land o' Eire, m'lord, whether we be prayin' t' de Blessed Mary or no. 'Tis our land. Our sweat gave it de dark smell. Our backs broke de rocks. An' our blood made it rich. Learn t' see de life in it, m'lord. 'Tis Irish. Until ye do, ye're more blind dan me. An' yer lassy's horse."

"Aye, ma'am," James said, then studied her closely, astounded. Annoyed, but astounded.

"Are ye noble yet?" she pressed on.

"Another riddle for me?" James had had quite enough. But Laura didn't seem particularly perturbed so he hated to show his own shortness. He decided to humor the woman once again. But just this once more.

The woman waggled her finger in his direction, yet slightly off to the right. "My father used t' say, true nobility, m'lord, is not about de business of bettering yer brothers and fellow men. True nobility is found in being better dan ye used t' be. Are ye better dan ye used t' be, m'lord?"

"He is," interjected Laura. "Mr. Annesley has traveled a lifetime journey that few could bear. I vish ye to know, ma'am, that he is noble in every sense of the vord."

James's eyebrows peaked. His cheeks flushed, smiling. He had never heard her gush such.

"Den mind he knows himself as ye know him." The elderly woman turned to face Laura square. "And lassy," she said, "yer horse smells o' Eire. Feels o' Eire. As if he has Connemara blood in him. Why'd ye give him an English name as Dover?"

Laura shrugged, with a wink toward James. "'Twas the first name I thought of, ma'am."

The old woman cackled infectiously. "Well said, lassy!" She reached for Laura's hand. Finding it, she gripped it tightly, and with her other hand she patted Laura's head. "Ye've got a fine lil' Swede here, m'lord. Ye should listen t' her. Pray ye take heed of what she says."

"Aye, ma'am," replied James.

The woman turned and began walking toward her cottage. "All right, ye said ye wanted t' eat. Let's see what we can find in de kitchen. Some tea. More if ye like. I'll say a prayer for yer *deartháir*."

James and Laura glanced at each other, then quietly followed her inside. "*Deartháir?*" Laura whispered.

"Brother," James replied with a shrug.

CHAPTER 34

The best of men cannot suspend their fate:
The good die early, and the bad die late.

— The Character of the late Annesley,
    Daniel Defoe, 1715

By four o'clock, James and Laura were riding again. As before, they were together on the one animal. Dinner, safety, guards, news, all were hours ahead. They passed the time thinking of a good Irish name for that Connemara horse—anything to eschew the thought, the mention, of Seán or the events at the track. They settled on Bhaldraithe, the blind woman's surname, and Laura half-laughed when James spelled it. It had come as no surprise to James when Mrs. Bhaldraithe had proffered the most detailed directions. She had even taken an iron poker and drawn a map on her dirt floor, explaining her cottage was a bit north of Kildangan, a few miles east of Monasterevian, almost to the River Barrow. Thus they "had done been sceedaglin' de wrong way, all considerin' their desired destinations." That made sense, James reasoned, why Bailyn and his men had not found them. No, Bailyn would be well ahead of them by now. So they rode northeast, passing south of Cherryville sometime after five, and by early evening they were within sight of the hamlet of Kildare. James led Bhaldraithe off the road onto the back cattle trails, then stopped on a hilltop overlooking the stone buildings. Bailyn might be at the crossroads with constables or soldiers, ready to arrest him for trespassing or horse thievery, or worse. James urged the horse along until they were past the town, then doubled back.

"We'll go to the Blue Crow," James whispered. "Let's see who's there." He pulled on the reins when they reached Main Street, slowing the hooves to a cautious clop. Several people were walking there, a few on horseback. An occasional carriage passed. As they turned on a narrow street lined with shop signs, he spotted the inn. Neither spoke as they approached. James studied the front door, the front windows, the upper balcony. He saw no one. They stopped. He hopped off and helped Laura down.

"Stay here, please," he began. "Let me see—"

"I know," she said, her eyes wide, her fear conspicuously hidden.

He leaned forward and took her hand, kissing it. "Stay here. Be prepared to ride off—"

"I'm not leaving," she whispered firmly. "I'll be right here."

He shook his head, sighed through an embracing smile, then turned and walked into the Blue Crow. It was quiet inside. Only a few men were reposed in the tavern room. No guard, attorney or witness for his trial. They didn't appear to know him, and he didn't recognize them. He moved toward the back, to the other room on the ground floor, the room Mackercher used as an office. Two men were in there, smoking pipes, drams in hand: a thin, young Highland guard and one of Mackercher's solicitors. Behind them was Laura's thick-legged aunt.

"M'lord!" the solicitor exclaimed, standing at the sight of James. A perfunctory bow.

"Gentlemen. Madam Kristin," James said, stepping forward.

"How is Laura?" the woman asked. Her Swedish accent eased like melted butter.

"She's all right," James said, nodding at the door. "A bit shaken. If ye don't mind, ma'am, will ye go and fetch her? She's awaiting outside."

"I was so worried. I'll go," she said, slipping out.

The solicitor continued, "Thought you'd been arrested along with Mr. Mackercher."

"Where are the others?" asked James.

"Left for Dublin, hours ago. Petitioning the court for a release."

"Good." James turned to the Highlander. "Ye were there today?"

"Aye, m'lord. I was with ya outside when—"

"Were ye? Ye escaped arrest?"

"Aye, m'lord. Blessings ya did as well."

"Mr. Mackercher?" asked James. "Was he hurt?"

"Not hurt, best I could see. I was watching from the racing stalls."

The solicitor rejoined, "I assure you, we'll have them released come morning."

James squared the older man. "Where are they?"

"Newbridge, sir. At the garrison."

"One was shot in the leg," said James. "Is he with them?"

"Aye, sir." The Highlander nodded. "Best I could see."

James turned hearing people enter. Laura came quickly to stand near him. He put a hand on the middle of her back and pulled her close. "Everything is fine enough," he softly said.

Madam Kristin was beaming. "I'm so very glad ya're both well."

"Thank ya." Laura smiled. "For waiting here, Auntie."

"Of course my dear," replied the grey-haired woman. "Shall I have tea brought in?"

James nodded, then returned to the young guard. "Tell me, did ye see Captain Bailyn?"

"Only heard ye speak of him. If I saw him, I wouldn't know it."

"He's short. Skinny face. Red infantry hat."

The solicitor smirked. "Aye. He came through here an hour ago or so." Then he said to the Highlander, "He was that ugly one." He scratched under his wig, then looked at James. "He came in, looked around, and walked out. Said nothing. Has the most dead eyes I've ever seen."

"I didn't see him," continued the guard.

James inhaled, then let it go. He saw Laura close her eyes. He sniffed, then looked at the floor. "Probably kicking himself for not shooting me today."

"But we heard ya shot one of them, m'lord," the guard said. "A constable at that."

"What?"

"Ya shot him dead, ya did. Right? With a bussy?"

"Dead?" James felt his gut kicked in. *Not Seán!* "Who said that?" he snapped.

"A man that'd been wagerin' there.

"Don't repeat such," barked the lawyer. "Mr. Annesley shot no one. He—"

"The man shot," James stared, "was he my age? My height?"

The guard shrugged, then saw James's deep frown. "Sorry, m'lord."

The older man was still glaring on the younger. "We can't have rumors such as that. If you hear it again, you say it was Captain Bailyn that did the killing. You understand?"

"Probably was Bailyn," James added softly.

The guard nodded, then tried, "Wish it'd been Bailyn, instead, I mean, that was killed."

"Aye," James growled, turning. He bit his bottom lip, then let it go. "Soon he will be."

A servant woman entered carrying a tray of teacups and saucers, Madam Kristin close behind. Everyone took a cup, pouring their tea into their saucers and starting to sip. James took one sip then set his down and leaned near Laura. "I must go find Seán."

She inhaled. "Why you?"

"They don't know him. If he's hurt, or worse, I'll need to bring him back."

"He's alive," offered Laura, forcing a small smile. "I believe he is."

"We can only hope." He picked up his hat and popped it straight.

Laura pressed, "Why don't ya vait till Mr. Mackercher's men arrive tomorrow?"

"Because it may be too late."

"Then take these men here. Please, James. Take them with ya."

"Nay, Laura." He raised his voice to be certain the other two heard. "These gentlemen will stay here and protect ye and Madam Kristin." He turned, giving them a determined look.

"Aye, yar lordship," they replied in near-unison. The younger added, "With our lives."

James gave Laura a quick kiss on the forehead. "I'll be back late tonight or in the morning." Her tears were welling. "I will, *Acushla*," he promised, squeezing her hand. Again, he kissed her forehead, as if not knowing what else to do. Then he stood straight, pulled his hat on firmly, winked at her nervously, and turned, walking quickly through the open door. He kept his face forward and firm, belying nothing of the knots contorting within him. Within seconds he was on Bhaldraithe, galloping away

But he didn't turn to the south, toward the Curragh. Rather he slowed two blocks up and surveyed around. No sign of Bailyn. He turned up a muddy alley—the Huntsman Inn just ahead. He was tired of running, hiding, playing the fool. Richard had done his damage, certainly, but the Dublin trial would right that, would settle that score. But Bailyn had killed his father, then Juggy and Higgins. And now Seán. James touched the dirk's sheath against his leg. It was there. He felt his rapier hilt. It was a good one. Sufficient for the task. A pistol. He had one, but it was not loaded. Perhaps he should load it. He gave the horse a slight nudge. He could not face burying Seán without knowing Bailyn was dead. Now he approached the Huntsman. The street was nearly empty, the inn quiet, its paned windows dark. He dismounted and tied off the reins. Then stepped up the porch. The heavy door creaked wide. Inside he slowed, his eyes adjusting to the lack of candles. The evening light glowed faintly on everything, yet illuminated nothing, giving the parlor a deep bluish haze.

"James Annesley. Ye're late, I must say."

"Damn ye," James growled, his eyes focusing. The man was alone at a table near the side wall. No one else was around. The whole inn seemed eerily empty. Except for Bailyn.

"I sent them away," said Bailyn, sneering.

James stepped closer, dropping his hand to the hilt. "Who?"

"Ah, ye know, James. Yer other lawyers. Everyone."

"Did ye arrest them as well?" James slipped his coat off and laid it aside.

"Who? Them? Nay, just turned 'em out."

"Turned them out? On whose authority?" Now he was unbuttoning his waistcoat.

"Oh, a friend of a friend of Lord Anglesea owns this old place. Ye know how it is."

"Nay," said James, "I don't know how it is."

Captain Bailyn smirked, then shrugged, saying, "Sure ye do."

"And Mackercher?" James pushed his sleeves up as he came to the edge of Bailyn's table. "Where's he?"

"That mongrel Scot?" he muttered. "He's just like his Scot farts: raisin' a stink all 'round, then won't go back where he came from." He reached for his tankard. "I should've shagged his sister when—"

James slapped the cup from Bailyn's hand, sending it rattling against the wall, its contents splashing to the floor. "I'll stand for no more of yer mouth, yer vile affronts."

Bailyn was quiet for a moment, expressionless, a fixed stare straight ahead. "Yer lawyer was arrested, as ye no doubt know, with that whole lot of Jacobites. Yer alone, or didn't ye know?" He turned, glaring up. "And yer poor friend. I reckon 'bout now the crows are havin' an eyeball feast."

Fire roared over James. He surged, grabbing Bailyn by the collar, lifted him into the air, then threw him away from the table. Bailyn smashed a chair, splintering it to pieces, and slid six feet before coming to a stop.

Recovering quickly, he stood and drew his rapier. "So, lad, ye're ready to die now are ye?" he snarled, wiping blood from a cut on his forehead, smearing red across his eyebrows.

"Ye've killed yer last." James pointed at the man. "'Tis yer turn now."

"We'll see."

James continued. "I know why ye want to kill me. 'Tisn't just Richard that drives ye mad. 'Tis cause ye know I'm right. Ye know I'm the Earl. That ye're in bed with the devil. And ye know that when I come into my title, ye'll have nowhere to hide. Ye'll be hanged for murder the very day."

"Keep mouthin' yer last words." Bailyn removed his coat, shifting the rapier between his hands as he did. "Better make 'em count for something."

James circled him, keeping an eye on the man's weapon. "What'd ye think? Thought ye'd whack my head again? Ye think I'm still a boy, do ye? Ye're an arse. Look, now 'tis your head that's bleeding." He smirked, then finally pulled his rapier. Then with his left hand came the dirk. "Ye recognize this?"

For a moment, Bailyn forgot himself and frowned at the weapon.

James flicked it, as if summoning Bailyn closer. "Let me show ye what's written on it."

"Ye gonna fuck with me all eve? Ye won't do anything 'cept shit yer britches. Ye're a milk coward. Ye'll run, just like yer wee da did. Ye'll be out in the mud dead, just like him. What are ye waitin' for?"

James stepped closer. "Just deciding the best way to kill ye."

"Shame yer whore's not here to watch ye die." They continued to move.

Though clearly fomented, James held it in. "Trying to provoke me?"

"I can see it's eatin' at ye."

"Nah, yer guile means nothing t'me. 'Tis yer time to die. And I think ye know it."

"Then what are ye waitin' for?" Suddenly Bailyn hurled himself forward, lunging. James jumped clear, a first twinge of fear jolting through him. Again they faced each other, blade tips neck high, eyes locked, feet stepping sideways, shoving chairs from their paths, moving in a slow circle, tracing that most ancient of dances. Seeing an opening, James thrust hard, but Bailyn parried with a bellguard clang of steel, then reposted swiftly. James recoiled as the other sword flashed by, slicing a large swath through his waistcoat. Grasping both blades in one hand, he jerked the garment off and flung it away.

They recovered their stances, both sweating in the dim, sultry room. James studied Bailyn's movements looking for a tell, anything that might betray the next lunge, the next thrust. Bailyn's right foot shot forward then down as he took a much longer step and lunged. James responded with a parry, then a repost that missed its mark. They disengaged, then rushed forward at the same time, their bellguards bashing together, both rapier tips gliding past their targets. James tried to stab with the dirk, but only slammed an elbow into Bailyn's nose, all before Bailyn could get his blade around. The man's upper lip turned red as blood flowed from his nose, and his eyes grew wide and wet. Another thrust, followed by another parry, then a riposte and more chairs crashed over, both men grunting, breathing hard. James retreated slightly, searching for a chance to rebut. Suddenly a glancing slash sliced cloth and flesh across his chest. He staggered, his wig falling off, then quickly regained his stance, his long blade up. He shoved another table with his hip, then saw Bailyn had a dagger drawn—that is what had cut him. He scolded himself for not seeing the weapon come out. Warm blood ran down his belly, soaking the white shirt. The pain came sharp, but caused his mind to narrow into a single focus. Bailyn grinned, his left hand up, palming the dagger, his thumb and finger two inches apart. "Just that close, Jemmy-boy." He pointed. "Next time, 'twill be yer heart."

James clenched his teeth. The room was growing darker with the dimming day, but they had no seconds to call the duel, to call quarter, even to light a candle. It would go on this way, getting darker and more dangerous. He had to end it soon, now, but how? He needed to spot a weakness, predictability in Bailyn's movements. He thrust again, but only a feint. Bailyn took it, tapping it aside, then on his right foot he lurched forward wildly and down into a lunge. James rocked back, then rejoined, knowing he had just seen it. He had seen it before, and there it was again—the man flopped his right foot leading into a lunge. Bailyn attacked again, but this time James was against a wall. He parried hard, shoving back, then furiously thrust around with the dirk, causing Bailyn to recoil from reach, backing the man away until James could free himself from the corner. Now in the open, James circled, eyes locked on Bailyn's eyes, but mind locked on Bailyn's foot. Then he saw it. In the instant that Bailyn stutter-jerked forward on his right foot, James sidestepped, expecting a lunge to follow. When it came, he was well out of the way, and Bailyn's rapier blade found only black, empty air. James swiftly dropped the tip of his rapier, then popped it up, slipping it under the man's bellguard, driving the tip forward, impaling it deep in Bailyn's left shoulder. The dagger dropped.

Bailyn cried out in pain, jerking back, wincing, trying to extricate himself from James's rapier, but James threw his weight behind it and leaned in, driving the steel straight through the flesh, feeling it rub by bone and out the other side. Then with all his strength he plunged the dirk into Bailyn's chest, cracked the sternum, shoving it downwards. Bailyn groaned angrily, careening back as blood spewed up the blood groove of the blade, speckling James's neck and face. He yanked the rapier free, but the dirk wouldn't give. The bloody brass grip slipped from his grasp as the man dropped to his knees, eyes open and straight-ahead. Then Bailyn fell backward, his head smacking hard on the wood floor. James watched him die, the primordial shudder, the blood pooling in the dark, the dirk's hilt reflecting the very last glimmer of the day. Finally he reached down and jerked the dirk from the body. Staggering back, he leaned against the wall, gasping for breath, blood streaming from the slice across his own chest, the sharp pain screaming up at him. He was panting hard, staring at Bailyn. But he didn't feel victorious. No triumph. What an awful thing it was to kill a man. Even one as foul as this.

CHAPTER 35

Then we shall rise
And view ourselves with clearer eyes
In that calm region where no night
Can hide us from each other's sight.

—from The Exequy, Henry King, 1657

James tied a small linen tablecloth around his chest, angrily cinching it over the wound. Though it was hurting worse, the bleeding had slowed. He could ride. That's all that mattered. He stared at Bailyn's body, infuriated. The bastard had killed with impunity, the son of a bitch. Impunity from the law. Impunity of the mind. But not of the soul. Bailyn was answering for that, right now. He had better be. But would he, himself, have to answer for this killing someday? No, this was duty. Yet reason didn't abate his rage—it boiled him where he stood. Hundreds of dead he had seen at sea, killing all around. But nothing equaled this, this death of his own. This man killed so many. He deserved to die this way. Not in a bed. It was right for his blood to be spewed on a dirty tavern floor, mixing with the spilt brew. He used a cloth to wipe most of the blood from his blades and resheathed them. He turned again to Bailyn. "I hope you can see yourself," he muttered, wishing the dead had ears.

How can such savage men kill people, good people, and not be affected? Why didn't they too get gnashing sick from their acts? How did they escape this anger? How could Bailyn have murdered countless people—his father, a woman, Juggy, a man like Higgins, now Seán, and undoubtedly others—yet stay so smug, so damned arrogant? As if unaffected. As if righteous. As if specially touched, ordained to do Satan's work. Perhaps that was it entirely. And just as accursed was Richard, who ordered the deaths. Directly or through some mad concordance. He was no less guilty of those acts, yet remained repugnantly aloof. The goddamned dog. Yet he, James, having killed the very rat that had infested so many, was tasting bile and felt his head pounding with pain and fury. To kill a man with your own hands. To watch a life depart. However awful Bailyn was, at one time he was a young woman's baby. Now dead, here. Here is where that life ended. Here is what that life left behind. No, he brushed the thought away. It was good to have killed him. It needed to be done. And it was good that he did it. He needed to be the one. But it was anything but satisfying. Perhaps that is how the callous keep some semblance of sanity: they don't watch their victims die. They don't let themselves see the horror they inflict, the last seconds of the dying, the last breaths on this earth. This animal should have watched his own death. He wished he had kept Bailyn alive longer, let him suffer more. No. He knew better, but for the moment it felt good to think it. He stared another few seconds, then turned and walked out.

For the first time he saw faces, about ten people, all boys and young men, at the front of the Huntsman, peering silently through the windows. As he pushed open the doors, they parted, giving him a path to his horse. Once atop Bhaldraithe, he said to the group, "He was a murderin' fiend. Had it comin' t'him." Seeing the blankness of their stares, he eased his horse around. Within a minute, he was on the main road, heading south toward the Curragh.

The path wound quickly into the woods and Kildare was soon gone behind him. It was nearly dark and the stars were beginning to join the half-moon, pouring themselves across the deep blue sky. Though James barely noticed. He was bent into a small slump over the horse as it clomped along. Occasionally glancing over his shoulder, he studied the dim woods, the fields beyond. Anyone was suspect. Anyone might be a soldier or constable, one of Richard's men. Seeing only a few in the distance, he dismissed them and kept moving, letting his mind jostle where it might. He had to return to that Curragh stable. Get back to Seán. To find Seán. The Huntsman was probably filled by now. That group would be hauling Bailyn out. And when the question was asked, they would describe James. Some probably could name him. But who will bring the charges? Richard? Not likely. Not this time.

Bhaldraithe lumbered along with an occasional snort, his hooves thrumming the worn road. He had gone many miles that day and a fair amount at a gallop. So James kept him at a lope. Besides there was, most likely and unfortunately, little reason to hurry. The frogs were out, calling, and a few crickets too. James shifted his weight, creaking the leather saddle, trying to ease the sharp, swelling ache in his chest. Quietly, he began deeply humming *Greensleeves*, letting the tune wash through him, calming him, soothing the aches, freeing his thoughts to drift across that day's morning. He and Laura had been on that same road, riding in a coach with Mackercher, laughing, anticipating a day at the races—out to find rest and fresh air. He let his head

sag side-to-side. What a horrible day. His thoughts could not sustain a singular path without quickly flexing back, as if pulled by the gravity of that
Curragh moment: Seán giving fire, and taking it, for them to escape. If that
coach was still there he would use it to bring Seán back.

He chuckled smugly, imagining Richard hearing of Captain Bailyn's
death. But would that end it? No. Richard would never stop. Not until sufficient force was brought to bear. And Bailyn's death would only incite him,
if it did anything. So what would be sufficient? A verdict against Richard? He
nodded to himself. This coming trial for the earldom was not only the best
way to beat Richard, it truly was the only way. Even then, Richard would
likely remain in Ireland, causing trouble. James would require him to leave.
He smirked, realizing that, after the trial, *he* would have the power to call
upon the English infantry, to have Richard escorted away. To have Richard
hauled into the bowels of a ship and transported if necessary. But to where?
America? No, America was his. He had earned America. He didn't want to
export such foulness to the Colonies, regardless of the act's irony. Probably,
the man should go to France, he reasoned. Richard spoke some French so—
Ah, the man could go to hell, for all James cared. Why be concerned for him?
Richard would be lucky not to be hanged upon reading the verdict. But then
again, what if Richard won? He and Laura would return to Virginia. Maybe
Mackercher would go as well. It was a pleasant thought.

The sound of an approaching carriage snapped James up. He eased Bhaldraithe off the road, into the cover of black trees. As it passed, he could see the
driver and was at first startled at how much the man looked like Mackercher.
But in the next instant, as the moonlight came more fully on the man's features, he could see it was no one he recognized. He returned to the road, his
thoughts turning to Daniel Mackercher. Good ol' Mackercher. He will be very
pleased to learn Bailyn was killed. Even more so when Richard is penniless
and ruined. Especially after a night in jail courtesy of the man. James smiled.
Mackercher was a good man. What an enormous sum he was spending on
attorneys, witnesses, inns and coaches. James had known Mackercher was
wealthy but never realized the extent. According to several, over the past few
years Mackercher had found great riches in the tobacco trade. Not to mention his solicitor fees. It was unfortunate, James reasoned, that Mackercher
had not been of such means in earlier years. Juggy might never have served
the Annesleys. Might never have suffered the insults of Arthur. Might never
have died. He wondered if Mackercher felt guilty for that. Maybe that was
why Mackercher was so willing to expend his fortune prosecuting James's civil

suit. Perhaps. Of course he and Mackercher would have their own reveng-
es, but this was about much more than that. It was about land and estates,
money and titles, what was rightfully his. Right? James could find no answer
that satisfied him. He thought about the old woman, Ms. Bhaldraithe. This
trial should be about right from wrong. Justice and injustice. What James did
with the land and title was another matter. How could he ever claim this land
as English soil, as his land? By what true authority? At least Richard would
have no claim to it. No claim to that Kennedy land around Dunmain. Where
Fynn was buried. And where, tomorrow, he would take Seán. The image of
Seán, lying dead in a filthy stall, brought a pall down—black dread merging
with the night air. He was alone on an empty road on an empty night. His
stomach ached, a lump the size of a fist stuck in his throat. It was almost too
much to bear: having to bury his friend without ever saying those words,
those things that needed to be said. How can we know the dead hear us? We
must say what we can when we can.

A distant clip-clop, and James reined Bhaldraithe to a stop. It was a horse
on the road, somewhere ahead, moving toward him. Who else would be out at
this hour? No one preferred to be out after dark. Certainly not in the woods.
After all, there were wolves and bandits to be feared. So was it a constable
on patrol? Looking for James or any of the escaped Highlanders? Most likely
with orders to shoot him, if he was caught alone. He dismounted stealthily,
led Bhaldraithe into the trees and tied him. Crouching low, he peered down
the path ahead, trying to see anything. Carefully, silently, he drew his rapier.
The horse was coming closer, its black image cast about by the meager moonlight and its sister shadows, playing a game with James's eyes, toying with his
mounting tension. But as the soft, slow sound of hooves came rhythmically
louder, he saw the beast in silhouette, its head drooped low and stolid. It was
as if the horse was unguided, not hurried, not ridden at all. Suddenly a twig
snapped under Bhaldraithe's hoof and James flinched, tightening his grip on
the rapier. But the approaching horse kept lumbering along. James couldn't
see a rider, only a bulk lying over the horse's neck. His heart pounded. Was
this a trap? Was that bulk really a man? Someone planning to rear up at the
last second and reveal a weapon? James decided to stay hidden. He should
have powdered his pistol. The horse quietly passed by. James resheathed his
rapier, untied Bhaldraithe, and pulled him gently back into the road. He
stopped and watched the other horse ambling on toward Kildare. What if
the slumped rider was drunk, or dead? He mounted up, turned his horse to
follow, and drew the sword with a resounding ring. "You sir!" he shouted,

startling himself. "In the drink, are ye?"

The other horse startled up to a trot, then slowed. The man never moved, just bounced along. James spurred Bhaldraithe to a canter, coming quickly alongside. But he still could not see the man's face. He touched the dark body with the flat of his sword. Still nothing. He reached out, collecting the other set of reins. The animal stopped.

"Up with ye, sir," he said, stretching across the man's arched back, grabbing him by the coat, pulling him upright. He felt a warm wetness on the man's back and realized the coat was soaked in blood. And now, in the moonlight, he could see blood down the horse's side. This man was clearly dead. James dismounted and walked to the far side. "Easy, there," he whispered as the horse started forward. The man's head was dangling limply in front of him. He lifted it, to see the face. "Seán! M'God, Sean!" he exclaimed softly, pulling him from the saddle, easing the body to the road. The wind was whipping the tops of the trees, causing more moonlight to fall sporadically through, shifting dark to light to dark across Seán's face. His eyes were open, set in a fixed stare. "Ah, nay! Seán! No." He shook Seán, but there was no response. Tears welled in James's eyes as he slowly reached to close Seán's. But then Seán blinked and gave a small cough, flicking a sprinkle of blood across James's face. "Ye're alive! Ah damned! Seán! Seán! Hang on, m'friend." James carefully moved him off the road and into the grass, then lifted his head, holding him in his arms. "Don't ye die on me, Seán. Ye damn well better not! Don't ye die! Ye hearin' me?" He sniffed, tears streaming down a cheek. Though he could not see Seán's wound in the darkness, he could feel it. The coat was ripped across Seán's left shoulder and blood was everywhere. Only grouse shot from a blunderbuss could make a wound like this, James thought. But there had been several shots that morning. He felt Seán's chest and legs for more wounds. Nothing. "Seán," he whispered. "Can ye hear me?"

Seán moaned faintly.

"Ye must stay awake." Again, he heard a feeble moan. "Ye've been hurt badly. I can feel it. Yer shoulder. Are ye damaged elsewhere?"

Nothing.

"Seán!" he shouted. "Wake up! Answer me. Where else are ye hurt?"

"Muhaa…." Seán tried.

"Yer what?" James leaned closer to hear.

"Haan…."

"Yer hand?" James felt for Seán's hands. When he reached for the left one, he paled. There was nothing there but a mangled thumb. Recoiling, he

tried to calm himself. "All right, all right. 'Tis all right, Seán. Ye'll be fine."
He jumped up, jerked the bloody tablecloth from his own chest and ripped
it in two. With one half, he tied off Seán's left arm, then wrapped the other
around the shoulder. "Stay awake, Seán. Let's sit ye up some. Keep the blood
in ye." James found a large hunk of wood and gently guided it under Seán's
head. When he propped up the left arm, Seán let out a wail. James stood
again, turning, looking, wondering what to do next. "We're goin' to load ye
in the next wagon that comes along. I'll get ye to a doctor, I swear it. Are ye
hearin' me?"

"Aye," whispered Seán.

"That's good. Ye're talkin' Keep talkin'."

"Sa...."

"What? Say it again, Seán."

"Jemmy? Seámus?"

James smiled nervously. "Aye, I'm here. I'm goin' to keep ye talking all
night if I have to. Can ye believe that? Used to couldn't get ye to shut yer gob
and now...now I don't want ye to stop." James heard his own voice cracking as tears overflowed his eyes. He clenched his jaw till it shook, driving his
emotions back, forcing himself to sound cheerful. "Aye, ye're goin' to talk
all night. Can ye believe that, Seán? Ye're goin' to talk all night and into the
morning if ye have to. Ye are indeed. Then ye'll be right as rain." Inside, he
felt the weight of his lie.

"Jemmy?"

"Aye?"

"I'm...sorry."

James took a deep breath, then collapsed his chin to his chest, silently
crying. Seán reached over and put his right hand on James's leg.

"I was," Seán began, his voice bare, a rhythmic whisper, "I was coming...
to Kildare." With a punctured lung, he was wheezing his words in short, faint
bursts. "I was coming to...to find ye...to tell ye...how sorry I am."

James nodded, a faint sob escaping before he could stop it. He placed a
hand over Seán's. "I know, Seán. I know. Ye did what ye thought ye had t'do."

"Took me a damn hour...just to get on...that horse."

James smiled, smearing his tears back. "I'm glad ye did."

"Can ye...forgive me, for what I did? Seámus?"

"Of course I do."

"I just had—"

"No more of it. 'Tis done with."

"I did ye wrong."

"Hush now. We'll never speak of it again."

"Ye said…ye said I had to keep talkin'…now ye're tellin' me to…to hush."

James chuckled softly. "I suppose ye're right." Again he wiped his eyes, taking another deep breath. "That thing, that misunderstanding. We'll just not speak on it, all right?" His voice peaked up at the end, full of emotion. He pulled in his bottom lip and bit down. Finally, he continued, "Let's talk about something else."

Seán was silent.

James sat for a moment, searching for something to say. "The trial will be soon, two months. November."

"I wish I could've been there."

"Where? You will be!"

"At your trial…to see Bailyn's face… when ye win."

"The bastard's dead."

"Ye kill him?"

"Aye."

Seán moved barely. "That's good."

"Aye. I suppose."

"Ye ran him down with…with a coach and six?"

"Nay," James answered though another smile.

"Well ye should have," breathed Seán. "Should've thrown…a centipede on him. Would've killed him…on the spot."

James chuckled. "Aye. But how could I find another with such long fangs?"

"Aye," Seán whispered. For the first time he gave a faint grin. Slowly, he reached out and touched James's shirt. "That yer blood, or his? Or mine?" Then he gestured at the splatters across James's face.

"All three, I think."

"Ye hurt?"

"I'll be alright."

Sean took a slow, pained breath, then asked, "Ye sure?"

"Don't be concerned. Laura will have me back in health."

"That's good. Someone needs…t' look out for ye. When did she arrive?"

"Last Spring," said James. He was watching the road, hopeful for any sign of a wagon or coach. Anyone. Maybe he should just put Seán back on that horse and head on to Kildare. But what if that killed Seán? How could he risk that? It was only luck that got Seán this far alive. But to let him die here? He had to do something.

"Is she Lady Anglesea?

"We plan to marry after the trial."

"That's good. I'm sure ye'll—"

"Ye'll be there, Seán. Ye will."

He groaned, readjusting his arm. "I'm of the doubtin'."

"She asked for ye t'be there. Ye don't want to disappoint her. Nay, ye don't." James stared off. He wished Laura was with him, yet was completely glad she wasn't. He glanced again at Seán, then to his shoulder. "Ye'll get through this night." In another flicker of moonlight, he saw the tablecloth was much darker than before. He pulled the bindings tighter. "There's no damn way I'm letting ye die out here. I won't—"

"She's beautiful," Seán interrupted.

James took a deep breath. "So she is. But you, ye'd best keep yer eyes off her! I don't want to lose her to some Irish Catholic who...." He trailed off, realizing there was no joke to be made there. "Just keep yer eyes and hands off her, if ye know what's good for ye."

"'Ach, now Jemmy....'" He tapped James's arm. "It'd only be the one hand."

"Alright then," James laughed. "But only the one."

CHAPTER 36

On the 11th of this Month came on the great Trial between
James Annesley, Esq; Plaintiff, and the Rt. Hon. Richard,
Earl of Anglesea, Defendant, before the Rt. Hon. John
Bowes, Esq; Lord Chief Baron, Hon. Richard Mountney,
and Arthur Dawton, Esqrs. Barons of the Exchequer, in the
King's Courts in Dublin.

> — *Gentleman's Magazine*, London, November
> 1743

The windows were still there, still dark and aged, still midair on the walls of
the Four Courts of Justice. James stood motionless, neck strained back as he
studied them, far overhead. Behind him, the footman helped Laura from the
coach. "What are ya seeing?" she asked, taking James's arm. Her creamy linen
dress crinkled against his side. The bulk of her hair was pinned up, letting a
few buttery tresses drape her thin shoulders.

"Wonderin' what's so interesting there," he replied. "Those windows."
He saw her confusion. "See the flagstones?" he asked, looking to the base of
the wall. "One sticks up a bit."

"Does it?"

"I followed my father's casket here," he explained, pointing along the
route the pallbearers had taken. "Came 'round this way, to get to the front
of that church there, Christ Church. Then, somewhere along here, I looked
up…at those windows, I believe." Another remembrance came to mind and
he turned toward the yard. "I was looking for my mother." His voice trailed
silent for a moment. "Whatever t'was, I tripped on that flagstone."

"Oh dear," she softly said. "What happened?"

"I knocked a bearer down, I did. He let go and my dead father nearly
crushed me." He leaned his head back again, considering the crusty panes.
"I'd forgotten that, till just now."

Laura patted his arm. "I'm sure this city reminds ya of many things."

"Aye." His brow peaked for a second. "Some be best forgotten." Then, with a wink, he added, "Some best remembered."

Another large hackney pulled to a stop and the driver leaped down to fly the door wide. Mackercher stepped out, followed by three other solicitors, all wearing black silk robes and long, bubbly, powdered wigs. "James. Miss Johansson," Mackercher greeted, walking briskly to them. "Glad ya're already here. Thought we'd passed ya near Naas." He turned fully to Laura. "Aren't ya the very beauty o' the mornin'." She gave a pursed smile, eyes sparking back. Then he plopped a big hand on James's shoulder, giving James's clothing an exaggerated review. "Not a grandee t'be."

James grinned. "Ye'll not get *me* under a plume." His fashionable blue suit was accented simply by a smattering of silver glints: his dress sword's hilt, the glimmer of buckles—shoes, breeches, and a small one on the crown of his royal blue tricorn hat. His wig, though fuller than his usual pintail, was nevertheless tied so firmly back that he more appeared to be sporting a white duck strangled with a black ribbon than wearing that singular beacon of wealth and peerage.

"I like it," announced Mackercher half-heartedly. He looked back at more solicitors and barristers disembarking their coaches. Then he refocused on James. "It is most appropriate, m'lord. Yar attire. Just as we'd wish this jury to see."

Now the crowd was thickening, people moving in large waves, rounding the corner to the front of the Four Courts, swarming the wide stone steps like seagulls squawking hungrily. Many of these were the working class of Dublin, mostly men, come to see a lord put down. Someone noticed James and yelled, "James Annesley! There he is!" Others reacted, some pointing, and James gave an embarrassed nod.

Mackercher barked, "Let's go," pressing firmly on James's back. James in turn grabbed Laura's hand and they moved quickly for the steps.

More cries followed them up. "Ye'll win, m'lord!" they shouted. "Don't believe his lies!" "Ye'll surely beat dat damned pretender!"

James turned back, acknowledging their words with an awkward wave of his hand, then stepped inside the courthouse. It was no quieter there. The main hall was filled with people, most of quality and expensively dressed, engaged in little pockets of conversation, waiting for the trial to commence. Many turned, saying, "Good morning, Mr. Annesley. We wish ye well." He smiled, nodding to them as well, yet kept walking, keeping a firm hold on Laura's hand. As they arrived at the courtroom's ironwood doors, two grim doormen opened them slowly.

"Go on," Mackercher urged with a whisper. "Please, m'lord."

Stepping inside the giant hall of the Court of Exchequer, they were immediately enveloped in the smell of aged, oiled oak and the coolness of the cavernous room. James's gaze drew upward, to the high arched ceiling soaring above them. Then down its lines to the enormous stone pillars supporting it, each reverently hugging a wall, as if fearing conspicuousness in this grand room. He and Laura, with Mackercher close behind, kept moving to the front, their light footfall echoing off the burnished floor and heavy walls. Directly ahead, along the back wall, stood a raised platform supporting a long judges' bench. Behind it were the tops of three tall, elaborately carved chairs, each examining the room, anticipating their charges, as if three temporary governors, rulers of an empty room, each to disappear when their kings arrived. Above them—high above them—were the same windows James had seen from the street. Yet now they appeared different, vivid and bright. Glowing. Not darkened at all.

He looked at the men near the front. A few of Richard's attorneys studied him as he approached, judgmentally frowning as if he had done something disgusting, as if he was not welcome, an intruder advancing on them. James gave them an obvious smirk. Mackercher stepped around to take the lead. They walked to the front of the gallery and stopped before the barristers' bar, the low wooden fence dividing the grand hall, separating the gallery from the court tables, jury and judges' bench. "Miss Johansson," Mackercher whispered, "Would ya be so kind as sit on that first row? James will join me in front of the bar." He pointed. "We'll be there, right in front of ya."

"Aya," she agreed with a demure smile, then sat down, arranging her dress.

"Will Madam Kristin be joining us?" asked Mackercher.

"I do expect her this afternoon."

"Then ya'd best save her a space. This will be a crowded room."

"I will." Laura smiled.

James was studying the faces in the courtroom. "Where's Richard?" he growled softly.

"He'll be along shortly," replied Mackercher as he swung open the gate in the bar rail. James followed him in, and they moved to the plaintiff's side, a long walnut table on the left. Behind it were seven chairs, all facing the bench. Mackercher took the middle seat, James to his right. Other lawyers were streaming in now, a few of them James's. All appeared intense and somber.

James turned, smiling at Laura, remembering her at the murder trial, in the Old Bailey's nasty little courtroom. But this was different. Though still under English law, this was the grand court of Ireland. And this was his fight, his trial. Here all would be set right. Finally. Here he would begin his life anew, recapture what had been stolen. He stopped on that. Such was impossible. He looked at the floor. To regain those stolen years, that stolen childhood. It could not be done. Winning here, winning this trial, that was the sum, the entirety of justice he could hope for—to have a jury say before everyone that he, James Annesley, was the Earl of Anglesea. That he had been wronged. That he was not a runaway felon, not an indentured servant. Not a murderer. Not a worthless bastard. He thought of Mr. Clowes and smiled to himself. The old man would be proud. He was ready to prove himself, his truth, his name, his birthright. Yet he most missed Fynn. If only. Had he lived to see this day, this dream fulfilled, this revenge obtained, this loyalty requited. He flinched, felt the blood. Moved away from the image's sharp edge.

Laura was holding him with a small smile, as only she could do. But he could see the concern, her tight brow, the flatness of her lips, the sloop of her eyes. She was worried. She should not be, he thought. He wasn't. Probably because of Mackercher. He glanced up at the man, now standing, consulting with their throng of other lawyers, papers in hand. Yes, it was Mackercher's presence, his irrevocable, unshakable strength. Mixed with the truth of the matter, the evidence, the history, it all formed a confidence in him that he could not otherwise explain. It would not be easy though—a point Mackercher had made time and time again. Richard had seventeen solicitors registered for his defense, including, most notably, the Solicitor General of Ireland himself. And he had a team of thirty-two barristers that had been combing the streets of Dublin, in fact the whole of Ireland, searching for witnesses, anyone who would testify that Joan Landy, "Juggy," was James's real mother. According to Mackercher, they had found over one hundred and fifty people to corroborate that story. James wondered how much of his money Richard had spent buying so many lies. Yet, what if they were not lying? Was it possible Mackercher was also his uncle? he wondered, studying the looming Scotsman. Would he be sitting between two uncles today, Mackercher on his left, Richard on his right? He shook his head. No, Mary Sheffield was his mother. He knew that. They had over one hundred witnesses to prove it. Though he had to admit to himself, a part wished he was related to Mackercher, that he had that man's unique strength in his veins. Laura blushed slightly as James looked back at her again. She would see. This would all end well. He could feel it.

When the giant doors to the courtroom creaked again, James sat straight, glancing up expectantly. More of Richard's attorneys were coming in, followed by the first group of spectators. James studied them. The room rumbled with indistinct voices, a few laughs, but most speaking in low serious tones. He felt alone and decided to sit with Laura until he was required to come forward. As he stood, the courtroom's doors again opened, more spectators streaming. Then he saw Seán walking toward him, his coat's left arm tied off at the elbow. They embraced awkwardly, James whispering, "Glad to see ye."

"I wouldn't have missed this, Seámus."

Laura was standing. "Seán! So good of ya to come. Are ya well?"

"Well enough," he smirked. "'Tis grand t' see ye again." He kissed her hand.

"Do ye remember her in Kildare?" asked James. "Ye were a bit muzzy that week."

"Remember her? Oh, Lord aye!" Seán turned. "'Tis you I can't seem to place."

James chuckled. "When did ye arrive?"

"Yesterday. We came through Kildare. Just after ye'd left."

"We?" asked Laura.

"Ach, aye, we. Where's me manners!" Seán turned to a young, pretty lady behind him and said, "Laura, Seámus, I'd like ye to meet Miss Ann Conway. She was my nurse in New Ross. Ann, this is Miss Laura . . .uhmm."

"Johansson," said James.

"Ach, aye, Laura Johansson."

"The pleasure's mine, ma'am," said Ann, duteously.

"Nice meeting ya as vell," Laura replied with her usual resplendent smile.

"And this rogue here," Seán went on, "is my good friend Seámus. Nay, rather…." He paused, glancing about, then raised his voice, "This is James Annesley, the Earl of Anglesea!"

James smiled self-consciously as all eyes focused on him. Ann curtsied, blushing a shade lighter than her red hair. "'Tis an honor to meet ye, m'lord."

"Ah, now," James said, "none of that. I'm pleased to meet someone willing to put up with this rapscallion." He grabbed Seán's right shoulder.

"Shall ya sit with us?" asked Laura.

"We'd be honored," said Seán.

—✲—

Half an hour later, James was once again beside Mackercher at the plaintiff's table. The courtroom was full of people, the gallery overflowing, the
area in front of the bar teaming with a sea of black robes and long solicitor's
wigs. When an extra table was brought in for Richard's seventeen solicitors,
James's six, including Mackercher, were clearly amused. Finally, the bailiff
and other officers of the court filed in, and the bailiff ordered everyone to
order and to stand. The courtroom emanated with squeaks and rustling
as the hundreds of spectators came to their feet. An odd hush followed as the
twelve gentlemen jurors entered, then stood before their seats in the long jury
box beside James's table. He watched them, each dressed in black, blue and
burgundy finery, each noble and proud. Though he noticed a few glancing at
him, others were clearly looking for Richard, who still had not arrived.

"There stands the rest of Ireland's wealth," whispered Mackercher.

James nodded, knowing Richard had obtained his due: a jury of equals.
There were no surprises there. He had been briefed on their identities weeks
ago. This one jury was rumored to be the wealthiest ever seated by an English
court. They consisted of five earls, six marquis, and one baron—all members
of the Irish and English Parliaments. And compiled, they represented almost
the whole of Protestant Ireland, save Richard's vast holdings. (Though most of
their lives were spent on English soil.) Whether or not they would be sympa-
thetic to James remained to be seen. A verdict for him would require devour-
ing their own. Supposing they saw Richard that way, as brethren. Mackercher
surmised it hinged on how many Richard had irreparably angered in Parliament—something impossible to ascertain with accuracy, rumors being as
abundant as the people who birth them.

As the jurors remained standing, the bailiff announced the three honorable judges as they solemnly filed in, each under bulky crimson robes
trimmed with white fur, a black sash around the waist, a long wig that draped
shoulders and chest. All three faces were aged and pale, firmly impassive. The
one who took the center seat, Lord Chief Baron, John Bowes, wore a thick
gold cord around his neck, hanging low like a giant necklace. He was broad
shouldered, with a long face around a Roman nose below deep-set eyes that
carefully betrayed nothing.

Once the robes were all settled, the bailiff turned, bellowing, "Hear ye!
Hear ye! Be it known in these parts and in this presence that the matter
of James Annesley, Esquire versus His Lordship Richard Annesley, the right
honorable Baron of Altham, the Earl of Anglesea—"

"Bailiff!" Justice Bowes commanded. "Leave off the formalities. For that is what we are here to determine."

"M'lord." The bailiff nodded, gathering himself again, then resumed, "Be it known in these parts and in this presence that the matter of James Annesley, Esquire versus…Richard Annesley, his lordship, is hereby heard before these honorable justices of His Majesty. Long live this court and long live the king!"

Justice Bowes motioned for all to sit and in a thunder they did. Cocking forward, he asked, "Sergeant Mackercher, are you ready?"

"Aye, my lord," replied Mackercher, resuming his feet.

"And is this Mr. James Annesley?" The judge frowned.

"Aye, my lord." Mackercher motioned for James to stand, to which he quickly complied.

Bowes turned to the mass of black robes against the other wall. "Prime Sergeant Malone, are you ready?"

"Aye, my lord." Anthony Malone, Richard's lead solicitor, was also standing.

"I see you have managed quite an army, but where is your client?" growled Bowes.

"My lord, I expect him momentarily."

"We'll start without him. Perhaps he does not take this matter seriously enough to dignify us for its commencement."

Malone stammered, "My lord, I can assure you, Lord Anglesea most certainly does."

"I will grant him one minute, but no more, Prime Sergeant!"

"Thank you, my lord."

"Prime?" James whispered to Mackercher, smirking. "We're up against another Prime Sergeant? Maybe I should've hired me one of those."

Mackercher grinned, shaking his head. "Yar bloody-well stuck now," he whispered back.

At that moment, the giant doors flew open and all eyes turned. In paraded four men dressed in gallant orange finery, followed by Richard, who high-stepped forward, shoes clicking, scarf in hand, chest first. The four stood aside and Richard kept moving. James smiled at the sight. His uncle was in grand fashion—bright purple coat, hat adorned with a plume of silver and green feathers, an enormous wig, a bright gold rapier. As Richard opened the barrister's gate, Justice Bowes bellowed, "Halt!" Richard froze, glaring. "Remove your hat, sir," ordered Bowes. Richard obeyed, slowly, giving the judge a long blink and short nod. "Are you a solicitor in this matter?" Bowes asked.

"My lord?" replied Richard.

"No man comes before that bar who is not a solicitor or a party in this case."

"Most certainly, my lord. I am a party to this case."

"State your name," barked Bowes.

"My lord," began Malone, "this gentleman is Lord Ang—"

"Silence." Bowes raised a hand, then pointed at Richard. "I'm addressing the dandy."

"Richard, Earl of Anglesea, m'lord. Not one to be pointed at, I assure you."

"Aye? Well, we'll see about that," Bowes grumbled. "Step forward."

Richard's face reddened, his jaw set. He opened the gate and quickly walked to his table.

"Lord Anglesea," Justice Bowes continued before Richard could sit, "you will not make a mockery of this court. If you want to parade in here with your hubris, like a peacock, and keep this court from commencing on time, I will have you arrested on charges of contempt. Do you understand?"

"My lord," Richard retorted, fuming, "I had no such designs."

"You did, indeed. And what's more, I've been informed that your flock of black sheep there has been roaming this city, offering money to those who would agree to testify here. I will not tolerate such criminal impertinence."

Malone blurted, "I must object, my lord. Lord Anglesea has done no such—"

Richard raised an imperious hand, silencing his attorney. "I'll deal with this man," he snarled, then marched toward the bench.

"Stand where you are!" one of the other judges commanded.

"Bailiff!" shouted Bowes. "Arrest this man upon the next step!"

James glanced to his side and saw Mackercher with an unabashed grin.

"This is an outrage!" shouted Richard. "To treat a fellow peer in this manner! I will have your appointment sir!"

"Lord Anglesea," said Bowes, lowering his voice. "This court is not below you. If you wish to speak to me again, you must have your counsel make the request. If you speak to me directly, one more time, you will be expelled from this court."

Richard was shaking with rage, glaring at Bowes, who returned it with equal fury. The entire room was silent. Grasping the hilt of his rapier, Richard spun back to his table.

"One more matter, Lord Anglesea. You shall leave your sword beyond the bar."

Without looking at the judge, Richard jerked the sword free and threw it over the railing, where it clanged down the aisle of the gallery.

James glanced down at his own rapier, then looked at Mackercher, who motioned him to remove it. James slowly complied, laying in on the floor. Another attorney used his foot to slide it under the bar to Seán. When James looked back at Bowes, the judge was staring at him. "Sergeant Mackercher," Bowes said quietly, "you may commence."

"Thank ya, my lord," Mackercher said, stepping forward as though nothing had just happened. He slowly approached the jury box. "If it may please my lords, gentlemen of the jury, I am Daniel Mackercher, counsel for the claimant, Mr. James Annesley, the only son and heir of Arthur, the late Fourth Baron of Altham and Sixth Earl of Anglesea, deceased, otherwise to be titled, the Right Honorable James, Eighth Earl of Anglesea. Eighth, as his uncle, the defendant in this case, deviously stole the position of Seventh. The issue to be tried before ya is one of grand consequence—whether or not Mr. Annesley is the child of Mary Sheffield, the wife of that same late Arthur. It will be claimed by the defense that Arthur never had a son by Mary, Lady Anglesea, but rather that James Annesley is the son of a woman by the name of Joan Landy, now deceased. Though it will no doubt be proffered to ya that Ms. Landy was my sister, let me assure ya that such fact is of no consequence." He paused for a moment, then went on. "In order that I may convince ya of the truth in this matter, I will prove to ya gentlemen that Mary, Lady Anglesea did indeed undergo a pregnancy, that she gave birth to a son, and that the plaintiff before ya is that very son." After another brief pause, he wet his lips and continued. "Numerous witnesses will be brought before ya who will relate their account of that pregnancy and birth, but it has been my experience that memories from that many years ago, twenty-eight years ago, can often be quite feeble indeed." Mackercher turned, facing Richard. "Unless, of course, they are financially encouraged to remember details not otherwise known." He returned his gaze to the jurors. "Most of the good people I will bring before ya will tell ya how Arthur treated James, how James was publicly regarded as his legal son and rightful heir. And a few will speak of the defendant, and how he treated the plaintiff. I am confident that once the plaintiff has brought his full case before ya, ya will have learned the truth—that which the defendant, Richard Annesley, knows full well. For as ya will see, had that evil, greedy man...." He gave a long purposeful point at Richard. "Had he not known in his black heart that the plaintiff was truly the rightful Earl of

Anglesea, he would never have gone to such detestable lengths to destroy him." Again Mackercher paused, then turned back to the jury. "I thank ya for yar wisdom in this matter," he concluded, then returned to his chair.

"Prime Sergeant Malone?" Justice Bowes prompted.

"May it please my lords," Malone responded, approaching the jury. "Gentlemen of the jury, this is a case of great importance. Many of you know the defendant, Richard Annesley, Earl of Anglesea, and you know the pride he maintains for his family's good name and lasting honor. He takes this matter quite seriously, indeed." He paused to glance at Justice Bowes, who was staring back implacably. Malone quickly resumed, "Quite seriously. As each of you does, as well. The facts will be presented and proven to you, clear and simple. The plaintiff is a bastard, an imposter, a desperate young man determined to steal what never belonged to him by birthright." He clasped his hands together and began pacing the length of the jury box. "Gentlemen, I bid you, think of yourselves as Isaac, who was so easily deceived because of his blindness, fooled into giving his blessing to the deceiver." Malone walked to the front of James's table and stood directly before him. "Here is Jacob, the deceiver, coming before you with his false lambskin and baseless offering." He took a step sideways, positioning himself in front of Mackercher. "And here...here is the form of Rebecca, the one who urged Jacob to deceive. It was this man's sister who gave birth to James Annesley." He pivoted back to face the jury. "Do you not find it queer that the woman's own brother is here to argue this case, no doubt fishing for a piece of the fortune? 'Tis obvious, gentlemen." Malone put both hands on the railing of the jury box and leaned toward the men. When he continued, he spoke so softly that James had to strain to hear him. "When I sit down the deception will begin," he said. "A parade of people will come before you. I ask you to see them as they are, the false *hair* (he waited for the few chuckles) of Esau, and the vile food which you will be asked to eat. I beseech you, use your eyes gentlemen. You have them. I implore you, do not make Isaac's mistake. Do not be deceived. Do not be the instruments for this black thievery." As Malone sat down, James watched anxiously, impressed yet chafed by what seemed a clever opening.

"Sergeant Mackercher, you may call your first witness."

Mackercher stood. "The plaintiff calls Mr. Thomas Rolph."

A pew creaked behind them, and James looked back to see an old man grappling to stand. A young woman helped him, then led him to the aisle. As Rolph's eyes met James's, James gave him an appreciative nod. Rolph had been the butler at Dunmain House during James's childhood there, and though James had no particularly warm memories of him, Rolph had been a pleasure to visit with during trial preparation. The elderly man's memory was strong and he had been useful in sorting through the countless dates and disparate witnesses. After shuffling forward, past the bar, he finally reached the witness box where a court officer was waiting.

"Raise yer right hand, sir, placing the other firmly on the Holy Bible," the officer ordered. Rolph did, his wrinkled, spotted hands shaking. "Do ye swear, sir, on this Holy Bible and before this court, and upon yer oath to King George the Second, that the testimony ye shall give unto this court this day shall be the truth and nothing other than the truth, so help ye God?"

"Aye. I do," Rolph muttered, then took the seat.

Mackercher smiled warmly. "Morning, sir. Yar name's Thomas Rolph, is it not?"

"Aye."

"Tell us, sir, how ya came to be acquainted with Arthur, the late Earl of Anglesea."

"I knew Lord Anglesea two or three years before m'lord married Mary Sheffield. She was daughter of the Duke of Buckingham. I was in his service then, and came t' m'lord's house in Dunmain at the end of 1714. Dunmain House, 'twas called."

"How is it, sir, that ya remember the exact year ya went to Dunmain House?"

"'Twas the year Queen Anne died, God rest her."

"What was yar service there?"

"I was butler t' the house."

"Do ya remember Lady Anglesea being with child?"

"She was. Gave birth t' Master James in the month of April. Year o' our Lord, 1715."

"And how, sir, do ya remember the month?"

"'Twas eclipsed the day James was born. 1715, best I remember. I know 'twas April."

"Did ya know my sister, sir—Joan Landy?"

"Aye. She was appointed wet nurse t' Master James. People referred t' her as 'Juggy.'"

Light laughter cascaded across the courtroom and Mackercher ignored it. "All right, sir," he said. "Was Juggy ever with child?"

"Aye. 'Bout that same time. 'Twas a boy. He died 'bout the time James be born."

"Do ya recall, sir, what she named that boy?"

"Named Daniel. Fynn said she'd named it for her brother, as I recall. That'd be you."

Mackercher smiled. "Ya mentioned Fynn. Do ya mean Fynn Kennedy?"

"Aye."

"Who was Fynn Kennedy?"

James watched as the venerable old man plodded through each of Mackercher's questions, telling the jury about Fynn and Catherine, and Catherine's death birthing Seán. He went steadily on, recalling details of James's birth, Juggy's cottage, and how Mary would visit James there. He had heard all this before, innumerable times over the past few months, from the different witnesses they had interviewed. But it was odd to hear old Rolph telling it in court, for the whole world to hear, as if he were talking about someone else, someone who was not sitting before him in the same room.

The minutes passed by, stretching slowly into an hour, and Rolph seemed to be tiring. "We didn't know for sure, Mr. Mackercher," he was now saying, "but I think m'lady was merely an acquaintance of young Tom…Thomas Palliser."

"That day, the day ya said Lady Anglesea was turned out, did ya hear her accuse Arthur of bringing forth a bastard child?"

"By virtue of my oath, I did not."

"Please sir, do correct any error, but she would've known if James was not her son, aye?"

Rolph smiled coyly. "I can't fathom how she'd have missed such an event." The gallery chuckled.

"And she referred to James as her son?" asked Mackercher.

"Aye. She did, indeed."

"And in the middle of this argument during which, as ya've told us, Arthur sliced off Tom Palliser's ear, and was hurling insults to Mary about being unfaithful, are ya telling this jury that not once did she accuse Arthur of being unfaithful by fathering James with another woman?"

"That's correct, sir. Not once."

Coldness came over James. They were a bare two hours into this trial, yet he was already wishing it over and done with. It was hard to listen to these people talk about him, about his mother and Juggy, about Arthur, about Fynn. Telling the world things he wished to forget, things he wished he had never known.

CHAPTER 37

Sit still, my soul:
Foul deeds will rise,
though all the earth o'erwhelm them,
to men's eyes.

— from *Hamlet*, William Shakespeare, 1601

Evening's amber light was streaming through the windows high over the judges' bench, angling across the open temperate air, dust floating in the golden shafts. James stared at the thousands of little specks glinting there, flickering like motes of hot ash rising from a fire. Lowering his gaze, he saw Mackercher and Malone still in the midst of a heated exchange at the bench, petitioning the judges on some point of law. It was late; everyone was tired. Over the course of the previous week, Mackercher had questioned ninety-six witnesses, most for no more than four or five questions, and most with little or no cross-examination. One had been John Purcell, the butcher, who testified about the murder of Juggy. Mackercher let another solicitor handle the direct of him. Now they were nearing the end of their case, to James's relief. This trial was requiring more painful patience than expected. He had envisioned the testimony as fascinating, but it was anything but that—it was dreary repetition of random remembrances. And soon would begin Richard's farce parade. It was arduous at best.

Suddenly Justice Bowes boomed, "That's satisfactory gentlemen, step back!"

Mackercher returned to the table angry. Clearly, he had been refused.

"Is your witness coming today, Sergeant Mackercher?" asked Bowes.

"Aye, my lord, he—" At that instant, the doors swung and a short, wiry, grey-haired Irishman came walking briskly to the front. James saw the left side of the man's head was deformed: a fleshy hole where an ear had once been. He was sworn in then stated his name as Thomas Palliser. Mackercher moved close to the jury box before asking his first question. "Mr. Palliser, for the past few days we've been hearing, in some detail, of an altercation ya had with the late Lord Arthur Annesley. I will spare asking ya the event particulars as it clearly did occur." Laughter came from the gallery. "I apologize, Mr. Palliser," he added quickly, "I meant no disrespect."

"None taken," replied Palliser, his accent thickly Irish.

"What I wish to ask pertains to the events following that day, that day at Dunmain House. Do ya know the defendant, Richard Annesley?"

"Aye, I know o'him."

"When did ya first meet him?"

"De day after I lost me ear, 'twas. He came t'me with some o'his men, a Captain Bailyn an' another. I believe went by de name Higgon."

"Might it have been Higgins, a Mr. Paul Higgins?"

"O' might've. I know not, but might've indeed."

"What did the defendant want from ya that day?"

"Asked me challenge Lord Anglesea, fer satisfaction. Fer his affront on me ear, ye understand. With pistols, he did."

"To a duel?"

"Aye, so he did. Had a challenge written fer me. Gave t'me t' post at de cross o' Ross."

"New Ross? About four miles from Dunmain House, aye?"

"I think 'tis more o' six," said Palliser. "Aye, twas a post front o' St. Mary's."

"And did ya?" Mackercher continued. "Did ya post it, yar challenge?"

"Most certainly. Didn't know an Earl wouldn't meet me."

"So Arthur never accepted yar challenge to duel?"

"Nay. Lord Anglesea said I should—"

"By Lord Anglesea, do ya mean the late Arthur Annesley or his brother, the defendant?"

"Him there," replied Palliser, motioning toward Richard with a finger. Richard's eyes went to slits at the gesture.

"Ah well," Mackercher said softly, "ya may refer to him as Richard. I think we understand he merits no higher address."

Malone jumped to his feet. "My lords this is outrageous! I object! Sergeant Mackercher is making arguments to the jury, entirely disregarding—"

"Enough Sergeant Malone." Bowes raised a hand. "Sergeant Mackercher, you will have your closing argument. Do not stir our wrath at this juncture."

"Apologies my lord." He turned back to the witness box. "Mr. Palliser, please disregard my comment. Ya may address the defendant in whatever way ya deem appropriate. Now, ya were telling us what he," he pointed purposefully at Richard, "the defendant, said ya should do."

"Aye. Well, he...Lord Richard...." Palliser grinned. "Said I shouldn't accept Arthur not meetin' me. Dat an honorable man would see justice done."

"And by justice, what did ya think Richard meant?"

"T' kill him," said Palliser. A collective gasp was heard. "By virtue o' me oath, he did."

"And at that time, did ya know Richard was Arthur's brother?"

"Aye, sir," the Irishman replied, shifting in his seat. "Been told dat, I had."

"Very well, that brings me to a most delicate question. A few days later, Arthur was shot in his drawing room, rendering him blind in one eye. Do ya know what villain fired the shot?"

Palliser glanced about, as if unsure what to say. "Nay."

"Nay? Do ya not know that it was Richard himself who pulled that trigger?"

"I must object, my lords!" shouted Malone. "This is beyond—"

Bowes leaned forward. "Sergeants, approach." Mackercher and Malone walked to Bowes, and James could hear Bowes lecturing Mackercher fierily. After a few moments, both stepped back.

"Mr. Palliser," Mackercher continued. "I am nearly done—" Suddenly, the bells of Christ Church Cathedral began to peel the six o'clock hour. Since the cathedral adjoined the Four Courts, the tolling resounded through the courtroom, muffling all other sounds, forcing whoever was speaking to yield, to let it pass. Mackercher shook his head as the bells finally hit six. "All right, Mr. Palliser, shall we try this again?" He asked a few more questions, of little consequence, then turned the witness over to Malone.

Malone stood behind the defense table. "Of what profession are you, Mr. Palliser?"

"Eh?"

Malone gave a slight shake of his head, then smiled as if acknowledging Palliser was toying with him. He approached the witness box. "I asked, of what profession are you?"

"I'm a Roman Catholic, sir."

Malone waited for the general laughter to die off. "Nay, sir. What business or occupation do you follow?"

"Oh. I'm a tanner."

"A tanner?"

"Aye. What o' it, sir?"

"Are you not also a builder of muskets?"

"I've tended t' 'em, sir, from time t' time. Never built one."

"Is it not true that you shot Arthur, the late Earl of Anglesea, after—"

"Nay!"

"—after he attacked you for your dalliances with his wife?"

"By virtue o' me oath, nay."

"Tell us true, were you and Mary Sheffield not involved in a relationship—"

Mackercher sprang to his feet. "I object, my lords. What Lady Anglesea did or did not do has no bearing in this case."

"My lord," Malone said, turning to Bowes, "Sergeant Mackercher introduced the subject on the day first of his prosecution, when he asked his witness, Mr. Thomas Rolph, if Lady Anglesea made comment of Arthur's unfaithfulness. 'Tis only fair for this jury to know if she herself was indeed so involved with Mr. Palliser here."

"I will allow it, for now. But not much further, Sergeant Malone."

"Aye, my lord," Malone said, then turned. "Now, I ask you again—"

"Nay, we weren't," Palliser said in a gruff tone.

"Nay?"

"On my oath."

"Then why did Arthur accuse her of such?"

"I know not."

"What do you believe, Mr. Palliser?"

"I believe in God," he replied, stiff-necked. Again the gallery chuckled.

"Order!" Bowes bellowed, though he too was restraining a grin.

Malone continued. "If you were not in such relations with Mary Sheffield, and yet her husband cut off your ear in the fury of an accusation of such, do you not have—"

"'Twas someone else," Palliser mumbled.

"Someone else?"

"Aye, but I know not who, so don't ye be askin' me."

Again Mackercher stood. "My lords, to what relevance is this questioning? To besmirch Lady Anglesea's fine name? To insult his Lordship, the Duke of Buckingham? Surely there is no value here. There is no merit to such a frivolous line of questioning, no purpose other than to draw us from the question that has brought us here, as to Mrs. Sheffield's maternity of the plaintiff, to which we have already proven—"

"Your stand is sustained and noted," answered Bowes. He turned to Malone. "Do you have more questions for this witness?"

"Nay, my lord."

"You may take your leave, Mr. Palliser. This court stands adjourned until eight o'clock on the morrow next." Everyone stood as the three judges rose and strode through their door.

James stretched, then turned, smiling at Laura. Mackercher leaned near him saying, "Nearly done, m'lord. One or two more tomorrow and we'll rest."

"Very good, Mr. Mackercher," James said. He stood before continuing, "I don't care for such talk of my mother. Keep it out. 'Tis useless."

"That's over, unless they bring it up in their direct examination, in which case—"

"No more," James half-barked. "Shut them down if they do. I want no further accusations of such infidelity."

Mackercher nodded confidently. "I'll do my best, m'lord."

James put a hand on Mackercher's shoulder. "We'll dine at Stag's Head?"

"If that's what ya'd like."

"Laura likes it, so 'tis fine. We'll visit with ye there." James started toward Laura, pushing past the black robes milling around the bar. Just then Richard blocked his path, glaring. James snorted with disgust. "What do ye want?"

Richard leaned close, whispering, "Ye'd better win this case, knave. If ye don't, I'll have ye done in for sure. B'Christ, I will."

"Oh?" James stood his ground. "Are ye already hiring more assassins?"

"I'll send ye to hell in an instant. I'll do it myself!"

"Ye're a rabid dog, ye are. Ye never stop. Well, I admire yer tenacity, but do please ply me no more with yer schemes."

"Damn yer blood!" Richard snarled.

"My blood?" snapped James. "Annesley blood runs through us both, lest ye forget."

"Ye don't deserve it."

James leaned into Richard's face. "Fortunes have been spent on both sides in this affair, but do ye know the highest price for me?"

Richard stepped back, glowering, lofty.

"Seeing it in print, for everyone to know I'm related to the likes of ye. Having to admit I was born into this godforsaken, honorless family."

"Blood and thunder! Where's my sword?" Richard shouted, spinning around.

"James!" Mackercher was there, along with Malone and a swarm of other lawyers.

"'Tis nothing," grumbled James. "Just family banter."

"Ye knave! Ye goddamned little knave!" roared Richard, struggling to free himself from his lawyers.

"Uncle! Black-eyed vermin," James fumed. "Hear me clearly. Though I'd sorely wish to kill ye, I'd rather see ye live in ruin and shame. To that end, when I've reclaimed my title, ye must go. Flee to France if ye wish, or any other place that'll harbor yer rotten kind, but ye'll not remain here or England. Do ye understand me?"

"Damn ye bastard," hissed Richard, "ye'll never win this."

"Do ye not understand me sir?" James shouted in the man's face.

"Come now," Mackercher urged, steering James away. Shaking, James allowed himself to be led to the door where Laura, Seán, and Ann were staring at him.

Malone followed after, asking Mackercher, "What if Lord Anglesea does not leave?"

Mackercher turned, smirking at the capitulating question. "He'll be hanged, Mr. Malone. On sight. No hesitation. No trial. No mercy. Is that not clear enough?"

"Outrageous!" Malone protested.

"Murder and kidnapping, Prime Sergeant Malone," said Mackercher. "A man's sins will surely find him out."

CHAPTER 38

But all-feeling Heaven, who hates injustice, would not
suffer that cruel usurper of another's right to proceed in a
manner which might secure him the possession, and for
his greater punishment rendered him accessory to his own
shame and confusion.

— *Memoirs of an Unfortunate Young Nobleman,*
James Annesley, 1743

The trial resumed the next morning as the bells of Christ Church pealed
eight. Mackercher rose. "My lords, the plaintiff calls his last witness, Prime
Sergeant John Giffard."

At once Malone was on his feet. "Sergeant Giffard may not be called to
testify, my lords. He was an attorney for the defendant in another matter, and
anything Sergeant Giffard can say would be privileged and inadmissible as
secrets between an attorney and his client."

"My lords," began Mackercher, his tone resolute. "We concede the veracity of that fact, that last spring, in London, Sergeant Giffard did represent
Richard Annesley in his meritless prosecution of James Annesley on the false
grounds of murder, but—"

"This is highly unacceptable," Malone cut in. "There is no evidence
to suggest that it was the defendant who prosecuted those murder charges
against the plaintiff. No such—"

"Prime Sergeant Malone," Bowes interrupted, "did you not just claim
this man's testimony to be privileged because of that very fact, that he represented the defendant in an earlier matter?"

Malone hesitated before conceding, "Aye, my lord."

"And is it not true that the earlier matter was the murder prosecution of
the plaintiff?"

Malone looked at his team of attorneys, appealing for a lifeline, but none
came. Instead, their gazes darted to the walls, dropped to the floors, examined
notes. "Aye," Malone finally muttered.

"Speak up, if you will, Prime Sergeant Malone," a different judge ordered.

"Aye, m'lords," said Malone. "I said, Aye."

"Then to that issue, the fact is so stipulated, Sergeant Mackercher," said Justice Bowes, appearing glum. "Yet," he continued, "I still see no room to allow such testimony."

"Thank ya, my lord," Mackercher said, then took a breath before continuing. "My lords, the witness's testimony may be allowed on the grounds that the defendant has previously waived his right to claim such testimony as duly privileged. Evidence exists—"

"My lord," Malone interjected, "may we not conduct these arguments at the bench, or more preferably in chambers, rather than before this jury?"

Justice Bowes leaned back, conferring with the other two judges. The courtroom fell dead silent, other than the indistinguishable murmur of the judges' deep voices. Finally, Bowes sat forward, saying, "We see no reason at present, Sergeant Malone. Sergeant Mackercher, please state your evidence of the asserted waiver."

"Thank ya, my lords. Sergeant Giffard was counsel to the defendant, Richard Annesley, in the previous instance, but as James Annesley was not found guilty in that criminal matter, the defendant refused to pay Sergeant Giffard for the legal services he rendered. Sergeant Giffard then took the matter to the Court of Exchequer in London where a waiver was executed by the defendant allowing Sergeant Giffard to divulge to that court what legal services he had performed, in order that Sergeant Giffard could prosecute his claim for payment."

"Do you have that waiver?" asked Bowes, his aged hand already outstretched.

"Aye, my lord." Mackercher stepped up, Malone following, and handed the paper over.

"My lord, may I see that?" asked Malone.

"Of course." Bowes allowed Malone to read it, then took it back. While Bowes read it, Malone turned his head and glared at Richard, who simply looked away. The paper was then handed to the other judges, who read it in turn. They put their heads together, whispered for a moment, then resumed straight postures. "All right, Sergeants, you may step back," announced Bowes. Mackercher and Malone returned to their tables as Bowes addressed the jury, "Gentlemen of the jury, you will now be hearing rather unusual testimony. The witness, Mr. John Giffard, is a prime sergeant solicitor who represented the defendant, Richard Annesley, in a prior instance. The witness is no longer counsel to the defendant and therefore will not be coming before you in his capacity as such, but rather as a witness only. As the defendant did not pay Sergeant Giffard's bill of...." He paused to read the waiver, then looked at Giffard, still waiting beyond the bar. "His bill of ten thousand pounds...."

The gallery gave a collective gasp.

"As Richard Annesley refused to make payment," Bowes went on, "he was sued by Sergeant Giffard in a London court for collection. In that suit, Richard Annesley waived all rights of privilege between an attorney and client." He lifted the paper. "This is that waiver." He gave Richard a disdainful look that, to James, seemed to say, 'you ignorant greedy man.' Then he resumed with the jury. "Therefore, we shall allow Sergeant Giffard to come before you and give testimony that would otherwise have been disallowed. Sergeant Mackercher, you may call your witness."

Mackercher waited as Giffard came forward and was sworn in. Then he began. "What is yar profession, sir?"

"I am an attorney of the Common Pleas in England and a Prime Sergeant Solicitor of the High Court of Chancery."

"Do ya know the defendant in this suit?"

"Aye, I do. I was retained by the Earl on the fifth of May of this year to carry on a prosecution for murder against the plaintiff, James Annesley."

"And when was that trial?"

"It was held in the Old Bailey on the third of June."

"So the conversations ya had with the defendant occurred during a one month period, sometime around May of this year? Is that correct?"

"Aye, that is correct."

"And as was mentioned before ya came to the stand, Richard Annesley was unhappy with yar performance in the murder prosecution and refused to pay yar fees?"

"Whether or not he was unhappy with my performance, I can only surmise. I do know he was extremely disconsolate that his nephew was not hanged."

"How do ya know this?"

"When the waiver was signed, one of his men, a Captain Bailyn, carried it to London and threatened to kill me if I further pursued payment from Lord Anglesea."

"Did ya pursue the suit for payment?"

"Aye, I did. And it was granted."

"Do ya know where Captain Bailyn is now?"

"Somewhere quite hot, I suppose." Giffard flicked a small smile at James.

Mackercher continued, "Most likely so. He's dead, correct?"

"That is my understanding." A nervous chuckle rose in the room, then faded quickly.

"What was the court's verdict in yar suit?"

"I was awarded my fees but have yet to be paid. Indeed, I'm certain I never shall be."

"Why is that, Sergeant Giffard?" Mackercher asked, stepping closer to the witness box.

"I must object, my lord," Malone said. "The witness's knowledge about the defendant's financial habits or property is not relevant to this proceeding."

"I will allow it," Bowes said, then glared at Mackercher. "But get to its relevance."

"Aye, my lord." Mackercher turned back to Giffard. "I asked—"

"I remember the question. I was never paid because Richard is penniless, best I can determine." A surprised muttering erupted throughout the courtroom.

Bowes raised a hand. "Continue, Sergeant Giffard."

"Aye, my lord. The man has so heavily encumbered the Anglesea Estate that there are more debts outstanding against it than its capital on the whole."

James slumped back in his chair, gut punched.

Mackercher was clearly surprised as well. "Ya are not saying the entire estate of the Earl of Anglesea is worthless, are ya?"

"Not exactly. 'Tis of great worth, valued at several million pounds, to be sure. But Richard, the current Earl of Anglesea, and quite probably his brother before him, has incurred debts of greater amounts."

James closed his eyes. "Sergeant Giffard," Mackercher continued, now more slowly, "how did ya come to know of such private finances? Have yar factors investigated the man?"

"Nay. I could be mistaken. I've looked into the matter as best I can, but the Anglesea estate is broad and grand, not easily assessed."

"I would think not."

Malone was standing. "I must object. This inquiry, ostensible as it is, into the defendant's private affairs is highly irrelevant."

"Sergeant Mackercher," said Bowes, "move this line of questioning back to the issue at hand or release this witness."

"Aye, my lord. Sergeant Giffard, did the defendant tell ya why he wished to prosecute murder charges against his nephew, James Annesley?"

"Aye. He said the man should be hanged, at any price. He and I traveled to London in late May, but once there, we stayed apart, generally speaking. He thought it inadvisable to be seen in my company. Most messages between us were conducted thereafter by Captain Bailyn."

Mackercher frowned. "The one who later threatened to kill ya?"

"The very same."

"Yet before ya went to London, ya had direct conversations with the defendant?"

"Aye. And one particular occasion in London."

"What did ya discuss in those conversations?" Mackercher moved close to the jury box.

Malone jumped. "My lords, this is privileged—"

"No," barked Bowes. "I have already ruled it allowable. Take your seat sir."

Malone complied, slowly.

"He said he had arranged a witness, a Mr. Seán Kennedy, the son of the man James accidentally shot. Mr. Kennedy was to testify that it had indeed been an intentional killing."

James winced, imagining Seán was uncomfortable as well. James knew Mackercher would not explore this issue regarding Seán. That was their agreement. Nevertheless, it was bad enough simply hearing this much said.

"Did he ever tell ya, sir...." Mackercher paused, facing the jury, lowering his voice. "Did Richard ever say that he knew James Annesley was the rightful heir to the title and property of the Earl of Anglesea?"

"Aye, he did. And he told me he had kidnapped the boy, sold him into slavery to remove him from Ireland." The courtroom flared with murmurs.

"Silence," warned Bowes.

"He did?" asked Mackercher, as if surprised. "The defendant...." He walked to stand in front of Richard, then pointed at him. "This man here, the defendant, he told ya that?"

"He said that was why James had to be hanged. He wanted to be rid of him. That since James returned from the American Colonies, the young man had been nothing but a nuisance. He said he wished to have killed James while still a boy, rather than to have transported him."

"All right." Mackercher gave Richard a wicked smile. "So, once again, Sergeant Giffard, ya're saying that Richard Annesley, in private conversation with ya, admitted James Annesley was the rightful Earl of Anglesea?"

"Aye. He told me so."

"Thank ya, Sergeant Giffard." Mackercher stood motionless, staring at

Richard, who met his gaze. Then Mackercher smiled, clapped his hands once, and turned back to the bench. "We pass this witness for cross-examination."

Bowes peered at the defense table. "Sergeant Malone?"

Malone stood, his face ashen. "Aye, my lord," he said.

Mackercher took his seat beside James, leaned over, and whispered, "We have him. All he can do now is assault the man's character."

"Sergeant Giffard," Malone said slowly, as if unsure how to begin, "do you know if Lord Anglesea was aware of James Annesley's innocence or guilt in the murder trial?"

"Aye. Richard knew James was innocent. He told me so."

"Yet he sought to have him hanged?"

"Aye," answered Giffard.

Malone advanced slowly. "Did you not believe that to be a most wicked crime in and of itself—to seek the hanging of an innocent man?"

Mackercher grinned, then whispered to James, "Here it begins."

"Nay. I did not," Giffard replied coolly.

Malone grasped the rail around the witness box. "Nay? As an attorney, a solicitor before the King's Court, one who sets himself out as a man of integrity and honor, how could you engage in such a prosecution without objection? How could you represent a client, carrying out his orders, when you had full knowledge of the lies being perpetrated?"

Giffard snapped, "I may as well ask you, sir, how you came to be here today? How you came to be engaged for the defendant in this very case? You no doubt know the truth of this matter."

Malone froze, staring at Giffard, mouth agape, then pulled his lips in tight.

"Sergeant Malone," Bowes barked irritably, "have you finished with this witness?"

"I have another question or two."

"Are you certain?" Bowes asked with an obvious nudge.

"Aye, my lord." Malone stepped back to his table. "Sergeant Giffard, did you not comprehend that your actions would be for a bad purpose, to unjustly compass the death of another man?"

"I was not there to undertake a bad purpose. I was there to conduct a prosecution. If there was any dirty work, I was not concerned in it." To that Malone gave a chuckle which to James sounded forced. Giffard continued, "Again, Sergeant Malone, I must ask how you came to be engaged in this suit without objection?"

Now Malone erupted, firing back, "I make a distinction between carrying on a civil defense and a murderous prosecution that has as its only objective the death of an innocent man!"

"Oh? How came you to that distinction—by your wits?"

Bowes intervened. "Gentlemen! This is not the forum for a debate of your legal ethics. Sergeant Malone, do you have anything else relevant to this trial?"

Malone took his seat, muttering, "Nay, my lord."

"Sergeant Mackercher?"

Mackercher stood. "My lords, with yar permission, the plaintiff rests his case."

"Very well. This court stands adjourned until one o'clock this afternoon, at which time we shall begin the defendant's case in prime."

James grabbed Mackercher's shoulder, giving him a warm squeeze, then turned to Laura with a smile. As she returned it, James saw a glisten in her eyes, a tear nearly formed. Glancing at Seán, he was stopped by the accession he saw there—a repressed chin, an embarrassed grimace. James shrugged with a three finger salute. "Through ice" he mouthed softly. Seán nodded a silent "thank you."

CHAPTER 39

O what is greatness, when purchased at the expense of all
that can render the possessor
deservedly respected by the world, or easy in himself? In
vain does the unjust aspirer
hope to cover his infamy with ill-got titles and the glare of
pomp—the base groundwork
is visible through all the tinseled outside. Man sees it with
contempt, and Heaven with abhorrence.

— *Memoirs of an Unfortunate Young Nobleman*,
James Annesley, 1743

Frigid dampness descended on Dublin in great grey blankets of drizzly fog. The courtroom was dark and chilly, and James looked back at Laura hoping the green cape he bought her was keeping her warm. She gave a weary smile. They were both tired, tired of the long hours, day after day, the cold room, the hard seats not made for weeks of sitting. Mostly they were tired of the unrelenting spout of lies that gurgled from the witness box throughout Richard's defense. At first James had maintained mild annoyance when witness upon witness took the stand relaying blatant fabrications about Arthur and Mary. Some, in fact, were so ludicrous they were laughable, like the two men with thick Hibernian dialects, whom James had never seen before, yet claimed to have been his childhood friends. One woman blustered on about being Arthur's mistress, until Mackercher got her to admit under cross that they had done nothing more than dance together at a Parliament ball. But James found none of the tales amusing anymore. They were beyond ridiculous. Now Mackercher was putting down the latest: "So, ya really don't know what Mary said about her son?"

"Aye, I do."

"Mr. O'Malley," Mackercher shouted as he spun, leading with an accusing finger, "I believe ya said yar father told ya these things. Is that not correct?"

"Aye. He did."

"So ya never heard these things yarself?"

"My da was no liar!" blurted the witness, his face reddening.

"Oh, I'm sure. But would you tell us things untrue?" Mackercher snapped. Malone jumped up, objecting. Bowes leaned forward slowly, resting his chin on his tented fingers, but didn't speak. Malone sat.

"All right, Mr. O'Malley," Mackercher continued. "Did you, with yar own ears, ever hear Mary Sheffield say James was not her child?"

"I already said, my da—"

"Nay!" Mackercher thundered. "I asked what you heard from Mary!"

"Umm" the quailing man began. "Not that I recall, but—"

"Finally. I'm done with ya," said Mackercher, huffing back to his table.

"Step down, Mr. O'Malley." Bowes gave a dismissive wave. "Sergeant Malone?"

Malone was already up. "The defense calls Charity Heath to the witness box."

"Very well," Bowes mumbled.

James watched the aging woman slowly stride the aisle, past the bailiff at the gate, then on to the witness box.

"Raise yer right hand, placing the other firmly on the Holy Bible," the court officer instructed. Charity did as she was told. "Do ye swear, ma'am, on this Holy Bible and before this court, and upon yer oath to King George the Second, that the testimony ye shall give unto this court this day shall be the truth and nothing other than the truth, so help ye God?"

"I do so swear," she muttered, then added faintly, "I will."

"Please be seated."

As Charity sat, she glanced nervously at Richard before settling her gaze on the approaching Malone.

"Madam Heath, you were the attending servant to Lady Anglesea?" he asked, rubbing his forehead as he spoke.

"Aye, sir. I was."

"During what years were you such?"

"Before she was married to Lord Anglesea, during that time, till she left Ireland." Her words were woven tightly.

Malone paced before the jury. "Did you live with her during those years?"

"Always. I always did. Aye, sir. I was with her constantly, I do say."

The steady click of Malone's shoes stopped, then he slowly turned to face Charity. "Then you should know. You should be able to settle this matter for us. Had Lady Anglesea a child at Dunmain House?"

Charity scooted a little sideways, glancing at Richard again, then down to

Malone's feet. "Nay, sir. She never did. Nor was she ever with child." A polite gasp from the spectators.

Malone continued, "And Madam Heath, you said, I do believe, that you were with Lady Anglesea always? The entirety of her time in Ireland?"

"Aye. I always dressed and undressed m'lady. And at Dunmain House, I always put her to bed, then attended at her rising in the morning, for she was such a person that wouldn't permit anyone else to do it. She couldn't possibly have been with child without my knowing it."

"Thank you, Madam Heath. Now tell us, do you remember the day your lady left Dunmain House?"

"Aye. Arthur, Lord Anglesea turned her out, and I went with her to New Ross. And then we moved here, to Dublin."

Malone advanced closer. "Just the two of you? Not James as well?"

She frowned, her lip quivering. "Aye. 'Tis true."

James eased forward in his chair, glowering at Charity, who had yet to look at him.

"Why didn't Lady Anglesea take James with her?" Malone pressed.

"I know not," whispered Charity.

"You know not? Surely Lady Anglesea told you why she wouldn't—"

"Nay!" Charity squalled, tears welling in her eyes. "She didn't."

"All right, Madam Heath. So…Mary Sheffield, the supposed mother of the plaintiff, left Dunmain House without taking him, her supposed son, with her. Is that correct?"

Charity dabbed her ashen cheeks, then sat straight, crossing her arms. "Aye."

"After she left, you say she went to New Ross, then on to Dublin?"

"Aye, she did."

"And during that time, did she ever receive James as a visitor?"

"Never." Charity's gaze was now fixed on the venerable oak walls.

"Did she talk of seeing the child, as if he was her own?"

Again Charity cut a long glance at Richard. "Nay." Tears dribbled again down her flushed cheeks. "She did not."

James lurched forward angrily, wanting to stand, wanting to shout at her, to call her the liar she was. Mackercher put a hand on his arm. "Settle," Mackercher whispered, "I'll have my turn with this witch."

"Did she ever attempt to see James?"

Charity clenched her jaw, then took a deep breath and answered, "Not that I was aware."

"Lying hag," whispered James.

Bowes cut his eyes to James, but said nothing.

"Madam Heath, I can see this is emotional for you. No doubt it has been difficult, caring for your lady as you did, while seeing an imposter attempt—"

"Yar lordships!" Mackercher protested.

Bowes shook his head at Malone, who nodded, continuing calmly, "We thank you for your candor." He looked at the bench. "I have no further questions for this good lady." He veered back to his seat.

Mackercher stood and slowly advanced on Charity. "Madam Heath, ya certainly have a fanciful story for us today, do ya not?"

"Nay, indeed, 'tis true," she murmured, not looking at him.

"When ya were sworn in, did ya not swear on the blessed Holy Bible that yar testimony would be the truth before this court and God?"

Again, her eyes flashed to Richard. "So I did."

"Madam Heath, no doubt all in this court have observed the most curious of things, that ya keep looking at the defendant before answering. And yet ya seem unwilling to look me in the eyes, or the plaintiff. Do tell us, how long have ya known Richard Annesley?"

She looked down, her hands clasped together in her lap. "Many years," she whispered.

"How many?" bellowed Mackercher.

"I don't know," she growled back.

"All right," snapped Mackercher, raising a hand. "Since when have ya known him?"

"'Twas many years ago. I'm not—"

Mackercher thundered, "'Twas since he assumed the title, Earl of Anglesea! Is that not correct?"

"I suppose, 'tis."

"Indeed ya met Richard on the very day Arthur was buried. Is that not correct?"

"I don't know. I had seen him at Dunmain, before, but...." She squirmed, as if physically entangled on Mackercher's hook.

"But in Dublin, that's where ya became Richard's bedmate, at that time, did ya not?"

"By honor, I must object!" Malone shouted.

Bowes flicked a hand haphazardly in the air. "Sit down, Sergeant Malone."

Mackercher leaned on the witness box railing. "Madam Heath, did ya, or did ya not, become Richard's bedmate at that time?"

Charity looked away, tears welling in her eyes.

"Madam?" asked Mackercher.

"You will answer the question," growled Bowes.

She began a slight nod, then whispered, "Aye."

"And did ya not stay in Dublin, specifically to be with Richard when Lady Anglesea left for England?"

"Aye." Her voice was barely audible now, her hands shaking.

"And are ya not currently employed by Richard in some capacity within his household?"

"Aye...I am." She sobbed.

"No more questions, my lords. I won't ask her in what capacity she now serves." He looked at the jurors. "I think that's clear enough." Though Malone sprang to his feet, he remained silent. Justice Bowes peered at him blankly, as if willing the man back into his seat.

—m—

Eight more witnesses were questioned that day. Then, at half past five, the defense rested. In the course of the prior week Malone had called seventy-three witnesses, all of dubious integrity—James could only hope truth would speak for itself, and that the lies would be equally manifested and clear.

Closing arguments commenced the next morning, each side allowed two hours to spin what tales they may. Their droning speeches palled James. Seemed to pall everyone. Even Mackercher's went on forever. Each witness was discussed punctiliously, their evidence weighed and argued, measured and discussed. Why did the jury need anything but Giffard, James wondered silently. Hadn't he said enough? But four hours of wearying argument ensued. Occasionally, the judge on Bowes's right nodded off before awaking with a snort. And one juror appeared to sleep through it all. Finally, just before one o'clock, it was over. Justice Bowes instructed the jury before sending them out to deliberate.

James stood and gave Mackercher a nervous grin. "Surely they've seen the truth here."

The man nodded but James could see he was worried. "I hope so," Mackercher whispered, fingering his eyebrows.

James decided to wait with Laura, who was still on the front row of the gallery, softly talking with Seán and Ann. He stepped around Mackercher and saw Richard standing frozen, leaning forward on his table. James started to walk by, but as he opened the gate, he stopped.

Richard looked over, scowling.

"*Parlez-vous Francais?*" James asked, smirking before walking on.

As they waited together, James and Laura, Seán and Ann, the drafty courtroom grew colder. They talked about trivial things. When the conversation waned, Seán relayed a naval story, then told Ann about the fanged centipede, giving them a welcome laugh.

Minutes turned slowly into heavy hours. Time became sap. Finally, three hours and fifteen minutes later, just after the cathedral bell rang four o'clock, the jury filed in and James hurried back to his seat. There he stood, watching the judges enter, resuming their places on the bench. His heart drummed. His hands became slick. Justice Bowes sat resolute, then leaned to one side, whispering something to one of his peers. James wanted to sit. For as laborious as this had been, it all seemed terribly quick now, at this moment. Here. Now. It was time. It would be said. It would end. James studied the jury. Most were looking at the judges. One flicked a glance at Richard, then to James, then to the bench again. James could read nothing in it. Throats cleared behind him. Someone sneezed. Then more silence, save the judicial whispering. Then Bowes abruptly straightened. He nodded at Malone, then to Mackercher, then addressed the jury. "Gentlemen of the jury, your service here over these two weeks has been of the greatest importance and most notable honor to your country, to this court and to your King. None of us (he indicated himself and the other judges) remembers nor has heard of a trial that persisted for such length of days. Your patience and enduring service is duly noted and most gratefully appreciated. Now, I ask you sirs, how do you find? For the plaintiff or for the defendant?"

The foreman stood. "We find for the plaintiff, my lords."

The courtroom exploded, cheers erupting, deafening, startling shouts. James dropped back into his chair, slumping forward, suddenly flushed and out of breath. His hands were trembling. He turned to Laura and grinned.

Mackercher spoke loud to be heard over the commotion, "My lords, I pray ya render a formal judgment on behalf of the plaintiff, and that it may be recorded, and that the effect of this judgment be announced."

Laura was standing now, leaning across the barristers' bar to James. He stood, embracing her as she happily cried. Then Seán was there, patting James's back, gripping him by the shoulder. "Ye did it, Seámus!" he exclaimed. "Ye bloody-well did it!"

Malone was shouting, "My lords, the effect of the judgment should not be rendered—"

"Nay, Sergeant Malone," Bowes said. "It should indeed. Silence! Order in this courtroom! Silence!" James and Mackercher returned to their seats as the room was rendered to a nervous hush. James glanced at Richard who was standing, staring at the floor, not blinking, not moving, just frozen and fixed, and yet in the same instance dissolving. A salt pillar in a torrential rain.

"Richard Annesley, in accordance with, and resulting from, the verdict of this jury, the title and property of the Baron of Altham and the Earl of Anglesea is hereby removed from you. You shall desist all occupancies and surrender all possessions of said property, resign your seat in the English and Irish Houses of Lords, and remove any and all such references from your title. Is that understood?"

Richard continued to stare at the floor without response.

"Is that understood, Mr. Annesley?" Bowes thundered.

When Richard still said nothing, Malone rose to his feet. "'Tis understood, my lord."

"When he returns to his senses, Sergeant Malone," Bowes grumbled, "make it clear to him that I shall hold him in contempt if he ever once violates, or attempts to violate, this order. And I am sure appropriate action will also be taken by the Earl."

"Aye, my lord," Malone conceded.

Bowes turned to face James. "The Right Honorable James, Sixth Baron of Altham, Eighth Earl of Anglesea, shall no doubt enforce my decree as well, aye?"

James popped up and enthused, "Most certainly, my lord."

"On that, I declare this matter finished. This court stands adjourned."

Again, the spectators clapped and cheered. James turned and clasped Mackercher's arm. "We did it! Well done, Mr. Mackercher. Well done, indeed! We did it!"

Mackercher stood, appearing stunned, then nodded slowly. "B'jingo, I guess we did."

"I can never thank ye enough—"

"Please, Lord Anglesea," Mackercher intoned, "I pray ya'll keep our bargain. I have been fully compensated today."

James beamed. "Ye're a great man, Daniel Mackercher."

Mackercher smiled, then looked at the noisy crowd. "Ya'd better go, m'lord. I'll see ya at the Stag's Head."

"Very well. We'll meet there," James replied, then walked away. As he came through the barrister's gate, people rushed him. People he had never seen before were bowing, curtsying, calling him Lord Anglesea, congratulating him on his victory. He looked for Laura and pulled her to his side. Seán went ahead of them, clearing the way. Though grateful for the kind words, he needed to get out, to breathe, to talk with Laura, with Seán. They left the courtroom only to find the foyer more crowded with shouting people. Pushing through the masses, James turned away from the main doors. "Here. In here," he said, pulling Laura around and down another corridor.

"I'll get Mr. Mackercher," Seán offered, with Ann close behind.

"Aye. Thank ye, Seán," shouted James. "He'll meet us at the Stag. And you two as well? Ye'll be there, won't ye?"

"Aye, we will. How will ye get out of here?"

"Isn't there a back way through the cathedral? There used to be."

"Best I remember. Ye'd better go," Seán said, smiling. "I am happy for ye, Seámus. This is a great day." Another quick embrace and Seán turned, disappearing in the crowd.

James held Laura's hand, pulling her down the hall until the throng was well behind them, the noises growing soft. "Somewhere back here is a passage that opens into the churchyard," he said. A bit farther they found it and stepped outside into the nippy, brumous air, and into the blast of the bells of Christ Church. Somehow, inside, over the dissonance of the crowds, the explosion of joy, they had not noticed the bells—which were not ringing rhythmically, as they would to announce a service, the hour, or even a death knell. They were clanging chaotically, jubilantly peeling the victory. Squinting up at the bell tower, tears welled in his eyes. Then he looked down, slowly shifting around, realizing the place. "This is the churchyard," he muttered. "This is the place, Laura. Right there," he pointed at the south transept door, "that is where I walked out. And here…." He released her hand and walked slowly forward. "This is where Richard rode up, those years ago." He studied the ground, the wet yellow grass. Laura cinched her cape tighter, watching him move about. "These benches weren't here then," he continued. "This was all open in this area. He rode up on us. And declared me a bastard. And I received this scar." He touched the right side of his face. "This is the place." Laura came behind him and put her hands on his back. James looked up again. "And those bells were ringing for my father." He turned to his right. "And Fynn was beside me. Juggy and Seán were over there." He pointed to the far wall near Fishamble Street, then fell silent, the velvety mist covering their faces.

"I'll ride with Mr. Mackercher, or Seán," she breathed gently.

He kept his eyes ahead, still envisioning the past. "Aye. Ye should get out of this dampness." He turned to her. "I'll walk ye."

"Nay, *Acushla,*" she said, her eyes replete with compassion. "Stay for a while. I'll go round that way. It leads to the carriages, aya?"

"It does. Promise me ye'll come back if ye don't see one of ours?"

"I will." She didn't move right away, but instead gave him a small smile, unblinking, as though her vivid blue eyes were seeing straight through him. "I love ya, James, Earl of Anglesea," she said.

He meekly whispered, "*Acushla.* Sweet lady of mine. I love you." As she turned to go, he reached for her hand and kissed it tenderly. "I'll see ye at the inn?"

"Aya, James."

"Thank ye for…. Thank ye," he said. She sighed with a smile and a slight shake of her head, then walked away. He watched her down the path until she disappeared around the corner. Then he walked quickly, farther into the churchyard. From there he could see her. She was at the street, a footman helping her into their carriage. James turned back, tilting his face up. The cathedral's gigantic, ashen stone walls towered over him, its sombrous buttresses stretching high into the Dublin sky, disappearing into the low, dove-grey clouds. He could not tell where the spire ended and the sky began. As he lowered his gaze, focusing on the transept door, the bells finally stopped. In the silence, a calmness fell, the sound of the mist, the sound of distant hooves on cobblestones, coach wheels rolling, faraway voices. It was quiet. It was peace. It was over. It was his. He walked slowly to the door, gravel crunching under his feet, then turned the big iron handle and went in.

CHAPTER 40

The great cause wherein the Hon. James Annesley, Esq.,
was Plaintiff ended today, when the jury brought in a verdict for Mr. Annesley. Never was a cause of greater consequence brought to trial; never any took up so much time in
hearing, nor ever was there a jury composed of gentlemen
of such property, dignity and character. Never was there so
universal a joy: the music that played in the streets, even
the bells themselves, being scarce heard amidst the repeated
hussas of the multitude.

— *General Evening Post*, Dublin,
November 25, 1743

The cold air followed him in. James walked to the front of the nave and
stopped. He could hear whispers, saw a few people moving in the shadows,
talking quietly, a few in the nave, on their knees. He looked back at the choir
chamber, then up, past the chancel screen, watching the organ's pipes stretch
for the vaulted ceiling.

"May I help ye, sir?" asked a man with an Orphean voice.

James turned. "Ah, nay sir. Thank ye kindly."

The clerk nodded, smiling, then slipped away.

"Sir?" James called after him. "Pardon me, but where is the chapterhouse?"

"'Tis outside, sir, between the south wall and the Four Courts."

James thanked him and turned to go.

"But ye may get to it through there, if ye wish," the man added, gesturing
to a small door under the darkly arched arcade.

"Good. I thank ye." James walked slowly down the middle of the nave,
then back to the south wall. He knocked on the door softly. When no answer
came, he eased it open. Entering, he noticed it was windowless, lit only by a
sole rush light flittering against the stone wall. He surveyed its tables, books
and assortment of chairs. It appeared more of a rector's study than what he
thought to be a chapterhouse. He walked to one of the tables, running his

fingers across its smooth coolness. "I'm finally here, Mum," he whispered. He leaned against the wall, exhausted, rubbing his forehead.

Suddenly a man in a minister's robe entered. "Oh, pardon me, son," exclaimed the man, obviously surprised to find someone there.

James stood straight. "Nay, Father. Pardon me. I was just leaving."

"Do ye have business with me?"

"Nay, I was leaving," whispered James, stepping past him. "Sorry to intrude. I was curious, and…. Pardon me." He walked into the nave, his footsteps echoing softly across the flagstones until he took a seat on an empty pew near the center. Above, he saw the stone arches curving into the dark overhead, then noticed the carvings at the top of each pillar along the arcade. The faces he had seen so many years ago were staring back at him now with their same implacable expressions. He considered each in turn, looking for one in particular. Then he found her. The young woman's face was still dead, her eyes still closed. He stared at her. Nothing happened. He glanced to his right, at the tombs of Strongbow and his halved son, and realized where he was sitting. He rose and moved up two pews, and over to the middle. Now he was in the same pew where he sat at his father's funeral. He closed his eyes, imagining Fynn beside him, then opened his eyes, picturing his father's casket at the front of the nave. Then he remembered his father was in the crypt below, but nothing lured him to go. Again he closed his eyes. He heard the swish of a dress from behind, feet treading slowly down the center aisle. His eyes eased open but he kept them down, hoping not to be recognized. The woman slipped in beside him, yet across the aisle. He heard the clump of an object being set on her bench.

"M'lord?" she ventured in a quivering voice.

James hesitated, then took a deep breath, preparing to say something cordial before standing and moving away. He scooted slightly to his right, away from the aisle.

"M'lord?" the wrinkled voice came again. He had heard it before but couldn't place it. Slowly, he turned his head to see Charity Heath, her gaze to the floor. Her bloodshot eyes flicked up at him, her sagging, flushed cheeks streaked with tears. She had appeared disheveled and tired in court, but now James saw her as old and broken.

"Madam Heath?" he said, his voice cautiously gentle.

She sniffed, wiping her cheeks with a handkerchief. "M'lord, I did ye wrong in there, in the court yesterday." She refused to look at him again, keeping her sad eyes down.

"Aye, ye did," said James. He scooted left, closer to the aisle, closer to her.

"They're going t' charge me with perjury, m'lord," she cried. Now she looked up at the glimmering candles, the light reflecting off her wet face.

"I suppose they will."

She hunched forward, fully weeping. He regarded her, feeling sorry for her, sorry that she had fallen into Richard's snare. She sniffed again, now loudly. "Ye can, m'lord...Lord Anglesea," she muttered, "you can grant me a pardon. Ye can have me forgiven."

James stood and moved across the aisle to sit next to her. He touched her slumped head. "I'll have to think about that." He observed a small amber chest sitting beside her, a dull floral print covering its humped lid. It seemed familiar somehow, a deep resonance, a distant memory. Far away, yet intimately close.

"M'lord?" she whispered.

"Aye, ma'am?"

"This is yers," she said, sniffing, glancing at the chest. She lifted it over her lap and placed it on the bench between them.

"'Tis mine?"

"Aye, m'lord." She looked up at him, tears coming in a torrent. He waited, silently watching as she collected herself and wiped her eyes. "It is...'twas yer mother's, Lady Anglesea's. She...."

James glanced at the chest, then back to Charity. "She what?"

"She wanted me to give it to ye."

James felt his heart cave. "And ye kept it all these years?"

"Aye, m'lord. I'm sorry. I'm so sorry, I am."

"What's in it?"

"I know not, m'lord. 'Tis locked, and I never.... I never tried t' open it."

He stared at her, this little breaking woman, and felt only pity.

"'Tis just that...I wronged ye, m'lord. I wanted t' come. Set things right. T' bring ye what's yers. I hoped ye might be here." She stood and he stood as well. As she went, he stepped to let her pass. "I'm terribly sorry," she said, softly crying as she moved.

"Thank ye," James murmured, knowing nothing else to say.

He watched her walk away, her sniffs echoing as she went. Then he sat again and stared at the chest. He ran his hands across its curved back, across the faint images, then touched the keyhole. With a sigh, he reached up and loosened his ascot, then pulled the key from around his neck. As he had done so many times, he ran his thumb over the "B," though it was now faint. Inserting the key, he turned it, hearing the light click.

A white damask cloth was folded inside, undisturbed. He gingerly touched it, his mind saturated with the image of his mother. Then he lifted the damask and found more cloth beneath it, then a locket on a gold chain, a pair of silver spoons, a small ring, and on the bottom, a yellowed sheet of parchment. Gently, he pulled out the parchment—a faded sheet of music titled *Greensleeves* at the top. He smiled, the sound of the melody swelling in his mind. Reaching back into the box, he pulled back a different layer of the cloth and found another piece of parchment, folded and sealed with wax. He held it up to the light, flipping it over, then back again, studying it, then gently broke the seal. Unfolding it, he saw it was a letter.

> *My dear Jamie —*
>
> *Where are you? I have waited here in the chapterhouse of*
> *Christ Church, but you never came. I am so sorry. I do not*
> *know what to write. I do not know what I should say to you,*
> *my dear boy. I do not know when I will ever see you again.*
> *I never wanted to leave you. My heart is broken from our*
> *parting at Dunmain. It has been nearly two years and now it*
> *seems we may be parted for much longer. I do not know where*
> *you are, my Jamie. But I pray you are safe and that you are*
> *well.*
>
> *I will go now, for England. If you read this letter today, or*
> *soon hereafter, I will be sailing to Bristol on the Courtmain. I*
> *pray you will be there, that somehow you will find me. But I*
> *must go home. I pray you will understand. Please come quickly*
> *to Kent, that you may find me there.*

James stopped. So she had indeed been there. *Damn. Why didn't she hear me? God, I yelled and yelled.* He read on.

> *My Jamie, there is always the chance we may not meet again,*
> *and I want you to know I have always loved you. Dearly. My*
> *life did not transpire as I would have desired. It has not been*
> *a happy one as I hoped it to be. I know yours has not thus far*
> *been either. But I hope that will soon change. For both of us. I*
> *hope you find happiness, find love, find everything God has to*
> *offer us here. All the good. All the peace of His love.*

*I must tell you one thing more. You are young now, and may
not understand, but I hope someday you will accept the words
I will impart. I was married to Arthur Annesley not by my
will. In truth, I never loved him. He is buried here, below
where I now sit, and yet I feel nothing for him. He has kept
you and I parted for these two years. He treated you wrong,
and me. He was an evil man who wronged us both.*

*Jamie, in the locket enclosed is the image of another man, the
man I love entirely. Please find it in your heart to forgive me,
but I must tell you the truth. This man is your true father.*

His breathing nearly stopped as he fumbled through the folded cloth
and grabbed the gold locket from the chest. He held it tightly as he finished
reading.

*I beg you, do not think unkindly of me, for the words in this
letter are from my heart. I want you to know the truth, to
know your father. I pray you will forgive us both. We pledged
to keep this our secret, not to rob you of your inheritance. I do
not know if we were right to do so, but please do forgive us. As
I am fortunate to be your mother, you are very fortunate to be
his son.*

*We all err, Jamie, even with those we love most deeply. Please,
do come to me, my sweet Jamie, as soon as you can. I must go
now, for it is a long journey home.*

> *Your loving mother,*
> *Mary*

Mouth agape and dry, eyes locked wide, James set the letter aside. He
pulled the locket up, his hand nearly shaking, the chain flopped over. He
paused, almost frozen, as if not opening it might change things, might erase
what he had just read. He began shaking his head, then suddenly went into
motion, frantically fumbling with the catch until it finally flipped open. Staring out at him was the ruddily young, distinctively handsome, unmistakable
face of Fynn Kennedy.

CHAPTER 41

To be, or not to be: that is the question:
Whether 'tis nobler in the mind to suffer
The slings and arrows of outrageous fortune,
Or to take arms against a sea of troubles
And, by opposing, end them.

— from *Hamlet*, William Shakespeare, 1601

Six Months Later
Dunmain, Ireland

As the coach lumbered along, James and Laura sat close together, enjoying the mild spring air gliding through the open windows, slipping over them, delivering the scent of primrose and larkspur in full bloom. He held her hand and turned to her.

"Will Seán already be there?" she asked.

"Aye, most likely."

Laura's hair was up under a small, straw hat, and her yellow and white linen dress rustled as she leaned close to James, whispering, "I love ya, husband." He kissed the back of her hand, then looked out, over her head, watching the verdant countryside drift by. They left New Ross within the hour and were close now. The coach moved smoothly, the ruts shallow and dry. As they arrived at Dunmain House, James glanced at the giant mansion, its grey walls, the turrets on the corners. Each time he had seen it since the trial, an odd, distracted feeling came over him, making him look away. This time was no different. As the carriage rolled through the main gate, he kept his eyes on the garden walls, noticing they were plush with ivy and ferns. Seán would tend to them, he thought.

"Whoa, there." The driver pulled the carriage to a stop on the gravel drive.

"There he is," said Laura, pointing to the stable.

"Aye. I see him."

She turned to James, grasping his hand. "Take yar time," she assured him. "I'll be inside with Ann."

He smiled, reaching across to lightly stroke her cheek with the back of his fingers. They kissed, then he stepped out. Walking quickly to the stables, he looked for Seán, whom now he didn't see.

"*Cá bhfuil tú*, Seán?" James called out.

"*Anseo*," Seán replied, saying he was there. "*Tá anseo orm.*"

As James came around a corner, he saw Seán standing in a stall, grooming a horse.

"*Dia duit*, Seámus," Seán greeted him. "I didn't expect ye so soon."

"*Dia duit*," replied James. "How are ye my friend?"

"As fine as can be, I suppose, and you?" Seán stopped brushing the horse.

"Good." James patted the horse on the rump, then ran his hand across its back and patted it near the withers. "How's Bhaldraithe?"

"Ach, there's no doubt he's a splendid animal, Seámus. I can't thank ye enough."

"'Twas nothing. Besides, he has too much Connemara in him t' ever leave Ireland."

"What do ye mean, leave Ireland?"

"Ah, well, Seán…."

Seán stepped close. "That why ye're meetin' me here today? To tell me ye're leaving?"

"Let's walk, shall we?" asked James, his voice yielding and kind.

They walked east along the carriage road, toward the tranquil hills and distant sheltering forests, fern-covered stone fences lining the way. Fynn's Hill, with its crowning stand of noble ash, was in the opposite direction. James would never go there again. After the trial, he spent one excruciating February morning sitting alone on that silent hill, under those wind-swept barren trees, weeping, wrestling with God, whispering to his father. No, he would never go back to Fynn's Hill. Certainly never with Seán. Thus they walked the other way.

"'Twas good to see Mr. Mackercher at the wedding," Seán said after a while.

"Ye remember anything about that night?" James laughed.

"Let's see, Mackercher was there, the ale was good, and something about you and Laura."

"Ha! Indeed. Laura and I saw him again a few days later, before he left for Scotland."

"He returned to Aberfoyle?"

"Aye," said James, his eyes to the road, feeling a knot in his stomach.

"All right, Seámus," Seán blurted. "We're walking. Where, I don't know. So tell me now. Are ye leaving?"

James looked up, away, out to an open field of meadowsweet in full yellow bloom. "Aye," he whispered.

"Where are ye going?"

James hesitated, unexpectedly overcome with emotion. "This is much harder than I ever imagined, Seán. Telling ye this." He felt his eyes tighten.

"The Colonies, eh?" asked Seán.

"Aye." He sniffed the tears back, clinched his teeth and for a moment felt better. "We'll build a farm in Virginia. 'Tis where we belong now."

Seán stopped walking. "What do ye mean, Jemmy? What about—"

"Ah, 'tis worthless, Seán," James said quickly. "The court completed their survey. Seems I've inherited more debt than land. The proverbial wind, so 'tis."

"The wind, eh? Perhaps if ye'd been more meek, ye'd have gotten the earth."

James smiled, shaking his head. "Ye're a funny rogue," he said flatly.

They chuckled nervously, then fell silent again. After rounding another bend in the meandering road, Seán finally spoke. "What will ye do?"

James shrugged. "Sell the land. Pay the debts."

"And the title?"

James stopped walking. "'Tisn't mine, Seán."

"What?" Seán stopped also.

"Nay. Never 'twas."

Seán came closer. "What the devil do ye mean?"

James reached in his pocket and pulled out the letter. He unfolded it, then handed it to Seán and looked away. Behind him he could hear the paper fluttering in the breeze. He walked to the stone fence and leaned on it, watching the sheep in the pasture beyond, seeing the wind caress the grass, remembering the Scottish Highlands, remembering Fynn.

"My God!" exclaimed Seán. "And the locket?"

James walked back to the road, took the letter, then handed the golden object to Seán. Realizing Seán couldn't open the locket with one hand, he took it back and popped it open. He held it out for Seán to see.

"M'God, Jemmy," Seán breathed, staggering back from the mythic image. "So, this means...."

"Aye, *dearthdiri*," said James, gently pronouncing the Irish word for "brothers." He snapped the locket closed, dropped it in his pocket, then carefully folded the letter along its worn creases.

"*Dearthdiri*," Seán repeated, incredulous, his eyes wide. "Does Laura know?"

James nodded, returning the letter to his pocket.

As they resumed walking, Seán asked, "And Mackercher?"

"He had his victory last November," said James. "The estate was of no concern to him. I didn't feel the necessity of telling him."

Seán looked at James. "Of course Richard doesn't know."

"Nay. And he never will. I'm asking ye to keep this in yer heart...to yerself. Let it remain only between us. If ye tell Ann, it must stay between ye both, as husband and wife. Can I trust ye to that?"

"Ye have my oath on it. Is Richard still in France?"

"I suppose he is."

They walked for a while without speaking, each immersed in his own thoughts. Until, over the smooth fertile pastures came the toll of a faraway bell, calling evening worship. "Remember being on this road before," James asked, "when we were wee lads?"

"Aye. We played in those forests," replied Seán, pointing off to his left.

"And Fynn...Da...." He waited for the Seán's nod. "He'd come fetch us, blowing his hunting horn." James smiled, remembering him, seeing him riding across the Dunmain meadows. As they trod slowly on, silently crossing their ancient land, the lagging sun slipped behind the trees, its waning light gradually giving way, striping the fields with long reaching shadows.

"Seámus," Seán said with a cracking voice, "I could never imagine having a finer brother."

"Ah, now," James muttered. They both stopped. "You were always my brother." Looking away, he clamped his jaw tight, trying to control his emotions. Then a lone tear fell to his cheek. "Brothers...*Dearthdiri*...I think I always knew that." He set his gaze to the northwest, across the green hills speckled with red clover. "Da was born just over those hills," he said.

Seán turned in that direction. "Aye. The cottage is between here and New Ross."

James looked at the setting sun. "And he rests over there...on Fynn's Hill."

"Aye," whispered Seán.

James took a measured breath, then spoke forcefully, "This is Kennedy land, Seán—always has been. So it will remain in our family. I've ordered the rest of the Anglesea Estate sold. But I've kept Dunmain House and these lands around it." He turned and faced Seán. "Ye're Ireland t' me, Seán. And Ireland is you. You should own Dunmain. 'Tis Kennedy land. I want ye t' have it."

"But I cannot possibly pay for—"

"I give it to ye Seán. Gladly," James said, cutting him off. "'Tis yers, *deartháir.*"

Seán took a deep breath, then looked in James's eyes and thanked him, saying, "*Go raibh maith agat.*"

"*Go meádaighe Dia dhuit,*" replied James, nodding with a smile. "Ye're very welcome, indeed. I hope you and Ann bring life to Dunmain House. A family. Happiness. That's all I ask in return."

"We will, Seámus. We will, indeed."

As they resumed their walk, talking quietly, a Gaelic wind whispered over them, through the trees, riffling their infant leaves. Then came the harking screech of a falcon, and James looked up, seeing her there. She floated across that azure sky, calling her young to follow, to stretch their fledgling wings, to let go, to engage their faith, to cling to hope, to trust the unseen air will hold them—out beyond the hills and all the way home.

EPILOGUE

This above all:
To thine own self be true.
And it must follow, as the night the day,
Thou canst not then be false to any man.

— from *Hamlet*, William Shakespeare, 1601

The great trial between James and Richard Annesley was, at that date, the longest, and sat the wealthiest jury in all of British history. Due to the uniquely-allowed testimony of Prime Sergeant Giffard, the famous Anglesea trial remains the basis of the modern "attorney-client privilege."

James never officially assumed the title Earl of Anglesea, and never took his seats in the Houses of Lords. The Anglesea Earldom ended with Richard's death in 1761. Charity Heath served five years in prison for perjury.

Daniel Mackercher became near bankrupt from the costs of the trial and forever refused payment from James. He soon rejoined the Scottish military and led a division at the battle of Culloden in 1745, the ill-fated, final battle for Scottish independence.

James and Laura built their farm in Virginia, and there had two daughters, Joan and Mary, and a son they named Fynn. Fynn Annesley later rose through the ranks of the American Colonial Army and was killed in Yorktown, Virginia in 1781, at the last major battle of the American Revolution.

James and Seán never saw each other again, though they wrote many letters to each other. Seán lived to an old age, seeing two more generations of Kennedys come to live on the land surrounding Dunmain. Eight generations later, a descendant of that Kennedy family became the thirty-fifth President of the United States. Today, land that was once part of Dunmain contains the John F. Kennedy Arboretum, and near its center is Fynn's Hill.

Dunmain House was eventually sold and fell into ruins during the Great Irish Famine. Eventually, during the late 1800s, the house was restored. Today it is once again the home of an Irish family.

James Annesley returned only once to the British Isles. In 1759, James,

Dear Reader,

Thank you for taking this journey through the extraordinary saga of James Annesley. It was a unique pleasure to discover James, research the facts, and write this book. My only wish was that I may have added footnotes explaining, "Seriously, this actually happened!" throughout the pages.

Fortunate Son is the premiere of a unique series of historical novels, each pivoting on the actual events encompassing a significant historical courtroom drama. I am an avid social historian, with a particular affinity for trials—perhaps as much for the dramatic stories as for their spectacle of colorful characters. Plus, reading transcripts from trials preceding audio or video recordings is enthralling and the nearest experience of time travel available.

Next up is *American Red*, centering on the 1907 trial of the deadly, one-eyed, union boss, "Big Bill" Haywood who was accused of ordering the successful assassination-by-bombing of the governor of Idaho (the first such in American history). Bonus: Haywood was represented by none other than the young Clarence Darrow. Today, few have heard of the case, though in its time it was above-the-fold from coast to coast and across the globe. It is a sweeping tale of murder, adultery, corruption, mountain mafia, the Pinkertons, domestic terrorism, government-sanctioned kidnapping, the last gunslingers, mining unions, and perhaps the greatest train race ever—all set on the backdrop of America's doomed thrust toward radical socialism as other countries such as Russia were embarking on their own "red" revolutions. Sounds like a outlandish adventure, right? I agree, and hope you will take that journey in late 2014.

For more information, to reach me, and to receive regular updates, please visit www.dmarlett.com.

Warmly,
David Marlett

Laura, and their children, traveled to Lee, Kent County, England for a special viewing of that year's appearance of Halley's Comet, and to visit the grave of his mother, Mary Sheffield, and the grave of Edmond Hillary, the famous astronomer for whom his discovery, Halley's Comet, was named. In 1742, both Halley and Mary had died within weeks of each other and were both buried in the churchyard of St. Margaret's of Lee.

After the visit in Lee, the Annesley family traveled to London, with plans to continue on to Ireland where they would visit Seán. But while in London, James fell from a horse and was severely injured. He died on January 5, 1760, at the age of forty-four. Seán and Laura laid him to rest in the churchyard of St. Margaret's, near his mother, finally reuniting them. Laura returned to Virginia and raised their children. She never remarried.

Though extremely well known at the time, these events were eventually lost to history, with only an occasional reference. The English author Tobias Smollett's novel, *The Adventures of Peregrine Pickle*, 1751, is most certainly based on Smollett's time with James Annesley in the Royal Navy. It is surmised that Smollett's earlier and more famous novel, *The Adventures of Roderick Random*, 1748 was also inspired by James. It is rumored that Sir Walter Scott's novel *Guy Mannering*, 1815, and Robert Louis Stevenson's novel, *Kidnapped*, 1886, were based in part on some elements of James's earlier adventures.